AF269278

BURN EVERY BRIDGE

FBI Series: Strike Team East #1

BARBARA FREETHY

Fog City Publishing

PRAISE FOR BARBARA FREETHY

"Barbara Freethy's first book PERILOUS TRUST in her OFF THE GRID series is an emotional, action packed, crime drama that keeps you on the edge of your seat...I'm exhausted after reading this but in a good way. 5 Stars!" — *Booklovers Anonymous*

"A fabulous, page-turning combination of romance and intrigue. Fans of Nora Roberts and Elizabeth Lowell will love this book." — *NYT Bestselling Author Kristin Hannah on Golden Lies*

"PERILOUS TRUST is a non-stop thriller that seamlessly melds jaw-dropping suspense with sizzling romance. Readers will be breathless in anticipation as this fast-paced and enthralling love story goes in unforeseeable directions." — *USA Today HEA Blog*

"Powerful and absorbing...sheer hold-your-breath suspense." — *NYT Bestselling Author Karen Robards on Don't Say A Word*

"I loved this story from start to finish. Right from the start of PERILOUS TRUST, the tension sets in. Goodness, my heart was starting to beat a little fast by the end of the prologue! I found myself staying up late finishing this book, and that is something I don't normally do." — *My Book Filled Life Blog*

"Freethy hits the ground running as she kicks off another winning romantic suspense series...Freethy is at her prime with a superb combo of engaging characters and gripping plot." — *Publishers' Weekly on Silent Run*

PRAISE FOR BARBARA FREETHY

"Grab a drink, find a comfortable reading nook, and get immersed in this fast paced, realistic, romantic thriller! 5 STARS!" *Perrin – Goodreads on Elusive Promise*

"Words cannot explain how phenomenal this book was. The characters are so believable and relatable. The twists and turns keep you on the edge of your seat and flying through the pages. This is one book you should be desperate to read." *Caroline - Goodreads on Ruthless Cross*

"Barbara Freethy is a master storyteller with a gift for spinning tales about ordinary people in extraordinary situations and drawing readers into their lives." *— Romance Reviews Today*

"Freethy (Silent Fall) has a gift for creating complex, appealing characters and emotionally involving, often suspenseful, sometimes magical stories." *— Library Journal on Suddenly One Summer*

Freethy hits the ground running as she kicks off another winning romantic suspense series...Freethy is at her prime with a superb combo of engaging characters and gripping plot." *— Publishers' Weekly on Silent Run*

"If you love nail-biting suspense and heartbreaking emotion, Silent Run belongs on the top of your to-be-bought list. I could not turn the pages fast enough." *— NYT Bestselling Author Mariah Stewart*

ALSO BY BARBARA FREETHY

FBI SERIES: EAST COAST STRIKE TEAM

BURN EVERY BRIDGE

CROSS THE LINE

OFF THE GRID: FBI SERIES

PERILOUS TRUST

RECKLESS WHISPER

DESPERATE PLAY

ELUSIVE PROMISE

DANGEROUS CHOICE

RUTHLESS CROSS

CRITICAL DOUBT

FEARLESS PURSUIT

DARING DECEPTION

RISKY BARGAIN

PERFECT TARGET

FATAL BETRAYAL

DEADLY TRAP

LETHAL GAME

SHATTERED TRUTH

For a complete list of books, visit Barbara's Website!

BURN EVERY BRIDGE

© Copyright 2026 Barbara Freethy
All Rights Reserved

No part of this book may be used or reproduced in any manner whatsoever
without written permission except in the case of brief quotations embodied in
critical articles and reviews.

This is a work of fiction. Names, characters, places, and incidents are products of
the author's imagination or are used fictitiously. Any resemblance to actual
events, locales, organizations or persons, living or dead, is entirely coincidental.

———

For more information on Barbara Freethy's books, visit her website:
www.barbarafreethy.com

CHAPTER ONE

Something felt wrong.

Kara couldn't pinpoint what it was—just a prickle at the base of her skull, the kind of instinct that had kept her alive through eight years on the NYPD and a year working for the FBI.

With her phone at her ear, her friend Jess rambling on about the challenges of being a new mom, she shifted her feet as she waited in line to order a coffee at the very busy counter of Brew & Mortar, a café near the courthouse where she'd just dropped off her final report for 26 Fed, the Manhattan FBI office that had been her home since she'd become an agent. But today started a new chapter.

Everything looked normal. The morning crowd was a mix of suited executives grabbing coffee on their way into the office, a couple of NYU students hunched over computers, and a trio of forty-something women who looked like they'd just finished a yoga class. The espresso machine hissed and gurgled behind the counter, while the barista called out orders in a steady rhythm. Outside the window, the January sky was gray, with foreboding clouds pressing down on the city.

"Honestly, Kara, I don't know how anyone survives on three hours of sleep," Jess said, drawing Kara's attention back to the phone. "Lily was up every two hours last night, and Brad somehow slept through all of it."

Kara smiled despite the unease crawling up her spine. "Despite sounding tired, Jess, you also sound happy."

"I am. I just can't stop staring at my beautiful baby. My old life as a cop seems very far away. Now I'm a realtor and a mom. How things have changed! But let's talk about your life changes. I can't believe you're already moving on to a special elite FBI team. It's very impressive, even for an overachiever like you."

"I'm excited to work for a smaller team that can move fast and without so much oversight," she admitted.

"Well, you were the smartest cop I ever worked with."

"Not everyone shared your opinion."

"Because they put loyalty above integrity, but that's all behind you now."

"Thank God! Hang on. I need to order." She lowered her phone as she ordered her usual coffee and then stepped aside to wait for her coffee.

It was crowded in the café, especially at this end of the counter, and a woman in a very expensive, tight-fitting black suit gave her a dark look as she encroached on her space, immediately moving away.

She put her phone back to her ear. "I'm back."

"So, what's your first case going to be?" Jess asked.

"Not sure yet. I'm eager to find out. The agents I've met so far seem impressive, and my new boss, Jason Colter, even more so. He came from a very successful elite team run out of LA, and he's modeling this team on that one. That unit has had tremendous success, so fingers crossed."

"It sounds great, and I think the team is lucky to have you."

Jess had always been a great cheerleader. They'd partnered together for two years until Jess got married and pregnant. Their lives were very different now, but if there was one person she could always count on to be in her corner, it was Jess. At the sound of a baby's cry, she said, "I think Lily is awake."

"And hungry. I'd better go."

"Give that sweet baby a kiss for me."

"I will."

As Kara slipped her phone into the outer pocket of her crossbody bag, the woman in the suit moved to the counter to get her drink, only to collide with a middle-aged man, who splashed his coffee, heavily laden with whipped cream, onto her sleeve.

She gasped in dismay, anger flaring in her eyes. "Watch where you're going."

"Sorry," the man muttered. "I didn't see you. Uh, do you need a napkin or something?"

"Just get out of my way." The woman grabbed her coffee from the counter, along with a pile of napkins, and headed toward the restroom.

The man shrugged and left. As he moved through the door, another man entered. Wearing black jeans and a black wool coat over a gray sweater, he appeared to be in his mid-thirties and had wavy, dark-brown hair and a very attractive face. His confident gaze swept the room for a long minute. Then he frowned and left. He must have been looking for someone. She couldn't imagine anyone standing that guy up.

Hearing her name called, she turned her attention away from the door and picked up her coffee. She took one sip and sighed in pleasure. Her morning coffee always tasted great, and the caffeine kick got her ready for the day.

As she stepped outside and onto the sidewalk, the world suddenly exploded behind her, a blast of heat throwing her to the ground. She landed hard, the concrete slamming into her palms and knees as glass and debris rained down on her head.

For a moment, there was nothing but white noise, the taste of copper in her mouth, and mind-spinning confusion.

Then the screaming started.

She forced her eyes open. Smoke poured from the shattered windows of Brew & Mortar, thick and black, and through the haze she could see flames licking at the counter, spreading fast. People stumbled out to the sidewalk, coughing and bleeding.

She needed to get up, to move, to help.

She pushed herself to her feet, her legs shaking, but determination gave her strength. As she moved through the open space where the door had been, the smoke was worse than she'd expected, choking and hot, burning her throat with every breath.

A table had overturned near the entrance, trapping a young woman. Her face was streaked with blood.

"Can you move?" She dropped to her knees, already assessing the situation. The girl was conscious but disoriented.

"I—I think so—" the girl stuttered.

She shoved the table aside, then pulled the girl to her feet and helped her outside, running into the good-looking man who had come into the café, then left.

"Do you need help?" he asked.

"There are more people in there," she returned as he moved past her.

There were a dozen or so people in the street, some bleeding, some burned, everyone dazed and terrified. Thankfully, fire engines and ambulances were arriving. She handed the girl off to a paramedic and then turned to go back into the building, but a firefighter blocked her way.

"We've got this," he told her.

As they went into the burning structure, the man she'd seen before came out of the smoke, his arm around a barista, who was crying but didn't appear to be too badly hurt.

Feeling helpless, she looked around the scene, wondering how she could best help, but before she could move, a firefighter ran down the sidewalk toward her. When she saw her Uncle Danny, wearing his turnout gear and chief's hat, his warm brown eyes filled with concern, she almost lost it.

"Kara? Were you inside?" he asked in shock.

"I'd just left," she said, pulling herself together.

"You're hurt. You're bleeding."

"It's nothing."

He ignored her comment, flagging down a paramedic. "She needs to get checked out," he ordered.

"I said I'm fine." But even as she protested, she could feel the sting of cuts on her hands, the ache in her shoulder, the pain in her knees from where she'd hit the ground.

The paramedic had her sit down on the curb while her uncle went back to work on the fire.

"Any trouble breathing? Dizziness? Ringing in your ears?" the paramedic asked as she checked her blood pressure and oxygen levels.

"No. Yes. A little." Kara let the paramedic work, too tired to argue, and her gaze drifting back to the café.

Brew & Mortar was a disaster. The windows were blown out, smoke was still pouring from the interior, and while the fire was easing now, it had destroyed the interior in only a few minutes. As her gaze moved away from the building, she noted that the street had been cordoned off, with police cruisers blocking traffic, and a growing crowd of onlookers pressed against the barriers.

She scanned the crowd for the man in the wool coat, but she didn't see him anywhere. She didn't really know why she was looking for him. Although it was strange that he'd entered the café, left quickly, then returned after the explosion. It probably meant nothing. It was just her years of investigative training making her suspicious of any action that seemed out of sync.

"Your oxygen levels are good," the paramedic said. "But you should go to the hospital, get checked out properly—"

"I'm fine. Please help the others. I'm okay."

As the paramedic left, she got to her feet, feeling more aches and pains now that the adrenaline surge was wearing off. Her throat felt dry and raw, but she was lucky not to be more seriously injured. She'd seen a few people loaded into ambulances who hadn't looked very good.

Pulling her phone from her bag, which was thankfully still hanging around her neck, she called her boss.

"Colter," he said crisply.

"Jason, it's Kara," she said, her voice shakier than she'd expected.

"You don't sound good. What's going on?"

"There was an explosion in a café by the courthouse. I was just leaving when it happened."

"Are you injured?"

"No, but there are casualties, at least a dozen. I'm going to stay here and see what I can find out, if that's okay with you. I don't know if it was a gas line or a bomb, but it's bad."

"Call me back when you know more."

"I will." As she put her phone away, she saw the firefighters beginning to shut down as the fire was basically out. Since the urgency of the scene had diminished, she moved down the street to speak to her uncle.

Danny Reid gave her a sharp look. "Are you okay?"

"Yes. I told you I was. Do you know what happened?"

"There appeared to be an explosive device in a trash can outside the door to the restroom."

His words confirmed her suspicions. "I had a feeling, but I was hoping it was an accident. Are there any fatalities?"

"One woman was in critical condition. She was pulled from the restroom. A few others with burns, but it could have been worse. Fortunately, the explosive was limited in range." He paused. "Is this incident tied to a case you're working on?"

"No. I just stopped in for coffee."

"You were lucky, Kara. I almost had a heart attack when I saw you." He shook his head, his lips tight.

She put a hand on his arm, seeing the concern in his brown eyes and knowing that it came from a promise he'd made her father a very long time ago. "I'm fine, Uncle Danny."

"You might not have been."

"But I am."

He gave her an assessing look, then slowly nodded. "Okay. I need to get back to work. Take care of yourself."

"I will."

As she turned away, she saw two FBI agents approaching the scene, Monica Greer and Cy Barash, who worked explosives response. She'd been on violent crimes the past year, so their paths had crossed a few times.

Monica gave her a look of surprise. "What are you doing here, Reid?"

"I was getting coffee. I had just left when the bomb went off."

"That's lucky. Do you know anything about the explosive?"

"It was placed in a trash can next to the restroom."

"Did you see anything? Anyone running from the scene? Watching the fire afterwards?" Agent Barash asked.

"No, I didn't see anything. The police have been talking to witnesses. Hopefully, one of them saw something."

"We'll coordinate with NYPD. Glad you're okay." Monica paused. "And good luck with Colter's group. He's a good guy. I worked with him a few years ago."

"Nice to hear," she said as Monica and Cy went to talk to the NYPD incident commander, Captain Lisa Rodriguez. She wanted to join them, but she wasn't working for 26 Fed anymore, and it was time to get to her actual job.

Hopefully, this explosion was a one-off and not the beginning of something more.

An hour later, after stopping at her apartment to shower and change clothes, Kara drove to her new team headquarters, a three-story building in Murray Hill. The central location made it easy to respond to issues anywhere in the city, but far enough away from 26 Fed to maintain its own independence. There was no sign on the building, nothing to draw attention to their existence, as their team would operate covertly when needed.

After parking in the underground garage, she used a biometric scanner to enter the elevator and a fingerprint scan to take it to the third floor. When the doors opened on an unimpressive hallway, she walked down the corridor and used another biometric scanner to enter through the double doors leading into the office suite. Inside, there was a reception desk with a computer and a phone, but it was more for appearances than anything else.

She entered through another armed door, arriving in the open-concept office space with eight desks in the central bullpen and two glass-walled offices at one end, with a large conference room that looked over the city.

There were two agents at their desks: Natalie Ramon, an agent who'd recently transferred from an office in Latin America, and Zane McDougal, a former Wall Street exec with a background in financial crimes. Natalie was on the phone, and Zane was on his computer. She set her bag down on her desk and headed toward the conference room, where she could see Jason Colter standing in front of the monitors, while Alina Volkov and Tyler Brennan sat at the table.

Jason was in his mid-thirties, tall and fit with brown hair and light-blue eyes. He had literally been born into the FBI. His grandfather and father had both risen to the top levels of the bureau, but Jason had chosen a less politically ambitious path, refusing to rely on his last name to get him ahead. He'd come up through the trenches, and in the past year, he had closed some big cases, leading to his new post as director of Strike Team East.

Alina Volkov was a stunningly pretty blonde in her early thirties, whose parents had fled Russia when she was a baby, but her Russian roots and fluency in multiple languages had taken her from a position in the State Department to the FBI. Next to Alina was Tyler Brennan, who had started his intelligence career with the Army's Delta Force before joining the FBI two years ago, working in both LA and Chicago. He had rugged good looks and an abundance of confidence.

As she opened the door, all eyes turned to her.

"Kara," Jason said with a nod. "How are you feeling?"

"I'm doing all right." She had some cuts on her knees and hands and a deep scratch on her forehead from some glass, which she'd put a small bandage over, but otherwise she was okay.

"You look better than I expected," Alina said, offering her a warm smile. "Considering you were at ground zero."

"Why were you in the café?" Tyler asked. "Were you meeting someone?"

"No. I had to drop off a file at the courthouse for my last case. I was just grabbing a coffee before I headed here. I've been to that café many times. It's still difficult to believe what happened."

"Did you get any more information?" Jason asked.

"The fire chief told me the explosive device was small and placed in the garbage can next to the restroom. Special Agents Greer and Barash from 26 Fed were at the scene, as well as NYPD." She pulled out a seat at the table, noting the monitor behind Jason contained photos from the scene, including a photo of a woman, the same woman who'd given her a dark look when she'd gotten too close to her. "Who is that? I saw her in the café."

"Samantha Barkley, federal prosecutor," Jason replied. "She was pulled from the restroom in critical condition."

"Oh my God," she murmured, her gaze locked on Samantha's professional headshot. "She went into the restroom because a man spilled his coffee on her."

"Deliberately?" Tyler asked sharply.

"I didn't think so, but...maybe."

"Who was the man?" Jason asked.

"Middle-aged. He had on dirty jeans and a Knicks sweatshirt. His hair was a mix of brown and gray, not styled, long and messy.

He apologized to her after spilling his coffee. She reacted with extreme annoyance. He shrugged and walked away."

"Did he stay in the café?" Tyler asked.

"No. He left. And Ms. Barkley went into the restroom. To be frank, she was irritated before the coffee spill. She was on the phone with someone, and when I got close to her, she gave me a glare and moved away. That's when I first noticed her, and their collision occurred right in front of me." She paused, wondering where this was all going. "Are we working this case?"

"Yes. Damon has asked us to take over," Jason replied, referring to Damon Wolfe, who ran the New York field office, commonly referred to as 26 Fed. "Apparently, Ms. Barkley has had conflicts with agents in Damon's office, and he wants a clean investigation. Since you were at the scene, Kara, you'll take the lead. You and Tyler can work with NYPD. Alina will connect with ATF. We need to find out if Ms. Barkley was the target, with the others as collateral damage, or if she was just in the wrong place at the wrong time."

She nodded, surprised but also excited to have the lead, especially for a case that had literally exploded right behind her. "Sounds good. There was another individual who stood out to me, besides the one who spilled the coffee. A man entered the café just after Ms. Barkley went into the restroom. He came inside and scanned the scene as if he were noting every detail. Then he walked out. He was probably inside for less than a minute. That said, after the bomb went off, he came back to the café to help rescue people. If he were connected to the bombing, he probably wouldn't have done that."

"Unless he wanted to throw suspicion away from himself," Tyler suggested.

"Possibly," she conceded. "I'm sorry I didn't get his name. I was helping someone when he went past me. We were both ordered out when the fire department arrived. I looked around for him later, but he had disappeared."

"Wes is pulling security footage from the scene," Jason said, referring to the head of their tech team, Wes Paulson. "Let's see if either of the men you described was caught on camera leaving the scene. If not, Kara, I'd like you to sit down with Elliott Briggs. He's not only an analyst; he's also an excellent sketch artist. Any kind of description would be helpful going forward. Let's get to work." As the others got up, he added, "Kara, hang back."

She waited as Tyler and Alina left, then gave Jason a questioning look.

"How are you really doing?" he asked, his sharp blue gaze running across her scratched-up face. "And I want an honest answer."

"Honestly, I'm fine."

"You were in an explosion, Kara. It's okay to not be fine."

"I know. But aside from a few scratches and bruises, I'm in good shape, physically and mentally. You don't have to worry about me."

"Good. But I want to reiterate that needing time to process an attack like this is not a sign of weakness. This team will only succeed if we trust each other to tell the truth."

"I agree. And I'm energized to get to work. I have skin in the game—literally."

"Thankfully not too much," he said with a small smile.

"Thankfully," she echoed. "And I appreciate your confidence in me to lead this case."

"Damon told me you're a superstar in the making."

"That's a lot to live up to."

"I believe you're up to the challenge."

"Thanks. I won't let you down."

His words pumped up her confidence, making her believe this unit would be the right place for her to develop her career. But she would have to do good work to make that happen. And that work would be with people she'd only met in the past week. Trust might be key, but they barely knew each other. Still, she was used to hitting the ground running, so that's what she was going to do.

After leaving the conference room, she made her way into the operations center where Wes and Tyler were already reviewing footage from security and traffic cameras near the café and around the courthouse on several large wall monitors.

Wes had come from the San Francisco office, an expert in technology and cybercrime. He was in his late thirties and seemed to have an intense, private personality. She knew next to nothing about him, except that he was supposed to be very good at his job.

Tyler was a mystery as well, which probably wasn't surprising since he'd spent years working covert operations in the military and during his first two years in the FBI.

When Jason had hired her for the unit, he'd told her that he'd assembled a team of agents who would be the best of the best. She was still a little shocked she fell into that category, but apparently her history with the NYPD and Damon Wolfe's support had made her a good candidate for the team, and she intended to prove Jason had made the right decision in hiring her.

Taking a seat at an open computer in front of a blank monitor, she spent the next thirty minutes looking for the two men who had stood out to her. Finally, she caught a break, squinting her eyes at a grainy image of a man in jeans and a sweatshirt three blocks away from the café. "Got something," she said. "This could be the man who spilled the coffee. The clothes look the same, but unfortunately, his back is to the camera."

"And his clothes are fairly standard," Tyler commented, as his gaze moved to her monitor.

"True. I can't see if the sweatshirt has a Knicks logo, but I think this is the guy." She saved the frame as a screenshot and sent it to her phone. If anything, she could use it when she sat down with Elliott to draft a sketch.

"We'll see if we can get another look at him," Wes said as he and Tyler went back to work.

Fifteen minutes later, she spotted the mysterious, good-looking stranger who had acted both suspiciously and heroically. He was standing about two blocks away from the café, on the other side of the street. The timestamp appeared to be a minute before the explosion. He was talking on the phone, but he froze when the flash of fire could be seen in the screen's corner. He said something else, and then put his phone away and rushed out of sight.

She froze the video. "This is the man who went in and out of the café without ordering anything."

Both men looked at the image, then Wes's fingers flew across the keyboard as he picked up the same image and ran it through their system. "Got him," he said.

She looked at his monitor as a man's image appeared with the name: Max Malone. He was the owner of a company called MG Security, based in Manhattan. It looked like the company had only been in business for about nine months.

"This is unusual," Wes commented. "Max Malone has a big gap in his life. Before the creation of his current company, there's no employment history for the previous twelve years. At that time, he worked as a journalist for the Associated Press after graduating from Northwestern the year prior to that."

"And then he's a ghost," she murmured, staring at his image.

"He has no social media," Tyler interjected. "I'm thinking he works in intelligence, maybe undercover work."

"For what agency?" she asked.

"Could be CIA, NSA, DEA. Hell, it could be the Bureau."

"We need to find out," she said, getting up from her chair. "I'm going to see what else I can dig up on him."

"I doubt you'll find much," Tyler said. "His slate has been deliberately wiped clean."

"Until nine months ago," she reminded them. "Maybe his reappearance in the world will provide some clue as to why he was in the café this morning." She returned to her desk, getting onto her own computer, as her mind raced with questions about the mysteriously good-looking man.

An hour later, she'd found little beyond what Wes had discovered in two minutes. Max Malone was thirty-four years old, a little over six feet tall, with dark-brown hair and green eyes. He'd been born in Chicago and had gone to college at Northwestern, where he'd played on the baseball team and graduated with a degree in journalism. His first job had been with the Associated Press. And then there was nothing until last year.

His company was also shrouded in secrecy. No official website. No employees. No known clients. He had a business bank account, a post office box, and a phone number that had gone to voicemail when she called. It wasn't much to go on, and she couldn't afford to spend all her time on someone who might not even be important, so she put him aside and turned to Samantha Barkley.

Samantha Barkley's job as a federal prosecutor could certainly have made her enemies. And Kara couldn't help wondering if Max Malone fell into that category. The timing of his entrance and exit was certainly suspicious, and raised the question: Had he been looking for Samantha when he'd come into the café the first time, or when he'd come back?

CHAPTER TWO

An hour later, Kara and Tyler headed to the DA's office to talk to Samantha's boss and coworkers. The DA, Clayton Montgomery, a smooth political operative in his fifties, described Samantha as fearless and ruthless, someone who wasn't afraid of anything or anyone. The bigger the challenge, the more she loved it. She'd received threatening messages off and on for years, but that had never made her shy away from a case.

Montgomery encouraged them to speak to Melanie Daniels, Samantha's legal admin, who told them Samantha was currently working on a financial fraud case, but it was in early discovery, and not all the players had been identified.

As they talked to Melanie, Kara couldn't help noticing that Tyler had a way with women. While the DA had focused on her, Melanie couldn't stop staring at the rugged man beside her, and Tyler leaned into her attention with a smile so charming, he convinced Melanie to show them Samantha's emails from the last twenty-four hours. Unfortunately, there was nothing noteworthy in that time period, and without knowing if Samantha was the actual target of the bomb or an innocent bystander, they couldn't dig too deep into her life without more evidence. Unless, of course, Samantha was able to give them permission.

With that thought in mind, they headed to the hospital, only to discover that Samantha's condition was critical. She'd made it through surgery, but she had suffered burns across her body as well as serious lung damage. She'd been placed in a medical coma, and the doctor was somber in his remarks about her long-term prognosis. He also told them he'd spoken to Samantha's sister, who was flying in later tonight. Julia had given him permission to discuss her sister's case with the FBI, but they might want to speak to her directly once she arrived.

As they made their way out to the parking lot, she said, "The doctor didn't seem optimistic."

"Even if she survives this critical stage, she's looking at a long recovery," Tyler said. "I don't know that her life will ever be the same."

"It definitely won't be." She shivered, thinking about how she could be in the same position as Samantha. If her drink had come a second later, if she'd gone into the restroom, if she'd been standing closer to the wall...so many ifs. But she couldn't focus on what hadn't happened. She needed to find out who had put Samantha into the hospital bed before they struck again.

"It's almost five," Tyler said as he drove out of the lot. "Do you want to go back to the office? Or I can drop you somewhere."

"The office is fine. I need to get my car. My uncle is a battalion chief with the fire department. He was on the scene this morning. Maybe he can tell me something we don't already know."

"So, you were a cop before you became an agent, and your uncle is a firefighter. Sounds like you come from a family of first responders."

"I do, and I know the best cop and firefighter bars in the city," she said lightly.

"Which group has the better bar?" he asked.

"I'll have to take you to a couple, and then you can decide."

"I'm in," he said with a smile. "Did you grow up in New York?"

"In Queens. How about you?"

"Small town in Iowa."

"Really? I wouldn't have guessed that."

"I enlisted in the Army when I was nineteen. The recruiter told me I could see the world. Of course, he didn't tell me what else I would see." His tone turned dark, then he cleared his throat. "That was fifteen years ago."

"Do you still have family in Iowa?"

"I do, but I don't go back very often."

"I heard you were recently in the Chicago office?"

"Yes. I liked the Windy City, but I was excited to come to New York and work with Jason. We spent a year together in LA, and he is very good at the job." As Tyler finished speaking, he turned into the garage under their building. He parked, then said goodnight and headed to his Ford Bronco, while she got into her small KIA SUV.

She'd asked her uncle to meet her back at the café. It felt a little eerie to return to the scene, but she needed to see it again without all the chaos of the morning. She parked at the end of the block and got out, her steps slowing as she walked down the street, each step taking her closer to the destruction.

What had been a bustling morning coffee shop was now a gutted shell. The large front windows were completely blown out, jagged shards of glass still clinging to the frames. Black scorch marks spread across the cream-colored brick facade in a starburst pattern, darkest near what had been the entrance. The cheerful red awning that had stretched across the storefront hung in tatters, one side completely torn away and the other dangling.

The buildings on either side were dark, their windows boarded up—collateral damage from the blast. The entire block felt abandoned. But as she drew closer, her uncle got out of a pickup truck he'd left in a loading zone and met her on the sidewalk. He was off duty now, wearing jeans and a jacket, his messy pepper-gray hair and weary eyes suggesting a long shift.

"Thanks for meeting me, Uncle Danny."

"Whatever you need, although I'm sure you'll see all the official reports from the investigation," he said.

"I will. Some reports have come in already, but I just want to go inside again, see it for myself without other officials around."

"Then that's what we'll do." He grabbed a crowbar from the back of his truck and walked to the entrance, where plywood had been nailed across the shattered doorway. Pulling the plywood off, he set the crowbar down and turned on a powerful flashlight before leading her inside.

As she stepped into the structure, a beam of his flashlight caught the charred walls and collapsed ceiling tiles. Everything was covered in soot and the chemical residue from fire suppression. The potent smell of burned plastic and wood made her eyes water. She had trouble even knowing where they were standing. All the familiar things were gone, turned to ash.

"The explosive was there," Danny said, directing the beam toward the back hallway where the restrooms were located.

She followed the beam of light, her mind reconstructing the morning, trying to remember who had been standing where, whether she'd overheard any conversation, whether she'd seen anything.

Samantha Barkley jumped into her head, her beautiful black suit, her impeccable style, her sharp, irritated gaze. She had spent time on the phone. Had she been angry with whomever she was talking to? Was that why she had been so short-tempered? They needed to get her phone records, find out who was the last person she'd spoken to.

Turning around, Kara tried to guess where Samantha and the man had collided. But that probably didn't matter, because she knew Samantha had gone to the restroom to clean up.

The man had immediately left the café. The other guy had come in and looked around. Her name had been called by the barista, and she'd picked up her coffee. She'd left a minute later, and the bomb went off.

She sucked in a quick breath, her body still feeling the reverberation and shock of that moment.

"Everything okay?" Danny asked as he turned the light toward her. "Are you reliving it?"

"Yes, but I'm fine. What do you think about what happened here?"

"It feels targeted. Big enough to do significant damage but not take out more than the immediate area. It also would have had to be small enough to fit inside a trash can and be placed there without anyone knowing. I assume there's no security footage from inside the building?"

"Not in that hallway, unfortunately. There were also many people who entered the café the previous evening and earlier this morning who had backpacks with them, including plenty of them who made a trip to the restroom. It could have been anyone."

"You have no suspects then?"

"Not yet. But the woman in the restroom is a federal prosecutor. It's possible she was the target. Or this could have been random."

"A federal prosecutor being critically injured by an explosive device doesn't sound random to me."

"Maybe not. But we can't assume anything."

They stood in silence for a moment, Danny's flashlight the only source of light in the gutted café. The building creaked around them, settling, and Kara could hear traffic in the distance, the normal sounds of the city continuing while this space remained frozen in the moment of violence.

"Do you like your new job?" her uncle asked.

"So far, so good. I'm just getting started."

"You deserve to be working with good people, Kara. People who have your back." There was weight behind his words, and she knew he was thinking about what had happened at the NYPD.

"My boss seems solid," she said carefully. "And the team is experienced. I like what I see."

"Good to hear." He paused. "Did you tell your mom you were here this morning?"

She shook her head, giving him a warning look. "No. And you don't need to tell her. It would just upset her, and I'm fine."

"I get it. Come on. Let's get out of here."

They made their way back to the sidewalk. Her uncle put the plywood back into place to secure the scene. "Do you need a ride somewhere?"

"No. My car is down the street. I'll see you later."

He gave her an impulsive hug. "Take care of yourself."

"I will." She waited until he'd hopped into his truck and sped away before crossing the street and moving in the opposite direction. She was curious about where Max Malone had been spotted and what he'd seen from that vantage point.

When she reached that location, she did a slow turn. From this spot, she could easily see the entrance to the café. Is that why he had stopped here? Had he been watching for someone to enter or exit the café? Had he been talking on the phone? Or had the phone triggered the explosion?

Pondering that thought, she suddenly started when a figure came down the street and moved toward the plywood-covered door of the café. The man wore black jeans with a black coat, and he looked exactly like Max Malone. She waited for a couple of cars to pass by and then jogged across the street, coming up behind him as he poked around the entrance.

"Looking for something?" she asked sharply.

"You?" he said in surprise. "You were at the café this morning. You went back inside to rescue people."

"So did you. I'm Special Agent Kara Reid. And you are?"

"Max Malone." A smile crossed his lips. "And there's nothing special about me."

His attractive charm did not go unnoticed, but she wasn't going to let it distract her. "Why are you trying to get into the building?"

"I wasn't trying to get in; I was just looking around. I was curious about what happened here this morning. What about you?"

"I'm looking into the explosion."

"Do you have any leads?"

"Just you."

He cocked his head to the right, giving her a speculative glance. "Why would I be a lead?"

"You walked into the café, looked around, then walked out. But you didn't go far. You were standing across the street watching the building when the explosion occurred."

"You seem to know a lot about my actions this morning."

"There are multiple cameras in this area. Want to explain your behavior?"

He hesitated, then shrugged. "I was looking for someone. I had a meeting at the café, but she didn't show up. That's why I didn't stay."

"Who were you meeting?"

"Does it matter?"

"Everything matters when a bomb goes off in a crowded café in the middle of New York City. Answer my question."

He studied her for a long moment, then said, "Samantha Barkley."

She straightened at his answer. "Ms. Barkley was in the café. She was in the restroom."

"I heard that later. At the time, I didn't think she was there."

"How do you know her?"

"Mutual friend. And I don't really know her. She asked me to meet her. I was a little late, so when I didn't see her in the café, I thought she'd gone."

"What did she want to talk to you about? Was it a case she was working on? And who is your mutual friend?"

"She didn't say what she wanted to speak to me about, but I run a security firm, so I assume it had something to do with that."

"What kind of security? Are you a bodyguard?"

"I offer a variety of services. I'm sure you already looked me up," he said, a knowing gleam in his eyes.

"Yes. And I found very little information about you. It's almost as if you've been doing a job that no one could know about."

"Or maybe I just stayed off the internet."

"You're very cagey, Mr. Malone."

"Really? I think I'm being quite forthcoming."

"Look, Ms. Barkley may not survive the night, and there's a good chance she was deliberately targeted. If you know something that can help find the person who did this, start talking."

"Why do you think she was the target?" he countered.

She was reluctant to answer his questions when he was stonewalling her, but maybe if she gave him a little, he'd give something back. "A man spilled coffee and whipped cream on her, which sent her to the restroom minutes before an explosive device planted near that restroom went off."

Something shifted in his expression, so subtle she almost missed it in the dim light. "Is that a fact?"

"It is. Now, your turn."

"I don't have any information."

"I don't believe you."

He gave her another assessing look, then said, "Ms. Barkley didn't say why she wanted to speak to me. When I heard she was injured in the explosion, I wondered if she was the target."

"How did you hear she was hurt? Her name hasn't been released to the public."

"Like I said, mutual friend."

"I'm going to need a name."

"You're not going to get it from me."

"Why not? Wouldn't Ms. Barkley's friend want to help with the investigation?"

"How did you happen to be in the café this morning?" he asked, ignoring her question. "Did you have an idea something was going to happen?"

"No."

"You were just there by chance, and now you're investigating? That's a coincidence, isn't it?"

"I'm an FBI agent, and I'd like to know who almost got me killed this morning. I'm very motivated to find that information, and I'm not going to let some shady security guy stop me from doing that."

"I'm not trying to stop you from doing anything. I hope you can find the perpetrator quickly."

"Who's the mutual friend?" she asked again.

"Goodnight, Agent Reid."

"This conversation isn't over," she said in annoyance, but he was already walking away from her. "I can bring you in."

He turned his head and gave her a smile. "I'd just ask for a lawyer, and since you have no reason whatsoever to hold me, that would be a waste of time for both of us."

She really hated that he was right. At least, he'd given her one clue—a mutual friend. Now, she just had to figure out who that was. Since he'd known about Samantha, that meant the friend was probably connected to Samantha's family. Perhaps the sister would know why Samantha had wanted to talk about security with Max Malone. Hopefully, she could speak to her in the morning.

———

Max couldn't get Agent Kara Reid's image out of his head as left the area. In fact, her face had been stuck in his mind since he'd seen her earlier in the day, long before he'd known she was an

FBI agent. She was not only a beautiful woman, with deep brown eyes, beautiful skin, and thick, wavy brown hair that would probably look spectacular if she let it out of her professional ponytail; she was also courageous. She'd run back into a burning building, with no thought to her own safety. He'd thought it had been pure bravery, but now he realized she'd also been trained to act in a dangerous situation. And that's exactly what she'd done.

His phone vibrated in his pocket, and he glanced at his watch, seeing another impatient text from Dominic Ashford. Since he was about to enter the lobby of Dominic's building, he ignored the text and headed inside, checking in with the security desk before heading up to the penthouse apartment on the thirtieth floor. He gave a quick nod to the guard, who knocked, then let him in.

"Where the hell have you been?" Dominic demanded as he met him in the foyer.

It was rare to see the thirty-five-year-old British billionaire in such an anxious state, but one that was completely understandable.

"What's the update on Samantha?"

"She's in critical condition."

Dominic ran a hand through his already messy blond hair. "But she's going to make it, right?" There was desperation in Dominic's eyes and in his voice, but Max had never been one to sugarcoat the truth.

"It's less than fifty-fifty," he replied.

Dominic swore, then waved him into the luxurious living room, which offered floor-to-ceiling views of the glittering city. "Do you want a drink?" Dominic asked as he walked over to a fully stocked bar and poured himself a shot from the open bottle of tequila.

"No thanks."

Dominic swigged the tequila, then picked up the bottle again to pour another shot. "I can't believe what is happening."

"I'm sorry about Samantha. I wish I'd gotten there on time."

"Then you would be in the hospital, too." Dominic drank down his second shot and said, "Was this about me? Or was it about her?"

"She was most likely the target of the bomb, whether that was because of her job or her relationship with you, I don't know," he said. "I spoke to the FBI agent investigating the explosion, and she told me someone spilled coffee on Samantha, which sent her into the restroom before the blast. That seems like a purposeful move."

Dominic stared back at him, his jaw tight, anger running through his eyes. "Doesn't sound like a coincidence." He walked over to the couch and sat down, his shoulders sagging with worry.

Max took the seat across from him, studying Dominic's face, his demeanor. Everything suggested genuine worry, heartbreak, and anger for what had happened to a woman he'd been seeing for a few weeks, but was it true?

He shouldn't have doubts. He'd known Dominic for years. Actually, that wasn't completely true. They'd met at prep school as teenagers, and for a couple of years, they'd been close, but that had been a very long time ago. They'd only renewed their friendship nine months ago when Dominic had asked him to consult on global security after a lapse by his current security team had resulted in an ambush, leaving two men dead.

But that situation had happened on the other side of the world, and Dominic had expressed no concern about his presence in New York City, where his corporate headquarters were located, or about his current girlfriend.

"Does the FBI have any suspects?" Dominic asked.

"If they do, they're not sharing."

"You said you spoke to an agent. Did you tell her you were supposed to meet Samantha?"

"I did."

"Did you mention me?"

"I did not," he said evenly. "But your connection to Samantha is not a secret. You've been photographed together. Her sister knows about you. Your name will come up, and they'll want to talk to you."

"What do you suggest I do?"

"Tell them what you know."

"Which is nothing."

"Then it's nothing," he said simply.

Dominic stood up and walked to the window, staring out at the city.

After a moment, he rose and followed him. The city was spread out before them, and he knew Dominic considered himself to be a power player, not only in the city but in the country, and also the world. Despite his stature, this incident had shaken him, and he didn't know if that was because Dominic was in love with Samantha or because something else was going on.

"I wish Samantha had told me what she wanted to talk to you about," Dominic said, frustration edging his voice. "Are you sure she didn't give you an idea of the subject?"

"Positive. Do you know what she was working on?"

"A corporate fraud case, I think, but she didn't talk about her work, and neither did I. We wanted to keep that part of our lives separate." Dominic turned to face him. "This was probably tied to her case, don't you think? My competitors, my enemies, they wouldn't have gone after her, would they?"

He could see the genuine fear in Dominic's eyes. "That's the second time you've asked that question. Is there some reason you think someone would have gone after her?"

"We both know what happened in Dushanbe six months ago."

"That was because of your potential infrastructure project cutting off smuggling routes," he said. "At least, that's what you led me to believe."

"That's what I assumed it was. I've never felt unsafe here in New York City."

"Even though you have a fairly heavy security presence surrounding you at all times?" he commented.

"Well, I can't be too careful. I'm a public figure and a rich man. That's why I'm concerned about Samantha. I need to know what happened to her. You need to figure it out, Max."

"Why me? I thought you wanted me to focus on your overseas trips. That's where I have the most expertise, not here in the city."

"You know how to get answers. And I need answers. I'll pay you extra. Just get it done. This is the priority."

He gave Dominic a long, speculative look. 'Are you afraid that whoever went after her is coming for you next?"

"It has crossed my mind. Or other people in my life could be in danger. That's why it's imperative we find out who's behind that bomb."

"The FBI is already on it, and I'm sure the ATF and the NYPD are also investigating."

"I want you on it, too."

"I'll do what I can. You're not holding anything back, are you?"

"How can you ask me that question?"

"Because you don't always play by the rules. We both know that. If you're aware of a threat, then telling me what that is will get us to the truth more quickly."

"I'm not holding back," Dominic said. "I—I care about Samantha."

He might have believed him more if Dominic hadn't stumbled through the sentence. Either he wasn't comfortable sharing his feelings, or he was lying.

"Her sister, Julia, is on her way to New York," Dominic continued. "My admin got her a suite at the Hilton near the hospital. Maybe you can talk to her tomorrow."

"What did she tell you?"

"Nothing. She hadn't spoken to Samantha in a couple of

weeks. She seemed a little awkward on the phone. I think Julia might feel more comfortable talking to you than to me."

"Why? You're the man Samantha has been seeing."

"She just seemed nervous to be talking to me. She gets in late tonight, but you should be able to reach her tomorrow."

"Okay, I'll speak to her."

"Hopefully, tomorrow we'll get better news and better answers."

"Hopefully," he echoed, but as he left the apartment, he didn't feel hopeful at all.

CHAPTER THREE

Tuesday morning, Max woke up to the familiar smell of ginger and garlic wafting up from the Golden Dragon restaurant on the ground floor of his building. He'd been living in this second-story apartment for almost three months, which, in his life, was a long time. Dominic had offered one of his corporate apartments for the duration of his consultancy, but he didn't like sterile and modern; he preferred warm and chaotic, and his neighborhood on the edge of Chinatown was lively and diverse, with real people who he felt far more comfortable with than those who were in Dominic's orbit.

After a quick shower, he grabbed his coffee mug and headed down the narrow stairs from his second-floor apartment to the restaurant's kitchen entrance. Stepping inside, the energy in the room did not surprise him. It was only eight, and the restaurant wouldn't open for lunch until eleven, but the Kim family was in deep prep mode. Mrs. Kim looked up from her knife work on a pile of scallions, her sharp gaze raking his face and body with the same critical expression she'd worn since the day he'd moved in above the restaurant.

"You look tired. You don't sleep, do you?" she asked, her

accent still notable despite living in New York for the past thirty years.

"Sometimes I do."

"Not enough. You need to eat. Not just drink coffee." She gestured at his empty mug with her knife.

"Coffee's fine—"

"Coffee is not food. You are too thin. Always working, never eating."

Her husband, Mr. Kim, emerged from the walk-in cooler carrying a crate of vegetables. He nodded at Max, his weathered face creasing in what might have been a smile. "Good morning."

"Morning," he said as a teenage boy entered the kitchen, phone in hand. Peter Kim was seventeen, the youngest of the four Kim children, and like his older siblings, he either helped in the kitchen or worked deliveries for the restaurant after school. "Hey, Pete."

"What's up?" the kid said.

"Not much. You?"

"Got a calculus test first period." Peter made a face. "Can't wait to graduate so I can do what I want."

"You go to college first," Mrs. Kim said sharply, not looking up from her prep. "Then you get a good job, and, maybe after that, you do you want."

Peter rolled his eyes, but didn't argue. He'd probably had this conversation a hundred times.

"Coffee's ready," Mr. Kim said, gesturing to the industrial coffeemaker in the corner. "Help yourself, Max."

He filled his mug, then headed back upstairs. His apartment was small—a main room that served as both living space and home office, a bedroom barely big enough for a bed, and a bathroom that had probably been renovated in the eighties. But it was more than enough for him, and it was also off the grid, which he preferred.

He'd just set his coffee down on the kitchen table, which he also used as a desk, when there was a knock at the door.

He opened the door to Kai Porter, a forty-two-year-old brunette with sharp eyes that didn't miss a thing and a sharp mouth that sometimes got her into trouble. They'd worked off and on together for years, and she was one of the few people in his life he could count on. She'd quit the agency last year to take care of her mother, who had recently passed. After Dominic had hired him, he'd hired her.

While Dominic had given him an office at his corporate headquarters along with an admin and a team of people he could use, he didn't entirely trust any of them. He wasn't completely sure that someone in Dominic's company hadn't sold him out on his last trip abroad, so while some things he could reveal to the bigger group, he wanted to keep specific details between him and Kai until they needed to go public.

Kai entered the apartment with her laptop bag over her shoulder and a plate of steamed buns in her hand. She gave him a smile. "I was going to complain about you wanting me to come here instead of Dominic's posh offices, but Mrs. Kim flagged me down on my way up, and these smell delicious."

"They are delicious," he said as he closed the door behind her. "And what I wanted to talk to you about is better said here than in the office."

"Fine. But Mrs. Kim said I had to make sure you eat, so you don't starve to death." She set the buns down on the table. "I told her I wasn't responsible for you, but she didn't seem to care."

He went into the small kitchen and grabbed two plates. "She has a kind heart."

"She certainly cares about you." Kai took a seat at the table, and he sat down across from her, sliding a pork bun onto her plate. She picked up her fork and took a bite. "So good," she mumbled with her mouth full.

He nodded, eating the bun in a few quick bites, then chasing it down with a swig of strong coffee. "Now I feel ready to go."

"And do what, exactly?" Kai asked, with an inquiring arch of her brow. "The trip to Tajikistan is now postponed for two more weeks because of the weather. Which gives us a month to work on Dominic's security detail and itinerary for the groundbreaking. That's more than enough time. In fact, if we smooth the way too soon, we'll have to do it all over again."

"This isn't about Tajikistan. Dominic's girlfriend, Samantha Barkley, was critically injured in the café bombing yesterday."

Kai's eyes widened. "Seriously? That's terrible. Is she going to be all right?"

"It's touch and go. Dominic wants me to find out who's responsible for the bombing, and whether it's connected to him."

"He's worried someone went after her because of him?"

"Yes. At least, that's what he tells me."

"You don't believe him?"

"I'm not sure. But that's the least of my concerns. If Samantha was targeted because of Dominic, then he could be in danger. I need you to see what you can dig up on Samantha's cases over the past few years. She's a federal prosecutor. There has to be some public information that can give us a potential enemy list."

"I'll do what I can using the limited resources we have. The FBI will have more access."

"I'm working on getting to share in that access."

"Working how?" she asked doubtfully.

"I'll let you know if I'm successful. At any rate, Samantha's sister has arrived from Colorado. Dominic set up a meeting with her for me this morning." He checked his watch. "I'm going to head out shortly."

"Is Dominic meeting you there?"

"No. He thinks the sister will tell me more than she would tell him."

"But Dominic is Samantha's boyfriend, or whatever you want to call him. Why would the sister hold something back from him?"

"No idea if she would, but that's what's happening this morning."

"All right."

She had a look on her face that told him she had more to say. "What?" he asked as he got to his feet. "Something on your mind?"

"I can't help feeling that this job is taking you further away from your original goal, Max."

"You're not wrong," he admitted. "But Dominic's money is going to fund that goal, and until I can get back overseas, I need to keep him happy. I also have a vested interest in what happened to Samantha. She asked me to meet her at the café. I was late. I thought she'd left, so I didn't stay. It turns out she was in the restroom because someone spilled coffee on her, which I think was deliberate."

"Now I understand. You feel guilty."

"Not necessarily guilty, but I was there. I saw the destruction, and Samantha Barkley wasn't the only one hurt. I want to know who set off that bomb and why."

"Then I'll help."

He nodded. "Great. If none of this is tied to Dominic, and it was just random, I'll back off and let the FBI do their thing, but until I know for sure, I'm all in."

"Let me know how it goes with the sister. I'll keep working on our actual work until I hear otherwise."

"Thanks."

Max headed out the door and into the January cold. The sidewalk was already jammed with people. The constant energy was something he loved about New York, but the density of people and buildings, and the international acclaim of the city had always made it a target. He just hoped the bomber from the café wasn't planning another attack.

After taking a cab downtown, he walked through the Hilton lobby and took the elevator to the twenty-third floor. The woman who opened the door was a softer version of Samantha

Barkley. Same dark hair, same bone structure, but Julia's warm brown eyes lacked Samantha's sharp intensity. Julia wore jeans and an oversized Colorado Rockies sweatshirt, and she looked exhausted and terrified.

"Hello, I'm Max Malone. I'm a friend of Dominic Ashford."

"He told me you were coming over. He said Samantha asked you to meet her at the café. Can you tell me why?"

"Why don't you let me in, Ms. Clemons, and we'll talk?"

She stepped back and waved him inside. The room held two double beds, one covered by clothes and an open suitcase, the other untouched. A laptop sat on the desk, and tissues were scattered across the nightstand. Julia gestured toward the small table and chairs by the window.

He sat down across from her. "First, I want to say how sorry I am about what happened, and I very much hope that Samantha recovers."

"Thank you," she said, fighting back tears. "Her doctor doesn't seem very optimistic."

"Did you speak to the doctor this morning?"

"Yes. He said her chances will improve if she can survive the next twenty-four to forty-eight hours."

"I don't know your sister well, but I know she's a fighter."

"I hope she can fight through this. But it's going to be a lot." Her voice broke on the last word, and Max gave her a moment to collect herself. "I'm sorry," she said. "What did you want to talk to me about?"

"I was wondering if Samantha mentioned anyone who was giving her trouble. Any threats she might have gotten at work or at home? Any reason she might have wanted to talk to me?"

"Dominic said you handle security for him. It seems like it would have been about that."

"But Samantha didn't ask Dominic for my help; she asked to meet with me separately, and he knew nothing about it. I'm hoping she told you why."

"She didn't. I haven't spoken to her in probably two weeks,

which isn't unusual. She's a very busy woman." Julia paused. "Are you suggesting she didn't trust Dominic?"

"Not at all, just saying she didn't ask for his help; she asked for mine."

"Maybe she was worried about herself. Samantha got death threats all the time. She said it was part of the job." Julia took a breath. "Is it true she was the target of the bomb?"

"That's to be determined. But her job might have made her a target, which is why we're starting there."

"My sister is very private. She doesn't open up to me or really to anyone. It's one reason her ex divorced her."

"I didn't realize she had been married."

"In her mid-twenties, right out of law school. They were married for only two years. They had little in common besides the law."

"What's their relationship like now?"

"They don't have one, but Victor is not a danger to her. He's remarried with two kids. I don't think they've spoken in years."

It didn't sound like the ex-husband was a factor. "What did she tell you about her relationship with Dominic?"

"She said he checked all the boxes: attractive, wealthy, powerful, and well-connected—all things she finds important. I asked her if he was kind and sweet, and she laughed. She said she didn't know him well enough to say. But she seemed pretty happy about their relationship." She paused, giving him a questioning look. "Is he a good guy?"

"As far as I know."

"Well, you would know, right? You're his security guy, aren't you?"

"One of them. And he is very upset about what happened to Samantha."

"I hope you can find out who did this. I can't help thinking that since she's still alive, someone might try again."

"Dominic has arranged for private security at the hospital. You don't have to worry about that."

"Well, that's good." She started as a knock came at her door. "Are you expecting someone?"

"No. Why don't I get that?"

He got to his feet and walked across the room. After looking through the peephole, he opened the door to Agent Kara Reid and another man, who looked familiar, but he couldn't quite place him.

"You again?" Kara said, surprise and suspicion in her deep-brown eyes.

He shrugged in reply. "Small city."

"Not really. We're here to see Julia Clemons."

Julia came up behind him. "I'm Julia."

"I'm Special Agent Kara Reid with the FBI, and this is Agent Brennan," Kara said, flashing her badge. "We'd like to speak to you about your sister."

Julia gave him a questioning look.

"You should talk to them," he encouraged. "They're trying to find out what happened to Samantha. We can speak more later." As Kara and her fellow agent stepped through the door, he slipped past them into the hallway. Before he could take another step, Kara came back into the hall.

"Mr. Malone," she called. "What are you doing here?"

He turned and said, "Looking for answers, just like you."

"For Dominic Ashford?"

Her question hung in the air as an odd tension sizzled between them. He noticed details he hadn't before—the intelligence in her big, dark eyes, the perfect shape of her nose, the fullness of her mouth, the slight catch in her breath that suggested she felt a tension between them, the same tension he was starting to feel whenever she was around.

When he didn't answer, she added, "We're going to need to speak to Mr. Ashford."

"You should," he said, then turned and walked toward the elevators, feeling her assessing gaze on his back every step of the way.

———

Max Malone had an agenda, but Kara didn't have time to figure that out now. She closed the hotel room door and joined Tyler and Julia, who were sitting at a table, with Julia dabbing at her teary eyes with a tissue.

"I'm sorry about your sister," she said as Julia composed herself. "I know this is an incredibly difficult time."

"Thank you. I don't know what I can tell you. I know little about Julia's work and even less about her relationship with Dominic. My sister and I spoke on the phone every couple of weeks."

"Were you the one to inform Mr. Ashford about Samantha's injuries?" she asked.

"Yes. He called me," Julia replied. "He said he'd been trying to reach Samantha and that he knew she often stopped in at that café for coffee in the morning. I had just heard from the hospital a few minutes before he reached out, so I told him what I knew. Then I got on a plane as fast as I could. Unfortunately, I haven't been able to speak to my sister. She's in a coma." Her voice caught once more. "They don't know..." She gave a helpless shake of her head. "It's bad. Even if she survives, it will be a long recovery. Someone needs to be punished for what they did."

"We're going to find out who set the bomb and determine whether your sister was the target," she assured Julia.

"I hope you can. Max said that Dominic sent his private security to the hospital just in case someone tries to hurt her again."

She nodded. They'd stopped in at the hospital before coming to the hotel and had met with the security guard.

Tyler cleared his throat. "Did you talk to Mr. Ashford about the explosion?" Tyler asked. "Did he offer a theory as to who might have been responsible?"

"No. He said he was shocked. He wanted to know if Samantha had told me about any threats against her, but she hadn't said a word. That wasn't unusual. She's my big sister. She wouldn't burden me with that kind of anxiety."

"What do you know about Max Malone?" Tyler asked.

"He works in security for Dominic."

"Samantha never mentioned him to you?" she asked.

"No. Why?"

"Just trying to figure out the relationships Samantha had with Mr. Ashford and Mr. Malone," she explained.

"Well, she was seeing Dominic romantically, and Max works for Dominic. Max said Samantha asked him to meet her at the café, but he didn't know why, and I don't either."

"What did Samantha say about her relationship with Dominic? Was it serious between them?"

"I don't know. She seemed excited about being in his life. She told me she was meeting interesting people and that he was charming, handsome, and rich. As for serious, it's only been a few months, and Samantha always looks before she leaps. She's a planner. She's not spontaneous. She doesn't fall in love easily." Julia swallowed hard. "But I hope she was in love, that she got to feel that, because...well, I just would hate to think she would never experience that." She got to her feet. "I really need to go to the hospital. I want to sit with her. Are we done?"

"One last thing," she said. "We'd like to look in Samantha's apartment. We're trying to get a search warrant, but if you would give your consent to her building manager, we could get inside now and see if there is any evidence in there that might help us get to whoever did this."

Julia gave her a conflicted look. "I guess I could do that. I want you to find whoever hurt her."

"That's all we're trying to do," she assured her. "If you want, we could stop by the apartment now and then drop you at the hospital."

"Okay. I just need to change. Would you mind waiting for me in the lobby?"

"Of course. We'll meet you by the elevators." She headed out of the room with Tyler. "This will be good."

"As long as she comes down the elevator and doesn't ditch us by getting off at a lower floor and then taking the stairs," he said.

She gave him a surprised look as they stepped into the elevator. "Do you think she would do that?"

"Probably not, but there was a slight shift in her gaze when she asked us to wait in the lobby."

"I think she just wanted to change her clothes in private."

"Maybe. We'll find out soon enough."

A few minutes later, they got off at the lobby level and then moved to stand slightly away from the crush of people. Tyler's gaze scanned the lobby, and she followed in kind, but she wasn't sure exactly what he was looking for or even why he was suspicious of the victim's sister.

"What are you thinking?" she asked. "You seem a little edgy for what's happening right now."

"That man—Max Malone—I've met him before."

Now she was surprised. "Seriously? Why didn't you say something yesterday?"

"Because he didn't look the same when I met him. He had a beard, and his hair was much longer. He also had a different name that I can't recall now. But today, when I looked at his green eyes, I recognized him."

"Where did you meet him?"

"I'm not sure. Afghanistan, Iraq, maybe Syria." His lips tightened. "It was three or four years ago, when I was serving overseas. I believe he was working with the CIA."

"That would explain why his work history has been scrubbed. But what does it mean for this case?"

"Maybe nothing. It's not unusual for a former CIA agent to go into private security, and Dominic Ashford has global interests."

"Since Dominic was seeing Samantha, it makes sense he'd be looking into what happened," she added. "But Max Malone is cagey. He answers questions with questions, and I'm not sure if he's trying to find out what happened to Samantha or make sure no one else does."

"As in protecting his boss?"

"Maybe. Although it seems unlikely Dominic Ashford would blow up a café filled with people to get rid of a girlfriend."

"Unless she had something on him, and he wanted it to look bigger than a targeted attack."

"Something to consider," she said, happy to see Julia step off the elevator. Getting into Samantha's apartment would be more than helpful, and not having to wait longer for a search warrant would be even better.

———

Samantha's apartment was in Tribeca, in an old but elegant building with a uniformed doorman out front. There was also a security person at the front desk, who alerted the building manager, and shortly thereafter, the manager appeared and escorted them up to the tenth floor. He opened the door for them, and they stepped inside.

The apartment was modern and bright with white walls, light-gray floors, and a mix and match of thick accent carpets. There were paintings on the walls, expensive pottery and sculptures in showcased alcoves. It felt more like a museum and less like a home. But that seemed to fit the person they were getting to know.

Julia wandered around, an awed look on her face. "I had no idea she lived like this," she murmured.

"You haven't been here before?" Kara asked.

"No. She moved in last year. She said it was nice, but this is beyond nice. God, she must feel like she's in the ghetto when she comes to visit me."

For the first time, there was an edge of bitter jealousy in Julia's voice, which surprised Kara. Maybe the sisters weren't as close as one might think. She made her way through the living room into a glass-partitioned office, while Tyler headed down the hall.

"There's nothing of us here," Julia muttered a moment later as she followed her into the office. "No family photos, none of the crayon drawings my kids send her. Maybe she just throws them away. She probably just humors me by saying she likes them."

As Kara flipped through the drawers in the filing cabinet, she found the aforementioned drawings in a pile and was relieved to have something to cheer Julia up. "She doesn't throw them away." She pulled the pictures out and placed them on the neat and organized glass desk.

"Oh," Julia said in surprise, picking up the first one. "Now I feel terrible for saying that, because she did keep them." Her lips trembled as she stared at the childish drawing of a family at a park. "She was supposed to come to this birthday party, but she couldn't make it because she had to work, so my son drew a picture and put her in it." She struggled to compose herself. "She might never be at another party." She shook her head in terrified grief. "I can't do this. I can't be here right now. It feels like we're cleaning things up after she's gone, and I don't want her to be gone."

"You can wait downstairs," she said. "We won't be long."

"No. I'm just going to go to the hospital. I need to see her. I need to sit by her bed. I'll take a taxi."

"Okay, but before you go, would you know any of her passwords? For her computer?"

Julia gave her a blank look, then shook her head. "No. Sorry. I wish I could help, but I can't." With the drawing in her hand, she whirled around and headed out of the office.

A moment later, Kara heard the front door close. Maybe that was just as well. She needed more time to go through Samantha's office.

Tyler joined her about ten minutes later, a frustrated expression on his face. "I got nothing. And everything is so neat it's unsettling."

"I agree. If anyone looked through my things, they'd find a lot more mess."

"Nothing in here?"

"Her laptop is password protected, so I can't get on it. I don't see anything in her files, which seem to be personal bills and such. But there is this one folder." She tapped the manila folder on the desk and then pushed it across the glass to Tyler. "It looks like an itinerary for a trip to Tajikistan. There's a note on the last page with the words danger and cost, with a question mark."

Tyler opened the file and read through the few pages inside. "Dominic Ashford's company is going to break ground for a bridge and highway project through a treacherous mountain region in Tajikistan, connecting poorer parts of the country with the city center." He paused and looked up. "I'm not surprised someone wrote danger and cost, because this project will disrupt the smuggling routes in that area. That will make many people unhappy."

"Maybe Samantha was concerned about Dominic's safety, and that's why she wanted to talk to Max Malone."

"Malone would be knowledgeable about that part of the world."

She nodded. Despite feeling like they'd found a clue, it really didn't bring them any closer to what had happened at the café. "This may not tie in at all to the bombing. Tajikistan is a long way from here."

"You're right. Hard to see the link between what happened at the café and this folder."

"Exactly. Let's go talk to Dominic Ashford and see if he can clear up a few of our questions."

"I thought we were waiting for his assistant to get back to us on a time," Tyler said dryly.

"Waiting time is over. If Dominic wants to find out what happened to Samantha, he'll talk to us."

CHAPTER FOUR

The global headquarters of Ashford Industries was located in a twenty-five-story high-rise in midtown that Dominic Ashford had built several years ago. While the top five floors of the building were reserved solely for Ashford Industries, the rest of the building was leased by other large and successful companies.

After passing through security, Kara and Tyler were escorted upstairs by a suited man who had little to say except that he'd take them to see Mr. Ashford.

When the elevator doors opened, they stepped into a luxe office suite, where their escort conversed with the receptionist before asking them to take a seat in the reception area. They didn't bother to sit down. She was determined to see Dominic as soon as possible and was prepared to use her badge to force her way into the office if she had to. Thankfully, the receptionist got up from her desk and took them through a pair of double doors and down a short hallway to Dominic's office.

Dominic got up from behind a massive mahogany desk and came around to greet them. He was a very attractive man in his mid-thirties, impeccably dressed in a gray suit, his blond hair perfectly styled, his face clean-shaven. He had that executive glow that spoke of expensive skin products. After they'd introduced themselves, he waved them toward a corner where two black leather sofas surrounded a coffee table.

"Please sit down," he said with a British accent.

"First, we're very sorry about what happened to Samantha Barkley," she said as they sat down. "We understand the two of you are romantically involved."

"Yes," he said shortly. "How can I help you?"

"How long have you been seeing Ms. Barkley?" she asked.

"About three months. We met at a charity fundraiser." He paused, his blue-eyed gaze reflective. "I have to admit I wasn't looking to date a lawyer. But Samantha was beautiful, smart, and passionate about her work. I couldn't resist. That said, I can't imagine the details of our relationship would be helpful to your investigation."

"Samantha texted Max Malone, who I believe works for you," she continued. "He claims he didn't know what she wanted to speak to him about. Do you know?"

"I don't. I was surprised she reached out to him directly. She must have had a question about something related to her caseload."

"Do you think she felt threatened?" Tyler interjected. "She didn't mention anyone with whom she had a problem?"

"No. Samantha is a strong woman with little patience for incompetence. I would venture to say she could have been easily annoyed by many people."

She didn't find that difficult to believe, remembering the dirty look Samantha had thrown her when she'd moved into her personal space.

"What about her current case?" Tyler continued. "Did she talk to you about it?"

"She mentioned that members of a renowned accounting firm in the city were under indictment, and she was going to prosecute them for fraud. We didn't discuss the details. I know you're looking for a lead, but I don't have one. Maybe one of her coworkers or the DA would know more, especially if this attack was related to her work."

His tone was smooth, his answers seemingly helpful, but he also wasn't telling them much. She needed to shake him up a little. "What if the attack was related to you? Do you have enemies who might see your girlfriend as a way to get to you?"

He stiffened at her words, but he quickly composed himself. "I haven't received any threats in recent weeks. And I pray she didn't get hurt because of me. I don't think I could live with myself if that were the case."

"We found a file in Samantha's apartment," she continued. "It appeared to be an itinerary for your upcoming trip to Tajikistan. There was handwriting on the last page; I don't know whether it belonged to Samantha or to someone else. But the note had two words: danger and cost, with a question mark."

Dominic's lips tightened. "Samantha was concerned about an infrastructure project my company is breaking ground on next month. The region can be dangerous, but I have a security expert who will make sure our event is as safe as it can be."

"And would that expert be Max Malone?" Tyler interjected.

"Yes, it would," Dominic replied, not offering any further details.

"The man Samantha wanted to talk to," Tyler continued.

"Well, now that you mention the file, I'm thinking it's because she was worried about me, about the trip. There was an incident last year with my security in a different region of that country. We were ambushed, and two of my security guards were killed. That's why we moved the project to a different area."

"But Tajikistan is not that big," Tyler said. "Do you really think the danger is gone?"

"We will have more support this time."

"And that will be expensive," she said.

"It usually is," Dominic replied. "But this is an important project. It will change lives. It's an enormous investment for the company, but it will be worth it."

He sounded passionate, sincere, or he might just be a great salesperson.

"Do you have any leads at all into the bomber?" Dominic asked, changing the subject.

"Not at this time," she answered.

"That's disappointing. I've been racking my brain trying to think of who might have wanted to hurt Samantha. While we didn't talk that much about her current case, she mentioned that the accounting firm had clients tied to organized crime. One of those clients is Armen Petroysan, who owns a chain of automotive dealerships."

She nodded. Armen Petroysan had been on both the NYPD and the FBI's radar for years, but there had never been enough evidence to bring him in on anything. "That's interesting. We're still trying to get the case files from the DA's office."

"What's the problem? Do I need to make a call? I know the DA. I can put some pressure on him."

"They're going to release the files; it's just a process," she said. "And to be quite frank, we don't know if Samantha was the target or just in the wrong place at the wrong time, so we have to look at everything. But we appreciate the tip, and we will look into that case."

"Is that it?" Dominic asked as he rose, clearly ready to end the meeting.

"One more thing," she said as she got to her feet. "How long have you known Max Malone?"

"Max?" Dominic echoed, surprised by the question. "A long time. We went to boarding school together in the UK—Harrow. We were there for two years together."

She hadn't been expecting that answer. "I didn't realize you were friends."

"Well, we lost touch for a long time, but we've reconnected, and Max is very good at his job."

"Because of his CIA background?" Tyler asked.

Dominic's eyebrows rose slightly, as if he wasn't sure how to answer that question, but he said simply, "You'll have to talk to him about his background. Let me show you out."

They were at the door when Tyler paused, "Mr. Ashford, can you account for your whereabouts Monday morning between seven and nine a.m.?"

Dominic's expression turned stony. "You're asking me for an alibi for an explosion that almost killed a woman I care about?"

"Standard procedure in an investigation like this," Tyler said calmly.

"I was here." Dominic said tightly. "I had a conference call with investors in Dubai at eight a.m." The warmth drained from his demeanor. "My assistant and my security people can confirm that." He pointedly opened the door.

"Thank you for your time," she said, noting how quickly the door closed behind them.

When they got into the elevator, Tyler said, "What do you think?"

"He answered our questions. His emotions seemed appropriate."

"But?" Tyler asked.

"I felt like there was something he wasn't saying."

"I felt the same way. I wouldn't be surprised if this bomb had more to do with him and less to do with Samantha. Maybe someone wanted to send him a message. We need to find out what happened on his last trip to Tajikistan."

"And maybe more about Armen Petroysan. I'd like to know how Samantha's case is going to affect him."

"Well, we should get her case files soon. Let's go back to the office."

———

The rest of Tuesday delivered little progress, Kara thought, as she stretched and rolled her neck around on her shoulders a little after five. The files from the DA's office would arrive in the morning, so she'd spent most of her time re-interviewing witnesses and using social media to find out more about Samantha Barkley and Dominic Ashford's relationship.

They'd spent a lot of time at philanthropic events and political fundraisers, with a few dinners and birthday parties with local politicians and CEOs, all of whom appeared to be friends with Dominic. But she wasn't as interested in his friends as she was in his enemies. When she'd asked him if Samantha could have been targeted because of her relationship to him, it was clear that he couldn't rule out that possibility. But it was going to be difficult to find real information about Dominic on the Internet. Which meant she needed to talk to Max again. He hadn't returned any of her calls, but she had managed to get Wes to trace his phone to a Chinese restaurant on the edge of Chinatown.

Maybe it was time to check that out. She put on her coat, grabbed her bag, and headed down to the garage. Twenty minutes later, she arrived at the Golden Dragon restaurant. There appeared to be a door next to the restaurant that led to an upstairs apartment. She wondered if Max might live there, although it didn't seem like the kind of a place a guy who owned his own security company and had a billionaire for a client would live. Although it did seem like the kind of place that a CIA agent might use as a cover.

She pushed the doorbell for the apartment. If she was wrong, at least she'd know. There was no answer. Pulling out her phone, she called him again. She was ready to leave a more urgent message when his deep voice came across the line.

"Max Malone?"

"Who's asking?"

"Agent Kara Reid. I've called you several times today. I need to speak to you."

"About?"

"Dominic Ashford and Samantha Barkley. I have questions."

"Dominic told me he already spoke to you. I doubt I can provide any new information."

"Oh, I think you can. Where are you? Can we meet?"

"I guess I could meet with you. On one condition. You pay for dinner."

"I'm not having dinner with you," she protested.

"Too bad. Because I'm hungry and I like to talk over a meal."

She drew an irritated breath. "Fine, I'll buy you dinner. Where?"

"How about here?"

His voice was no longer on the line; it was coming from behind her. She whirled around in surprise, her heart beating a little too fast when she saw him standing on the sidewalk with a smirk on his too-handsome face.

She put her phone into the pocket of her jacket. "Funny," she said.

His grin broadened. "I hope you like Chinese food."

"I do. And I will buy you dinner, but you have to promise to actually speak."

"No promises. We'll see how things go."

She didn't like his response, but at the moment, he had the upper hand. She had no grounds to bring him in for an official interview yet, so she had to take what she could get. Waving her hand toward the restaurant, she said, "After you."

He led the way into the Golden Dragon, opening the door for her and motioning her inside. The space was small and unpretentious, with a dozen tables covered with bright red tablecloths. Paper lanterns hung from the ceiling, and the air was thick with the smell of garlic, ginger, and other spices.

A woman who had to be in her sixties came out of the kitchen, her face breaking into a wide smile when she saw Max.

"Max! Finally, you come to eat!" She came around the counter, already talking rapidly in a mix of English and, what Kara assumed, was Cantonese. "And you bring someone!" Her sharp eyes turned to Kara, assessing her with the kind of directness that would have been rude anywhere but in a Chinese family restaurant. "Girlfriend?"

"No, Mrs. Kim, this is—"

"A colleague," Kara said quickly.

Mrs. Kim waved her hand dismissively. "Colleague, girlfriend, it doesn't matter. You both need to eat. Sit, sit." She gestured emphatically toward a table in the corner. "I make you something good. Best dumplings in New York."

"Mrs. Kim, we can order—" Max said, once more interrupted.

"No, no. You sit. I cook." She was already heading toward the kitchen, calling out something in Cantonese that made an older man appear in the kitchen doorway. He looked at Max, then at Kara, and said something that made Mrs. Kim laugh and swat at him with a dish towel.

Kara raised an eyebrow at Max as they headed to the corner table. "Sounds like you're well-known around here."

"I live upstairs. But you knew that, right?"

"I knew your phone had been in this location quite a bit."

He smiled and tipped his head. "Very good. But I wasn't trying to hide."

"Could have fooled me. You have no business address outside of a post-office box, no website, no client testimonials anywhere. How do you sell your services?"

"Personal referrals. You're going to love the food here; it's great. I have to warn you, though, Mrs. Kim will bring enough food for four people."

As she sat down, she took in the restaurant from a new vantage point. It felt warm and comfortable, not trendy, not trying to be anything other than what it was, and she felt instantly at home. She was, however, a little surprised by how much the family seemed to like Max. The more she learned about him, the more intrigued she became.

"So," she began. "Dominic Ashford mentioned you went to

Harrow together. I didn't take you for a UK boarding school kid."

A flicker of surprise ran through his eyes. "I'm surprised he shared that with you."

"Is it a secret?"

"No. But I don't understand why you'd be talking about that."

"He said he'd known you a long time."

"Well, we certainly met a long time ago."

She wondered about the distinction he seemed to be making. "Does that mean you don't know each other well?"

Ignoring her question, he said, "What else did Dominic tell you?"

"That you used to work for the CIA."

He sat back in his chair, giving her a speculative look. "I don't think Dominic told you that; I think Special Agent Brennan did."

"Tyler mentioned he remembered meeting you somewhere overseas when he was in Delta Force," she admitted. "Why did you leave the CIA?"

He shrugged. "Why does anyone leave a job? I felt like making a change."

"And now you run security for Dominic Ashford?"

"I'm handling international security for him. He already has a team in the US."

Mrs. Kim appeared with a pot of tea and two cups, setting them down with a flourish. "Green tea. Very good for you. Make you strong, healthy." She poured for both of them, then disappeared again.

Kara wrapped her hands around the cup, grateful for the warmth. "How did you end up living in this neighborhood?"

"Does it matter?"

"Just curious. It would be an excellent cover for a CIA agent masquerading as a private security consultant."

"Are you writing yourself a story here, Agent Reid?"

"Am I wrong?" she challenged.

"The rent was cheap, and I like the neighborhood."

Everything about him was frustrating—the way he deflected questions, the way he kept showing up in her investigation, the way her heart jumped every time she saw him. "Why all the secrecy, Mr. Malone?"

"There's no secrecy. You're trying to make me part of your case, but I'm not."

"You work for Dominic Ashford, who dates Samantha Barkley. You were in the café. You're in this whether or not you want to be. Did you see anyone in the café when you came inside, anyone you recognized, anyone that seemed out of place, who caught your eye?"

He stared back at her. "I saw you."

Goose bumps ran down her arms at his very direct reply. "You didn't even look at me," she countered.

"I did. And you were staring right back at me. I thought we had a moment."

"We did not have a moment," she said, even though she was staring at him now and couldn't seem to break his gaze. "Are you trying to be charming?"

His smile broadened. "Is it working?"

"No."

"Too bad. I did see you, Special Agent Kara Reid," he drawled, using her full name and title. "Although I had no idea you were FBI."

"And I had no idea you were CIA. Odd that we should both be there at that moment."

"You seemed determined to make it odd. As for the rest of your question, I didn't notice anything out of the ordinary. I've actually been replaying the scene in my mind to make sure I wasn't forgetting something. Contrary to what you might think, I'm angry about what happened, not only to Samantha but to everyone else who was injured, both physically and emotionally."

"Then help me."

"How? You know more than I do. I have no idea what you want from me."

"I don't think you're telling me everything."

Before he could reply, Mrs. Kim returned with plates of dumplings, scallion pancakes, kung pao chicken, and fried rice. Far too much food for two people, just as Max had predicted. She set everything down, nodded with satisfaction, and left again.

The smell was incredible. Kara picked up her chopsticks, suddenly starving.

For several minutes, they just ate, and then Max said, "What's your story, Agent Reid? You seem to know more about me than I know about you."

"Barely," she retorted. "All I know is that you went to boarding school with Dominic Ashford, and you were or are a CIA agent."

"When did you join the FBI?"

"A year ago."

He raised an eyebrow. "You're a newbie then. And yet you seem in charge. That's impressive."

"I might have a short tenure with the FBI, but I was a police officer for eight years before changing careers."

"Here in New York?" he asked as he put another dumpling on his plate.

"Yes. I'm a native New Yorker, born in Queens."

"And do you come from a family of cops?"

"No. Firefighters. My dad, my uncle, and a couple of cousins."

"But you didn't want to follow in their footsteps?"

"I believe in service and helping people, but I do not like fire. That blast yesterday...it shook me."

He gave her a thoughtful look. "Yet, you ran back into a burning building. Sounds like you're as brave as the rest of your family."

"No, I'm not, but the firefighters weren't there yet, and I had to do something. I also didn't have time to think about it, which was a good thing."

"If you'd thought about it, you would have made the same decision."

"Maybe...maybe not." She saw the questioning gleam in his eyes and had a feeling she'd revealed too much to backtrack now, so she finished the story. "My father died on 9/11."

"Oh. I'm sorry," he said, his tone sounding genuine for the first time. "That's terrible."

"I was only six, but I can still remember that day. It started out normally, and then the world fell apart. My mom picked my little brother and I up from school and daycare. We spent all day watching the news, and family kept showing up at the house, crying, scared, hopeful. We didn't know about my father for a long time. He was in one of the towers. He rescued a lot of people before..." She cleared her throat, not sure why she'd told him such a personal thing. "Anyway, I couldn't become a firefighter after that. Not that it stopped others in the family. My uncle is a battalion chief, and his kids followed in his footsteps. I took a different path."

"That's understandable. Your father sounds like a hero."

"He really was. Not just that day, either. It was the way he lived his life." She took a sip of her tea. "We have gotten way off topic."

"Do you want more rice?" he asked as he picked up the bowl.

"No, you go ahead," she said, relieved with the change in subject. "I have to say, it was delicious. Do you eat here all the time?"

"Once or twice a week, but Mrs. Kim is often sending food upstairs. I've had just about everything on the menu. So, have you learned anything about the bombing, about the man who bumped into Samantha?"

"Actually, I spoke to a barista this afternoon. She told me she remembered the guy with the coffee topped with whipped cream because he asked for extra whip. She thought his name was

Jonas. She said he'd been there a couple of times that week, but he'd never ordered coffee with so much whipped cream before."

"Maybe he was checking the place out," he murmured.

"That's my thought. We're going back in time to see if we can catch him on a camera and try to get a last name and an address. Unfortunately, the camera on the front of the building has been out for the past week. Someone smashed it, and they hadn't gotten it fixed yet."

"Well, that sounds like too big of a coincidence."

"It does." She wiped her mouth as she finished eating and took her phone out of her pocket. "In lieu of a photo, I worked with a sketch artist, and this is what he came up with." She pulled up the image and handed him the phone. "Do you recognize him?"

His lips tightened. "Yes. He was leaving the cafe when I arrived."

"Do you know who he is?"

Max looked at the sketch once more, his jaw tightening. "No, but I think I saw him outside Forge Fitness last week."

She sat up straighter. "Where's that?"

"Soho. I was leaving Dominic's apartment building, and I saw Samantha on the street. She was waiting for a cab to take her to the gym, and I offered her a ride. I'm fairly sure this guy was standing in front of the fitness center when I dropped her off."

"Did Samantha talk to him?"

"No. I only noticed him because while she was in my car, she'd gotten a phone call, and she was finishing up. I double-parked until she was ready to go, and I was just looking around."

"When she got out of your vehicle, did they interact?"

Max shook his head. "I don't believe so, but I'm not sure I watched her go all the way into the gym."

"I need to go to that gym and show the sketch around, see if anyone can identify him. If I can get a name, that could be a huge break," she said with excitement.

"I'll go with you. Let me get the check."

"It's my treat," she said, more than happy to pay for dinner, because she might finally have a significant lead. "But I have to say that if you're sending me on a wild goose chase, you will regret it."

"Do you think I'd misdirect a federal agent?"

"I don't think I have any idea what you'd do, Max Malone, if that's even your real name."

He simply smiled and waved to Mrs. Kim to bring the check.

CHAPTER FIVE

As Kara drove to the gym with Max in the passenger seat, she had a few more questions. "When you gave Samantha a ride and she was on her phone, could you tell who she was talking to, or what they were talking about?"

"I only heard her side of the conversation, but it sounded like work. She was asking about discovery, timelines, and whether someone was going to talk. She didn't mention names, and I didn't ask."

"How many other times were you alone with her?"

"Zero," he replied flatly. "I spoke to her a few times when she was with Dominic, but that was about nothing in particular. I really didn't know her, Kara."

"We found a file in her apartment with an itinerary for a groundbreaking event in Tajikistan. She or someone had scribbled words about safety and cost. Was she concerned about Dominic being in danger on that trip? Do you think that might be why she wanted to speak to you?"

"I suspected that might be why she wanted to speak to me, but I don't know."

"Why does Dominic want to go in person to such a

dangerous place? Doesn't he have hundreds of employees who could do that for him?"

"I've asked that same question. It's difficult to protect a billionaire in that part of the world. But in case you don't know, billionaires can be stubborn about getting what they want."

"Oh, I'm aware," she said. "Sometimes to the point of reckless stupidity."

"Sometimes," he agreed. "Dominic feels it's important for his brand to be on the ground and in front of the cameras when it comes to big projects. Every time he does that, he gets attention and more investors."

"So, it's not completely selfless."

"Not even a little," he said with a laugh.

"Have you tried to talk him out of going?"

"That's not my job. He's aware of the risks. And it's up to me to minimize those risks. Anyway, none of this has anything to do with Samantha."

"I'm not entirely sure of that. Dominic is a wealthy public figure who probably has enemies. Hurting his girlfriend might give someone leverage over him. Are you concerned that he might also be in danger from this same bomber?"

"It has crossed my mind. I'm hoping you can find the bomber fast so we can put that worry away."

Max was being very agreeable, but she didn't completely trust his change in attitude. "Why you?" she asked abruptly, shooting him a quick look. "Why did Dominic hire you? What special skills do you bring to this job?"

"I have connections in that part of the world."

"From your CIA days?"

He shrugged. "I don't think that matters."

"You're a very frustrating man," she muttered.

"Getting back to Samantha, is there any update on her condition?"

"Still the same. They may try to wake her up later tomorrow, but it could also be Thursday. I would love to talk to her, to find out if she knows who might have tried to kill her."

"That would be a big help. I will say one thing about Samantha: she's not Dominic's usual type. He dates models, socialites, not women with serious, high-profile jobs. Not prosecutors who work seventy-hour weeks and probably don't have time for his charity galas."

"Maybe he was tired of shallow relationships."

"Maybe." Max didn't sound convinced.

"You don't think they're actually in love?"

"In love?" he echoed with a laugh. "They've only been seeing each other for a few months; I don't think either of them sees it as love."

"Some people fall fast."

"And that's usually a hard fall."

She wondered if his cynicism about love came from personal experience or just observation, but she wasn't going to ask him that. They weren't together to share personal stories; they were investigating a bombing, and she needed to focus on that.

"There's the gym," Max said, pointing ahead. "Let's see if anyone recognizes our mystery man."

Forge Fitness had a pristinely clean and nicely decorated lobby, with solid doors presumably leading to the actual fitness center.

A young guy sat at the front desk, maybe early twenties, scrolling through his phone. Behind him, through a glass door, Kara could see a dark-haired man doing paperwork in a small office.

Kara pulled out her badge when they reached the desk. "FBI. We need to ask you some questions."

The desk clerk's eyes widened as he put down his phone. "Is something wrong?"

"What's your name?"

"Spencer."

She pulled up the sketch on her phone and showed it to him. "Do you recognize this man, Spencer?"

Spencer's face turned pale. His eyes flicked nervously toward the office, then back to the phone. "I'm not sure. You should talk to Elias—he's the manager." He gestured toward the office, his hand shaking slightly. "I'll get him." He got up from the desk, knocked on the door, stepped inside, and then shut the door behind him.

Spencer emerged a moment later with a dark-haired Hispanic man in his late forties.

"I'm the manager. Elias Costa. How can I help you?"

"I'm Agent Reid," she said, introducing herself. "We're looking for this man. Do you know him? Have you seen him?"

Elias looked at the sketch on her phone. "This is just a drawing."

"But a good likeness of who we're looking for."

His gaze moved back to the photo. Then he lifted his head and gave a negative shake. "Sorry, I don't know who that is." Elias's gaze moved to Max. "I didn't catch your name."

"Max Malone. My client, Dominic Ashford, works with one of your trainers."

"Yes, he does. Is this man in the sketch tied to Mr. Ashford?" Elias looked even more concerned now.

"No, but he might be tied to an explosion that occurred yesterday," Max said.

Elias started, surprise moving through his gaze. "An explosion?"

"Are you sure you don't recognize him?" she interrupted, not wanting to give Elias any more information. She didn't trust him, and she couldn't help noticing that the desk clerk was listening avidly to their conversation.

"I'd like to help, but I can't. This image could be anyone. Is there anything else?"

"No," Max said before she had a chance to speak. "Thanks."

As Elias headed back into his office, Spencer picked up the phone to take a call. "Forge Fitness."

Max waved her toward the door, and she reluctantly followed. "You give up way too easily," she muttered as they reached the sidewalk.

"Elias wasn't going to give up that guy."

"You mean the one he didn't recognize?" she asked sarcastically.

"He definitely recognized him," Max said. "I think Spencer did, too, but the kid isn't going to tell us anything in front of his boss."

"You're right," she said with a sigh.

"The facility closes at nine," Max continued. "That's twelve minutes from now. Why don't we wait in the car and see if we can catch Spencer when he leaves work?"

"Fine." She got into the car, which was thankfully facing the gym, so unless Spencer left through a back door, they should be able to see him.

They sat in silence for a few minutes, then she said, "So what was it like working for the CIA?"

"It was a lot of things."

"That's vague. How did you get into the CIA?"

"It was so long ago, I barely remember."

"I'm sure you remember." She sent him a pointed look. "You just don't want to tell me. I'm not the enemy. We both want to find the person who blew up the café. Unless that's not really your goal?"

"What other goal would I have?"

"Protecting your client. Finding out what we know so that you can help him." She didn't want to believe that, but she couldn't ignore the possibility that Max had a hidden agenda.

"Dominic had nothing to do with that bomb," he said.

"I'm not saying he tried to kill his girlfriend. But that doesn't mean she wasn't targeted because of him, or that he doesn't know more than he's saying, or that you don't know more than you're saying."

"I am legitimately trying to help you, whether you believe it or not."

"And once again, you're not addressing what I just said."

"You're speculating based on nothing. I like to look at facts."

"So do I, and the fact is you're acting shady."

"I'm really not, Agent Reid. But you don't have to trust me to work with me. And I don't have to trust you."

"Why wouldn't you trust me?" she asked in surprise.

"I don't know you."

"I'm a federal agent."

"That doesn't automatically make you trustworthy," he said with a cynical smile. "At least, not from my experience."

She couldn't really argue that point because her own experience had also taught her that sometimes a badge could be used as a cover. "That's a fair point."

"It is?" he commented, surprise in his voice. "I thought I'd get an argument."

"No, you're right. Labels mean nothing. Neither do words. It's all about actions. That's when you see who people really are. Maybe I'm a little suspicious of you because my coworker told me he met you overseas several years ago, but you had a different name then."

"He did, too," Max said.

Now she was taken aback. "Really? He didn't mention that. What were the circumstances of your meeting?"

"That's classified."

"So, it had something to do with intelligence?"

"I can't answer that. I'll just say that we met at a time of intense secrecy. I think we were on the same side, but I'm not completely sure."

She didn't think Tyler was sure either, but the door to the gym had just opened, and she straightened in her seat. A man and a woman filed out. A moment later, Spencer came out the door, a backpack over his shoulders, a phone in his hand.

"There he is," Max said.

"Hopefully, Elias isn't right behind him."

"I don't see him. Let's go."

They reached the sidewalk just as Spencer got to them. Max grabbed his arm and pushed him into the nearby alley so that Elias wouldn't see them if he left the gym through the front door.

"What's going on?" Spencer demanded, pulling the AirPods out of his ears.

"We just want to talk," she said, keeping her voice calm. "You're not in trouble, Spencer."

"I don't know anything."

"Then this will be a brief conversation," Max said.

"If Elias knows I talked to you, he'll fire me," Spencer said. "I need this job."

"We're not going to tell Elias anything," she reassured him. "But we need to know about the man in that sketch. You recognized him. I know you did."

"I don't want any trouble."

"Neither do we," Max said. "Tell us what you know. The sooner you do, the sooner you can leave."

Spencer drew a worried breath and let it out. "His name is Jonas. He comes into the gym once or twice a week, but he doesn't work out. He meets with Elias, and then he leaves."

"What's his last name?" she asked.

"I don't know."

"What do they talk about?"

"I don't know," he repeated.

"But you know something," she pressed.

Spencer shifted his weight from one foot to another. "Elias runs high-stakes poker games in the back room on weekend nights when we close at six. They're private, invitation-only."

"And Jonas is part of that?" Max interjected.

"Not necessarily part of the game, but he usually shows up on Fridays and Mondays. I think he might be moving cash or doing other things for Elias. I don't know for sure. I just hear things sometimes."

"Where can we find Jonas?" Max inquired.

"I have no idea where he lives."

"Do you know anything about him that might help us find him?" she asked. "It's really important, Spencer."

"Well, last time he was in, I heard Jonas tell Elias he should come to the Crimson Club, that they have some new girls working. I got the feeling he's a regular there."

"Sounds like a strip club," Max commented.

"It is," she confirmed, all too familiar with that club from her days as a cop.

"I gotta go," Spencer said. "That's all I know."

As Spencer hurried out of the alley, she turned to Max. "Want to check out the Crimson Club?"

"I thought you'd never ask."

"I probably should send you home. This is an FBI investigation."

"You think you're going to get rid of me now? I am absolutely coming with you. If you don't take me, I'll show up there anyway and probably mess up your investigation. But your call."

She'd gone this far with him; she might as well go the rest of the way. "Fine, let's go."

"I'll look up the address."

"No need. When I was with the NYPD, I worked a case a few years ago that involved the club. The owners are two brothers from Belarus, Alex and Sergei Novik, although Sergei is rarely there and appears to be more of a silent partner. We believed they had ties to organized crime, but we couldn't prove it. At the time, we were more interested in one of their customers being a murderer, so we turned over our intel to the FBI. I don't know what they did with it."

"You could probably find out now."

"Maybe, but let's see how Jonas is tied to the club."

"Hopefully, he's a regular because we need someone to give us more information about him than just his first name."

———

The Crimson Club had changed little in the three years since Kara had last been there. Same red neon sign out front, same heavy door with a bouncer checking IDs, same dark interior pulsing with bass-heavy music. The main floor was crowded, men in suits mixing with guys in leather jackets, all of them watching the stage where a woman in silver heels and not much else moved around a pole with practiced grace.

She didn't bother to show her badge to the bouncer. Taking a low-key approach seemed a better way to go. Inside, the air was thick with smoke and cologne.

She recognized Alex Novik behind the bar with a female bartender. Both were slammed with customers waiting for drinks. She doubted Novik would talk to them and scanned the room, looking for another option.

Movement caught her eye—a blonde woman coming down the back hallway wearing a tight mini-dress that showed off her cleavage and her ass. Even in the low light, Kara recognized her.

"I see someone who might help us," she said.

"Good, because I don't think showing your badge around will get us anywhere in this club."

"Just the opposite," she agreed.

Ava stopped abruptly as their eyes met. Recognition flashed in her eyes, quickly masked by wariness.

"I need to talk to you," Kara murmured.

Ava glanced toward the bar, then made a slight gesture and walked toward the hallway she'd just come from. There were four doors in the corridor. Ava stopped in front of one of them, opened it, and then motioned them inside with a sultry smile on her lips that did not reach her eyes.

The lighting was dim, and Ava flipped a switch to turn on some music with a sexy beat. There was a leather bench along one wall, a small table, and mirrors lining the other three walls, and a pole in the center of the room.

Ava moved closer, her voice dropping to barely a whisper. "Cameras, no sound. You can talk while I dance for you. I need to make this look good."

"Understood," Kara said as Ava stepped back and began to dance.

"This will be fun," Max murmured. He slid closer to her, taking her hand, as he leaned in and shockingly placed his lips on her neck.

It was all she could do not to jerk away from that heated kiss. "What the hell was that?" she said tersely.

"Relax. We need to look like we're enjoying this."

She forced a smile on her face as she put her hand on his thigh and then looked at Ava. "Do you know a customer who goes by the name Jonas?"

Ava moved closer, offering her back to Max. "Can you help me with my zipper?"

"Of course," he said as he slid the zipper down her back.

She stepped out of her dress. It pooled around her feet, revealing a stunning body encased in barely-there lingerie. She kicked the dress aside with her high heel and said, "I know Jonas." She moved back to Max, cupping his face as she whispered, "He does favors for Alex."

"What favors?" she asked, her voice stuttering a little as Ava turned to her, sliding her hand down her face.

"Whatever Alex wants. Collections, deliveries, who knows what else." Ava straightened, then moved back to the pole, where she spun around.

"Do you know his last name, where he lives?" Max asked.

"Jonas Cray. He lives on the corner of Eighth and Monroe, a gray building, apartment 3C. I was sent there one night to do a private show for him and a friend."

"Who was the friend?" she asked.

"Don't know. But he was younger than Jonas, mid-thirties, dark-skinned. He didn't say anything to me; he just watched."

Ava unhooked her bra with practiced ease, tossing it toward Max with a sultry smile as she continued to dance.

"When did you last see Jonas?" Max asked.

"Yesterday. He was flush with cash. Threw me a hundred, made my night."

"Did he say anything to you?"

"Nothing that wasn't sexual. Why are you looking for him?"

"We think he might have been involved in a bombing yesterday."

Her movements faltered. "At the café?"

"Yes. Do you know anything about that?" Kara asked.

"No." She turned her back to them as she swayed her ass. "I don't know anything." A moment later, she turned around. "Leave me out of this."

"I will," she said, meeting Ava's gaze. "Just like I did before."

"That's why I gave you his name."

Ava danced for several more minutes, giving both her and Max a little lap dance, which made Kara far more uncomfortable than it seemed to make Max, but she tried to show enjoyment, knowing they were being watched. She was more than a little relieved when it was over. Max took out his wallet and slipped a hundred to Ava before they headed out the door.

They left the room, walking back down the hallway and through the club. The music seemed louder now, the crowd even bigger, and Kara was acutely aware of Max beside her, his presence somehow larger than it had been before.

Outside, the January air hit her like a shock, cold and clean after the stale heat of the club.

"Well," Max said. "FBI work is more interesting than I expected. But you really need to loosen up, Kara. I'm not sure you sold that very well."

"I did fine, and we know where to look for Jonas. That's what matters."

As they got into her car, her personal phone buzzed. She pulled it out of her bag and saw her mom's number. She sent the call to voicemail and started the engine, and then the phone buzzed again. She didn't pick up as she navigated into traffic. Jonas's apartment building was only a mile away, so it was a quick trip. As she parked, her phone buzzed once more, and she sighed in exasperation.

"Maybe you should get that," Max suggested. "It feels urgent."

"It's my mother."

Surprise ran through his eyes. "Really? Then you should definitely pick up."

"I know what this is about. She probably heard about the explosion from my Uncle Danny, who promised not to say anything, but I'm sure she heard the news and went straight to him."

"Uncle Danny?"

"He was the battalion chief at the fire yesterday."

"That was your uncle? Is that why he took you into the building last night?"

"Yes. And I thought you got there after we came outside." Her phone buzzed again.

"Just take it," Max said.

"Fine. I'll just tell her I'll call her back." She punched in her mom's number as Max pulled out his phone, checking his own messages. "What's going on, Mom?"

"You tell me," her mother said. "I saw the news about the bombing at the café, and Danny told me you were there."

"I was outside the building, and I'm fine. I told him not to share that with you."

"That's what he said, but we don't keep secrets from each other." Her mother's voice was loud, and she could see a smile playing around Max's lips.

"Well, I'm okay. I'll tell you all about it tomorrow. I'm working right now."

"On finding the bomber? That sounds dangerous."

"Don't worry about me. I know how to take care of myself. I'll call you back."

"You're really not hurt?"

"I'm not."

"I love you, Kara."

"I love you, too." She ended the call and put her phone back in her bag. "Sorry about that."

"Don't be. You have a mother who cares about you. No reason to apologize for that."

He was being nicer than she would have expected. "Do you have a mother who worries about you?"

"Not anymore," he said shortly. "She passed away seven years ago. Before that, she annoyed me with inopportune calls, but now I miss them." Before she could say she was sorry again, he opened his door. "Let's go find Jonas."

They got out of the car, walked across the street and down to the corner. The building Ava had described was run-down and not at all secure. In fact, the front door was ajar.

They took the stairs to the third floor and quietly approached the apartment. She pulled her gun out from under her coat, as Max did the same.

She shook her head. "You don't have authority here; I do. Put it away."

"If he comes out shooting, authority won't matter. I'm just backing you up."

She lifted her hand to knock on the door, realizing it was partly open. She knocked anyway, but there was no response, no noise of any kind. She glanced at Max, who gave a nod, obviously on the same wavelength as her. They didn't have a warrant, but if the door was open...

Grasping the knob, she opened it fully and stepped into the apartment, gasping at the bloody scene. A man was lying on the floor, his throat slit, a pool of blood under his body, his gaze fixed on the ceiling.

Max swore under his breath. "Is this him? The man you saw in the café?"

She nodded. "It's him."

"Someone didn't want him to talk."

Before she could agree, she heard a noise from the bedroom. She lifted her weapon, and Max did the same as they both moved in that direction. She got into the room just in time to see a hooded figure halfway going out of the window. They both rushed across the room.

The man had taken the fire escape down a floor and then jumped to the ground. She crawled out after him, and Max followed. They sped down the fire escape and sprinted through the alley. The man was very tall, and his long strides took him quickly down the alley. When they got to the street, he was gone.

"Dammit," she said breathlessly. "We were so close. I need to call this in." She had barely pulled her phone out of her pocket when she heard the roar of an engine.

As she whirled around, she was blinded by headlights as a car roared toward them, and it didn't look like it was going to stop...

CHAPTER SIX

Max shoved her to the side, and they tumbled onto the ground next to a dumpster as the car screamed past, so close Kara felt the heat of the engine, and the smell of exhaust choked the narrow alley as the vehicle disappeared as fast as it had come.

She was still catching her breath when Max jumped to his feet and sprinted down the alley after the car. By the time she pushed herself up and brushed the gravel off her clothes, he was already walking back, shaking his head, anger in every tight line of his expression.

"Gone," he said. "Are you okay?"

"I'm fine. Thanks for the save." She was a little disappointed in herself for not seeing the danger as quickly as he had, but she wasn't going to tell him that. "Did you catch a number on the license plate?"

"No."

She pulled out her phone. "I need to call this in. Let's go back to Jonas's apartment."

As they walked down the alley and around the corner to the front of the building, she made a note of the street address. Once they had reentered the apartment, she called her Team Ops Center, which was manned 24/7, while Max looked around.

He clearly knew not to touch anything, skirting the path around the victim and ignoring Jonas's phone, which was lying in a pool of blood. There could be important evidence on that phone, but it might take time to open it.

After the dispatcher confirmed NYPD and EMS were on their way, she ended the call and walked over to the body, squatting down beside the victim. Her experienced gaze took in the details of the attack. The attacker had probably come up from behind Jonas, and the knife had been quick and deadly.

There was no other apparent bruising on Jonas's face, no evidence of a fight. Since there had also been no sign of forced entry, it appeared Jonas had let his attacker in. Whether that was because he knew that person or because it was an expected delivery or meeting that had gone south, she could only speculate.

Getting to her feet, she texted Tyler that she'd found Jonas, the man who'd spilled the coffee on Samantha Barkley, and that he was deceased. She would fill him in tomorrow. While she knew the ops center would contact Jason as a matter of protocol, she didn't want to leave Tyler out of the loop.

A moment later, her phone rang. "Tyler, you didn't need to call me back. I know it's late."

"It's fine. How did you find him?"

"Long story," she said as sirens lit up the air. "I showed Max Malone the sketch. He recognized Jonas as someone he'd seen at a gym where he'd taken Samantha. One thing led to another. I can fill you in later. The police are here."

"Give me the address."

"You don't have to come."

"I'm not doing anything else."

She gave him the address and ended the call as Max came out of the bedroom.

"I'm going to take off," he said.

"Now? You need to wait for the police."

"Why? Aren't you in charge of the investigation? You know

what I know, and you also know where to find me. I don't need to be in the middle of this." He was already moving toward the door.

"Max—"

"I'll call you tomorrow. Be careful, Kara. The killer could have made a cleaner exit. He didn't have to come back down that alley and try to run us over. Someone knows we're not far behind them."

"I just wish I knew who that someone was," she said, but her words fell into the void of silence left by his quick departure.

Her lips tightened as she wondered why he'd exited so quickly. Was it just about staying away from law enforcement? Or had he found something while she was on the phone? She hoped it was the former and not the latter, because she had thought they were on the same side. Maybe that thought had been premature.

She walked into the bedroom, which was a cluttered mess with an unmade bed, clothes, and empty snack bags. The bathroom was in the same state. There was a desk with a couple of half-open drawers, which she carefully opened with her sleeve. But the mess inside didn't seem worth digging through.

If Jonas was part of a bigger plot, and it certainly appeared that he was, she doubted any evidence of that was in this mess. It was more likely that they would find some kind of digital or payment trail.

The sound of voices sent her back into the living room as two uniformed police officers arrived. She showed them her badge and then stepped back as they moved toward Jonas.

"Messy," one of them commented. "Was he dead when you got here?"

"Yes."

A moment later, an older man in a wrinkled suit came through the door. Detective Stuart Margolin was a seasoned detective with twenty years under his belt and a man who was more loyal to his fellow officers than to the truth.

She let out a small sigh as he saw her, and his dark eyes immediately turned suspicious.

"Reid," he said shortly. "What are you doing here?"

"The victim is a person of interest in a federal investigation."

"Heard you were a fed now. Guess you had to go somewhere."

She ignored that comment, wanting to keep this encounter professional. She explained what she'd found when she'd entered the apartment, the chase down the fire escape, and the near miss with the speeding car. As she finished speaking, an EMS team arrived and, after making a cursory inspection of the body, immediately notified the ME's office.

"So, who exactly is this guy?" Margolin asked. "And what are you investigating?"

"I'm investigating the bombing at the café yesterday. As for his involvement, it's unclear at this point."

"Well, someone didn't want him to talk."

"We'll be handling the investigation into Mr. Cray, but we'll need your help to find his killer."

He gave her a sour look. "Yeah, sure," he said, which was code for *I'm not going to help you any more than I absolutely have to.* "In the meantime, this is my scene. You can go."

As the detective went to confer with the officers, she took another look around Jonas's living room, but again there weren't any clues to suggest he'd recently made a bomb or was involved in other criminal activity.

The CSI team arrived at the same time as the medical examiner, and as the room grew more crowded, she took the stairs down to the lobby where several tenants were talking to more police officers.

As she stepped outside, she ran into Tyler.

"How's it going?" he asked.

"Everything is under control. NYPD will take control of the evidence and deliver Jonas's phone, computer, and any other relevant items to us early tomorrow morning."

"Do we know for sure he was the man in the café?"

"Yes. As for whether he set off the bomb, there's no definite evidence of that, but I'm sure he was involved."

"How did you find him?"

"After I showed Max Malone the sketch, one thing led to another." She told him about the gym, the Crimson Club, and chasing Jonas's killer down the fire escape before losing him, finishing with the car almost running them down in the alley.

"You've had a busy night," Tyler said, an odd note in his voice. "Where is Malone now?"

"He left before the police arrived."

"He didn't want to make an official statement.'

"Well, we were together, so he didn't see anything I didn't see."

"Are you sure about that?"

She didn't like the suspicious doubt in his question. "I'm absolutely sure."

"He didn't have a chance to remove anything from the apartment without your knowledge?"

She wasn't about to tell him Max had spent time alone in Jonas's bedroom while she'd been on the phone, because she doubted he'd found anything in there, and she was already feeling like she was being interrogated by a man who was supposed to be her equal.

"Max didn't take anything. Look, I don't know you, Tyler, and you don't know me, so we're going to have to earn each other's trust. But I'm telling you the truth."

"It's not that I don't trust you, Kara; I don't trust Malone. There's something about that guy that bothers me."

"Because you saw him in a war zone under another name. I get it. He saw you, too. And he doesn't trust you either. I don't know what happened back then, and I don't care right now. I'm only concerned about the present. Do you want to go upstairs and look around?"

"I do, but you don't need to come. You've had a long day. Go home, get some rest. I'll see you in the morning."

Tyler didn't wait for a reply as he hurried into the building. Clearly, he wanted to check out the crime scene on his own, and she didn't quite know what to think about that. But she was tired, and there was nothing more for her to do tonight, so she headed to her car, new questions racing through her mind. Jonas Cray seemed like a big lead, but he couldn't tell them anything. Hopefully, something on his phone or computer would.

———

Max arrived at Dominic's apartment just before nine on Wednesday morning. Dominic was working from home, and he came out of the kitchen, dressed in workout gear, drinking a green juice, and looking like he'd just finished a workout.

"I hope this isn't bad news," Dominic said warily. "Because after speaking to Samantha's doctor a few minutes ago, I was feeling hopeful. Then I saw your text that you were coming over."

"I'm glad to hear Samantha is doing better."

"I don't know if better is the right word, but she's hanging in there, and if she remains stable, they'll try to bring her out of her coma on Friday or Saturday."

"That's good news."

"You're not going to ruin my momentary optimism, are you?" Dominic asked as he motioned for him to have a seat on the couch.

"There's been a break in the case," he said as he sat down across from Dominic. "The man who spilled coffee on Samantha at the café is dead."

"What?" Dominic asked in shock. "You found him? And he's dead?"

"Yes. Let me back up. I saw a sketch of the man and recognized him. Last week, when I dropped Samantha at Forge Fitness, the same guy was standing outside the gym."

"So, he goes to the gym?"

"The manager said he didn't recognize him, but one of his employees did. His information led us to the Crimson Club and a stripper who gave me a name and an address. Unfortunately, when we arrived at his apartment, Jonas Cray had his throat slit."

Dominic sucked in a quick breath. "God!"

He nodded. "His killer escaped out the window." He was still pissed at himself for not being more aware when they'd entered the apartment, not being faster on the stairs or down the street. But he would find another way to catch him, because he was even more motivated after the near attempt on his own life and on Kara's.

"So, what happens next?" Dominic asked. 'Who do you think killed him?"

"Someone who didn't want him to talk. Does his name ring a bell?"

Dominic shook his head. "I've never heard that name before."

"Well, the FBI will find out everything they can about him, and I'm going to do the same. "

"You gave this information to the FBI?"

"I was with the FBI agent, Kara Reid, when she found the body."

"Wait. You were with her? Why?"

"She showed me the sketch. Since I was in the café that morning, she thought I might recognize him, and I did. Getting back to Forge Fitness, I know your trainer works there."

"He does, but he always trains me here, in my personal gym."

"Have you ever met the manager, Elias Costa?"

"No. I've never actually been to Forge Fitness. Samantha recommended Mitch, and she had his number, so I spoke directly to him."

"But the manager knew Mitch was working for you."

"It wasn't a secret."

"Why didn't Samantha work out here with you? In your private fitness center?"

"She had a membership there long before I met her. She enjoyed the classes more than just lifting weights and using cardio equipment."

"Did she ever mention Costa or Jonas to you?"

"No. What are you trying to get me to say?" Dominic asked with annoyance.

"Nothing. I'm just trying to connect the dots. Jonas was at the gym at the same time as Samantha. That's not a coincidence."

"Do you think he was stalking her? It sounds like the bombing was targeted to her and not because of her relationship with me?"

"I'm not sure we can make that assumption," he replied, seeing the eager light in Dominic's eyes to do exactly that. "She could have been targeted because of you, and you both have a connection to Forge Fitness. Elias Costa runs high-stakes poker games out of the club. Have you heard about those?"

"No."

"Mitch never mentioned it?"

Dominic shook his head. "I said no, Max."

"What about the Crimson Club? It's a strip club, owned by two brothers from Belarus, Alex and Sergei Novik."

Dominic's expression shifted with surprise. "Sergei Novik? I didn't realize he owned a strip club here in New York."

"But you know him?"

"Yes. We've been both rivals and partners in various projects."

Max wasn't thrilled to find a connection between Dominic and Novik. "You said rivals. Would he have a problem with you?"

"He's won a few bids over me; I've won a few over him. And sometimes we've been part of a joint investment group. There's no way he's involved in what happened to Samantha."

"No way? The man who spilled coffee on her was a frequent customer at Novik's strip club."

"Sergei has never mentioned anything to me about owning a strip club, but he has told me that his brother Alex always needs his money and his help. And he's been supporting him his entire life. He probably bought the club to give Alex a job. You should look into Alex."

"I'll look into both of them. I have to say I don't like the connection between you and Sergei, and I guarantee the FBI will dig into it."

"They won't find anything." Dominic stood up, pacing around the room as he ran a worried hand through his hair. "None of this makes sense, Max. If the bombing was about getting to me, where's the message? Where's the demand for cash? For power or access? What do they want?"

"Maybe they're not after money or leverage. It could be about revenge. You hurt someone; they want to hurt you back. Have you pissed anyone off lately?"

"I probably do that daily," Dominic said candidly, with little regret in his eyes. "You don't get to where I am without making waves."

He stared at the man who had once been a teenage friend, someone who had been born into wealth but had then become determined to quadruple that wealth, using whatever means necessary. He didn't know what lines Dominic had crossed to get to this penthouse apartment, to his globally big life, and that was the problem.

"Maybe you should come up with some names for me to look into,' he said. "People you compete with. People you beat. People who wanted something from you and didn't get it."

"That would be a very long list."

"What about your team? What if we focus on your top-level executives? You told me when you first hired me, you were concerned someone in your inner circle had leaked your security plans in Dushanbe."

Dominic's lips twisted into a frown. "I am still concerned about that, but to blow up a café with not only Samantha in it, but a lot of other people...that seems unbelievable." Dominic paused. "Why don't you come to dinner tonight? My top three executives will be there along with investors I have done business with in the past. Maybe someone will reveal something to you I haven't been able to see."

"I could do that."

"But don't come as security. Let's make it look friendlier. Some of my team know you're working for me, but that you're also an old friend. Why don't you bring a woman with you? Maybe Kai could come."

"I guess I could ask her," he said, not thrilled about attending a dinner party that would probably yield few to no results. But if there was someone on Dominic's executive team who wanted to take him down or ruin his life, it would be good to get to know them all better.

"Cocktails are at six thirty. Dinner is at seven thirty. You can tell people you work security for me, but don't scare off my investors. Reassure them that Tajikistan is the best place in the world to invest their money."

"I'm not a salesman," he said dryly. "That's on you. But I will be discreet. In the meantime, I'm going to see what else I can find out about Jonas Cray and his possible employers. Because he was hired to spill that coffee. There is no doubt in my mind about that. And whoever hired him for that job probably also killed him.

CHAPTER SEVEN

The Crimson Club was closed until five, and Elias Costa at Forge Fitness was taking a sick day on Wednesday, which had made Kara's two stops on her way to work completely pointless.

After a morning debrief with the team, she dug into Jonas Cray's life, which was completely unimpressive. A high school dropout, Jonas had joined the Army at eighteen but received a bad conduct discharge before his twenty-second birthday. His employment after leaving the service had been spotty. He'd worked as a bartender, a bouncer, a parking valet, and a handyman. But there was no evidentiary connection between Jonas and Elias Costa or Jonas and Alex or Sergei Novik. No transfers into his bank account, no emails, nothing...

Jonas had been caught on camera entering and exiting the Crimson Club several times a day and also going into Forge Fitness, which certainly made Elias Costa's claim that he'd never seen him before a flat-out lie. But that wasn't proof of anything. They needed more.

Her team, especially Alina and Zane, who had embedded themselves in the dark web over the past year had been haunting online forums for chatter about the bomb or the victims, but so far nothing had come up.

By four o'clock in the afternoon, she was tired and hungry, so she headed into the break room for coffee and a snack. She grabbed a banana first, then moved to the coffeemaker to pour herself a cup.

Alina Volkov came in a moment later, giving her a smile. "I need one of those, too."

She slid the mug across the counter to Alina. "Take this one. I'll get another."

"Thanks." Alina took a sip and let out a sigh. "I needed this."

She smiled and took her mug to the kitchen table. "Me, too. How's it going?"

"Not great. I feel like I need a shower after reading the posts in the last forum of sickos. What about you?"

"Nothing yet. Jonas Cray seems like the perfect guy to hire to do a dirty job, but I can't link him specifically to someone targeting Samantha. By the way, did you get an update on Samantha's condition?"

"Just a few minutes ago," Alina replied. "She's stable but critical. Samantha's sister has been there all day. Dominic Ashford also spent about thirty minutes with her. No sign of trouble at the hospital. Ashford has security outside her room."

"I'm glad Samantha is hanging in there." She peeled her banana and took a bite.

"The hospital released the other two victims today," Alina added. "That there have been no fatalities is very fortunate."

"So far, anyway. Samantha still needs to survive."

Alina sipped her coffee as she nodded in agreement. "Hopefully, she will. So, what's the story with the ex-CIA agent who keeps showing up in the middle of this case." Alina asked curiously. "Tyler doesn't seem to be a fan."

"Apparently, they met overseas when Tyler was in Delta and Max was in the CIA, but no one will talk about that. They're just very distrustful of each other. But Max is helpful to me, because he's tied into Ashford and Samantha Barkley. He has access to their world which we don't have."

"That makes sense. Do you know why he left the CIA?"

"He said he needed a change," she said dryly. "He's not big on answering questions. And, honestly, he could still be CIA; I have no idea."

Alina smiled. "That sounds about right. I've never found anyone in the agency to be helpful."

"Well, he's the least of my concerns." She took a bite of her banana, chased it down with coffee, and then said, "I keep asking myself why anyone would choose to blow up a café just to kill one person? I know murder doesn't always make sense, but my logical brain wants to find an answer."

"We'll find the answer," Alina said confidently. "We won't stop until we do."

"We won't," she agreed. "I don't give up."

"Neither do I. A quality instilled in me when I was a child," Alina added. "You don't quit, and when you lose, you learn."

"That's a good philosophy."

"I'll tell my father you said that. He likes to believe that even though I didn't follow his dream, I got something out of it."

"What was his dream?" she asked curiously.

"My parents brought me here from Russia when I was four and my younger sister was two. They decided we were going to be professional tennis players. They sacrificed a lot to get us into the top camps, and I was pretty good, better than my sister, who didn't like the heat and didn't like to run and just hated to compete. But I loved the fight."

"How long did you compete? Did you play professionally?"

"You don't want to hear this."

"I really do. Tell me." She was more than a little curious to know more about her new team.

"I won the US Nationals when I was seventeen and got to play at the US Open. I made it through the qualifying and into the second round before I lost. I was on my way. I had a full ride to Stanford University. But in my first year at school, I went on a ski trip, and I fell down the mountain and broke my leg in two places. I also injured my wrist and a couple of ribs. It was a nasty accident."

"That sounds awful."

"I had to have multiple surgeries, and my tennis career was put on a long hold. When I tried to come back two years later, I wasn't the same, not physically or mentally. Having that time away, to not think about being my parents' hope for a better life, I started to have fun. I made new friends. I got a boyfriend. I realized how narrow my life had been. And I didn't want that life anymore."

"Were your parents crushed?"

"They were sad. But our relationship actually improved when I wasn't just thinking of my dad as my coach, when he wasn't telling me how to hit a backhand or what to do against a wide serve. It was like we started to just be a normal family, and eventually, after a brutal string of lessons, my father took my racquets away one day and said he was going to keep them until I said I wanted them back. And if I never said that, it would be okay."

"And you never said that?"

She shook her head. "I didn't. It wasn't what I wanted anymore. I wanted to be an FBI agent, and that's what I did." She laughed. "I don't know why I told you all that."

"I'm glad you did. I enjoy having tough competitors on my team, people who like to win, because I definitely want to win."

"You'll have to tell me your story sometime, Kara."

"I will, but now I'd better get back to work."

As she reentered the bullpen, she was surprised to see Jason and Tyler standing by her desk, deep in conversation.

"What's going on?" she asked.

"The police have a witness who claims he saw someone go into Jonas Cray's apartment," Jason replied. "He's a food delivery guy who dropped off an order to the apartment down the hall from Cray's."

"Where is he now?"

"Currently doing food deliveries, but he said he will meet you between drops. I've asked Kate to send you his number," Jason said, referring to his admin. "His name is Omar Radishka, and he's working the Hell's Kitchen neighborhood today. He says he delivers food to that building all the time."

"That's great." She looked at Tyler. "Are you coming?"

"Not if you don't need me. I've found a link on Sergei Novik to Dominic Ashford that I'd like to explore."

"What's the link?"

"In addition to the Crimson Club, Sergei owns an international construction and engineering firm. That firm has gone up against Dominic Ashford twice in the past year, including a project in Tajikistan that Dominic won. That links Novik to Dominic Ashford, Samantha Barkley, and Jonas Cray."

"It certainly does," she said with excitement. "Keep going. I'll check in with you later."

She grabbed her bag and headed down to the garage to get her car, feeling more optimistic than she had been. They had a possible witness to Cray's killer and a link between Dominic and Novik, a person who would certainly have the money and power to hire someone to make a bomb and blow up a café with the girlfriend of one of his competitors in it.

Thirty minutes later, she'd made her way to a parking lot in Hell's Kitchen where the delivery driver was waiting in his car for his next pickup. She parked a few spots down and then texted him.

He got out of his car, a young twenty-something Indian male wearing a sweatshirt with an NYU logo and baggy jeans. His hair was long, and a somewhat scraggly beard covered his cheeks.

She walked over to him, giving him a nod. "Omar Radishka?"

"Yes."

"I'm Agent Reid. Can you tell me what you saw last night in the building on the corner of Eighth and Monroe?"

"I had just delivered food next door, and I saw a guy go into 3C. He was tall, like professional basketball player tall. He had black hair and was dressed all in black. He looked creepy."

"Did he knock on the door?"

"Yeah. And someone answered. The man went inside. I heard someone ask what the hell he was doing there. But I didn't hear the reply. I was halfway down the stairs when I thought I heard someone yell. I waited for a second, but I didn't hear anything else, so I left the building." Omar paused. "I heard the dude inside got killed. I can't believe I saw who did it. Do you think I'm in danger? He saw me, too. My dad said I shouldn't have said anything to the police, but when I was delivering lunch to the building next door today, a cop stopped me and asked me if I'd been working last night."

"You did the right thing. I don't believe you're in danger. But I would take a few extra precautions. If you can avoid delivering to that block, I would do that. If you can take a few days off or stay with a friend, that might be helpful as well. Just be alert and don't talk to anyone else about this. Don't tell your friends, your family, no one. We'll keep your name out of our reports as well."

"Okay. Will you let me know when you catch him?"

"I will." She gave him a reassuring smile. "Did you hear a name by chance? Did the person inside greet the man?"

Omar thought for a minute. "I think he called him Cal. But I'm not positive."

"That's helpful. Anything else you remember? Was he wearing clothes with an insignia of any kind?"

Omar slowly shook his head. "I don't think so. I didn't want to stare at him too closely."

"Thank you." She handed him her card. "If you think of anything else, or if you have any problems, call me."

Omar got back into his car and pulled out with a squeal of his tires.

She got into her vehicle and punched in Tyler's number. He picked up almost immediately, and she updated him on what she'd learned from Omar. "The name Cal is unique," she added. "If we can find a Cal working with the Novik brothers or Elias

Costa, we might be able to connect Jonas Cray with one of them."

"I'll dig into that," Tyler said. "I contacted Ashford to set up a meeting to discuss his ties to Sergei Novik. His assistant told me Ashford is not in today and will return my call tomorrow."

"That's disappointing."

"Why don't you see if you can reach Malone?" Tyler suggested. "He has access to Ashford that we don't. And he seems open to working with you. I'd call him, but I don't think I'd get the same response."

She didn't think so either. "All right. Email me with what you know about Dominic's ties to Novik, and I'll contact Max." As Tyler ended the call, she put in Max's number, happy when he picked up. "I need to talk to you. Can we meet?"

He hesitated. "I'm going to be tied up for the next few hours. What do you need?"

"I want to talk about Dominic's relationship with Sergei Novik. I learned today that they have been rivals in business."

"Dominic mentioned that to me as well," Max said. "But he said they've also collaborated on projects, that their relationship is friendly."

"Maybe not as friendly as he thinks. I really think we should compare notes. When will you be free?" Silence followed her question. "Max, are you there?"

"I have to go to a dinner party that Dominic is hosting at Ceylon tonight."

"That's an expensive restaurant. I thought you only handled security overseas."

"He just wants me there to observe. In fact, he asked me to bring a date to look more like a friend than a security consultant."

"Why?"

"Because he's rattled by everything that's happened. He's not the only one wondering if Samantha's attack is connected to him."

"Who else will be at the party?"

"City officials, potential investors for his various projects, some of his executive team. I think there will be about twenty-five people there."

"So, who are you taking? Do you have a wife or a girlfriend?"

"No. I was supposed to take a coworker, but she really doesn't want to go."

"You should take me," she said impulsively.

"I don't think Dominic wants me to show up with an FBI agent."

"The only person who would know I'm FBI is Dominic. If he's agreeable, I could just be your date. I could also be another pair of eyes if he feels the need for more security."

"I don't know."

"Why don't you run it by him? Tell him I want to protect him as well as Samantha, that I'm concerned about him being a target."

"I thought you were more concerned about him being tied to the bomber."

"Well, I wouldn't tell him that," she said dryly.

Another hesitation followed her words, then Max said, "Do you have a fancy dress?"

"I think I have one in my closet that will work."

"I have to be there at six thirty."

She glanced at her watch. It was almost five o'clock. "I can make that."

"Text me your address. I'll pick you up."

"I can meet you there."

"You'll look more like my date if we arrive together."

"Fine," she said, rattling off her address. "Do you want to check with Dominic first?"

"I'll run it by him, but I can convince him," Max said, with nothing but confidence in his voice. "I'll see you soon."

As she hung up the phone, she couldn't believe she'd just suggested a date to Dominic's posh dinner party with a former

CIA guy she didn't trust at all. But this was a great opportunity to get a better look into Dominic's life, and she was going to take it.

———

He was out of his mind, Max thought, as Agent Kara Reid answered the door to her brownstone apartment building wearing a form-fitting champagne-colored dress that hugged her cleavage and her hips and showed off a pair of beautiful legs. Her brown hair was no longer pulled up in a ponytail but flowing down her shoulders in a silky brown cascade of waves that framed her beautiful face.

He'd known as soon as the words left his mouth that inviting her to come along was the worst idea he'd had in a while. Dominic's response had been just as negative, but he'd convinced him that having the FBI on his side could only be a good thing. So here he was, his heart pounding a little faster than it should.

"Hi," she said as she pulled the door closed behind her and came down the steps.

"You look...amazing," he murmured.

She flushed a little at his words. "I had to wear this dress for a friend's wedding."

"It looks good."

"You look good, too." Her gaze moved across his face to the black suit and tie he'd put on for the occasion. Then, as if realizing she'd been staring too long, she cleared her throat and put on the coat she'd been carrying.

He was sorry to see her cover up the beautiful gold dress, but maybe it was a good thing. He needed to remind himself that this wasn't an actual date. He led her to his car and opened the door for her before moving around to slide behind the wheel.

As she fastened her seatbelt, she said, "Did you tell Dominic you were bringing me?"

"I did."

"And he was..."

"Fine with it." He gave her a quick smile. "That might be a bit of an understatement."

"I'm not planning to cause problems."

"And yet I'm expecting at some point we'll run into one," he said.

"I guess that depends on how the party goes. Can you tell me anything about the guest list?"

"Caroline Rowe, Vice-President of Business Development; Sebastian Hanover, Executive Vice-President of Operations; and Hamid Azani, Vice-President of Global Operations, will represent the executive team, along with Dominic, of course. From the city side, I believe Supervisor Randall Hollingsworth will attend, and then there are about a dozen investors from various companies and some of Dominic's wealthy friend group."

"That sounds impressive."

"It's probably going to be boring as hell."

She laughed. "Not your scene?"

"Not at all. But the food and the alcohol should be good."

"I'm sure. What did Dominic tell you about Sergei Novik?"

"What you said earlier—that they've been rivals, that they've been part of investor groups, and that he doesn't believe Novik has a problem with him. Dominic also mentioned that he hasn't gotten to the top without making some enemies. He probably has as long a list of potential enemies as Samantha Barkley does."

"Great," she murmured. "I love a long list."

He smiled. "You mentioned you talked to a potential witness this afternoon?"

"Yes. Someone who delivered food to the apartment next to Jonas's. On his way out, he said he saw a tall guy with jet-black hair wearing all black clothing. He thought he heard someone say Cal and what the hell... But that was it."

"Well, that knife attack was quick and silent," he said.

"My team is looking into whether they can find anyone

named Cal tied to the gym or the strip club. But you should run it by Dominic as well."

"I will, but we're not talking about the case tonight, remember? This is observation time."

"I already agreed," she said.

"You did, but I don't know if I can trust you," he said, flinging her a sharp look. "I know how much you want to solve this case."

"I do, but I'm also an excellent investigator. And I know when to watch and when to talk."

He liked her confidence, her intelligence, and also how damn pretty she was. It was a deadly combination, and he needed to be more concerned about keeping his own focus than worrying about Kara keeping hers.

CHAPTER EIGHT

The valet took Max's keys as they stepped out onto the sidewalk in front of Ceylon. The restaurant occupied the ground floor of a historic building; its facade was dark-red brick with iron-detailed accents. Warm light spilled through tall, diamond-paned windows. A discreet brass plaque beside the entrance was the only sign that this was one of the city's most exclusive dining establishments.

Max's hand found the small of her back as they approached the entrance, and Kara felt the warmth of his touch through the thin fabric of her coat. She told herself the flutter in her stomach was just nerves about the investigation, nothing to do with how good he looked in that perfectly tailored suit or the way his green eyes had darkened when he'd seen her in this dress.

Stop it, she thought firmly. *This is work. He's a potential witness. Possibly even a suspect if Dominic is involved.*

But damn, he wore that suit well.

The maître d' greeted them. "Welcome. Mr. Ashford's party is upstairs in the private dining room. Isla will take you there."

An attractive blonde led them up a thickly carpeted staircase to the second floor. The private dining room was everything she'd expected: high ceilings with ornate molding, chandeliers that probably cost more than her annual salary, floor-to-ceiling windows overlooking the street below. About fifteen people were already there, champagne flutes in hand, engaged in polite conversation that came naturally to people who regularly attended twenty-five-thousand-dollar-a-plate fundraisers. Not that this was a formal fundraiser, but it certainly had to be about money.

Dominic spotted them immediately and crossed the room, his expression carefully neutral. He looked every inch the billionaire host in a navy suit, his blond hair perfectly styled, his smile practiced and somewhat cool.

"Max," he said, shaking his hand. Then his gaze moved to Kara, and she saw the brief flicker of wariness before he masked it. "Kara. Max mentioned you might join us."

"Thank you for including me." She extended her hand, and his grip was firm, assessing.

"Of course. Let's get you both some champagne." He waved a server over, who offered them champagne, and then moved toward a trio of men who had just arrived.

She sipped her champagne as her gaze scanned the room of rich and beautiful people. "So, who's who?" she murmured to Max.

Before he could answer, a striking blonde woman in an emerald cocktail dress made her way toward them with a purposeful stride that suggested she wasn't about to be ignored. She appeared to be in her mid-thirties, with sharp cheekbones and even sharper eyes.

"Hello, Max," she said with a British accent. "I didn't realize you'd be joining us tonight."

"Dominic invited me," he replied smoothly, his hand finding Kara's waist. "Caroline Rowe, this is Kara Reid. Caroline is Dominic's Vice President of Business Development."

"It's nice to meet you," she said.

"You too," Caroline replied, although she didn't seem interested at all as her gaze turned to Max. "Is there any positive... news?"

"No," he said.

"That's unfortunate." She paused as her gaze moved to a new couple entering the room. "Excuse me."

Kara thought Caroline might go to greet the new arrivals, but she went over to Dominic and whispered in his ear, then pulled him away from his group. Her hand lingered on his arm in a way that felt possessive, territorial.

"Caroline is in love with Dominic," she murmured.

Max gave her a surprised look. "I don't think so."

"I do. When she asked for news, I assumed she was speaking about Samantha."

"Yes, and she's also aware that Dominic asked me to look into the bombing."

"Have you ever seen her interact with Samantha? I wonder what the vibe is between them?"

"I couldn't tell you," he said. "Dominic has never mentioned any romantic involvement with Caroline, but she seems to be very close to him, very loyal. She's always concerned about his security, but I'm sure many people are after what happened six months ago."

"What happened then?" she asked.

"It was overseas in Dushanbe. Dominic's security team was ambushed. He wasn't hurt, but two of his bodyguards were killed. That's why he hired me. He was afraid that someone might have leaked his security plans or his itinerary."

"That's interesting," she mused. "But how private was that itinerary? I found one for his next trip in Samantha's apartment."

"He gave her the itinerary. I was there when he did,' Max replied.

A loud voice interrupted their conversation.

"Dominic," a man repeated as he moved through the crowd,

his face red with what appeared to be anger. He appeared to be in his forties with pepper-gray hair and a stocky build. Two men in suits were following him, as well as an older man, who appeared to be in his seventies or eighties.

"Richard," Dominic said, his tone neutral, as he moved forward. He turned to the older man. "Joseph. I didn't realize your son was coming."

Regret ran across Joseph's face. "I couldn't stop him."

"I've been trying to get you on the phone for three weeks, Dominic," Richard said, his voice carrying across the room. "Why are you dodging my calls? Why did you hand our contract to someone else?"

"Richard Greco," Max whispered in Kara's ear. "And his father, Joseph Greco. They run Greco Electrical. They've acted as subcontractors on many jobs."

"I haven't handed anything to anyone," Dominic said, his pleasant tone edged with steel. "We're still finalizing contracts for Tajikistan."

"Finalizing?" Richard's laugh was harsh. "Bullshit. You're going with Ridley Aames. Twenty years of loyalty, and this is how you repay it?"

"Richard, please." Joseph Greco's voice was calm and diplomatic. Clearly, he was used to smoothing his son's rough edges. "Dominic, I apologize. I wanted to bring this up with you at a different time."

"But you don't make time for us," Richard interrupted. "Your assistant said you're completely booked for weeks."

"Let's talk tomorrow," Dominic said. "I'll have my assistant call you in the morning."

"Or we could do it now," Richard said. "Why wait?"

"Tomorrow will be fine," Joseph interrupted. "We're leaving now."

Richard spluttered protests, but his father and the security detail escorted them out of the room.

Dominic exchanged some private words with a tall, lean man

with dark hair and dark eyes as the conversations in the room resumed.

"Sounds like Richard Greco has a beef with Dominic," she commented as she sipped her champagne. "Who's Dominic talking to now?"

"Sebastian Hanover, Executive Vice President of Operations and longtime friend. And Greco was definitely not happy about losing a big contract."

"After that scene, I'd be surprised if his company gets another one in the future."

"They won't," he said with certainty. "I suspect Richard's father, Joseph, knows that."

"Well, we can put the Greco's on Dominic's enemy list."

"As I said before, that list will be long."

She didn't doubt that, but she could also see a lot of fawning smiles in this room. "He seems to be surrounded by love here."

"Looks more like attention to me, and he does love that." As Max finished speaking, a Middle Eastern man in his fifties approached. He had brown hair, brown eyes, and a neatly trimmed beard.

"Max," the man said, a surprised gleam in his eyes. "Didn't take you for the party type."

"Dominic's request. Good to see you, Hamid. This is Kara Reid."

"He turned to Kara with warmth in his eyes. "Hamid Azani. I'm VP of Global Operations for Ashford Industries."

"Nice to meet you."

"The pleasure is mine." Hamid turned back to Max, his expression shifting to something more serious. "I was going to text you earlier about setting up a meeting to discuss next month's trip. I have concerns."

"About what?" Max asked.

"I think we're being too cautious. Too hidden." Hamid gestured with his champagne glass. "The whole point of going there is to show the local community and investors that we're committed, that we're not afraid. If we skulk around in armored vehicles and avoid public spaces, what message does that send?"

"It sends the message that we want everyone to survive the trip," Max said dryly.

"I understand security is your priority, but mine is the success of this project." Hamid's jaw tightened slightly. "And that requires presence. Dominic shaking hands, being seen, showing confidence. Otherwise, why bother going at all?" He paused. "Can I steal you away for just a moment?"

Max gave her a questioning look.

"Go," she said. "I'll be fine."

"We won't be long," Hamid promised her.

She nodded as she sipped her champagne. The crowd was growing bigger, and as a new group descended on the room, she had to back away. Unfortunately, she ran into another body, a man who appeared to be in his early forties with dark-framed glasses and a pleasant expression.

"I'm so sorry," she said.

"No problem. It's getting crowded. I'm David Hartford."

"Kara Reid. Do you work with Dominic?"

"Sometimes. I run an investment company."

"Are you an investor in the Tajikistan project?" Kara asked.

"I am, yes." David pushed his glasses up his nose. "Dominic's work is inspiring. He's going to change lives, and it's exciting to be a part of that. What about you?"

"Oh, no. I'm just here with a friend." At his questioning glance, she added, "I'm a middle school teacher. This is not my usual scene."

His smile broadened. "Middle school teachers change lives, too. I've always believed teachers to be our unsung heroes."

"That's nice of you to say, and of course, I agree," she said. "My mother was a teacher, too."

"Mine as well," he said, tipping his champagne glass to hers.

She gave him a smile as Max rejoined them. "Max," she said, "Do you know David Hartford?"

"I don't," Max replied as he shook hands with David.

"Are you a teacher as well?" David asked.

Max blinked, but he was a quick study. "No. I'm in security. Nothing as noble as teaching."

"Well, security is important, too. Would you excuse me? I see one of my associates looking a little lost."

"No problem," she said, watching David move across the room to greet a rather plain-looking woman in a simple dress, who would have definitely faded into the background of this glittering crowd.

"So, you're a teacher?" Max asked.

"Middle school. I borrowed my mom's profession. Turns out his mother was a teacher, too, so we had a moment."

"Your mom was a teacher?"

"Still is, actually. She teaches sixth-grade math and is very popular. Her students love her, and she loves them, despite their often bratty pre-teenage bravado."

"Sounds like it's the perfect job for her."

"Did your mother work?"

"Yes. She was a diplomat for the State Department."

Surprise ran through her. "Really? Is that how you ended up at prep school with Dominic?"

"We lived in the UK for a couple of years."

"Where else did you live?"

"All over. We moved every few years. It was both annoying and kind of exciting," he said. "I didn't like changing schools and countries. Not only was I the foreign kid, but I rarely spoke the language. That made it tougher. Although I did sometimes go to the American school wherever we were."

"What an interesting childhood you must have had. What did your father do?"

"He wrote books about history and travel articles about where we were living. He still writes and publishes now."

"That's cool. Do you see him often?"

"No. He lives in the UK and rents a cottage in Bath."

She wanted to ask more questions because Max was finally opening up to her, and she was even more intrigued, but dinner was about to begin, and they had to find their seats. There were two long tables, and they were seated at the end of one table. Olive Elliott and her husband Brent were next to Max, while Kyle Travers and his girlfriend Eliana Ribera were seated next to her. Kyle introduced himself as the owner of JQ Properties, which was currently developing a new high-rise in Hudson Yards.

Despite her not asking questions, Kyle told her about how his company was changing New York's skyline one building at a time, how he'd tripled his company's profit in the last eighteen months, and how his father, who had founded the company had now stepped aside to an in-name-only position on the board. His Brazilian model girlfriend sat next to him with a bored look on her face as she looked at her phone while Kyle did everything he could to impress her with his brilliant money-making skills, and his complete disregard for any local regulations that might slow him down. Because he was making history, and if those idiots at the planning department couldn't see that, then they were just being stupid.

She wasn't at all impressed. And she really wished she could switch seats with Max, who was talking to Olive Elliott about the biography she and her husband were co-writing about Dominic's life.

As Kyle rambled on, she heard Olive mention how sad she was to hear about Dominic's girlfriend being in the hospital, how she'd recently had drinks with Samantha, and was so impressed with her intelligence and her sharp wit, how she thought she might be the perfect match for Dominic, because she wouldn't fawn all over him the way so many others did.

"Don't you agree?" Kyle asked.

Having no idea what he'd just said, she simply nodded, and that's all he seemed to need. Thankfully, his girlfriend called his attention to something on her phone, and she could eavesdrop more openly on Max's conversation.

Olive's husband Brent said, "I'm not sure they're the right match, Olive. I think there are reasons Dominic mostly dates cheerleaders. And I can't see how Samantha's job wouldn't get in the way of Dominic's ambition."

Olive nodded. "That's true. Anyway, I'm sorry about what happened to her. I pray she recovers. It's just tragic. I really hope they find whoever did it. It's scary to think you can just stop for coffee and end up fighting for your life."

Max nodded. "Life is unpredictable. Did Samantha talk about what she was working on when you met with her? I'm just wondering if someone she was trying to prosecute wanted to get back at her."

"We've been thinking about that," Brent cut in. "Samantha was very vague about specifics. And we're writers. We like to dig. She was happy to chat about Dominic and her general life, but not about herself. Although she did say once it's tough to be so tough all the time...something like that."

"Like she was tired of being that cold, sharp prosecutor," Olive added. "I actually told her I would love to write her story one day. Now, I'm worried her story will be cut tragically short." Olive paused as someone called for their attention, and Dominic stood up, and all attention turned to him.

"Thank you all for joining me tonight," he said. "As you know, we're approaching a significant milestone with the Pamir Highway project. In six weeks, we'll break ground on what will be the longest high-altitude tunnel in Central Asia."

A polite round of applause followed that statement, and Dominic seemed happy to soak it in. Then he continued, "We'll be opening routes that have been dangerous or impassable for decades, connecting communities that have been isolated, bringing opportunity and infrastructure to one of the most challenging regions in the world." He paused, his gaze sweeping the table. "This project represents everything Ashford Global Development stands for—vision, persistence, and the belief that the right infrastructure can transform lives."

More applause followed, and she had to admit she felt a little energized by his words, his vision. Dominic was definitely a charismatic man.

"I also want to acknowledge that this hasn't been an easy week for me," Dominic continued. "Many of you have reached out to me about Samantha, a woman I care a great deal about. She was injured in an explosion on Monday at a café. She was just getting coffee, and now she's fighting for her life. I ask that you keep her in your thoughts and prayers. Thank you." He raised his glass. "I'd like to make a toast to Samantha's recovery, to the Pamir Highway project, and to partnerships that make impossible things possible."

She tipped her glass to Max's and said, "He's a powerful speaker. I got chills when he started talking about changing the world."

"Dominic has always been a good salesman."

"You don't think his project is as good as his pitch?" she asked in a quiet voice, not that anyone was paying them any attention anymore. Olive and Brent were talking to the couple next to them. Kyle had gotten up and moved down the table to chat with someone else, while his bored girlfriend played on her phone.

"Actually, this project is going to be great for the region, if he can pull it off," Max said. "But he's going to need more money to take that tunnel and road as far as it needs to go, so if these investors don't pony up, he may end this project at one bridge."

"Well, he'll probably get the investment. Everyone here seems to be very interested and engaged."

"That's his hope."

"Olive and Brent might be able to give us more information," she murmured. "They've been talking to Samantha and Dominic and digging into their lives. Could be worth a follow-up chat at some point."

"Possible. Although I sense they're searching to dramatize the story as much as they can."

She tipped her head. "I can't disagree."

"What about the guy who was sitting next to you?"

"He's a developer, very cocky, thinks a lot of himself, and likes to share."

Max smiled. "Sounds like you two didn't hit it off."

"Are you kidding? I smiled my ass off, and he thought I was fascinated by his amazingness. But then he got bored and moved to find someone else to impress."

"He's talking to Sebastian Hanover now, Dominic's Executive VP of Operations."

"Another British guy?" she mused.

"Yes. And one of the few people in the company who seems able to tell Dominic the truth and not just what he wants to hear. In fact, sometimes I think Sebastian relishes problems a little more than he should."

She was surprised by that comment. "As in he wants Dominic to fail?"

"Maybe. He'd be next in line if he did."

"Could be a motive for something."

"Or nothing," he said with a shrug.

She sat back as a server put a salad in front of her, the first of many courses, and she turned her attention to that. While she was here to observe, she was also excited to try food in a restaurant she could never afford or probably even get into on her own.

One course followed another, each plate small but elegant, each bite absolute perfection.

"This is amazing," she told Max as they made their way through the fourth course. "But how many more courses do you think we're getting? I'm pretty full."

"I think there are at least two more," he said.

"Do you always eat this well on Dominic's dime?"

"On his dime? Absolutely. On mine, not so much. What about you? Are you a foodie?"

"I like to eat, but this kind of meal is nothing I'm used to. I can't wait to tell my cousin about this place. She's an aspiring chef and has a food channel on social media. She would love this."

"Do you have a lot of family in New York?"

"A ton," she said. "My immediate family is small, just my mom and my younger brother, Hayden."

"How old is he, and is he also in law enforcement?"

"No. He's twenty-nine, and a newly minted doctor of orthopedics. My mom said it was a great specialty for him because he broke a lot of bones when he was younger. Hayden loved skateboarding, and he was great at it. But he liked to do tricks, and he took a lot of falls," she said with a smile. "My Uncle Danny and his wife, Beth, have four kids ranging from their early thirties to their early twenties. And my Aunt Nancy and Uncle Tim have three kids ranging from twenty-five down to fifteen. And my Uncle Joe and Aunt Linda have five kids ranging from twenty to eight."

He shook his head. "That's a lot of family."

"And a lot of fun," she said. "I miss my dad terribly, but it has been great to have so much support from everyone else. My mother has been a single mom for much of my life, but it hasn't ever really felt that way. What about you? What's your family situation beyond your dad and you? I haven't heard about any siblings."

"No siblings. A couple of cousins, but I haven't seen them since I was probably twelve. Our extended family fizzled out years ago. The traveling put too much distance between us, and now my dad doesn't seem to even care about trying to keep up with any of them."

"That's a little sad."

He shrugged. "It is what it is."

She sat back as the server put a fancy cheese plate in front of her. "Cheese, really?" she whispered.

He laughed. "It goes with dessert."

"I've never understood that."

"You don't have to eat it."

"Oh, I'm eating it," she said. "When in Rome, right?"

He laughed and picked up his fork. "When in Rome."

As they finished their cheese plates, Olive engaged Max in conversation once more, and she found herself studying his profile: the firm jaw, dark brows, the slight crook in his nose that suggested it had been broken at least once. He really was handsome, in that dangerous, unpolished way that made her pulse quicken. He was a sexy chameleon who could probably blend into any environment, become whoever he needed to be.

Max suddenly turned and caught her eye, raising his brow in a silent question. "Everything okay?"

"Yes." She picked up her water glass and took a long drink, feeling a little too warm, but it had nothing to do with the heat in the room and everything to do with him.

"You're supposed to be observing the room, not me," he added quietly.

"I wasn't looking at you."

"Yes, you were. What did you see?"

His challenging gaze held hers. "It looks like you broke your nose at some point," she said

"Bar fight in Dublin."

"What were you doing in Dublin?"

"Drinking. Which led to the fight." His smile was crooked. "I was younger and stupider."

"And now?"

"I'm older and marginally less stupid."

"I think that's still to be determined."

As he gave her a sexy smile, she felt a catch in her throat, and a shiver ran down her spine. She needed some space, some air. Putting down her napkin, she said, "I'll be back."

She headed into the nearby restroom and found Caroline reapplying her lipstick. She caught her gaze in the mirror. "Are you enjoying yourself?"

"I am. The food is incredible," she said, moving to the sink to wash her hands.

"Ceylon never disappoints." She capped her lipstick with a click. "How long have you known Max?"

"Not long," she said vaguely.

"Mm." Caroline studied her reflection in the mirror and turned to face her. "He never brings dates to business events."

"Is that what this is? It seems very social."

"With Dominic, everything is business." Caroline paused. "I know who you are."

"Who I am?" she echoed.

"You're an FBI agent. I looked you up online, and then I confirmed it with Dominic. He said Max told him he was bringing you, but I don't understand why."

"I'm trying to find out who planted the bomb that injured Ms. Barkley."

"And you're going to find that person at this dinner party?" she challenged.

She didn't flinch at Caroline's accusatory tone. "I wanted to get some insight into Dominic's world. There's a possibility one of his enemies went after Samantha."

"He mentioned that, but it seems unlikely to me. And it's not like Samantha and Dominic are really that close. They've been dating a few months. It's not like Dominic is in love with her."

She wondered if Caroline was trying to convince her or herself.

"Have you worked with Dominic for a long time?"

"I've known him for almost ten years and worked for him for the past two. He's brilliant, one of the smartest men I've ever worked with."

"What do you think about Richard Greco?" she asked. "He caused quite a scene, and his dislike of Dominic was palpable."

"Richard is a wild card who has a short temper and drinks too much; that's one reason Dominic has been leaning away from working with Richard. He enjoyed a good relationship with Joseph, but the son is an entirely different matter."

"Richard told Dominic he'd be sorry for cutting him out. Do you think he's capable of hiring someone to plant a bomb in a café and hurt someone close to Dominic?"

Caroline didn't act surprised by the suggestion. Instead, she seemed to consider the idea. Finally, she said, "Maybe. I guess that is possible. It seems extreme, but Richard is going to lose a lot of money. Still, I would think he would go after Dominic before Samantha."

"Samantha was a lot easier to get to. Dominic has a ton of security."

"Well, they didn't stop Richard from bringing drama here," she said sharply. "Something Dominic needs to address with his team and with Max. I know this party wasn't his responsibility, but with everything going on, he needs to be on top of his game." As the door opened and two women walked in, she said, "It was nice chatting with you. Have a good night."

She smiled, reapplied her own lipstick, and then left the restroom.

When she got back, she found a beautiful chocolate dessert waiting for her.

"That took a while," Max said. "I was about to eat yours."

"That would have been fine. I'm stuffed. I ran into Caroline and had a little talk with her. She knows I'm an FBI agent."

"I'm not surprised Dominic told her. They're close."

"I definitely think she has a thing for him. But we can talk more later."

"Let's get out of here," Max said. "I think we've seen all we need to see."

She grabbed her coat and slipped it on as they made their way down the stairs. Max handed the ticket to the valet, and she shivered as they waited for his Jeep.

"You're cold," he said, shrugging out of his coat to drape it over her shoulders.

She started with surprise at the gesture. "Now you'll be cold."

He shrugged. "I'll survive."

As she met his gaze, she felt another sizzle between them, and she found herself unexpectedly wishing this was a date, that they'd met under different circumstances, that this wasn't about a case, because she'd really like it to be about something else.

"Kara," he murmured. "You shouldn't look at me like that."

"Like what?" she whispered, knowing she was playing with fire.

His gaze darkened, but before he could reply, the valet pulled up with Max's car, breaking the spell between them. The valet opened the door for her, and she slid inside as Max moved behind the wheel. Neither of them spoke as he pulled away from the curb, and the silence continued, growing tenser with each passing block.

She'd started something...something she couldn't finish. And she didn't know what to do about that. Max didn't seem to know either.

When he finally stopped in front of her building, she let out a sigh of relief and jumped out of the car so he wouldn't have to park. Unfortunately, she realized she still had his jacket on her shoulders when she reached the sidewalk. She turned around, and Max was right there.

"Your coat," she murmured, putting up her hands to slide it off her shoulders. But she wasn't fast enough.

His hands covered hers, stopping the movement. Then he lowered his head and kissed her. It wasn't gentle or sweet; it was hot, deliberate, a little possessive, and she loved every second. But she had to end it soon...now. Finally, she forced herself to pull away.

She gave him a breathless look, fighting the urge to go right back into another kiss. "We can't do this. You know we can't."

"I know."

She stepped back, slipped off his coat, and handed it to him. "Thanks."

"Kara—"

"Goodnight, Max," she said, cutting him off. She ran up the steps to her building without looking back. But she could feel his gaze on her the entire way. And when she finally reached her door and glanced back, he was still there, still watching.

She went inside before she could do something stupid, like go back down those steps.

CHAPTER NINE

Thursday morning started with frustration. After a sleepless night tossing and turning, her mind racing with clues that seemed to lead nowhere and an increasingly long list of suspects, not to mention a hot memory of a kiss that had shaken her to her core, Kara had dragged herself out of bed and down to the office. But the morning briefing had only added to her feeling of restlessness.

Sitting in the Strike Team conference room, listening to updates that felt more like a list of dead ends than progress, she couldn't believe that it had been three days since the bombing and they still had no idea who the perpetrator was or the motive behind the attack.

Samantha Barkley remained in critical condition. Jonas Cray's phone had yielded nothing useful. Tracking down the elusive "Cal" who might have murdered Jonas had also led nowhere. Cray's building had no security cameras, and so far, Cal had not been spotted walking around the area.

"Tyler, what about the Novik brothers?" Jason asked, interrupting her thoughts.

"I went to the Crimson Club last night," Tyler said. "Neither Alex nor Sergei Novik was there. The manager said Alex was out of town, and Sergei is rarely at the club. I left my number. I haven't heard back."

"What about Sergei Novik's construction company?" Jason asked.

"Offices are in Midtown, but Novik is traveling. His assistant said I'd need to go through his attorney for any meetings." Tyler's frustration was clear. "His attorney has also not returned my calls."

"What about Elias Costa at Forge Fitness?" she asked.

"The gym said Costa is on vacation. Won't say when he'll be back."

"So everyone is disappearing," she muttered.

Jason turned to Alina. "Any progress on the bomb components?"

"ATF traced the materials to three different suppliers across two states. All purchased with cash over the past six months. No security footage, no leads."

"And Samantha's case files?" Jason continued.

"The DA's office is still deciding how many files to send over, but we have some information on the current case," Alina replied. "It involves an accounting firm accused of fraud on behalf of their clients. The biggest name on the client list belongs to Armen Petroysan, as Kara mentioned the other day. But there's no sign Samantha had any personal contact with him."

"What about her phone?" Kara asked. "Are we into it yet?"

"Unlocked it this morning," Wes said. "Going through it now, but preliminary review shows normal texts and calls. Work stuff, personal messages with Dominic and her sister. The one text to Max Malone about meeting at the café. But they had no further contact."

"All right, let's keep digging," Jason said. "Someone wanted Samantha Barkley dead, and they're still out there. Jonas Cray's murder proves they're willing to kill to cover their tracks."

The team dispersed, and Kara returned to her desk, feeling

the weight of too many questions and not nearly enough answers.

Her phone buzzed with a text from Max: *Need to meet. May have a potential lead.*

She stared at the message, then typed: *What is it?*

Not sure. Meeting at one thirty with one of Samantha's friends, if you want to join.

I'm in, she typed.

Max texted her the address for a diner in Chelsea. As she jumped to her feet, Tyler looked up from the computer next to her. "Did you get something?"

"I'm not sure. Max says he's meeting with one of Samantha's friends and invited me to join him, so I'm going. I'll text you when I know more."

———

Lou's Place was a classic New York diner—vinyl booths, laminate tables, and a menu that probably hadn't changed in a couple of decades. Max was already there when Kara arrived, sitting in a back booth with a cup of coffee in front of him. He was gazing down at his phone, which gave her a moment to see him without him seeing her, to quickly relive last night's unexpectedly passionate kiss, one that should never be repeated.

He lifted his head, as if sensing her stare, and she gave him a brief smile and then slid into the booth across from him. "Hi."

"Hello," he said, his sexy mouth curving into a smile that made her heart thump against her chest.

She'd spent most of the night trying to tell herself he was really not that good-looking, the kisses they'd shared had not been that great, that it had just been too much expensive champagne...but all those excuses seemed completely stupid now that she was sitting across from him again and feeling that same surge of desire that had made her act so recklessly the night before.

His gaze darkened, and she realized too late that she was

staring at him. Judging by the expression in his stunning green eyes, he knew exactly what she was thinking.

Clearing her throat, she said, "So, I'm here."

"I can see that."

She felt like a fool for suddenly feeling so tongue-tied. For God's sake, she was a federal agent, and she was meeting him because he had a lead on a case. She needed to get a grip. "Who are we meeting?"

"Claire Donnelly," he said. "You should probably sit on this side with me, so we can both see her face, assess what she has to say."

The last thing she wanted to do was slip onto that bench seat next to him. "I'll move when she gets here."

A knowing gleam entered her eyes. "Afraid you might kiss me again?"

"You kissed me."

"I think you made the first move."

"I did not. And I don't want to talk about it. It was a mistake."

"It was good," he countered. "Memorable."

The word only made her feel more unsettled. "Let's keep this professional. Last night was last night. It's business from here on out."

"You've never mixed business and pleasure?" he teased.

"No," she said flatly. "I don't mix the two. And I'm not starting now."

"Maybe later."

She sighed and forced a change in subject. "Tell me more about Claire Donnelly and why she wants to talk to you."

He sat back in his seat, gave her a thoughtful look, and then, thankfully, answered her question.

"She said she might have information about someone who was threatening Samantha. She apparently knew Samantha had wanted to meet with me that day, so she wanted to talk to me and not to the FBI. She may try to bolt once she realizes who you are."

"I'll make sure that doesn't happen. What's her relationship to Samantha?"

"Former college roommate. She moved to New York last year, and they reconnected. They had lunch together last week."

"And she knew you were meeting with Samantha. It's interesting that Samantha would tell her that. Hopefully, she told her more." The server came over to the table, pausing their conversation.

"What can I get you?" the woman asked.

"An iced tea," she said.

"You can get lunch if you want," Max put in.

"Let's see what Claire has to say first."

"I'll take a refill," Max said as the waitress refilled his mug. "You can leave the menus."

The diner's bell chimed, and she turned to see a blonde woman enter the diner wearing casual slacks and a black sweater. She didn't seem nearly as sharp or professional as Samantha.

As the woman looked around the diner, Max got up and went to greet her. She seemed a bit startled when she saw Kara, but Max firmly ushered her to the table, waving her to the bench he'd just been sitting on and then sliding in next to her.

"Claire, this is Kara Reid with the FBI. She very much wants to help find out who hurt Samantha."

"Okay," Claire said. "I really wanted to talk to you on your own, though. I'm not sure..."

"You don't have to worry," Kara cut in, giving Claire a reassuring smile. "We all want the same thing—to find out who hurt Samantha."

"I've been going crazy," Claire said. "I'm not sure that what I saw means anything, and Samantha is so private. She'd be furious with me for sharing her business with the FBI. Plus, I kept thinking that a bomb going off like that couldn't possibly be about her."

"You're here now. Just tell us what you saw," she encouraged.

"Samantha and I were college roommates. We're both really busy, but we try to have lunch every couple of months. Last week we met at Bistro Verde in Tribeca. We'd been there maybe twenty minutes when this man walked up to our table and told Samantha, 'You need to stop.' Samantha stiffened and told him to leave, and she immediately waved to the waiter to come over. The man said, 'You'll regret it if you don't', and then he walked out."

"Can you describe him?" Kara asked.

"He had dark hair with an olive complexion. He was wearing gray pants and a black leather jacket. He was probably in his forties, looked a little overweight with a beer belly. His eyes were cold and mean. I was immediately intimidated, but Samantha didn't seem concerned. She said if she stopped working every time someone told her she'd be sorry, she wouldn't have closed any cases. Despite her words, I thought she was rattled."

"And she didn't tell you what the man was threatening her about?" Max asked.

Claire shook her head. "No. She said she wasn't sure, that her current boyfriend had had some trouble lately, and it might be tied to him. Or it could be one of her cases. I suggested she talk to the police, and she said she was going to meet with a private security guy who worked for her boyfriend about something else, but she'd bring it up with him. After what happened, I thought I'd try to find you."

"Julia, Samantha's sister, gave me your number. I didn't tell her what happened because she was already upset." Claire paused, her gaze searching. "I want to know if what happened in the restaurant is tied to the bombing. I keep thinking it isn't possible because other people were also injured. My husband told me I should stay out of it. If it was about that guy, maybe I could be in danger, and that danger would come to him, to our kids..." Claire gave them a look pleading for understanding, absolution. "I didn't know what to do. But I haven't had a good night's sleep since that bomb went off." Claire blew out a breath. "Anyway, that's what I wanted to say."

"Is there anything else?" Kara asked.

"No. That's all of it. Maybe the manager at the restaurant or one of the waiters could verify what happened. I know people were watching."

"Bistro Verde, you said?" Max asked.

She nodded. "It was last Friday, just three days before everything happened."

The day and time helped, Kara thought. Hopefully, there were some cameras near the bistro that could help identify that person.

"I have to go," Claire said, sliding out of the booth.

Max got up, barring her from leaving immediately. "One second, Claire. Kara may need you to look at footage we can find from the restaurant to help us identify that man."

"I don't really want to be more involved."

"It will be completely private. No one will know you helped us," she said, a little surprised that Max had taken the initiative, but glad that he had.

"Okay. You have my number," she said as she hurried away.

Max moved around the table and sat down across from her. "What do you think?"

"We need to find that man," she said, already texting the information to her team so that they could start looking for him. "This could be the break we've been looking for." She finished texting, then lifted her gaze to his. "Thank you for including me. You didn't have to."

"I thought it might help. I'm not your enemy."

"You have been more helpful than I expected, but I still don't completely trust you."

"Well, I don't completely trust you either," he returned.

His comment surprised her. "Why not? I've been completely transparent with you."

"I doubt that." He paused. "I have a friend in the NYPD. He said you weren't a very popular cop."

"You looked me up?"

"I asked a few questions. It's not like you haven't been trying to find out about my past."

"But your past is redacted. And mine is not. I'm sure you know exactly why I wasn't popular."

"I'd like to hear about it from you."

She paused as the server returned to ask if they wanted to order anything else. "I'll take a chicken Caesar salad," she said. If she were going to talk about her past, she might as well have lunch while she was doing it.

"I'll take the French dip." As the server left, he said, "Since we'll be waiting for our lunch, this seems like a good time to talk."

"I'll tell you what happened. And then you're going to answer one of my questions."

He shrugged. "Let's see how it goes."

"After almost eight years in the NYPD, I made detective after closing a big case, which was very exciting. Unfortunately, the seasoned and cynical detective I was assigned to work with did not share my enthusiasm."

"Because you're a woman?"

"It was more because I wasn't someone who was going to look the other way. Three months into our assigned partnership, which was almost two years ago now, we started working on a joint interagency case with the FBI and the DEA that involved drugs and money laundering. During the investigation, I realized that my partner had stolen money and drugs from a stash house. I turned him in, and he and his friends turned on me. I'd broken the code. Not only because I'd reported him to Internal Affairs, but because I'd also talked to the FBI and the DEA."

"You had no choice. If you hadn't turned him in, you could have been charged as a co-conspirator."

"If anyone had ever found out, which they might not have,"

she said candidly. "And to be completely honest, there were other, far more dangerous, far more violent people to take down, which was repeatedly stated to me after the fact. That I had ruined the career of a man who had been on the force for over a decade, who had been overworked and underpaid, was unforgivable. And he had been overworked and underpaid, but that's the job we all signed up for. I couldn't let him walk away because he would have kept committing crimes, and that's not why I became a cop."

Max nodded, a gleam of respect in his eyes. "That was brave."

"And a career killer. No one wanted to work with me after that. Even the people who knew me well, who privately said I was right, felt tainted by any connection to me. My fellow officers said I was too self-righteous, too ambitious, that I just wanted to get him out of the way so I could rise in the ranks. The smear campaign was superb," she said, unable to hide the bitterness in her voice. "I started to feel like I had done the wrong thing."

"But you hadn't. Surely, there were some people on your side."

"More than came forward publicly. It was a tough time for me, and when one of the FBI agents I had worked with on the case suggested I join the bureau, I said yes."

"Sounds like you ended up in a better place."

"In some ways." She frowned. "I don't want to give you the wrong idea. There are more good people than bad in the police department, and some incredibly smart and brave unsung heroes. I just ran into one bad cop and some of his unforgiving friends. But I have a lot of respect for the NYPD, and I loved working there for a long time, but that time was over."

"And what do you think about working for the bureau? Although you're working for some special team, aren't you?"

She was surprised at how much he actually knew about her. She'd been so focused on finding out about him she hadn't really thought about him wanting to know more about her. "Yes, I recently joined a special unit that moves more quickly and with less red tape."

"How did you manage that?"

"I guess I impressed a few people."

"Well, that doesn't surprise me."

"I don't know why you'd say that. I don't feel like I've done anything impressive on this case. It's been three days, and I'm still trying to find a lead that will help us find the bomber."

"You found Jonas Cray."

"Too late," she said.

"But we were close." He paused, his gaze shifting. "It is odd how close we were."

"As in you think someone realized we'd found Jonas?" She wiped her mouth with her napkin as she considered that. "We went to the gym. We talked to Elias and Spencer. And then we hit the Crimson Club."

"And Ava told us where to find him," Max finished. "But I don't think there was enough time between our appearance there and someone silencing Jonas before we could talk to him."

"It had to have been someone from the gym. And Elias Costa has basically disappeared, so that makes him look guilty."

"Well, it is also possible that the plan was always to take Jonas out. He was the one with the most visibility in the café. If he's dead, and the trail goes to him, then it ends there."

"We've been looking for Cal, but we haven't spotted him anywhere in the area." She picked up her fork and made her way through her salad as they both ate for a few minutes.

When she finished, she took a sip of iced tea and said, "I think it's your turn to talk."

He gave a heavy sigh as he sat back on the bench. "What's the question?"

"Same one I asked before. Why did you leave the CIA? And this time, I want the real reason."

"Everything I did for the agency was classified, Kara. That is the truth."

"Then paint a picture in broad strokes that won't break any laws."

He thought about that for a moment, clearly conflicted, then he said, "I brought in someone I'd been chasing for a long time, someone who had hurt many people. I thought I'd finally get justice. But this individual made a deal with the powers that be, suggesting he would be a better asset than an inmate."

"So they let him go?"

"Yes. They sent him back into the field. He had a handler, of course, and he was under threat of immediate confinement if he stepped over a line." Anger burned through his green eyes. "He agreed. And I quit."

"I can understand why you did that. Has he stayed behind that line?"

"No. Two months after he made the deal, he vanished. No one has seen him since, and it's believed he's now leading a terror network that has gotten a lot more dangerous with him in it."

"I'm sorry. That's terrible," she said, realizing that the man who had almost seemed completely devoid of emotion since she'd met him actually had a lot of rage hiding just under the surface. "The agency must be trying to catch him."

"Well, it took me five years to catch him the first time, so who knows how long it will take this time."

"Did the agency try to get you to stay?"

"They wanted to reassign me, but I was done. Logically, I know that intelligence works better with embedded assets, but there are some people too evil to be turned, and I knew all along that no matter what he said, he would never work with us. They said it was a calculated risk. I don't think they calculated a damn thing." He picked up his coffee mug and took a drink.

"When did you decide to work with Dominic?" she asked.

He suddenly smiled. "I already answered your question. You don't get another one."

"Fine. I have to get back to work. Let's get the check." She'd no sooner finished speaking when the server dropped off their bill.

"I've got this," he said. "My turn."

She shrugged as he put down cash, and then they walked out of the diner together.

It was a wintry afternoon with a gray sky threatening rain or possibly snow. She zipped up her jacket. "Did you drive?"

He nodded. "I'm parked that way. Kara—"

"What?" she asked warily, not liking the look in his gaze.

"What you did at the NYPD took a lot of guts. I'm impressed."

His words warmed her soul. "Thanks."

"I think your choice to leave an agency that you couldn't believe in anymore was also brave."

"Some would say I threw my entire career away."

"Well, maybe you did. But I reinvented myself, and it looks like you're doing the same." She paused. "Although I have to say there's still something about your one and only job with Dominic that doesn't ring quite true to me."

"You're a very suspicious person."

"And I suspect," she said, playing on his word, "that you have secrets."

"Everyone has secrets."

"That's true. I just want to believe that those secrets aren't part of a hidden agenda that's going to prevent me from finding out what really happened to Samantha."

"I want to find out what happened to her, too."

"What if the truth becomes a problem for your old friend, Dominic?"

"I don't think that will happen."

Before she could ask him what he would do if it did, her phone buzzed. She took it out to read a message from her team.

"Is that about Samantha?" Max asked.

"Yes. My team pulled security footage from Bistro Verde, and it looks like the man who threatened Samantha is Vincent Castellano, a mechanic at a Jersey automotive shop owned by the Petroysan Group." She looked up at Max. "Tyler is headed to his apartment now. It looks like this is about Samantha's current case."

"Do you have the address? Should we meet him there?"

"I don't think *we* need to do anything," she countered.

"I just got you the lead. Don't cut me out."

Before she could respond, the earth rocked beneath her feet with a massive blast. She stumbled forward, Max's hand catching her arm to steady her. Ears ringing, heart pounding, she turned her head to see people running down the street toward them, screaming as shards of debris fell from the sky and thick black smoke rose into the sky from only a few blocks away.

She sprinted toward the chaos, with Max right next to her. She had no idea what they would find when they eventually turned the corner...

CHAPTER TEN

Kara's lungs burned as they made their way through the panicked crowd rushing toward them, but eventually they got to the end of the block and around the next corner, where a scene of destruction arose before them.

The blast had shattered a mid-rise building under construction in a residential neighborhood. Out of the six stories, the top three floors were engulfed in flames. Scaffolding had collapsed onto the street, with twisted metal and wooden planks scattered across the pavement. Windows were blown out, glass glittering on the sidewalk like deadly confetti. Smoke and fire were visible through multiple openings, black and thick, blotting out the afternoon sky.

There were already emergency vehicles on the scene, with more arriving by the second—fire trucks, ambulances, police cars. Crews from the FDNY were on their way into the building while other units attacked the fire from the outside. The police had established a perimeter, officers pushing the crowd back, as well as evacuating people from the buildings on either side of the damaged structure.

They made their way through the crowd, flashing her badge whenever someone tried to stop them, but they could still only get so far, the last officer directing her to the scene commander, where a man in an NYPD captain's uniform stood amid a cluster of police vehicles, talking into a radio.

She recognized him not from her days on the force, but from his relationship with her uncle. Captain Hank Ridgemont played cards with her Uncle Danny every other Thursday. He was a good cop, twenty-five years on the job, and had worked his way up from patrol. He was also someone who'd stood by her when many people had not. She wanted to talk to him, but the priority now was getting people out of the building and putting the fire out, so she and Max stayed clear of the emergency operations but close enough to see what was going on.

"What the hell?" Max muttered, his gaze moving from the fiery scene to her. "Is this connected to the café?"

She didn't know how to answer that question. "I was just thinking that the bomb at the café definitely had Samantha's name on it, but now..."

"Maybe this was construction related. A gas pipe explosion or something..." He turned his gaze back to the scene as firefighters were bringing people out of the building.

Most were wearing reflective vests, a few with hard hats on. EMTs rushed to meet them, triaging on the sidewalk.

"At least there are survivors," she said, feeling good about that, until she saw one person being carried out on a stretcher and rushed to a waiting ambulance.

She swallowed a knot in her throat and called Jason, explaining what little she knew about the explosion. "I'm waiting to talk to the incident commander," she finished. "I'll hopefully get more information from him."

"I'm on my way," Jason said.

"Okay."

Max was on his phone when she finished the call. She gave him an inquisitive look. "Who were you talking to?" she asked.

"A woman who works with me. I asked her to see what she could find out about this building."

"As in whether it's tied to Dominic?"

Max's gaze hardened, and so did his jaw. "That would be one question."

"If this building ties to Dominic, and he ties to Samantha, then these explosions are connected."

"Which is a big if," he said.

She wasn't so sure that was true. Dominic had a global empire, but he also had buildings in New York, and this could be one of them. As the urgency of the scene diminished, she made her way to Captain Ridgemont.

"Kara," he said in surprise. "What are you doing here?"

"I was a few blocks away when I heard the explosion. I'm concerned it may be tied to the one at the café on Monday. I'm the agent in charge of that investigation. Can you tell me anything about what happened here? Was it a bomb?"

"It appears that way. Probably located on the fourth floor. That's where most of the serious injuries occurred."

"How many people were inside?" she asked.

"Six."

Surprise ran through her at his response. "So few? On a construction site?"

"It was inspection day. Most of the crew wasn't here. Two victims with minor injuries were treated on scene. Four were sent to the hospital, two critically. Several people on the street suffered injuries. I don't have that number at the moment. One of those was a woman who works for the building department. She had just walked out of the building when it blew up, so she knew how many were inside." He tipped his head to a disheveled woman sitting in the back of an ambulance. "There's a lot to unravel. We'll have a longer conversation later."

"Of course. Thanks, Captain."

As he moved away, she and Max headed toward the ambulance, where a woman covered with dusty debris and some blood on her forehead stared in shock at the building.

"Ma'am? I'm Special Agent Reid with the FBI. And this is Max Malone. Can you answer a few questions?"

The woman looked up, her eyes red-rimmed but focused. "I —yes. I think so."

"Can you tell me your name?"

"Whitney Holden. I work for the Building Department. Administrative assistant." Her voice shook slightly. "I was here with the inspector. James Cooper."

"What happened, Whitney?"

"It was a final inspection. I came back to our car to get some paperwork we'd forgotten to take inside, and I was about to go back when the building blew up. I—I don't know what happened. And I'm afraid James is badly hurt." Her voice broke. "I saw them put him in an ambulance, and it looked like he had been burned. Do you know if he's okay?"

"He's on his way to the hospital. They'll do everything they can to save his life," she said soothingly. "Can you tell me who else was inside?"

She cleared her throat, struggling for composure. "There were five besides James, the general contractor and his foreman, and subcontractors for plumbing and electrical. When I left them, they were on the fourth floor." Whitney looked at the burning building, tears sliding down her cheeks. "I was in there minutes before. I could be dead right now."

"But you're not," she said firmly, drawing Whitney's gaze back to her. "You're okay. And you can help us figure out what happened so that whoever did this doesn't get away with it."

Whitney drew a deep breath. "How can I help?"

"Who owns this building?"

"Wexler Properties. James has inspected their buildings before. The construction is always very good. He never has problems with them."

"Did he have any problems today?" Max asked. "Anything he thought wasn't up to par?"

"Not when I was there. It seemed routine. We spend all day,

pretty much every day, at job sites. I never imagined something like this could happen."

"How long have you worked with the inspector?" Kara asked.

"Two years." Fresh tears spilled over. "He's a good man. James really cares about making sure buildings are safe."

"Did you see anyone else on site or when you came out to the car? Was anyone standing out front, looking at the building?" she asked.

"There were people on the street when I came out, but I didn't pay them any attention." Whitney took a breath. "Do you think someone was watching the building?"

"That's what we're trying to find out."

Whitney looked at the crowd that had gathered behind the police tape to watch what was going on. Then she shook her head. "I don't remember anyone in particular. I'm sorry. I want to help."

"Did someone send you out of the building?" Max asked. "Or did you suddenly realize you were missing paperwork?"

Whitney started at his question. "Uh, James asked me for something, and I couldn't find it. I thought I'd left the folder in the car."

"Was it in the car?" she asked, because there didn't appear to be anything in Whitney's hand.

"I—I don't know. I had just opened the car door when the explosion happened."

"Where's your car?" Max asked.

Whitney's gaze darted down the street. "It's that silver sedan in the loading zone."

"The one with the door closed?" Max asked.

"I—I think I closed it when I got up. I was knocked onto the ground. I was dazed. I don't remember exactly what I did. Why are you asking me all these questions about the car and the file?"

"We're just trying to set up a timeline," Kara assured her as Max headed down the street.

"Is he going to my car?" Whitney asked. "I don't know if the file is in there or not. I might have left it at the office."

"It's okay," she said, growing more suspicious of Whitney by the moment. "We'll figure it all out. How are you feeling? Does your head hurt? Were you injured by the explosion?"

"My ears are still ringing. And I hit my knees pretty hard on the ground. I need to call James's wife." She dug into the purse sitting next to her and pulled out her phone. "I need to talk to her before she hears what happened on the news."

"Of course, go ahead." She stepped back as Whitney made her call, her gaze moving down the street to the silver sedan. She'd thought she'd see Max nearby or inside, but he wasn't there, and then she glimpsed him running down the street, as if he were chasing someone.

She moved away from Whitney, following in his direction, not sure what he'd seen or who he was after, but she needed to find out. She moved into a fast jog, finally catching up to him at the end of the block. He was breathing heavily as he stared in frustration across the busy intersection.

"Who were you chasing?" she asked.

"I saw a very tall man with black hair staring at the building. I think it was the guy from Cray's building. When he saw me, he took off, jumped into his car, and disappeared into traffic. But this time, I got at least a partial plate." He rattled off a couple of numbers and letters, along with the make of the vehicle.

"Hang on." She pulled out her phone and asked him to repeat it, then sent the info to Wes. "This is good, Max."

"We'll see how good it is. He could have jacked that vehicle, and he might have already dumped it a few blocks away."

"That could still give us a clue. What about Whitney's car? Did you see anything inside?"

"Her doors were locked, and I saw no evidence of a file on the seat or the floor. I was about to come back and ask for her keys when I noticed the man looking at the building with a pleased smile on his face."

"If it was the same guy who killed Jonas, then the bombings are definitely connected."

"We know they are, Kara," he said, not a hint of doubt in his voice.

"We do," she agreed. "I also wonder if Whitney's early exit was just good luck, or if she knew she needed to be out of that building at a certain time."

"She definitely stumbled over her answers, and her car was locked."

"Let's talk to her again." They made their way back down the street, but Whitney was nowhere in sight, and her car was now gone. "She disappeared fast, but she shouldn't be difficult to find."

As she finished speaking, she saw Jason and Tyler get out of a black SUV and head straight to Ridgemont. "My team is here," she murmured.

Max gave a curt nod. "I'm going to take off."

"You should stay. You're part of this investigation."

"I doubt your team wants me to be a part of it, and I need to speak to Dominic. We'll catch up later. Let me know if you get a hit on the car. Or if you find Vincent Castellano."

"I will," she said, turning her head as she heard her name called. She walked down the street to meet up with Tyler. "Did Captain Ridgemont fill you in?"

"He did. Jason is talking to Damon Wolfe now as well," he said, motioning toward Jason, who had met up with Damon, who had just arrived on the scene with several other agents.

"This is connected to the café bombing," she told him. "I don't know how yet, but Max thinks he saw the man from Cray's apartment on the street here, smiling with pleasure at the destruction. That ties this blast to the last one." She paused. "Did you find Vincent Castellano?"

Tyler shook his head. "Wasn't home, and the super said she hadn't seen him since last weekend. She thought he might be out of town. His employer said he's been out sick all week, but he's definitely not sick at home. She let me into his apartment, because I don't think she likes him very much, and it looked like he hadn't been there in a while. She didn't let me do much of a search, had second thoughts about that when I started opening closet doors, but I found nothing noteworthy."

"Every lead we have disappears," she said in frustration. "Including a woman from the Building Department, who had the good fortune to come outside to allegedly retrieve something from her car before the bomb went off."

"Allegedly?"

"Her story had a lot of holes in it. But I have her name, and she shouldn't be too difficult to find. She was anxious about her boss, so it's possible she went to the hospital. I want to go there next and see if I can talk to any of the people who had minor injuries."

"Good idea. So, how far away were you when this happened?"

"Two blocks away. Near enough to feel the impact, but not close enough to see anything."

"You were with Malone?"

"Yes. We had just finished our meeting with Samantha Barkley's friend, and we were walking to our cars."

"Where's Malone now? I thought I saw him talking to you when we pulled up."

"He went to speak to Dominic."

"Why? Does Dominic own this building?"

"Not according to the woman from the Building Department. She said it's owned by Wexler Properties, but maybe Dominic has a link to that company." She turned as Jason joined them with a serious gleam in his eyes.

"What's your assessment, Kara?"

"This is tied to the café. But we need to figure out how and why before something else blows up. Unless we're no longer taking the lead?"

"We're still running with this, but we can tap into Damon's team as needed."

She was thrilled to hear that. "Good. Also, it's possible the man who killed Cray was here today. I sent Wes a partial license plate to track down. If he was here, he links to both bombings. In the meantime, I want to go to the hospital and talk to the survivors."

"I'll go with you," Tyler said.

"Keep me posted," Jason said.

"My car is a few blocks away," she told Tyler.

"That's fine," he said, falling into step alongside her. "So, Malone seems to be helpful."

"You sound surprised," she said dryly. "What is it about him that bothers you so much?"

"Maybe you should ask him what it is about me that makes him flee whenever I arrive," Tyler countered.

"Now you sound like him. Answering a question with a question. What was going on when you two met overseas? Was it something that involved both of you?"

"I can't say. It's classified."

"Well, that tells me something." She thought for a moment. "You both barely remembered each other, but when you did, your reactions were equally suspicious. Something happened that neither of you was happy about, maybe blaming whoever else was involved."

"I don't know exactly how Malone was involved," Tyler said. "But something went wrong, and I don't know whose fault it was. That's all I'm going to say about it."

"Fair enough. But we're not in the Middle East right now; we're in Manhattan, and Max is a conduit to Dominic Ashford. We need his access." She paused as they crossed the street and walked down the block to her car. The street was much emptier now, but the smoke still hung thick in the air. "I was thinking when we heard about Vincent Castellano and his link to Petroysan, who is linked to Samantha's current case, that the café bombing was just about her. But if that building doesn't tie to Samantha, then...I don't know. If it connects to Dominic, then she was targeted because of him and not her case."

"That would mean Petroysan is also tied to Dominic."

"Dominic mentioned his name when we first spoke to him, but that was in connection to Samantha. He didn't mention that he had a relationship with him?"

"It's interesting that there were so few people in the building," Tyler said. "Even though the blast was bigger, the body count was still small."

"Which isn't the way it usually goes," she agreed. "I wonder what any of those people would have had in common with Samantha."

"We need to find out if she worked on any cases that involved the Building Department. I'll text Alina and see if she and Zane can turn their search through Barkley's case files in that direction," Tyler said, pulling out his phone.

They got into her car a moment later, and as she drove to the hospital, she thought about everything she knew. The low body count was a good thing, but also slightly puzzling. Why wouldn't the bomb have gone off at a time when more people would be on-site? And if someone was targeted, as Samantha might have been, why would anyone blow up a building just to get to one person? It seemed excessive.

"Maybe there's something significant about the manner of the attack," she murmured, glancing over at Tyler as she stopped at a light. "Someone wants the big blast, but they're not trying to kill a large number of people. What's the psychology, the motivation?"

"I don't know, but we need to figure it out."

"I hope Whitney Holden is at the hospital. She was the woman who got out of the building right before the explosion. She kept changing her story, and she took off the second my back was turned. Maybe her being out of the building was just a lucky break, or maybe it wasn't."

CHAPTER ELEVEN

When they arrived at the hospital, Kara showed her badge to the intake nurse and asked for an update on the victims from the construction site. The nurse checked her computer. "Larry Russo is in surgery. Robert Torres and Will Baxter were treated and released. Anthony Perola has been admitted and is being treated for burns and smoke inhalation. He's on the second floor."

"What about James Cooper?" she asked.

The nurse's expression turned sympathetic. "James Cooper was pronounced dead twenty minutes ago."

She let out a breath. James Cooper was dead. He hadn't been as lucky as Samantha Barkley, although maybe she couldn't call Samantha lucky, since she was still in a coma.

"Is anyone from Mr. Cooper's family here?" she asked.

"You can check the burn ward on the second floor. That's where he was taken upon arrival, where Mr. Perola is now."

"Thanks." They made their way to the elevator, and she jabbed at the button in frustration. If they'd been able to find the café bomber before now, James Cooper wouldn't be dead.

"It isn't your fault," Tyler said.

She shot him a dark look. "That sentiment has never made me feel better."

"You're right. But even if it doesn't make you feel better, it's still true."

"We need to work faster."

"We're working as fast as we can, and you know that."

"Aren't you angry?" she asked in frustration.

"It's a waste of energy. I'm focusing on what we need to ask Mr. Perola, if he's able to speak to us."

"You're right. We don't have time for emotion." Despite her words, she was still feeling pissed off with herself as they got on the elevator. She hated to fail, and this felt like failure. But the only way to turn things around was to find the bomber.

After checking with the nurse's station, they were taken to Anthony Perola's room. He appeared to be in his late forties, with bandaged arms and minor burns and cuts on his face. His eyes were closed, and he had oxygen tubes in his nose.

"Is he asleep?" she asked the nurse.

The man's eyes opened at her words.

"Just a few minutes," the nurse said. "He needs to rest."

"Who are you?" he asked.

"I'm Agent Reid. This is Agent Brennan. We're investigating the explosion. Can you tell me what happened right before the bomb went off?"

"We were on the fourth floor," he said, his voice raspy. "James wanted to look at the electrical panel one more time because the elevator had shorted out on our way up. The backup system had worked, but he was concerned, and so was the electrical contractor. That had never happened before. Larry went to get something, and James went into the closet, and the next thing I knew, I was on my back, and there were ceiling tiles falling on my head and fire and smoke, and I couldn't see anything. I couldn't hear anything either." He paused, licking his dry lips. "I think someone was screaming, but I don't know. I started crawling, and I ended up in a stairwell, and the next thing I knew, there was a firefighter there, and he got me out of the building."

"Why didn't you go into the electrical closet with Mr. Cooper?" she asked.

"It wasn't my area. I did the plumbing. How is everyone else doing? No one will tell me anything."

She didn't want to tell him either. Fortunately, the nurse stepped forward. "That's enough for now," she said firmly. "You can talk more later."

"I need to know how they are," Anthony protested.

"The doctors are doing everything they can," the nurse told Anthony.

He looked to her for confirmation, and she went along with the lie. "Everything they can," she said.

They walked out of the room and into the hallway. She heard voices coming from the waiting room, and she saw Whitney Holden talking to a gray-haired woman. They were both crying.

Whitney got to her feet and came forward when she saw them. "James is dead," she said, her face pale, her eyes and nose red from crying. "That bomb killed him."

"I'm so sorry," she replied. "Is that Mrs. Cooper?"

"No. That's Larry Russo's wife. He's in surgery. They don't know if he's going to make it. James's wife is sitting next to him —his body," she stuttered. "I can't believe what's happened."

Whitney was genuinely distraught, which made Kara want to believe her, but she also found it odd that Whitney would be so close to the spouse of one of the contractors, but that question was at the bottom of her list. She waved her hand to Tyler. "This is Agent Brennan. I'd like you to tell him what you told us earlier. Now that you've had a few minutes to catch your breath, you might remember more details."

"I already told you everything," Whitney said, sounding panicked. "I'm sorry. I need to go. I have to go back to work and tell everyone what happened to James. Later, okay?"

Before they could agree, Whitney was gone, practically running from the room.

Tyler met her gaze. "Okay, now I know why you doubt her story."

"Right? She could just be in shock, but..."

"It feels like more. Do you want to talk to Mrs. Russo?"

She glanced at the woman who was now on the phone to someone, her tears still flowing. "I don't think she can help us."

As her phone pinged with an incoming text, she pulled it out of her pocket. "It's Wes. The vehicle Max spotted is owned by Steve Kowalski. He lives in Chelsea." She frowned. "He's seventy-four years old. That doesn't sound like the man who killed Jonas Cray."

"Well, Chelsea isn't far. Let's go check it out."

She drove across town, and while Chelsea wasn't far in miles, it took close to forty-five minutes to get through the traffic. Finally, just after six, they made their way up to the front door of Mr. Kowalski's home. When the door opened, the older man with white hair and weathered skin gave them a suspicious look.

Tyler introduced them and showed his badge, then asked him where his car was.

"I sold the car last month," he replied. "My wife doesn't like me driving anymore, and it's too damn expensive to buy gas."

"Who did you sell the car to?" she asked. "The registration is still in your name."

"The guy who bought it said he'd take care of it."

"Who was that?"

"I think his name was Cal. Yeah, that was it. Big, tall guy. Very nice, though. Gave me cash. Said he didn't want me to have to wait for a check to clear."

"How did Cal find you?" Tyler asked.

"My son put the car up on some social media site. I don't know which one. The next day, I had a buyer. It worked out great." He paused. "Why are you asking about my car?"

"The person who bought it is a potential witness in an investigation," Tyler returned. "Do you have his phone number?"

Mr. Kowalski thought for a moment. "No, I don't. I think my son did everything online. You could talk to him. He's in London right now, but I can give you his number."

"That would be helpful," she said.

"Hang on a second."

As he disappeared back into his apartment, she turned to Tyler. "I had a feeling we were going to hit a dead end. I hope the son has contact information."

Mr. Kowalski returned a moment later and gave them the number handwritten on a piece of paper. "Hope it helps," he said as he closed the door.

"It's after midnight in London," she said as they walked back to the car.

"Yeah. I'll work on this in the morning." Tyler paused when they reached her vehicle. "You don't need to take me back to the office. I'm meeting up with a friend of mine not far from here. I'll just hop on the subway."

"Are you sure I can't drop you somewhere?"

"With this traffic, the subway will be faster. I'll see you tomorrow." He smiled. "Hopefully not before then."

As Tyler headed down the street, she got in her car and was about to start the engine when she got a text from Max asking for an update.

Instead of texting him back, she called him, happy when he answered. "I was just going to ask you the same thing," she said. "Is Dominic tied to Wexler Properties?"

"We should meet. Where are you?"

"Chelsea."

"What are you doing there?"

"Just met with the old man who sold his car for cash to someone named Cal, who was going to handle the registration for him."

"So there's no change of ownership record."

"Nope. Tell me you have something to go on."

"Where are you headed now?"

"Home."

"I'll meet you there."

She wasn't sure that was the best idea, but she wanted to hear what he had to say, so she said she'd see him soon and started the car.

———

Max stood on the sidewalk in front of Kara's building, a four-story brownstone on a tree-lined street in the Lower East Side. The neighborhood had that lived-in feel he appreciated— bodegas on the corners, people walking dogs, the mix of old and new that made New York feel real instead of polished. He pressed the buzzer for apartment 1B.

"It's me," he said when she answered.

The door buzzed open, and he found her apartment to be the first door on the left. She opened it before he could knock, still wearing her work clothes, but she'd taken off her jacket and pulled her hair out of its ponytail. She looked tired, and he had to fight off an inexplicable urge to give her a comforting hug, which she would probably not find comforting at all. In fact, he wouldn't put it past her to flip him flat on his back if he tried anything because, despite the way she'd kissed him last night, she now seemed determined to make that a distant memory. But for him, it wasn't distant at all, and that brought a faint smile to his lips, which made her gaze narrow in suspicion.

"What's funny?" she asked.

"Nothing," he said. "Can I come in?"

She waved him inside, and as he stepped into the room, he found her home to be small but also colorful. Her tough federal agent exterior was missing in a living room filled with a soft, puffy sky-blue couch and matching armchair, with a colorful rug, and walls covered with art and pictures of New York.

There was a small galley kitchen off to the side of the living room, and through an open doorway, he could see a bedroom and bath.

"Nice," he said.

"Messy," she countered as she moved some books off the armchair.

"It looks like you're a reader."

She nodded. "Always."

He picked up the top book from the stack she'd just moved. "Suspense? You don't get enough of that on the job?"

She shrugged. "I read everything."

He could see that as he moved through the stack. Everything included romance, a historical novel, and a biography on Lyndon Johnson that looked to be over a thousand pages. "Wow, this one would make a great paperweight."

"Why are you here?" she asked. "Do you have new information? Did you talk to Dominic?"

"I did. Do you have anything to drink?"

"Uh, water, juice, and maybe a beer."

"Really? I'll take a beer. I hadn't figured you for a beer drinker."

"One of my cousins stayed with me for a few days last week, and he brought the beer," she said as she moved into the kitchen.

He turned toward a bookshelf, filled with books, but also packed with framed family photos on top. He picked up the photo of a man in FDNY gear, standing in front of a fire truck with a little girl by his side. "This must be you and your dad," he said as she handed him a beer bottle. "You have his eyes and the same determined jaw."

"That's him," she said. "I was six. The photo was taken a few months before he died. The last one I have of us together."

"Sorry again. I didn't mean to make you sad." He could see the sudden gleam of pain in her eyes, and he didn't like that he'd put it there.

"You didn't. It's just been a long day, and explosions give me a little PTSD."

"You're in the wrong business, Kara."

"That's what my mother says. She doesn't understand why I couldn't be a teacher like her, or a doctor like my brother, or a fashion designer like my cousin Sylvie, really anything else but law enforcement or the fire department."

"But you had other ideas."

"I think growing up in the shadow of that horrible attack made me want to protect my family, my city, even my country. It was a thought that took hold when I was really young. It never let go of me. And it's not always explosions and fire. In fact, it's mostly a lot of other stuff."

"But not lately."

"Not lately," she agreed.

He looked back at the next photo, which was a family picture of her mom, dad, and brother around the same time period. The next one was at her high school graduation with her mother and brother. And then there were family photos of all the aunts and uncles and cousins. He felt an odd sense of yearning for that kind of big family experience, but his very small family had gotten even smaller after his mother died, and now there was just him and his dad, and they barely saw each other. "I love these photos. Everyone is so happy."

"We have a good time together. So, tell me what you found out. I could really use some good news now that the license plate has led us to another dead end."

He wasn't entirely surprised. "I had a feeling the car wasn't going to lead us to Cal. He has probably already dumped it and moved on to another vehicle. What did you do after I left?"

"I went to the hospital and talked to Whitney Holden again. Her boss, James Cooper, passed away at the hospital, and she was distraught. She didn't want to talk to me again and bailed as fast as she could. I'll follow up with her tomorrow, and I'll talk to her coworkers, see what else I can find out." She took a sip of her beer. "There are a lot of little threads that could lead somewhere or nowhere. It's possible Whitney is just reacting from shock and fear of almost being blown up, or she knew to get out of that building early. Tell me what Dominic said."

"Dominic doesn't own Wexler Properties or that building, but he is friends with Martin Wexler, and he has worked with James Cooper on multiple occasions. In fact, James has been the inspector on several of Dominic's projects in the city in the last five years. He's definitely a link between Samantha and James, but I don't see why anyone would blow up two buildings to get to those two in order to get to him."

"I don't either," she said, disappointment running across her face. "It doesn't make sense. We're missing something." She stood up and paced back and forth in front of the window. "And Dominic is a common denominator, but how does he really play into this?" She paused, and he could see the new idea jumping into her gaze.

"He's not responsible for the bombings," he said.

"He could be. Maybe Samantha wasn't just his girlfriend; she was investigating him, and he needed to take her out, but not in a way that would make him a suspect."

"That's too far out there."

"And what if James Cooper was a thorn in his side? What if they weren't friendly? What if Cooper was standing in Dominic's way of getting a building approved? Maybe he was also an enemy to Dominic's ambition."

"You're painting a picture, but I don't think it's the right picture."

"You don't know that it's wrong," she argued.

"I know you want all this to make sense. But think about what we've seen. If Dominic wanted to take these two people out, is this how he would do it? He can afford to buy whatever he wants, and I've seen no evidence of him being violent or choosing a violent means to an end. I'm not saying he's never crossed a line. But he uses money, not bombs, to get what he wants."

"Money could buy a bomb maker."

"Too public," he said. "Not Dominic's style."

She sat back down. "Are you basing that on now, or on the guy you first met in school?"

"Perhaps both."

"What was Dominic like when he was a teenager?"

"He was as confident and arrogant as he is now, but he was also fun, friendly, someone who had a lot of big ideas and carried many people in his wake. Because being around him felt like being part of something really cool."

She gave him an interested look. "So, you wanted to be cool back then?"

He smiled. "Doesn't every teenager want to be part of the in-group?"

"Maybe. But you don't seem like someone who is concerned about peer pressure or being liked. Unless you changed..."

"I had to change schools a lot. Every time my mom got a new post, I had to start over, and it was never easy. That school, filled with all those rich kids, was definitely one of the harder groups to break into. But when Dominic befriended me, my life got easier. And I was always grateful to him for that. But I could see through him better than others could. I could see the vulnerability, the insecurity."

"Where did that come from?"

"His father. He was hard on Dominic, always disappointed in him. Whatever Dominic did wasn't good enough. That attitude drove Dominic to higher heights than he would have reached if he hadn't had a father like that. Dominic has always had something to prove to his father."

"Is his father still alive?"

"Yes. He lives in London, and even with all of Dominic's success, the man still asks him when he's going to do more for the world and not just for himself."

"Is that why he's investing so much in Tajikistan and other countries?"

"I think so. And it's also why he wants the press to cover his philanthropy. He wants to make sure his father knows without having to tell him."

"So odd that Dominic would still care so much about impressing his dad."

"His father is a narcissist. He's never going to be impressed by his son. He's never going to give Dominic the validation he craves. But even if Dominic logically knows that he can't stop trying."

"I guess I can understand that. The need to be seen by the people you love can be powerful." She paused. "What about you? Did your parents push you?"

"No. My parents were very involved in their own careers, not that they didn't care about me, but they weren't all that concerned with how I was doing in school or what I wanted to be when I grew up. They just told me I should find my passion and follow it."

"But you didn't start at the CIA. You worked as a journalist, right?"

He smiled. "I almost forgot you looked me up."

"Why did you want to be a reporter? And why did you stop wanting to be that?"

"I'd been traveling the world my entire life; I figured I'd just keep going, be a foreign correspondent. I had some language skills, and I couldn't see myself behind a desk working a nine-to-five job, so that's where I started."

"And the CIA recruited you? Or...was the reporting job always just a cover?"

He smiled. "It was an actual job that I did for almost two years. But I got tired of showing up after the damage had been done. Filming the aftermath, interviewing the survivors, documenting the destruction." He picked up his beer and took a swig. "One day, a guy approached me in Istanbul. Said he worked for the CIA, that they could use someone with my access and my cover. Someone who spoke the languages, understood the cultures, and had the State Department connections. It felt like a chance to be more proactive, so I took it. Occasionally, I still used the cover, but I had other covers as well."

"And you liked it for a while?"

"Almost ten years," he said.

"And you got to see a lot of the world."

"Too much of some places," he said, a little darkness leeching into his voice.

She immediately frowned. "Like..."

"I think we've had enough honest talk for a while. I'm hungry. Do you want to order a pizza?"

She thought about that for a moment. "You could just go home and eat."

"I have nothing to eat at my apartment."

"You live above a restaurant."

"And I need a change from dumplings. You don't feel like cooking, do you? And I suspect you don't want to go out, so let me buy you a pizza."

"Only if we can keep talking about Dominic. I can't just do nothing the rest of the evening."

"Then let's work on the case together," he said. "Because I'd like to find some answers, too, so I can get back to my real job." Pulling out his phone, he pulled up a food app. "What do you like on your pizza?"

"Everything," she said.

"Are you sure, because I might take you seriously. And I haven't had the greatest experience with ordering when a woman says she doesn't care."

She laughed. "Okay, no pineapple or anchovies. Anything else is fair game."

"Great. I love specifics. Makes it so much easier." He ordered an extra-large pizza and then said, "It should be here in about twenty minutes."

"Perfect. I'm getting hungry. It's been a long time since that Caesar salad. The days feel like they're flying by, but we're not getting a lot done." She paused, confusion in her gaze. "I have to say, today's explosion was shocking. I really thought the café bombing was a one-off, that it was about taking out Samantha Barkley. But it wasn't."

"No, it wasn't."

"I'm tired, but I also feel wired, you know?"

"I know. It's part of the job," he said with complete understanding.

"What was it like being a secret agent?"

He smiled at her words. "It was exciting."

"Really? I thought you were going to lie and say it wasn't at all interesting."

"Are you kidding? I was living a hundred different lives all over the world."

"That sounds both fun and exhausting. Maybe even a little lonely," she ventured, giving him a questioning look.

"Sometimes. There were jobs when there was a lot of waiting around, sitting in a hotel room until a meeting could get set up, but I always had a mission. And that focus made the waiting more tolerable, the isolation more acceptable. I'm sure you can relate."

"In the NYPD, I always had a partner, and most of them were great. They became close friends. The FBI has been harder to find that kind of connection, but I went to Quantico and then to 26 Fed and now to a new team, so I haven't been anywhere long enough to forge a close relationship. And to be honest, I'm also more wary after what happened to me. I don't trust as easily as I used to. Maybe that's a good thing."

"Probably," he agreed. "Trust can be used as a weapon."

"Sometimes you say very dark things."

He tipped his head in acknowledgment. "Sometimes I feel very dark things."

Her expression grew more serious. "You have a wound, something that hurts, and I'm guessing it's not just about the criminal who was turned into an asset. Something else happened, something more personal."

His gut tightened with each word as she came dangerously close to a truth he didn't want to talk about. His phone dinged, and he took a grateful breath. "The pizza is almost here. I'll go get it."

"Saved by the pizza," she said dryly as he stood up. "But I don't think I'm wrong."

"I didn't say you were."

"You didn't say anything."

"We have enough to talk about in the present; we don't need to go into the past." He headed out the door and down the hall and opened the front door just as the delivery guy walked up the stairs. He took it inside and found Kara pulling out plates and napkins, and he was relieved to be done with a conversation that had gotten far deeper than he'd wanted it to.

CHAPTER TWELVE

After a delicious, filling pizza, of which she ate far too many slices, Kara grabbed her computer and brought it over to the table while Max finished eating. They hadn't talked about the case or their pasts over pizza, keeping the conversation to more neutral topics. Although she had learned that he loved baseball, was a big fan of indie films versus commercial blockbusters, had read a fair amount of history books, and had favorite foods in probably six different cultures. He was smart, well-read, and one of the sexiest men she'd ever met, and the more she got to know him, the more she liked him.

She told herself not to get carried away, not to trust everything that he said. He'd admitted to being a spy. He knew how to create a persona, and she'd made mistakes before believing someone to be good when they were anything but good.

Forcing herself to stop thinking about Max, she put Whitney Holden's name into the search engine. While she didn't have access to her team's resource databases on her personal computer, she could still do a little digging.

"What are you looking up?" Max asked.

"Information on Whitney Holden."

"She really bothered you."

"She bothered you, too."

"She did," he admitted. "But she could have just been shaken up by her close call with death. It's not surprising she wasn't thinking clearly."

"Look at you, giving her the benefit of the doubt," she said dryly.

He smiled. "I try not to see anyone as just one thing, because no one ever is."

"No, they're not," she murmured as her gaze scanned Whitney's profile. "This is interesting. Whitney is into fitness. She goes to the gym three to four times a week and has a personal trainer named Giannis, who works at..." She looked over the top of her computer. "Wanna guess?"

"Forge Fitness."

"You win. Whitney also goes to the gym where Samantha went, where Jonas Cray was seen, and where Elias Costa lied to us about knowing Jonas. I need to talk to her now."

"Now?" he echoed, glancing down at his watch. "It's after nine."

"I don't care. It can't wait until tomorrow. She could run." As she finished speaking, she opened the email Wes had sent her earlier, which contained Whitney's personal information, including her phone number and address. "She lives in Brooklyn. I'm going to see if I can catch her at home, maybe before she has time to call her lawyer."

"She probably already did that," he said, getting up along with her. "I'll go. You might need backup."

"I can call Tyler to meet me there."

"Or I can just go with you. I will have your back, Kara."

She didn't believe everything he said, but she believed that. And she didn't want to waste time trying to reach Tyler, who'd already told her he was meeting a friend. "Let's go."

"I'll drive," he said. "You can keep digging into Whitney on the way, just in case we don't find her at home. We need to know who her friends and family are, and who might take her in if she were in trouble."

She nodded, grabbing her jacket as she followed him out the door.

On the drive to Brooklyn, she researched Whitney. "She lives her life online," she told Max as he sped through the dark city streets. "She's thirty-five years old and single now after her last boyfriend cheated on her. She loves working out, nutrition, manifesting, and poker."

"That's quite a combination," Max muttered. "Maybe she played poker with Costa."

"I don't think she's a high roller, but she's a pretty, single woman. They might have wanted her in the game." Her gaze moved down the page. "Turns out the cheating boyfriend made a living online playing poker, so she probably learned a lot from him."

"Wonder if she's racked up some debt."

"And maybe needed a quick payout," she said, following his train of thought. "She doesn't seem violent or dangerous or ideologically anything. But she seems to like attention, and her social media pages are full of rants about being used or taken for granted. I both can and can't believe she puts all this online for anyone to read."

"It wouldn't be difficult to manipulate her after hearing what you just told me."

"No, it wouldn't," she agreed. "Maybe that will help us get her to open up."

"We're almost there," he said, checking the GPS.

She straightened in her seat, scanning the addresses. "That's it."

As Max pulled up in front of a duplex and turned off the lights, she saw a woman come out of the front door carrying a suitcase. She was on her phone and didn't notice them at all as she headed to the car parked in front of the garage. She opened her trunk and struggled with the phone in one hand and what appeared to be a heavy suitcase in the other.

"She's running," she said, her hand on the door. She sprang out of the car, with Max right behind her. They were at the car before Whitney realized they were there. She squealed in alarm as she dropped her phone.

"Oh my God, you scared me," she said, reaching down to pick up her phone.

The screen was dark. Whoever had been on the call with her was gone. "Where are you going, Whitney?" she asked.

"I—I'm going to my mom's house. She lives in New Jersey. I'm too scared to stay here." Whitney's gaze flickered from her to Max and back again. "What are you doing here? I told you everything I know."

"You didn't tell me you go to Forge Fitness, that you know Elias Costa and Jonas Cray."

"Jonas? I don't know a Jonas."

"But you know the others," Max interjected. "Do you play poker with Elias?"

"I don't understand why you're asking me these questions about the gym?"

"The gym is tied to the bombing, which means you're tied to the bombing," she said. "You didn't just accidentally forget something before that bomb went off. You knew it was coming. You knew when to get out."

Whitney's face paled in the shadowy light, and she put a hand to her heart. "I—I didn't know. I swear. I had no idea there was a bomb."

"You're lying," Max said. "You set your boss up to be killed."

"I didn't know," she repeated, desperation in her voice.

"You didn't know they were going to kill James?" she asked, bringing Whitney's attention back to her. "That's good, because then you may escape a murder charge. But there could be other charges unless you help us. Tell us what you know, and I'll make sure you get the best deal possible. Make no mistake, Whitney, you are in a hell of a lot of trouble. A man died today."

Whitney bit down on her lip so hard that she drew blood. "He just told me to make sure the inspection was today, and to make sure James checked the electrical panel on the fourth floor before he left."

"Who told you to do that?"

"His name is Cal. I met him at Forge Fitness at one of Elias's poker games," she admitted.

"So you did play," she said.

"Yes, and I lost a lot. I owed Elias forty thousand dollars. He said he'd clear my debt if I did this one small favor for his friend Cal. I couldn't say no. I didn't think anyone was going to die." Her voice broke. "I thought they just wanted to sabotage the inspection, delay the building project. Cal said that someone wanted James to understand his decisions could be painful. And that I should stay out of the electrical closet. I thought maybe there was a hot wire or something in there. Or they wanted him to find something to delay approving the inspection."

"You thought it was worse than that," Max said sharply. "That's why you ran, isn't it, Whitney?"

"Something felt off," she admitted. "I was afraid of whatever was coming, so I said I needed to get a file, and I left. I had barely reached the car when the building blew up. It felt like the world shattered around me." She turned from Max to Kara, giving her a pleading look. "I realized I was supposed to be in there when it happened. That I was supposed to die, too. I have to leave tonight. I have to get out of here."

"You're not going anywhere by yourself because you're not safe," Kara said. "You're a loose end. And someone will want to make sure you never talk. The only way for you to ever be safe again is to work with us."

The sound of an engine revving snapped her head toward the street. A dark sedan was speeding down the block. The window opened.

"Gun," she yelled, grabbing Whitney's arm and pulling her back behind the car as gunfire erupted, shattering the windows above their heads.

Max was on the other side of the car, firing back, but the car had already disappeared around the corner. Dogs barked, and lights came on as the neighbors reacted to the shots.

She looked down at Whitney, who was crying, her eyes filled with terror. "Are you hurt?"

She shook her head. "No. I'm terrified."

"He's gone."

"For now."

Max came around the car, his weapon still in his hand. She hadn't realized he had a gun, but she was happy that he did, because she'd been too busy shielding Whitney to fire her own weapon.

She called 911 to report the incident and to verify she was an FBI agent on scene so the police wouldn't draw their weapons when they saw them. The dispatcher told them that cars were already on the way.

"The police are coming," she said.

"Are the police going to arrest me?" Whitney asked.

"No. I'm taking you into my custody," she said decisively. "We'll get you into a safe house tonight." She called Ops to report what had happened and request a safe house. She was given the address of an apartment in Midtown and was assured that two agents would meet her there as soon as they could. In the meantime, she needed to deal with the police.

She greeted the officers when they got out of the car. She wasn't familiar with either of them, which made everything easier. While she spoke with them, Max kept a protective eye on Whitney.

He'd put his gun away, and she didn't want to explain who he was, so she let them think he was also FBI. Fortunately, her badge, the lack of injuries, and the damage from the gunfire being contained to Whitney's car and garage door gave the officers little to be interested in. After her explanation, they left.

Max grabbed Whitney's suitcase and put it in the back seat next to her, while Kara slid into the passenger seat and gave Max the address for the safe house. Then they headed back into the city.

Whitney seemed in shock, an endless rain of tears pouring down her face, and hiccupping sobs racking her body. She seemed genuinely terrified and upset, but Kara had little compassion for her. She'd sold out her boss to pay off a gambling debt, and she didn't believe for one second Whitney hadn't suspected something was going to happen. Maybe the thought hadn't occurred to her until she was standing in that building, but her instinct had told her to run, and if she hadn't, she might have ended up like James Cooper.

Turning in her seat, she asked her again, "Tell me again exactly what Cal said to you, Whitney."

"I already told you."

"He said he wanted James to understand that consequences can be painful. What do you think he meant? Was he talking about revenge?"

"I actually thought he was talking about me, about having to pay for my losses, for the advances in cash Elias had given me so I could keep playing."

"But he wasn't talking about you; he was talking about James," she said.

"I see that now."

"Do you know Samantha Barkley?" Max interjected.

"I know a Samantha who works out at the gym. I think that might have been her last name. She's a lawyer."

"She's actually a federal prosecutor, and she was injured in a bomb blast at a café on Monday," Kara said.

Whitney stared at her in confusion. "Are you saying that Cal did that, too?"

"Pretty sure he did," she replied. "What do you know about

Cal? Do you know his last name? Where he works? Where he lives?"

"I just know he works with Elias, and he sometimes helps with the poker games. I don't think I ever heard his last name. And I have no idea where he lives. He's kind of creepy, super tall, and had mean, cold eyes that match his black hair." Whitney paused. "He has a faint accent. I'm not sure where it's from."

"Who else plays in the games?" Max asked.

"There are two groups: people who have money, and people who look good. And there are men and women in both groups. That's how I got in. Elias said they needed some single ladies who knew how to play."

"Was there more involved in these games than just poker?" she asked. "Were you supposed to entertain some of the other players in a more private way?"

"No," Whitney said. "I just played cards and flirted a little, mostly to throw the men off their game. I like to win. And it's hard to stop when I'm not winning. I keep thinking I'll get it all back on the next hand."

"Is your ex-boyfriend part of this group?"

"No. And why are you asking me about him?"

"Wondering if he knows Cal or Elias," she asked.

"I started going to the gym after we broke up. He plays with a different crowd and mostly online." Whitney took a ragged breath. "What's going to happen to me?"

"We're going to put you in a safe place for a few days. You'll answer a lot more questions, and the more help you give us, the easier things will go for you."

"I never thought James was going to die," she said as she burst into tears again.

Kara glanced at Max, whose hard profile didn't show any hint of compassion for the woman in the back seat, and she couldn't blame him. Whitney wasn't innocent. She'd walked her boss into the closet that had gotten him killed. But they needed Whitney to keep talking. Now that she'd confirmed Elias and Cal had worked together, along with Jonas Cray, they were getting a better idea of who was involved in the bombings, but the why was still to be answered.

When they arrived at the doorman-controlled building, they received a key and a unit number. Then they took Whitney up to the eighteenth floor. The one-bedroom apartment was small and furnished with the basics: a couch, coffee table, and TV in the living room, a small kitchen, a bedroom with a queen-sized bed, and an adjacent bathroom. The windows didn't open, and there were no buildings or windows facing them. The doorman and security manager provided an extra layer of security, but there would be an agent outside the door and one in the apartment with Whitney.

"This isn't bad," Max commented as Whitney went into the bathroom. "I assume your team is sending someone over."

"Not sure if it's my team or someone from 26 Fed. I guess we're working together now because there are multiple crime scenes. What do you think about Whitney's story?"

"She has a gambling addiction. She sold her boss out for money, and now she's worried that decision might cost her life."

"It might have if we hadn't gotten there before Cal."

"She's lucky you tracked her down tonight."

"I never should have let her leave the hospital."

"I find regrets to be a waste of energy, Kara. You do what you do with the information you have. Second-guessing won't make you feel better or change anything."

"You're very pragmatic, Max."

"I've been down the same road more times than I can count."

He understood the challenges of her job, probably because they were like those he'd faced in the CIA, although she suspected they were very different, too. Her phone rang. Tyler was on the line.

"Do you ever just go home and go to bed?" he asked dryly. "I thought that was the plan earlier."

"I started looking into Whitney and found ties between her and Forge Fitness. I couldn't wait until tomorrow to talk to her. And it was a good thing I didn't."

"Your instincts were on the money," Tyler agreed. "Damon is sending two agents from his team to take turns watching over her tonight. They should be there shortly."

"Okay, good. I'll wait here until they come."

"Are you on your own, or is Malone with you?"

"He's here, too. By the way, Max told me that Dominic is not tied to Wexler Properties, but he has worked with James Cooper on several of his buildings."

"That's interesting."

"Maybe. I'm not sure it matters." She gave him a brief recap of what Whitney had told her and suggested they focus on Costa in the morning.

"I'll see you at the office," he said. "Try not to get into any more trouble tonight."

"I'll try." She walked over to the bathroom door and gave a knock. "Whitney, is everything all right?'

A moment later, the door opened, and Whitney came out, her eyes and nose red and swollen. "Am I really going to be safe here?" she asked.

"Yes, you will be." She'd no sooner said the words when she got a text that the agents were on their way up. A moment later, there was a knock at the door.

Whitney jumped and moved back toward the bathroom door.

"It's your protection. Don't worry." She walked over to the door, checked the peephole first, and saw their badges before she opened the door to a male and female agent, who introduced themselves as Agents Capwell and Young.

After introductions were made and assurances were given to Whitney, she and Max left the apartment with Agent Young, who had put a chair next to Whitney's door. The other agent would remain inside for the first shift, and then they would switch.

They made their way downstairs and into Max's vehicle. He quickly pulled away from the curb, arriving at her building a short time later. It was after midnight now, and the street was quiet. She thought he would keep the engine running and drop her off, but he insisted on parking and coming inside to check her apartment.

"I can take care of myself," she told him as they walked up to her door.

"I know. But two pairs of eyes are better than one," he said as he scanned the street.

She unlocked the door to her building and then made her way into the hall and unlocked her apartment door. She could take care of herself, but it was rather nice to have him by her side as she flipped on the lights. Her apartment was so small it took only a few minutes to search, and everything was exactly as she'd left it.

"It's all good," she said

"Yeah," he muttered, his words not matching the frown on his face.

"You can go now."

"I don't think so."

"What?" she asked in surprise.

"I believe it was Cal who tried to run us down the other night, who shot at us a few hours ago, and also saw us at the scene of the blast earlier today."

"Was that today?" she asked wearily. "It feels like we've lived a year in the past few hours."

"I agree, but my point is Cal knows we're on his tail. We're getting to potential witnesses either right before him or right after him."

"So he might want to slow us down."

"Or take us out. I think we should stay together. I'll sleep on your couch."

She thought about his offer, wondering why she liked it so much. She'd always been fiercely independent and worked hard to be a strong woman in a dangerous field. She would usually have said no to his idea before he'd finished the last word. But she didn't want to say no. She wanted to say yes to him. And that made a shiver run down her spine.

His gaze darkened as if he'd just read her mind, which maybe he had, because they had gotten incredibly close in a very short amount of time.

"Kara?" There was a question in his voice, and she didn't think it really had anything to do with sleeping on her couch.

But she couldn't say yes to anything else. She probably shouldn't even say yes to that, except she really wanted to. She liked the idea of him being close by.

"Nothing is going to happen," he said, filling the silence.

"I know that. I don't want anything to happen."

"Well, I do want something to happen, but not tonight, not like this..."

Her breath came faster at his admission. "You really should go home. I'll be fine."

"You will be fine. But I'd just like to make sure that we're both fine."

"I'm not going to believe you're afraid to go home alone."

He smiled. "Is that a yes?"

"Yes," she said, the word slipping off her tongue before she could stop it. "I'll get you a blanket and a pillow."

She disappeared into her bedroom and came back a moment later. "I'll say goodnight. Help yourself to anything you want or need." She flushed as his gaze glittered with amusement. "I mean...you know what I mean."

"It's going to happen one day," he said confidently. "You and me."

"I don't think so."

"Yes, you do," he said.

"Goodnight, Max." She had to get out of this room before that *one day* turned into tonight.

CHAPTER THIRTEEN

Friday morning, Kara emerged from her bedroom, showered and dressed in dark jeans and a blazer, her hair still damp. She'd managed maybe three hours of broken sleep, her mind cycling through Whitney's confession, Cal's cold efficiency, and thoughts of Max sleeping only a few feet away from her.

The smell of coffee hit her first.

Max was in her kitchen, two bagels in the toaster, a container of cream cheese open on the counter, fresh coffee already brewed. He was still wearing yesterday's clothes—dark pants and a button-down that was slightly rumpled now—but he looked more rested than she felt.

"You went out?" she asked. "Because I know I didn't have bagels."

He glanced up, and something in his expression softened when he saw her. "Deli on the corner."

The gesture caught her off guard. It was unexpectedly thoughtful, almost domestic. She wasn't used to anyone being in her space like this, making coffee, buying her breakfast.

"Thanks," she said, meaning it.

The toaster popped. Max plated the bagels and brought them to her small kitchen table. They sat across from each other, and for a moment it felt oddly normal—two people having breakfast together, starting their day.

Max took a sip of coffee. "Sleep at all?"

"Not much. You?"

"Same."

They ate in comfortable silence for a moment. Kara spread cream cheese on her bagel, aware of him watching her.

"What's your plan today?" Max asked.

"Back to the safe house first thing. Get Whitney's full statement on record—everything we can use." She took a bite, swallowed. "Then the office. Dig into James Cooper's life and his inspection history. Figure out what he did that needed consequences."

"And how he possibly ties to Samantha Barkley," he added. "I need to check in with Dominic, see how she's doing."

"Don't talk to him about Whitney," she said, realizing how much information Max had that he could share with Dominic.

Anger ran through his eyes. "Do you think I'd do that?"

"You do work for him."

"That doesn't mean I'd protect him if he's guilty of something. He buys my services, not my undying loyalty."

"That hasn't always been my experience. I doubt it's been yours. We both know that loyalty can be bought along with a lot of other things."

He gave her a long look, then tipped his head. "Fair point. But my integrity isn't for sale. When I can't support something, I don't."

Considering he'd left a long career in the CIA because of a decision he couldn't support, she wanted to believe him. But trust didn't come easily to her. "Okay," she said finally.

"Okay," he echoed.

A tense silence fell over them as they finished eating, and finally, she had to break it. "What are your plans for today besides talking to Dominic?"

"I'm going to check in with some friends. See if anyone

knows anything about Elias Costa or Cal. If Cal has ties to the Middle East, someone may have heard of him." He sipped his coffee. "Has your team found anything on Costa?"

"Nothing noteworthy. He has no criminal record, no online presence. He started out as a personal trainer, working at several gyms and also with wealthy individuals. Apparently, he trained Marco Tilan, a wealthy French businessman who ended up buying the fitness center that became Forge Fitness. He encouraged his other wealthy friends to sign up for memberships, and then Elias became the manager."

"What did you find out about Tilan?"

"He died three years ago, and his widow, Fiona Tilan, inherited everything. But she lives in Paris and hasn't been to the US in years. Elias basically has free rein."

"Maybe you should look deeper into Marco Tilan," Max suggested. "He may be dead, but his network might be interesting."

"Now that we're zeroing in on Elias Costa, I agree. I'll do that as soon as I get into the office. Who are you going to talk to? Someone still at the CIA?"

"Someone who's well connected," he said vaguely.

"You're not going to tell me anything about him, are you?"

"I can tell you I trust him not to steer me wrong, that I've worked with him many times before."

"I thought you said you don't trust anyone."

"I have a few exceptions to that rule."

"Well, I'm making an exception for you. Don't make me wrong."

He gave her a long look, then said, "I hope I won't."

"I prefer the last two words over the first two," she said with annoyance. "Why can't you make the promise?"

"Promises can't always be kept, even when you want to."

There was a heaviness behind his words, and the shift in his gaze seemed to move into the past. He wasn't thinking about the promise he couldn't quite make to her anymore; he was thinking about someone else.

"Did you break a promise to someone you cared about?" she asked.

"I need to get to work, and so do you." He got to his feet. "Be careful, Kara."

"You, too," she said, but she wasn't sure he'd heard her because he was already out the door.

His actions reminded her how little she actually knew about him, and also how much she wanted to know more. But Max Malone was not the puzzle she needed to figure out right now. She needed to check on Whitney, then get to the office. The race to stop another bombing was on...

———

Max arrived at Tompkins Square Park in the East Village a little before noon. This meeting shouldn't be dangerous, but he had learned a long time ago to expect the unexpected. His gaze swept across the park. Everything looked normal—dog walkers, parents and nannies with kids, a few homeless people on benches, a couple of young lovers making out on a blanket. The day was warmer than the past few, with sun streaking through the tree branches, creating a more optimistic feel, one he'd like to hang on to for a while.

But he doubted that was going to happen. Things were escalating, building in intensity, and he doubted the attacker was done. He was afraid he or she was just getting started.

A man walked into the park wearing a Yankees cap, a navy-blue windbreaker, and jeans. He was lean and wiry and moved with a careless purpose that had always been his trademark. Reza Barech looked the same as he had the last time Max had seen him in Istanbul nine months ago. He was in his late thirties, olive-skinned, with dark hair and a beard. He was handsome enough to be charming, but his attractive face and easygoing manner made him easy to underestimate.

Reza walked over to the water fountain a few feet away from him and took a drink. Then he lifted his head and gave him a smile as he moved closer. "You look better than the last time I saw you," he said. "New York agrees with you."

"It's only a temporary stop."

"So I've heard. You're working for Dominic Ashford now. And you'll be back where you shouldn't be in a month."

"As his private security," he said, knowing Reza didn't believe him for a second.

"Sure. If you reached out because of Qadir—"

"I didn't," he said, cutting him off.

Reza looked surprised. "You didn't?"

"No. I'm working on something here in the city. Ashford's girlfriend was critically injured in a bomb blast on Monday."

Reza nodded. "I read about that. And yesterday there was another bomb. Related?"

"Absolutely."

"And connected to Ashford?"

"Still to be determined. There's a man who goes by the name Cal, well over six feet tall, black hair, black eyes, described as having a Middle Eastern accent. He works jobs for Elias Costa, who runs Forge Fitness, and possibly the Novik brothers, who run the Crimson Club. He's connected to a murder and a hit on a witness to the bombing yesterday. Anything about him sound familiar?"

"You said this wasn't about Qadir."

He looked at Reza in surprise. "It's not."

"Caleb Azrani fits the description you just gave me. He's the younger brother of—"

"Malik Azrani," he finished, one of Qadir's best friends. "But how could Caleb be here? The Azranis have been on the watch list for years."

"Only Malik. Caleb is his much younger brother. He came to

the US with his mother when he was a child. Malik stayed with the father. Do you have a photo?"

"There's a sketch, but I don't have it with me." A dozen thoughts raced through his mind. If Cal was Caleb Azrani, the brother of one of Qadir's best friends, it seemed likely that Qadir was involved in this. But there was no way he would set foot on US soil. However, that didn't mean he wasn't running things from afar. But the bombings weren't his signature, his style. Qadir liked chaos, mass hysteria, and explosions on a much larger scale. He wanted mass destruction, not single targets. "The two bombs don't sound like Qadir."

"Cal might run his own group here."

"Or be working for someone else. He seems more like a middleman to me. Can you do some digging?"

"If these events are tied to Qadir, this is the last thing you should work on, Max. Qadir has already stolen so much of your life. Look what you've lost."

"Which means I have little else to lose," he said harshly. "And this is more about Dominic, my employer, than anything else."

"For now, but not if the group is tied to Qadir." Reza gave him a sharp look. "You can't tell me that Ashford isn't a cover to get you back into a region that you should not be going to again. Or that his money isn't fueling your obsession."

"Can you help me or not?" he said.

"I'll look into it," Reza said, then dug his hands into his pockets and walked away.

His heart was still pounding as he watched his friend leave the park. There didn't appear to be anyone following him, but as his gaze moved around his surroundings, he very much hoped that no one had followed him here. He'd been careful. Hopefully, careful enough. But if these events were tied to anyone in Qadir's network, things were going to get a lot worse.

He pulled out his phone and called Kara.

———

Kara ignored her buzzing phone. "Is Whitney all right?" she asked Jason, who had just called the team into the conference room for an urgent briefing, which revealed an attack at the safe house.

"Ms. Holden is scared but unharmed," Jason said tersely.

"How the hell did this happen?" Tyler demanded.

"Obviously, the location was leaked. The agent in the hallway was knocked unconscious. The gunman shot the lock off the door. Fortunately, the agent inside reacted quickly, hitting him with gunfire before he could get to Whitney. The attacker was injured and retreated down the hall, where he disappeared into the stairwell."

"Description?" Alina asked.

"Medium height, ski mask over his head and face, oversized jacket, dark pants, and he had a large ring on his left hand. Wes and Charlie are going through security cameras now. The jacket and mask were dumped down the laundry chute. We may get lucky with DNA evidence."

"And Whitney?" she asked.

"The U.S. Marshals will take over," Jason replied. "I'm meeting with Damon in an hour. The information about the safe house most likely came from either his team or ours. Going forward, we'll set up our own safe house, but in the meantime, we need to tighten the circle. Damon and I will discuss how best to divide up the work, but for now, continue on as you've been doing." He let out a breath, turning to Kara. "Are there any updates?"

She hesitated, almost afraid to say anything now that she knew the safe house had been breached. Her team might be comprised of experienced agents, but she didn't know any of them well. In fact, she knew the agents at 26 Fed better, and she couldn't imagine one of them being a mole. But Jason was waiting for an answer, and she had to say something.

"I've been digging into Samantha's case files, looking for a connection between her and James Cooper, but nothing yet. I also contacted Wexler Properties, the owner of the building in the second blast. He is in Tokyo with his executive team and will be back tomorrow. I'll speak to him then."

"I've been researching James Cooper and his financials," Tyler interjected. "He's had several unexplained large cash deposits in the last several years. All for different amounts, all cash, none reported on his taxes. I spoke to his wife, who said she didn't handle the banking. She barely knew how to get into their accounts. I also talked to another woman in the Building Department, Grace Wilcox. She said James was a quiet man, kept to himself, did his job, and never had any arguments with anyone."

"The cash deposits are interesting," she muttered. "Maybe someone was bribing him to sign off on work that wasn't quite right."

Tyler nodded. "I haven't found a trail yet, but I'm looking into it. Also, followed up on Vincent Castellano. Hasn't been home or at work. But he used his credit card at a bar in Brooklyn yesterday, so I'm going to follow up on that."

"Castellano's employer, Petrosyan Automotive, is under investigation for tax fraud by Samantha's team at the DA's office," she interjected. "But there's nothing to tie that case to James Cooper."

"Alina?" Jason said.

"I've been looking into the Novik brothers," Alina replied. "Sergei Novik has been in Prague for the last month. He's expected back in the US this weekend. Alex Novik has been MIA at the Crimson Club since Cray was killed. He's allegedly sick, but he's not at home, and he hasn't used any of his credit cards since Tuesday night when he bought dinner in Soho. Judging by the bill, the meal was shared by more than one person. I was just about to start looking at cameras by that restaurant to see if I can identify him or his companions."

"And Cray's shooter—an individual possibly named Cal?" Jason asked.

"The car he was using was dumped in Chinatown," Alina said. "He's in the wind."

"All right. Let's get back to work," Jason said. "We need to figure out what connects those two bombings so we can prevent a third."

After the meeting, Tyler followed her back to her desk.

"I'm going to meet with a friend of mine at the ATF," Tyler said. "He's going to go over the explosive devices with me, see if we can find a signature, a part we can trace to a common buyer. After that, I'll follow up at the bar in Brooklyn, see if anyone knows Castellano. Do you want to come, or..."

"I want to keep going through these files, unless you need me."

"No, I've got it." He paused, looking like he wanted to say more.

"What?" She gave him a searching look.

"What's the situation with Malone?"

"What do you mean?"

"He was with you last night when I gave you the location of the safe house."

Her eyes widened as she realized what he was suggesting. "Max didn't leak the information."

"Are you sure? He drove you and Whitney to the building, right?"

"Why would he leak the address?"

'Because he's working for Dominic Ashford,' Tyler said with irritation in his voice. "He has a conflict of interest."

"There's no conflict. Max is trying to find out what happened, same as us. And I don't believe Ashford is involved in the explosions."

"You don't know that for sure. Ashford could be responsible for everything that's happening. He worked with Cooper, and he was dating Samantha. He's the link between those two. And Max is his protector. Haven't you considered the fact that staying close to you keeps him in the loop on information that he can then feed to his boss?"

She didn't like his tone or his question. "You need to back down, Tyler. I know what I'm doing. And you have reasons for disliking Max that have nothing to do with this case. If you want to share what those actually are, maybe I'll be more interested in listening to your opinion."

Tyler's jaw tightened. "I can't tell you. But I know he doesn't always stay on the right side of the line. You're going to have to trust me on that."

"And you're going to have to trust me not to make poor decisions."

As the air grew heavy between them, Alina came over. "Everything okay here?" she asked, making Kara aware that several people in the room had stopped what they were doing to listen to their discussion.

"It's fine," she said, sending Tyler a pointed gaze that he should think twice about contradicting her.

"Fine," he echoed. "I gotta go."

As Tyler walked away, Alina turned to her. "What's going on between you and Tyler?"

"We're just getting to know each other," she said. "There's no problem."

"Tyler can be a hothead, but he's a smart guy. If he's worried about something, you should listen."

"I always listen, but his concerns are not valid."

"Are you talking about Malone?"

"They have a history, Alina. Neither one wants to tell me exactly what that history is, but something happened in the Middle East, when Malone was CIA and Tyler was Delta. None of that is pertinent to now." She took a breath. "And I don't like being second-guessed or accused of letting someone use me for information."

"I'm sure Tyler didn't mean it like that."

"I hope not. But none of us know each other well. We're going to have to give each other leeway, find a rhythm. I'm sure we can do that, but right now I'm only concerned with this case."

Alina nodded. "Me, too, so I'll get back to it."

As Alina walked back to her desk on the other side of the room, Kara let out a breath. She didn't need to get into fights with her team, not when they were in the middle of a case. But she also didn't need a fellow agent questioning her decision-making. She knew what she was doing, and she felt like she knew Max better than she knew Tyler. With what had happened at the safe house, the only person she was going to trust was herself and her own gut instincts. Those instincts told her that Max was genuine in his desire to help.

Despite that affirmation, she couldn't ignore the tiny seed of doubt that Tyler had planted. Ashford was a link between Cooper and Samantha, and Max did work for him. But she could see no reason why Dominic Ashford would want to kill anyone or blow up two buildings.

She needed to find another connection, something that would lead them to the bomber.

Picking up her phone, she called Max back, wondering if he'd already found something, but his phone went to voicemail, so she hung up and got back on her computer.

Several hours later, her eyes were blurring from reading through the lengthy files the DA's office had sent over. She still had a couple more years to go through, but it was almost five, and she needed to get out to Queens for her uncle's birthday. She sent the remaining files to an encrypted folder she could access from home and would dig into that after she spent a little time with her family.

She had just gotten into the car when Max called her back. "What's up?" she asked. "Did you find anything?"

"I have some information. It's not verified yet, but I want to talk to you about it."

"That sounds a little mysterious."

"Can we meet?"

"I'm just leaving work. I have to go to Queens for my uncle's birthday bash."

"Maybe after?"

She hesitated. She didn't want to wait to hear what he had to say. "Or you could come with me..." She regretted the invitation as soon as it left her mouth, but it was too late to take it back.

"Are you sure your family won't care?"

"The family mantra is the more the merrier. Are you at home? I can pick you up. I'm just leaving work."

"I'll be waiting."

A little tingle of excitement ran through her. She told herself this was just about work, but she knew that was a lie. She just hoped he didn't know it, too.

CHAPTER FOURTEEN

Max was waiting in front of the Golden Dragon, looking so deliciously sexy in dark-gray slacks, a navy sweater, and a black coat that her heart flipped over in her chest. He hopped into her SUV and gave her a warm smile.

"Hello," he said as he fastened his seatbelt.

"Hi." She cleared her throat, feeling oddly uncomfortable, not by anything he was doing but the unexpected attraction that seemed to intensify every time she saw him. "Lots of traffic tonight."

"Not surprising," he murmured. "How did your day go?"

"It wasn't going great until about an hour ago. Tyler found Vincent Castellano."

"That's great."

"Castellano admitted to threatening Samantha at the bistro, but he has a rock-solid alibi for the café bombing. He was clocked in at work in Jersey during the blast. And he was out of town for three days before the blast at a family wedding. He said his threat was only about the fraud case Samantha was building against the auto shop. He was terrified of losing his job, and he didn't even know what the Meridien Tower was. He's a thug, but he's not our bomber."

"Why did he run and hide then?"

"After the bomb blast, he realized his threat might get him into trouble. When you think about it, his actions were not well thought out. He threatened Samantha in a public place with lots of witnesses and security cameras. He's not that smart."

"No," Max agreed. "And I can't see a tie between Petroysan and Cooper. Anything else?"

"James Cooper has unexplained cash deposits in his bank account. We're following the money."

"That's good," he said with a nod. "If he was taking bribes, maybe someone didn't feel he held up his end of the bargain."

"Which would go with what Whitney said about him needing to understand consequences." She paused. "Oh, there's another thing. Someone tried to break into the safe house. Whitney is all right. The agent outside is recovering from a concussion. The agent inside got off a couple of shots, striking the attacker, who unfortunately escaped. He ditched his clothes in a laundry bin, and there was blood on them. We're tracing the DNA now. Hope to have a hit soon. Things are moving along, just not as fast as I would like."

"You've made some progress."

"Some," she agreed. "What about you? You said you had news?" Her pulse was steadier now. Focusing on business had put her back on a more even keel.

"I spoke to a friend of mine. He believes that Cal is Caleb Azrani. Caleb's brother, Malik Azrani, worked with Ali Qadir, who is—"

"On every most wanted list," she finished, surprised by his words and the connection of Cal to a terrorist. "I'm familiar with Qadir and his extensive network. We busted a small terror cell about eight years ago that was loosely tied to him."

"This one may be as well. But the bombings don't exactly fit. Qadir's groups go for mass casualties, maximum chaos. These are too surgical, too targeted."

She thought about that. The explosions didn't seem to match the work of a terrorist organization, but the precision strikes might just be the beginning of something bigger. "Do you think your contact can find Caleb?"

"He's working on it."

"Is your contact CIA?"

"I really can't say, Kara."

She frowned, giving him a disappointed look. "Because he's covert?"

"Yes. And because he wouldn't give me information if he couldn't trust me to keep his secrets."

"I really hate secrets."

"Then you're working for the right agency," he said cynically. "Because my life has been one secret after another. Some days, I could barely remember who I was."

She glanced at his hard profile, thinking that was one of the most revealing things he'd ever said to her. "That couldn't have been easy. I only did one undercover stint at the NYPD, and it lasted two days. I can't imagine having to keep up a cover for a long time."

"It becomes a part of you. And when you live in filth, you get dirty. You can't see the lines anymore."

There was a hard edge to his voice. "It sounds like you're glad you're out."

"I have mixed feelings about it. But we don't need to discuss my career choices."

"I'm curious about those choices."

"I know I'm going to regret asking this, but why are you curious?"

"You don't seem like someone who stops before the job is done. The man you captured and brought into the agency was turned into an asset and then disappeared. Now you know he's somewhere out there causing mayhem... That can't sit well."

"I quit before he disappeared. I couldn't stand seeing his

smug face when he told me he was on my side now. I knew he was never on my side or America's side. As for dealing with the knowledge that he's still out in the world running his network once more, it makes me sick, and I would like to bring him down, but I don't have the resources to do that." He cleared his throat. "And that's all I'm going to say about him. We're almost to Queens, and I want to know what I'm walking into."

She didn't really want to change the subject, but Max was clearly done talking about it for now, and she needed to prep him for what he was about to walk into. "It's my Uncle Danny's birthday, and the party is at Hannigan's Pub, which is a firefighter bar owned by my uncle and two of his fellow firefighters, Jack Hannigan and Ray Connover. They bought the pub when Hannigan's father retired. They didn't want to lose their favorite drinking hole."

"Sounds like a fun place."

"It will be packed with family and friends. My uncle is very popular." She smiled. "Fair warning: They're going to ask you a million questions, so if you're having second thoughts, you can still bail and take a rideshare back to Manhattan."

"I'm not afraid of questions."

"You just don't like to answer them," she said dryly.

"Well, I don't think we're talking top-secret level questions, are we?"

"They'll be very invasive, but they won't be about you; they'll be about why you're with me. Whether we're dating. If we're in love. If you're my boyfriend. If they can start putting you in the family pictures."

"Wow, that's a lot."

"Like I said, you can change your mind."

"So, why don't you have a boyfriend?" he asked curiously. "Or do you? I didn't see any evidence of a guy at your apartment, but maybe you spend time at his place."

"I'm not in a relationship now. And I haven't been for almost two years, which has actually been a good thing."

"Two years, huh? Isn't that about the time you left the NYPD? A lot of changes in your life at the same time."

"You're very perceptive. My last boyfriend was a cop. We were together for over a year, talking about moving in together, but he didn't like any of the decisions I made during that time. He wanted me to look the other way, get a transfer, just focus on myself and on him, because whatever I did could damage him, too."

"Sounds like a great guy. Someone you could really count on," he said dryly.

"He definitely revealed his true colors. I understood I was making a choice for both of us. But I couldn't just ignore what I'd seen. I was supposed to be on the side of the law. We all were. That was our job. He told me if I was going to take my partner down, then we were done."

"It was your integrity or him."

"Yes," she said. "He left that night, told his buddies the next day that we were over, that I wasn't someone he could be with. That protected him a little when I went to Internal Affairs. They believed he'd tried everything he could to talk me out of it and to convince me I was wrong. He kept his friends and his job. It all worked out for him."

"For both of you," Max corrected. "You got a better job, and he didn't deserve you."

"He didn't. And I don't regret my decision. I do regret not having seen who he really was before that. It makes me cautious now. I haven't been in a hurry to get back into the dating world. It feels so fake most of the time. And I have a job that I can't really talk about, which complicates matters. I also work long hours, and men don't always understand that."

"Women, either," he commented.

She gave him a quick look. "Does that mean you're also single?"

"Yes. And in no hurry to change that."

"Because..."

"Because I have a job and long hours that would complicate a relationship," he said, echoing her words. "Maybe someday, but not now."

"That's how I feel, too," she said, a little voice inside her head suggesting that she might make an exception for the right man, maybe even the man sitting next to her. But she immediately pushed that thought out of her head. "So, back to the party... My mom and her sister-in-law, Beth, Uncle Danny's wife, will be the worst. They'll want to know all about you, so let me know what you want me to tell them. I can say we're just colleagues, let them assume you're FBI. That should shut them down. Then they'll be off you and trying to set me up with every single guy in the bar."

"Well, since you don't want to get set up, and I don't want to be your coworker, why don't we say we're dating?"

Her hands tightened on the wheel so hard she had to pull back from a speedy swerve. "What? Why would we do that?"

"To save you from having to talk to someone's single friend. And to stop them from asking me about work."

"They'll still ask you about that. They'll want to make sure you're a good catch."

"We'll tell them part of the truth. I work for Dominic Ashford's company, in his security department; keep it vague. A good cover has a few details, but not too many."

"I don't know. I'm not sure anyone would believe we're together, because we're not together."

"We have chemistry. You know that as well as I do," he said pointedly. "And I can be a convincing boyfriend. At least for a few hours. Give me a chance."

She stopped at a light, not trusting the playful smile on his face. "This seems like a terrible idea."

"It will be more fun this way."

"I think you're just missing being a spy."

"Maybe. But I'm doing this for you. Your family will love me, and they'll get off your back for a while."

"It would be nice to go to a party and not be the perpetually single girl. Okay, let's do it. But nothing too over the top. We're just seeing each other. It's casual."

"Casual," Max repeated. "Got it. No grand declarations of love."

"Absolutely not."

"No getting down on one knee."

"Max!" she said with alarm.

He laughed. "Just teasing."

She shook her head. "You are enjoying this idea way too much."

"I'm just getting started. This will be fun."

"I shouldn't be having fun. I'm in the middle of a case."

"That's why you need a break, a few hours to not think about it. I find the puzzle pieces fit better when I stop trying to shove them together in a desperate attempt to go faster."

"Speed could save lives. It's hard for me to let go when I know what's at stake, how a minute can make a difference."

"It can make a difference, but you're not Superwoman. You can only go as fast as you can go. And you can only do so much on your own. You have a team behind you, who are also working hard. And I have people who are trying to get me information, too. For the next few hours, let's take a break, have a drink, maybe some food, talk to your family, convince them that your future is bright, and when it's over, we'll go back to work."

That sounded really nice. She pulled into the public parking lot across the street from Hannigan's Pub and shut off the engine. "Are you ready? Because I'm not sure I am."

"Absolutely. Come on, fake girlfriend. Let's convince your family you're not going to die alone."

"I hate you a little right now."

"No, you don't."

And the terrible thing was, he was right. It wasn't going to be that difficult to pretend she was interested in him. It would be much harder to pretend she wasn't.

As they crossed the street, Max grabbed Kara's hand.

"We don't have to start yet," she protested.

"You never know who's watching," he replied as he wrapped his fingers around hers, enjoying the simple contact more than he probably should.

He'd never been a hand-holder. It wasn't something he thought about, and when his girlfriends had wanted to take his hand, he'd always felt a little awkward. But tonight, he wanted to hold Kara's hand, probably because she didn't want him to. She prized her independence. She fought for her own identity, and he admired that. He also wanted to see a more relaxed version of her, one who wasn't racing against time, desperate to find a bomber, obsessed with work. And if he were being honest, he wanted to see that version of himself, too, a version he'd forgotten about over the last decade.

"Here we go," Kara said, taking a deep breath as he opened the door to the bar and they stepped inside.

Hannigan's Pub was exactly what Max had expected—dark wood, brass fixtures, Guinness signs, and walls covered with firefighter memorabilia and faded photographs. The place smelled like beer and fried food, and the air was loud with conversation and laughter. Jimmy Buffett played from the jukebox in the corner, and a huge three-tiered sheet cake sat on the bar. There was energy and friendship and love in the room, and when Kara's face lit up when she spotted her uncle across the room, he felt something he couldn't quite name—envy, maybe. A longing to be a part of something like this, but it wasn't real, and he shouldn't forget that.

"Kara," the tall, broad-shouldered man said as he broke into a huge grin and walked through the crowd to give her a big hug.

As she let go of his hand, he felt very much like an outsider, but he couldn't afford to show that emotion on his face.

"Happy birthday, Uncle Danny," she said as they broke apart.

"Wasn't sure you were going to make it."

"I couldn't miss it."

Danny's gaze shifted, assessing him with the practiced eye of someone who'd spent decades sizing up people in dangerous situations. "And who's this?"

"Max Malone. Danny Reid," Kara introduced.

He extended his hand. "Happy birthday. Thanks for letting me crash the party."

Danny's handshake was firm, measuring. "A friend of Kara's is always welcome. How do you two know each other?"

Before Max could answer, a woman in her late fifties with Kara's dark hair and eyes appeared at Danny's elbow, her gaze moving between them with undisguised curiosity.

"Kara, you made it," the woman said.

"Hi, Mom." Kara gave her mother a big hug.

Apparently, this was a hugging family.

"Who's this?" her mother asked as she let her daughter go.

"Max Malone. My mother, Maggie Reid," Kara said. "And my aunt, Beth Reid," she added as another woman edged Danny out of the group.

Beth was a curvy blonde with bright blue eyes. "Hello. It's nice you brought someone, Kara."

"A nice change," her mother added, still giving him a speculative look. "Please tell me you're not just one of her coworkers who is going to drag her away in five minutes to finish some job."

"Mom," Kara protested.

"I'm not her coworker," he said. "And I can't imagine leaving a party as fun as this after only five minutes."

"Good," Maggie said with approval. "I like him, Kara."

Kara rolled her eyes. "Don't get carried away, Mom. We're just getting to know each other."

"Well, I know you, Kara, and you wouldn't have brought him here if he wasn't a little special," her mother said.

"Oh, he's special, all right," Kara said as he put his arm around her shoulders.

He gave her mother and aunt a smile. "Actually, Kara is the one who's extraordinary," he said. "I feel like I won the lottery."

"You are so sweet," Maggie said. "And you're right, my daughter is extraordinary. I'm glad she finally met someone who can see that."

"Okay, that's enough," Kara said. "I'm going to get us some drinks. Anyone else need anything?"

"No," Maggie said, waving Kara away as she urged him to take a seat at a nearby booth.

As Kara fought her way through friends and family to get to the bar, he was peppered with questions by Maggie, Beth, and a younger woman named Ria, who was apparently Beth's daughter and was planning a wedding in May. Her first concern seemed to be whether Kara would bring him to the wedding, since she had said she was coming alone. Her mother instantly cut her off, saying they could always make room for him, which sparked a bit of a tense discussion between the two before Ria left to find her fiancé.

Wanting to change the topic, he asked Maggie about her teaching job, and she blossomed with his questions; her passion for her career and her students more than clear. She also mentioned that Beth did music therapy with her students, which led Beth into a conversation about how music could help kids get over trauma.

Kara eventually made it to the table with two beers, and he gave her a smile as she handed him a frosty mug and sat down next to him. Putting his arm around her shoulders, he said, "I missed you."

She flushed a little. "Sorry, I kept getting stopped to chat."

Beth slipped out of the booth. "I need to say hello to someone. I'll speak to you later."

She'd no sooner left when Kara's cousin Sean slipped in next to Maggie. And as he sipped his beer and met various family members over the next thirty minutes, he felt more and more comfortable. While a few people asked him about his work, he was able to stall any deep dives into his business by just making everything sound a little boring.

He couldn't help noticing that everyone was eager to talk to Kara, too. Apparently, she hadn't been spending much time with family since she'd joined the FBI, and everyone was eager to catch up. He enjoyed seeing her relaxed and loved. She seemed softer than she had before and very, very real—in a way that made his chest tight. She belonged here, in this loud, warm, chaotic place where everyone knew her favorite food and teased her about her terrible karaoke skills and asked about her job with genuine pride and concern. She had roots so deep they were unshakeable. He had never had roots like that, not when he was a kid, and not when he was an adult.

The time passed quickly with food dropped off at their booth: burgers, fries, chicken fingers, salads, an assortment of other side dishes, as well as beer and wine, and they ate their way through many conversations.

But eventually, they found themselves alone in the booth, and that's when Kara gave him an apologetic look. "I told you it would be a lot."

"I'm not complaining. Your family is great. You're lucky."

"I know I am. Sometimes I forget." She paused as the crowd hushed and her Uncle Danny stepped up to thank everyone for coming.

As Danny talked about his family and friends, the support he'd always had in his life, calling out his wife and kids, he got a little emotional. Beth put her arm around his waist as he said, "I have to say that every birthday is bittersweet without my brother."

At his words, he felt Kara tense and impulsively put his arm around her shoulders again. She didn't seem to notice as her jaw tightened, and her gaze was fixed on her uncle.

"Jimmy was one of a kind. My older brother was my best

friend. He's the reason I became a firefighter. He's the reason I keep going even when it's hard. He sacrificed his life, and he's an inspiration every day. But it's not just his bravery that I remember, it's how funny he was, how adventurous he could be, how he was the first one to say yes to any idea, and how he loved his family, no matter how crazy they could be." His voice choked for a moment, and Max saw a lot of people wiping their eyes. "To Jimmy," Danny said, raising his glass.

"To Jimmy," everyone echoed, except for Kara. She'd raised her glass, but the words seemed to be stuck in her throat.

He gave her shoulders a squeeze.

She turned to him with moist eyes. "He says that every year, and it always gets to me."

"Understandable."

"I barely remember my dad, you know. I was six when he died. It feels like I know him more through other people's stories than through my memories. That seems wrong."

"It seems right, too."

She gave him a watery smile. "I really hate being emotional."

"Afraid it makes you look weak?"

"Yes," she said honestly. "In my line of work, female tears are not an asset."

"Well, you're not working now, and I'm not judging you."

She tipped her head. "You're a nice guy for a spook."

"Not a spook anymore."

"We should get going. Get back to work."

"Whenever you're ready."

Before she could say she was ready, her uncle slid into the booth across from them.

"Haven't had much of a chance to talk to you," he said. "Are you having fun?"

"Yes," Kara said. "And thanks for saying that about my dad."

"I meant every word." Danny paused. "This isn't party conversation, but since we're alone for a minute. I've been thinking about you since the explosion in Midtown yesterday. Same bomber?" he asked.

"I think so," she said. "But we're still digging into it all. Do you know anything about it?"

"The building is owned by Wexler Properties. They have had a couple of fires in the last ten years and have gotten a reputation for cutting corners during construction."

"Were those fires explosions?" she asked.

"Not deliberately set as far as I know, but you should look into the company. The Meridien Tower fire had numerous casualties."

"Meridien Tower," she murmured. "I remember that fire. It was a while ago."

"Seven or eight years, I think," Danny agreed. "I'd look into Wexler."

"I've already reached out to their executive team. They're on their way back from a meeting in Japan, so hopefully I'll be able to speak to them soon."

"I'm not sure I'm giving you much to go on. A bomb is different than a construction defect, but maybe someone had it in for them."

"Maybe. But Wexler has nothing to do with the café, so it's hard to say."

"You'll figure it out. You're a smart woman," Danny said. "I have confidence."

"Thanks."

As a roar came from a crowd near a dart game, he said, "I better go show the kids how it's done."

She smiled. "Keep them humble."

"Always," he said with a laugh.

As her uncle left, she turned to him. "We should go."

The determined look in her gaze told him she was already thinking about work, and that was fine, because he was, too.

"Let's do an Irish goodbye," Kara said as she led him through the bar. "It's faster."

"What's an Irish goodbye?"

"You just slip away. Otherwise, it will take us an hour to leave."

"Won't your family care?"

"They'll still be thinking how happy they are I had a date," she said dryly. As they left the bar and hit the chilly night air, she added, "You did well, by the way. Very convincing."

"I told you I would be," he said as they got into her car. "Although I'm disappointed that I didn't get to throw in a kiss before we left."

She rolled her eyes. "That would have been even more over the top. Seriously, you were way too complimentary and adoring. No one acts like that."

"You mean your last boyfriend didn't act like that?"

"None of them have."

"That's kind of sad," he said as he fastened his seatbelt. "Your mother is right; you deserve better."

"I don't think anyone acts that loving and protective unless they're putting on a front, as you were. Have you ever treated anyone else like that when you met their family?"

"I haven't met many families," he said, seeing an interested gleam flit through her eyes. "I usually get out before that happens."

"Then why were you so confident you could charm mine?"

"Because I am good at being charming, at knowing what people want to see and to hear. Your mom and your family want you to be happy, so I wanted them to know that was my goal, too."

"But it was an act."

"Well, it's not like I want you to be unhappy."

"You really never had a relationship that lasted long enough to meet the parents?"

"There was one girl back in college. She took me home for Christmas vacation because my parents were out of the country. Her family was nice, but very proper. Everything was perfect.

The food was impeccable, but no one talked to each other, and it felt so awkward. I didn't grow up in a family like yours, but my parents could banter. They were intellectually challenging to each other. They'd argue about some random fact in history that no one else would even know for an hour straight before they'd finally laugh and call it a draw."

She gave him a quick look. "That's the first thing you've said about them."

He shrugged. "It's not like we've had a lot of time to share stories."

"It sounds like they were in love."

"I think they were," he said. "My father was broken up when my mom died. It was the first time I realized she was the rock in the family. He had the strength, the big laugh, the firm voice, but she was the one who kept us steady."

"Do you still see your dad?"

"Not very much, maybe once a year."

"Why so rarely?"

"He lives in Bath, as I mentioned. And I've spent a lot of time in other parts of the world."

"Is he remarried?"

"No, but I noticed he has a female friend who seems to spend time with him. We don't have the kind of relationship where I would ask him outright, or he would ask me, for that matter. Not like your mother and aunt, who are very nosy."

"I told you they would be."

"You weren't kidding. Where was your brother tonight?"

"Working. Hayden is a second-year resident at St. Mary's. He works long shifts. He would not have been nearly as nosy as my mom if he had come. He's more private, and that's why we get along. He doesn't ask me a lot of questions, and I return the favor."

'Well, I think your family is great. And not just the family, all the friends. You're part of a community. It's very cool."

"I think so," she agreed. "Sometimes I find the personal

questions annoying, but I know they come from a good place. Anyway, that's enough family talk. I need to refocus. I want to dig into Wexler Properties when I get home and also renew my memory of that tower fire. I worked that day, and it was a significant event, but I don't remember the details."

"The details may not matter. There's no tie between Wexler and the café, as you told your uncle. The tower fire could mean nothing. The connection is between James Cooper and Samantha Barkley."

"Dominic also had a working relationship with Cooper. Every time we turn a corner, we run into Dominic's connections. Have you noticed that?"

"He has a vast network. I still think he's innocent, though."

"I hope you're right. How's Samantha doing? My last update was early this morning, and they hadn't taken her off the breathing tubes yet."

"They postponed until tomorrow. They don't think she's stable enough."

"How is Dominic handling it all?"

"He's been to the hospital just about every day, checks in on her for a few minutes, and then goes back to work."

"But he's not sitting by her bedside for hours on end."

"He doesn't have hours on end. His schedule is packed. And to be fair, he and Samantha have only been dating for a few months. I think he cares about her, but I don't know how deep their relationship is."

"I sometimes wonder why she was dating him," Kara murmured. "She's not his type; he's not her type. I wonder if she had a hidden agenda, like maybe she suspected he was involved in something illegal."

"Maybe. Who knows? Their relationship doesn't make sense, but sometimes the best ones don't make sense."

"That's true. Sometimes you catch feelings when you shouldn't."

He wondered if she was talking about her feelings about

someone in particular...maybe even him. There was a spark between them. And they had connected on a much more personal level now. But he was the wrong man for her, and she was the wrong woman for him. At least right now. Maybe one day when he'd accomplished his mission, when he'd vanquished his demons, maybe then...or maybe not. Because who knew if that would ever happen.

CHAPTER FIFTEEN

Kara knew she should take Max home instead of to her apartment, but he wanted to work on the case together, and she was tired of living in her own head. He might also have insight that she didn't have. He might not be FBI, but he was well-trained in intelligence gathering, and she trusted him to be honest about what made sense and what didn't. It felt a little wrong that she wanted to work with him more than with her own team, but after what had happened at the safe house, she needed to keep things tight.

Tyler's words still rang through her head. He'd pointed out that Max had known the address of the safe house. He'd been there with her. He'd seen the agents, knew how many they were, and how they were positioned. She couldn't deny that he'd actually had more information than her own team, although there were many people at 26 Fed who would have known that address and that protocol.

She just had to go with her gut, and for now, her instincts were telling her that Max was on the right side. Until they told her otherwise, she was going to go with that belief.

Her apartment was just as she'd left it, including the pillow and blanket that Max had used the night before when he'd slept on her couch.

She moved over to her dining table and opened her laptop computer while Max sat down across from her, pulling out his phone. "What are you searching for?"

"Information on Wexler Properties and the Meridien Tower. You?"

"Same, but I'm also going to finish my search through Samantha's case files. I've already gone through five years, but maybe there's something further back, something to do with Meridien Tower."

For the next half hour, they worked in comfortable silence. It didn't feel nearly as boring knowing Max was trying to help her find the answers she desperately needed.

Finally, she found the case she was looking for. "Here we go," she said. "Seven years ago, Samantha prosecuted a case against Redstone Technologies, a company that made smart systems for high-rise buildings. But that system failed in the Meridien Tower, resulting in an explosion on the nineteenth floor and a fire that killed six people and injured seven others." Her gaze skimmed the cover page. "The Meridien Tower was owned by Wexler Properties."

"What happened? Did anyone go to jail?" Max asked.

She shook her head. "No. The defendants made plea deals, and a civil case resulted in a significant cash settlement to the affected families."

"But no one was actually punished."

She lifted her gaze to his. "No, they weren't punished. And the city Building Department was named in the civil suit as well."

"Let me guess, the inspector was James Cooper."

'Yes, but according to the city's defensive statement, the building was up to code, and they had no way of knowing that the smart system would fail, as it was a new technology and had met all the requirements." She thought for a moment, seeing the wheels turning in Max's gaze as well. "Samantha let the case drop. James Cooper might have approved something that wasn't quite right."

"And someone has been looking for justice for a long time."

"Not justice anymore—revenge. That's what this is about. That's why the strikes are targeted, with minimal collateral damage."

"But an explosion," he continued. "Just like the one that killed those people. Who were the deceased?"

She turned back to her computer and pulled up the list of names. "Lauren Canejo, age sixty-one, homemaker, Ron Canejo, age sixty-three, software engineer, Angie Palmeri, age forty-three, tax accountant, Harry Faulkner, age thirty-nine, manager of the Franklin Art Gallery, and..." Her voice caught in her throat. "Tori Hartford, age thirty-six, a homemaker, and her six-year-old daughter, Ariel. They were survived by David Hartford, age thirty-seven, a venture capitalist."

"Hartford?" Max questioned as she met his gaze. "As in Dominic's friend?"

She nodded. "I had no idea he was a widower, that he'd lost his wife and child, but it makes sense. He had a sadness about him. But he couldn't be behind this. He seemed like such a meek and mild-mannered man."

"One who has money to buy whatever he wants. What about the other surviving family members?"

She glanced back at the page. "The Canejos had an adult daughter, Alexa, twenty-three. Both Palmeri and Faulkner were single but had parents and siblings."

"Here's some more detail," Max said, interrupting her. "This is from a follow-up article on the lawsuit, which was brought by the named survivors: Alexa Canejo, Palmeri's father, Joseph Palmeri, and Faulkner's father, Wilson Faulkner, also David Hartford." He paused. "I know Wilson Faulkner, too. He plays golf with Dominic. He's an investment banker."

"Any of them could want revenge. Maybe all of them."

"I'm betting the settlement was extremely substantial. This wasn't about money."

"No, I don't think it was. And the fact that two of the survivors have plenty of cash doesn't mean they don't want revenge. They also have the money to finance it. What's Faulkner like?"

"Loud, likes to name-drop and brag about his bank account."

"And Hartford is the opposite." She frowned. "I hope it's not him, because he seemed nice when I met him." She held up a hand. "And you don't need to remind me that a lot of killers seem nice, which is how they disarm you."

"Exactly."

She thought for a moment. "Okay, we've narrowed things down to the tower explosion, to the victims and their survivors. Let's focus on the targets."

"Samantha dropped the ball, let the defendant plead out," he said. "Cooper signed off on the project."

"Redstone Technologies," she muttered, glancing back at the file. "The owner is Mason Redstone. At the time of the explosion, he was forty-four years old and living in Tribeca."

"He's fifty-one now, still in Tribeca," Max said, keeping up with her search on the Internet. "His company changed its name to RK Sensor Solutions several months after the settlement."

"And then there's Stan Wexler, the owner of Wexler Properties. We haven't been able to talk to him yet. But since one of his buildings was blown up, he is probably no longer a target. Who else?" An odd expression moved through his gaze. "What are you thinking?"

"There's a conference at the Nexus Forum in Hudson Yards on Tuesday. It's called *The Future of World Cities*. The focus is infrastructure, capital, and politics all in one place, and Dominic is one of the featured speakers. Wexler Properties and some of the other targets might also be involved."

She opened a new window to search for the conference, and it popped up immediately, the list of speakers and attendees ranging from local to state and world leaders, as well as private equity firms, builders, and technology companies. "This will be a target-rich environment."

"With a great deal of security," he reminded her. "And so far, the strikes have been surgical in nature. An attack on the summit would be completely different."

"Wexler is attending. Redstone is as well. I'm betting Hartford and Faulkner will be there, too. This sounds like the climax."

He nodded, his expression serious. "It could be. At least it's a few days away. We have a little time."

"Three days. That's not much. And what if we haven't reached the climax yet? What if someone else, some lower-level participant needs to go down first, someone who won't be at the summit?"

"Good point. Let's see if we can find someone considered culpable but who wouldn't be at the summit. They could be the next target."

They spent another half hour trying to find out everything they could about the tower fire. "There are several possibilities," she murmured. "It depends on who someone would find the most responsible. There was an architect and several different contractors in addition to Redstone Technologies involved with the building of the tower. There was the smart system installation team, too. And then you could look at the DA's office. Samantha wasn't the only attorney involved. A judge signed off on the plea deal," she said, her fingers flying across the keyboard. "Judge Michael Androni. He wouldn't be at the conference on Tuesday. If someone wanted to get to him, they'd have to find him at home or at the courthouse." She paused, looking at Max. "Obviously, I don't know if he's next, but he could be."

"There are a lot of people who could be next," he said, fighting off a yawn. "It's almost midnight. I think we should call it a day, because the calendar is going to turn in three minutes."

"I can't believe it's that late," she murmured, having lost all track of time.

"You definitely know how to go all in on something," he said with a smile.

"Which is why I'm still single."

"If I leave, you're not going to stop working, are you?"

"I might just do a little more," she said honestly. "But you should go home. I'm sure you didn't sleep that well on my couch last night."

"Actually, I slept fine." He took a breath. "In fact, I was thinking I might try the couch again."

"You don't have to stay here and watch over me, Max. I'm a federal agent. I'm armed. I'm good."

"I know. But I'm tired, and it's cold outside, and I'll have to get a cab or a ride... Can I buy another night on the couch?"

"Well, you don't have to buy it. I owe you for putting up with my family, so if you really want to stay, you can stay." She wasn't sure that was the best decision, but she also didn't really want him to leave.

"Then I'll stay." He got up from the table, walked over to the couch, and sat down.

"Are you going to sleep now?" she asked. 'I can take my computer into my bedroom."

"I think you should close the computer and come sit over here."

She gave him a wary look. "Why would I do that?"

He laughed. "You're very suspicious, Kara."

"And you're giving off shady vibes again."

"I just want to talk to you. We're both wired with too much information right now. Sleep won't come easy. Let's try to calm our brains down by discussing something else."

He had a point. She was so tired, the names were starting to blur in her mind.

He patted the couch next to him. "Come. Sit."

After a moment, she joined him on the couch, careful to

keep a good foot between them. As he kicked off his shoes and propped his feet up on the coffee table, she took off her shoes and pulled her legs up under her as she faced him on the sofa. "What shall we talk about? Your time in the CIA? Qadir? I'm interested in both those subjects."

"We're done with shoptalk," he said firmly. "Tell me what you like to do for fun."

"I mostly work."

"Try harder, Kara."

She let out a sigh. "Well, I work out because I need to stay fit."

"That sounds like it's related to your job."

"You're being very picky, Max."

"It's not a hard question."

She thought for a moment. "I like to bicycle through Central Park. The Lake is one of my favorite spots. There are a bunch of flat rocks to sit on, and when you look out over the lake, you can see the city reflected in the shimmering water. It's really pretty and peaceful. It makes the city feel less chaotic. Not that I don't love the chaos. There's an energy here that I've never felt anywhere else. I know it makes people cranky at times. That's why New Yorkers can sometimes seem rude, but this city is filled with passion. People come from all over the world to chase their dreams. I love the art scene and off-Broadway. I love going to shows in the smaller theaters where beginning playwrights are putting on their first plays. Some of them are bad. But some are brilliant, and you're right there watching someone's career take off." She paused. "I am rambling."

"I liked the ramble. And I think you described the city exactly right."

"It's my home," she said simply. "Where do you think of as home?"

"There's no one place. I don't have a family home in my mind when I think of Christmas or some other holiday. I have places I remember, houses I liked, but I always felt like I was just a guest.

I never had roots. Not like you. Yours go deep. I saw that tonight at your family party. It made me a little jealous."

"Really?" she said with surprise.

"My family is small, even smaller now that my mom is gone."

"How did she die?"

"Cancer. She worked through most of it. She loved her job, her posts with the State Department. She taught me to love the world. Actually, she taught me to love the people in the world, and to protect the innocent whenever I could."

"She sounds inspiring."

"A little like your mom, actually," he said with a warm gleam in his eyes. "My mother wasn't a teacher, but she was passionate about helping others."

"My mom is passionate about a lot of things. Teaching, gardening, baking..."

"Her daughter," he added with a knowing gleam in his eyes.

"She's always wanted the best for me. I think because she had to raise my brother and me on her own, she felt like she had to be everything, and she was. And when she wasn't, everyone else stepped in. I missed my dad horribly. But I did have a village raising me. And I didn't always like having everyone in my business."

"That's how they show their love."

"That's what they tell me. Were your parents in your business? Did they like that you went into the CIA?"

"They taught me to make my own decisions, and they supported most of them, including my stint in the CIA. But we weren't a super close family. We didn't call each other all the time. We weren't hugging each other every time we got together."

She saw the humor in his eyes. "We are a hugging family. But I don't hug as much as everyone else, except when I'm with them."

"Because it doesn't fit the tough, determined mask you like to wear?"

"You have no idea what it's like to be a female cop and then a female FBI agent. If I'm not tough, I get walked over. I can't let that happen."

"I understand. Obviously, I've never been in your position, but I've seen women at the agency face the same challenges. For what it's worth, I've found female agents to be extremely good at their jobs."

"It's possible I overcompensate at times. Probably more so since I upended my career by telling the truth. I've felt pretty judged since then."

"Even with your new team?"

"I just don't know them that well. And after the safe house location was leaked, I'm concerned about whether or not that came from us or from the other office."

"That is concerning."

"Tyler suggested you could be the leak. You were there, and you probably shouldn't have been because you're working for Dominic. He implied that I had made an error in judgment, and maybe he wasn't wrong about that. I never actually thought about taking Whitney there on my own, and I should have."

"Things were moving fast," he said quietly. "But I didn't leak the location, Kara."

She met his gaze and saw nothing but truth there. Or maybe that's what she wanted to see.

"You don't entirely believe me," he said with disappointment.

"I want to believe you. But someone leaked, and if it wasn't you, then it was someone on my team, which I don't want to be the case, and if it was someone in the other office where I used to work, that will be disappointing, too. I just want to be able to trust everyone."

"Hard to do in the business you're in."

"It is," she agreed. "But we'll see what happens. In the meantime, I'm going to trust my gut more than anyone else."

"And what does your gut say about me?" he asked quietly.

She didn't answer right away because her gut was saying a lot of things. "I don't know," she said, because that was easier than telling him what she did know.

Disappointment ran through his gaze. "You do know; you just don't want to say."

"It's complicated."

"It doesn't have to be. Sometimes, life is a lot simpler than we think." He suddenly moved, sliding down the couch until he was right next to her, and then his hand was cupping the back of her head, his eyes asking a silent question that she could only answer in one way.

She lifted her mouth to his, and the sparks between them ignited as soon as their lips touched. All the feelings she'd been fighting for the past few days caught fire, and the heat was too enticing to run away. She wanted to kiss him, to touch him, to connect with him on a more physical level. And while her head was screaming caution, her body was melting into his.

After several passionate kisses, Max pulled away, this time putting the question into words. "Do you want me to stop?"

"No," she said. "I don't want you to stop, and I don't want you to sleep on the couch." She got to her feet and held out her hand. "Come with me."

"You're sure it's not too complicated?"

"I'm sure it is, but I don't care," she said as he got to his feet. And then she was in his arms again, and they kissed their way into the bedroom, stripping off their clothes along the way, stopping briefly to find protection before falling into bed together and pushing all the stress and anxiety and complications away.

Because it really was simple. She wanted him, and he wanted her, and neither of them had any idea what tomorrow would bring.

CHAPTER SIXTEEN

Saturday morning, Kara slipped out of bed carefully, trying not to wake Max. The mid-morning sunlight streaming through her bedroom window was bright and warm, and she felt ridiculously, foolishly happy. It was dangerous to feel this way about Max Malone, dangerous to let her guard down with a man whose past was still largely a mystery.

But the night with him had been good. Better than good. Earth-moving.

She pulled on a robe and padded to the kitchen, starting the coffee and opening her laptop. She wanted to get back into the case, and the judge, Michael Androni, was weighing on her mind. If their theory was right, if someone was systematically going after everyone connected to the Meridien Tower case, the judge who'd signed off on those plea deals could be next, and she needed to warn him.

Grabbing her phone, she called her office, hoping Wes would be working today. He was not, but Kelly Moran, one of the other techs, picked up her call.

"I need a phone number and address," she told Kelly. "For Judge Michael Androni. He presided over the Meridien Tower case seven years ago."

"Okay," Kelly said. "Hang on."

She tapped her fingers on the table, waiting for Kelly to come back. Thankfully, she didn't have long to wait.

"Here it is," Kelly said, giving her phone numbers for the judge, his wife Paula, and his clerk, Drew Emerson. She also gave her an address on Long Island.

"Morning." Max's voice, rough with sleep, made her look up from her laptop.

He stood in the doorway wearing only his boxer shorts, hair messed, looking unfairly attractive for someone who'd just woken up.

"Coffee's almost ready," she said, trying to keep her voice steady as memories of the night before flooded back.

He walked over and kissed her, soft and lingering. "You're already working."

"I'm trying to reach Judge Androni. I just got phone numbers. I need to warn him that he might be a target."

He nodded. "I'm going to grab a shower. Unless you want me to wait so you can join me..."

That offer was more than a little tempting, but she managed to resist. "I really need to make these calls. It's time to get back to work."

"Of course," he said with a nod, but she didn't miss the disappointed gleam in his eyes.

As Max left, she punched in the judge's number. It went straight to voicemail. She left a message, then tried his wife's number. Fortunately, she answered.

"Mrs. Androni? This is Special Agent Reid with the FBI. I need to speak with your husband about a potential threat."

"Oh my goodness! He's not with me right now. I'm at the wedding venue. He's still at the hotel. What's going on?"

"The wedding venue?" she echoed.

"Yes. We're in St. Barts. My daughter is getting married today. Is my husband in danger?"

"Not if he's in St. Barts," she said. "This is more of a New York problem, but can you have him call me?"

"Yes, I will. You're sure he's not in danger?"

She didn't quite know how to answer that, because there were no guarantees. "It's unlikely. Please don't stress about it. Enjoy your daughter's wedding."

"Okay. I'll make sure he calls you back," Mrs. Androni promised.

She ended the call, feeling relieved that the judge and his wife were out of the country. She doubted he would be targeted on an island in the Caribbean, not that she could completely dismiss that thought, but she liked the odds.

As she debated what to do next, the sound of the shower running sent her thoughts in a different direction entirely.

Impulsively, she got to her feet and walked into the bedroom. She knocked on the bathroom door, then pushed it open. "Want some company?" she asked, shedding her robe as she entered the steamy room.

Max opened the shower door and beckoned her inside with a smile. "I thought you wanted to work."

"I changed my mind," she said, stepping inside.

"Did you find the judge?"

"He's in St. Barts. I think he's safe for the moment. So..." She put her hand on his shoulders, pressing her body against his.

"So..." he echoed, sliding his hands down her hips as he gave her a heart-stopping kiss that drove everything else out of her mind.

She was fast becoming addicted to his taste, his touch, to everything about him. The reckless, passionate madness would have to end sometime soon. But not now. Not yet...

———

An hour later, they were dressed and sitting at the table, drinking coffee and eating avocado toast, which were two ingredients she actually had in her kitchen. Despite the stress surrounding their relationship, she felt pretty relaxed right now. It was nice to have Max around. She could get used to this, she thought idly, then immediately told herself she definitely should not get used to it. Max had already told her he didn't do long relationships, and she'd told him that work always took priority. This was just a fling. It couldn't be anything else.

But if she was going to make work less of a priority, he wouldn't be the worst choice: smart, handsome, sexy, knew how to drive her crazy, and was happy to do so over and over again. She flushed at that thought.

Max also understood her in a way no one else ever had. Which didn't make sense. She'd dated a cop for a year, but even though they'd done the same job, she'd never felt as close to him in all that time as she did with Max, whom she'd known for a week.

"What are you thinking about?" Max asked, startling her with the question.

She looked at him in surprise, then lied, "The case."

"Really?" he challenged, giving her a doubtful look.

"Why? What are you thinking?"

"That I wouldn't mind spending the day in bed with you."

Her body shivered at that thought. "I can't. I want to. But I can't."

"Yeah, I know. But you asked what I was thinking, and I told the truth. You didn't."

"We need to stop...this, whatever this is, and focus. In fact, maybe you should go home. You're distracting."

"Good," he said with a smile. Then he surprised her by pushing back his chair. "I'll go home and change my clothes, check in with my contacts, and also with Dominic, and then I'll be back. Because I think we work better together." He paused. "Will you still be here?"

"Probably. If I go out, I'll text you." She met his gaze. "I think we work well together, too. But we need to actually work."

"We will," he said. "I want to close this case as much as you do." His jaw tightened, his gaze taking on a faraway expression.

"Because it might tie to Qadir?" she asked.

"Well, that would certainly be one reason, but not the only one. I'd like to clear Dominic, too. Make sure he's not the next target. Because he's certainly friends with many people who appear to be on that list."

She nodded, but as he left, she couldn't help wondering if Dominic was on the list or working the list. But that didn't really make sense. What on earth would Dominic have to gain by blowing up buildings in the city? And he hadn't lost anyone in the Meridien Tower fire. But it was interesting that he was friends with two people who might have a motive for revenge. She needed to find out more about Harry Faulkner and David Hartford.

———

Max couldn't stop thinking about Kara. He couldn't remember the last time a woman had been on his mind so much and so often. He'd thought after the night they'd had, the edge would be off, but that wasn't the case. He just wanted her more. But she was right. The night was over, and he needed to get his head together.

After changing clothes, he texted Reza, who told him to meet him at St. Mark's Church, which was a few miles from his house. On the way, he called Kai, who had left him several messages in the last twenty-four hours.

"Finally," Kai said. "Where have you been, or do I need to ask? The pretty FBI agent seems to be your best friend these days."

There was a tart note in her voice. "Jealous?" he asked, knowing that wasn't the case since Kai had just told him she was moving in with a woman she'd met a few months earlier.

"Annoyed," she returned. "I don't like to be ignored."

"What's up?"

"I've been looking into Costa and the Novik brothers as you requested, and last night Elias Costa died in a solo car crash in southern Maine," she said.

His pulse leapt. "Seriously?"

"Someone is cleaning up or taking over," Kai said. "Have you talked to Reza again?"

"On my way to meet him now."

"What about Dominic? What does he have to say about what's going on?"

"I'm going to talk to him today, too. He's very concerned."

"He should be," Kai said. "And not just about what's happening here. I spoke to Milos," she added, referring to a mutual friend of theirs still with the agency. "He said things are heating up in Tajikistan around Dominic's project."

"What else is new?"

"What's new is that Malik Azrani was in Tajikistan last week."

Excitement ran through him at that piece of news. "Which means Qadir might be there as well. This is good. This was the plan. Flush him out, take him down."

"But you're still going to make sure that Dominic doesn't actually go. You can use his money, use his resources, use his project, but you can't risk his life."

"You don't need to remind me of that," he said. "I have no intention of risking Dominic's life, but everyone needs to think he'll show up, that the groundbreaking will happen. So, we'll stay the course."

"You haven't been on this course all week."

"Well, I need to make sure Dominic is safe here, too, and at the moment, that's the priority. I don't like that Malik's brother is here. If Malik is in Tajikistan, maybe Caleb is carrying out some part of the plan here. I gotta go. I need to talk to Reza. I'll be in touch."

After hanging up, he parked and entered the church. It was

empty on a Saturday afternoon, with one older woman on her knees in the first pew. He went up the stairs and into the choir loft, where he found his old friend. He sat on the pew next to him. "Getting more creative," he said.

Reza smiled. "Confession starts in twenty minutes. Figured I might as well kill two birds with one stone."

"You're going to confession?" he asked with surprise. "Since when are you Catholic?"

"Since last year, when I met someone at a mass."

"Someone, as in a woman?"

"A beautiful woman," Reza said. "I'm who she needs me to be."

"Is this business or personal?"

"A little of both."

"What do you have for me?" he asked, more interested in Reza's information than anything else.

Reza took his phone out of his pocket, opened his camera, and showed him a photo of a man at a train station. "Malik Azrani was in Berlin yesterday."

"And he was in Tajikistan last weekend," he muttered. "He's on the move."

"I checked the train schedule. Looks like he was headed to Munich."

He studied the image. He hadn't looked at a picture of Malik in over a year, but it definitely appeared to be him. He wasn't as tall as Caleb, and his hair was much lighter, but he had the same long and lanky limbs. "He's not avoiding the cameras. He wants to be seen," he murmured. "Maybe to get us away from Tajikistan. Or to make us think he's going somewhere in Europe, somewhere that isn't the US."

"That was my thought," Reza said. "But none of my sources seem to think he's headed to the US or that he's involved with Caleb. The brothers were estranged a long time ago. Caleb is eight years younger than Malik. When their parents divorced, Caleb went to the US; Malik stayed in Istanbul with his father.

Caleb hasn't been on anyone's radar until now. I don't know if he's working with his brother or making his own name."

He nodded. "I'm going to find out." He got up. "Thanks. And good luck with that confession. I hope the priest doesn't have a heart attack."

Reza smiled. "I'll go easy on him."

He smiled back and headed down the stairs. He'd wanted information, and he'd gotten it, but he wasn't sure what to do with it. When the café bomb had gone off, he'd never imagined it could be tied to anyone connected to Qadir, but maybe this wasn't about the Meridien Tower at all. Maybe it was about Dominic.

Maybe it was about him...

It was a little past noon when Max showed up with deli sandwiches, chips, side salads, and a couple of cookies. Kara was almost as happy to see the food as she was to see him. Oh, who was she kidding? He won hands down.

She smiled to herself as she unpacked the food. And smiled even more when Max came over and stole a kiss.

"What was that for?" she asked.

"I was hungry."

"Well, you did bring food," she said with a laugh.

"I wasn't only hungry for food."

Her stomach fluttered at the sexy banter, reminding her how long it had been since she'd shared this happy feeling of attraction and intimacy. "Well, I think food is the only option right now," she said, giving him a stern look. "Work, remember? Did you get information from your contacts? Did you speak to Dominic?"

"Dominic is attending an overnight executive retreat at a very private, very exclusive lodge in the Hudson Valley."

"Who's at the retreat?" she asked with interest.

"I believe Caroline Rowe and Sebastian Hanover were going to be there with some unnamed individuals, who I suspect are in town for the conference on Tuesday."

She frowned at that thought. "That could be dangerous. How secure is this location?"

"It's very secure, and Dominic has his own security with him as well."

"That's good. As long as you can trust the security. Didn't you say there was a breach on Dominic's last international trip?"

A cloud crossed his expression. "I did, but that area of the world is much harder to protect."

"Did you learn anything else?"

"Not related to your case. I did find out that Malik Azrani, Caleb's brother, and someone who has been high up in Qadir's network was in Tajikistan last weekend and spotted at a train station in Germany yesterday."

"That doesn't sound good for Dominic's project. But I'm not too unhappy that Caleb's brother is in Germany and not in New York." She took their food from the counter to the table and pushed her laptop to the side so they could eat. "You don't think Caleb is working with his brother or Qadir, do you?"

"There's no evidence of that," he said as he unwrapped a sandwich. "Oh, one other thing. Elias Costa was killed in a solo car crash in southern Maine last night."

"What?" she asked in surprise. "Seriously?"

"That's what I was told. I'm sure your office can get the details."

"Damn. I wasn't expecting that."

"There's no way it was just an accident. What have you been working on?"

It took her a minute to move her mind away from Elias Costa. She needed to have Wes find out more about Costa's death. Realizing Max was still waiting for an answer, she said, "The Meridien Tower case."

"How's that going?"

Before she replied, she took a bite of her turkey sandwich. "This is good," she said happily. "I was just thinking I was hungry when you showed up with a banquet of food. You must have read my mind from afar."

He gave her a lazy smile. "My mind-reading skills are not that good. I was hungry, too. So, have you learned anything new?"

She popped the cap on a bottle of flavored sparkling water, took a sip, then said. "Yes. I've been reading up about Redstone Technologies, the company that made the faulty smart building system that trapped the residents in the tower during the fire." She picked up the notebook next to her computer, where she'd been jotting down notes. "Ashford Capital invested two million in Redstone's Series A funding round. That's a division of Ashford Industries."

"I'm aware," he said, his gaze narrowing.

"Dominic was one of the first investors, but he didn't invest in any of the other rounds," she added. "Which might raise the question: Did he know there was something wrong with the technology?"

"It's more likely he invested as a favor to Mason Redstone to get him started."

She tipped her head in acknowledgment. "They seem to move in the same circles. I saw several photographs of them as well as David Hartford and Harry Faulkner."

"Which means Hartford and Faulkner probably know about that investment. If they think he profited from their families' deaths, and one or both of them are behind this terror track..."

"Then Dominic could be a target," she finished. "I know he's at a retreat, but I think you need to talk to him, Max."

He pulled out his phone. "I'll send him another text, telling him it's urgent we speak today."

"I'm a little surprised he left the city with Samantha coming off the ventilator today."

"Not today. Now they're talking Monday. I did get that much information from him when we texted earlier."

She ate the second half of her sandwich as he was sending the text, glancing at her own phone as she did so. She had no new texts, but she'd been in touch with her team earlier in the day, going over what she'd learned about a link between the tower fire seven years ago and what had happened the past week. She didn't want to leave them out of the loop, but she didn't go into too much detail.

When she'd asked Jason if he had any more information on the safe house leak, he'd said no, and she could feel his frustration as deeply as her own. She was sure he didn't want to believe anyone on his team would have done such a thing, but Damon probably felt the same way about the agents working under him.

She hoped that the location had been leaked by someone in the building and not someone working for the bureau, because she didn't want to believe that anyone was compromised. But until she knew for sure, she needed to keep her guard up.

"Dominic said he can squeeze in a quick meeting at three o'clock, ten minutes tops," Max said. "But I'll have to meet him at a park nearby. Apparently, no one can be on the property but secured and vetted guests."

"That sounds very secretive. I wonder who is with him.'

"Could be anyone. He knows all the powerful people."

"And he is powerful himself. I want to go with you, Max."

She'd thought he'd immediately say no, but after a brief hesitation, he nodded. "Okay."

"Really? I thought it was going to take more effort to get a yes."

"I thought I'd save my energy," he said, a knowing gleam in his eyes. "And I've kind of gotten used to having you around, which is strange, because I am very used to working on my own. But there is one condition. I'm driving."

She smiled. "No problem." She grabbed the bag of cookies. "I'll bring these for the ride. Did I mention I love chocolate chip cookies? Or was this a lucky guess?"

He grinned. "Actually, your mother mentioned it to me at the bar last night."

"No way. When did she do that?"

"When you went to get me cake after telling me you didn't want any. She said that you never ate cake, that every birthday she had to make you a giant chocolate chip cookie to share with your friends."

She shook her head in embarrassed amazement. "I can't believe she told you that. Did she also show you my naked baby picture she finds so amusing?"

"No, but I'd like to see that," he said with a laugh.

"Never."

"Never is a long time. And your mom likes me. I bet she'd send it if I asked."

"You're not going to ask, and you don't have her phone number."

"You don't think a super spy like me could get her number?" he teased.

"Well, you're not going to do that. And I was lying before. There aren't any naked pictures, but I'm sure my mom has other embarrassing things to share. So, you two don't need to talk again."

"I think you're lying now, and your mom and I will talk again. I am your fake boyfriend after all."

"Who will disappear like all the others," she said, getting to her feet. "And you don't do long-term relationships, remember?"

"I remember," he said, an odd expression coming to his eyes. "But that could change."

His words made her a little nervous, taking the moment to a more serious level, and she wasn't ready for that. "We should go. We don't want to miss Dominic's ten-minute break."

CHAPTER SEVENTEEN

Stone Ridge Mountain Lodge was nestled in the Hudson Valley between rolling hills covered in thick trees. She only saw the lodge from a distance because Max turned off the highway into an empty, winding road that led to a parking lot at a trailhead. There were two black vehicles in the lot, and two men waiting at the entrance to the trail.

They got out of Max's Jeep, and one of the men gave him a nod, while the other escorted them down a gravel trail toward a gazebo, which overlooked a small lake. Another was standing in front of the gazebo where Dominic and Caroline Rowe were standing. She was surprised to see Caroline. Although she was one of Dominic's top executives, it still felt a little odd. Dominic was dressed casually but expensively in slacks and a sweater, topped with a warm coat. Caroline wore black pants with a button-down blouse visible underneath a wool coat. Her blonde hair was pulled up in a loose bun, and her made-up face was flawless. They were a striking couple, even though they weren't really a couple. Although she wondered if Caroline wanted to change that. She certainly seemed very interested and protective of Dominic.

The man stepped to the side to allow them to pass. Dominic

gave Caroline a nod, and she turned to them with an expression of both irritation and concern. As she moved down the two steps leading into the gazebo, she paused and said, "Make this quick. Dominic has to be back in fifteen minutes. He shouldn't have even agreed to this meeting."

She didn't bother to reply to that, ignoring Caroline's very speculative look as she followed Max into the gazebo.

"I didn't know you were coming, Agent Reid," Dominic said.

"I wanted to make sure you were alerted to a possible threat," she replied. She glanced toward Caroline, who was clearly within hearing distance. "This conversation needs to be private."

"Caroline is a trusted employee."

"Tell her to go back to the car," Max said, a hard note in his voice.

Dominic looked at Max, weighing his words, then said, "Caroline, I'll meet you at the car."

She didn't look at all happy to hear that, but then she turned and walked away.

"Now talk," Dominic said. "What's happening?"

"We think we know who's behind the bombings," Max replied.

Dominic stiffened. "Who?"

"Kara," Max said, motioning to her.

She was surprised that he wanted her to take the lead, but she grabbed the opportunity, sensing they had little time. She told Dominic about the Meridien Tower connection, about Hartford and Faulkner losing family members, about the suspected pattern of revenge targeting everyone involved in the case, and how he was connected to everyone.

"I can't believe David or Harry would do something like this," Dominic said in disbelief. "They're not killers."

"Revenge is a powerful motivation," Max said.

"But I wasn't involved in the tower being built," Dominic argued. "And neither was Samantha."

"She didn't prosecute the case," Kara put in. "She made plea deals."

"That had nothing to do with me. I didn't even know her then."

"But you are involved, Mr. Ashford. Your company invested in Redstone Technologies," she said. "You provided the funding that got them started."

"That was years before the fire. I'm not sure either of them would even know about my investment. And why would they wait so long? It's been what? Eight, nine years?"

"Seven," she said. "I'm not sure what the trigger was. That's why we wanted to talk to you. Have you had any conversations in the last several months with either of them that would lead you to believe they were worked up about something, upset, angry with you or anyone else?"

"David doesn't get angry. He's one of the calmest people I know. And Harry is the opposite. He's always blustering about something, but if you're asking me if anyone mentioned that fire or their lost loved ones, no, never."

"James Cooper was also named in the lawsuit against the city," Max said. "And he's dead now, while Samantha is still clinging to life, but barely."

"You don't have to remind me," Dominic said tersely. "But you're asking me to believe that two people I consider to be friends might want to kill me. That's difficult to believe."

"They may have already tried six months ago, when your team was attacked in Dushanbe," Max said.

"That's not related. That was about Tajikistan and my infrastructure project."

"Maybe," Max said. "But we can't discount anything. You need to increase your security, and you need to back out of the conference on Tuesday."

"I can't do that. I'm the keynote speaker."

"For a summit where a lot of the people involved in the Meridien Tower development will be present," she interjected. "Imagine what a bomb could do there."

"The building will be swept thoroughly. The security will be intense. No one will get into the venue," Dominic said. "And if you are so sure you know who's responsible for the attacks, Agent Reid, why haven't they been arrested?"

"We don't have evidence," she admitted.

"Exactly. You just have theories," Dominic snapped. "I don't make decisions based on theories or on fear. If you want to warn someone, talk to Mason Redstone, and whoever else is on the hit list."

"We are talking to everyone," she assured him. "But you are the biggest public figure. We need to make sure you understand the risks. We also wanted to speak to you because you know David and Harry. Have they ever spoken to you about the fire? About the loss of their loved ones?"

"No. I wasn't in the country at the time of the fire. I was in London. I sent condolences, of course. But we never discussed the losses beyond that." His lips tightened. "David has always been a big supporter of mine. He's investing in my project in Tajikistan. Why would he do that if he blames me for the death of his wife and child?"

"What about Mr. Faulkner?" she asked. "When did you last talk to him?"

"A few weeks ago. He's attending the conference on Tuesday; they both are."

"Which means they'll have access that someone from the outside would not," Max suggested.

"They would also be there," Dominic said. "You think they're going to blow themselves up?"

She actually wasn't positive that wasn't part of the plan. "Hopefully, we'll have answers before Tuesday," she said. "But until then, you need to be on your guard."

"As you can see, I'm always on my guard," Dominic said, waving toward his security guy. "Look, I appreciate the heads-up.

But I have to go. The people I'm meeting with can't be kept waiting."

"Who are you meeting with?" Max asked curiously.

"I can't tell you that," Dominic replied in a voice that didn't waver. "Do you want me to reach out to David or Harry?"

"That's a possibility," Kara replied. "But not yet. Right now, we would prefer that you keep this conversation private. That includes not discussing any of this with Caroline or anyone else on your team."

"Fine. I need to return to the lodge. I'll be in the city tomorrow if you need to speak to me again."

As Dominic left the gazebo and hurried down the path with his bodyguard, she said, "He's a stubborn man."

"Used to getting what he wants."

"Well, hopefully he'll at least consider David Hartford and/or Harry Faulkner to be threats."

"Dominic made a good point. It has been a long time since the fire. He's seen David and Harry many times since then. If he was a target, why would they be so close to him? Why would they be giving him money? We could be on the wrong track," he said.

"Really? I thought you were pretty convinced about the track we're on."

"Well, you're very convincing," he said with a smile.

"I wasn't trying to persuade you. I was just following facts, making connections. And I still think the case against one or both of them is strong. They have money, access, and motive."

"They do."

"But?"

"I don't know. I keep thinking about what happened to Dominic's security team six months ago. Maybe there are other reasons someone would want him dead."

"But what would Samantha and Cooper have to do with any of Dominic's overseas projects? That sounds like a completely separate thing."

"They wouldn't. You're right. Let's take a walk. I'm not ready to get back in the car yet."

As they wandered down the path and through the trees, Max seemed quiet and introspective, and she wondered about that. It felt like he was gathering his thoughts, that he wanted to tell her something but wasn't completely sure he should. She didn't like that he had some secret in his head. Whoever he'd spoken to this morning had obviously suggested some other theory to him, one he didn't want to share.

As they neared the lakeshore, she couldn't stand the silence anymore. It was also getting cold, and the afternoon shadows were lengthening. She wasn't going to find any answers here in the woods. Max could wrestle with his thoughts on the way back.

"I want to drive home," she said.

He gave her a surprised look, almost as if he'd forgotten she was there. "What?"

"I feel restless and frustrated, and I'd prefer to drive than sit in the passenger seat. You seem in a more reflective mood, so how about I take the keys?"

He hesitated, then reached into his pocket and handed her the keys. "Fine."

"You can talk to me, Max. It seems like you have something to say."

Max opened his mouth to speak, then froze, his gaze fixed on something in the woods to their left.

Before she could turn her head to see what he was staring at, he shouted, "Gun!"

He grabbed her hand and shoved her toward the trees as the sharp crack of a rifle split the air. Max cried out as the bullet caught him in the left shoulder. He stumbled but stayed on his feet, one hand pressed against the wound, crimson seeping between his fingers.

"This way!" She drew her weapon, laying down covering fire as another shot splintered the bark inches from her head.

They ran through the trees, Max stumbling beside her, his breathing ragged. As it stayed quiet, she prayed the gunman was on a different path and further away. Finally, they reached the gazebo, dashing down the path to the parking area.

The two black SUVs were gone—Dominic's security had left with him. Only Max's Jeep remained. She shoved Max into the passenger seat, his face pale and slick with sweat, then jumped behind the wheel.

The engine roared to life as their attacker emerged from the woods—a tall figure in dark clothing, rifle raised. Kara floored the accelerator, tires spinning on gravel as they shot forward onto the mountain road.

"Are you all right?" she asked him.

"It's nothing," he said, his head lolling back against the seat as blood seeped through his fingers, which were pressed against his wound.

It wasn't nothing. He was bleeding badly, and she needed to get him help.

"I'll find a hospital," she said. "Hang in there."

"No hospital. Too public. I'll be okay. It's not a big deal."

She didn't argue with him because she was distracted by the sudden appearance of a gray sedan on the road a half mile behind them. "We have a tail," she said. "I'm going to lose him."

She pushed the Jeep harder, driving the winding roads as fast as she could. Fortunately, the Jeep had more power than the car behind them, and she gained ground. But it wasn't enough. She needed to change things up. Then she saw it—a narrow dirt road disappearing into thick forest.

"Hold on." She turned the wheel sharply to the right, and the Jeep bounced violently as they hit the dirt track, branches scraping the windows. She drove deep into the woods until she found a small clearing, then killed the engine and waited.

The sedan flashed past on the main road, then came back a few minutes later, moving slowly, searching. But the dirt road was barely visible from the asphalt, hidden by overhanging branches.

She sat in silence, her hands shaking on the steering wheel, listening to Max's labored breathing. He was conscious but barely, and his skin was gray and clammy. After several minutes, she thought the danger was over. She got out of the car and went around to Max's side of the car.

"Nice driving," he murmured, giving her a pained smile.

She pushed his jacket back so she could see the damage. The bleeding had slowed, but she needed to get it to stop. She took off her jacket and then her long-sleeved T-shirt.

"Hey, I'm not really up for a strip show," he said, trying to joke.

"Too bad." She rolled her shirt up and pressed it against his wound. "Can you move forward just a little? I want to check your back."

He grimaced as he did as she requested, and she was happy to see an exit wound. "Looks like the bullet went through you."

"Awesome. I like having matching holes."

"Hold this against your wound. I'm going to get us to a medical center." She put her jacket back on and zipped it up, then jumped back behind the wheel. She checked the GPS for alternate routes and made her way back to the highway. In five miles, they would pick other highways, leading in different directions, and she would have a better opportunity to blend into traffic.

But those five miles were nerve-wracking, as she drove as fast as she could, tensing every time she saw a car coming in the opposite direction or up behind her, but there was little traffic, and finally, she took one of two exits, hoping she'd chosen the right one.

It was another twenty minutes before the traffic thickened, and she felt calmer. Max hadn't said anything in a while, and his breathing was still labored. But as she glanced at him, his eyes flickered open.

"Is he gone?"

"I think so. I need to get you to a doctor."

"No. We can't risk it. He knows I'm hurt. He'll be looking..."

He wasn't wrong, but she couldn't just keep driving. It would take an hour to get back to Manhattan. As the miles passed by, she went through what she needed to do, which included getting a first aid kit and finding a place to stay that wasn't in the city.

Mason might know of a safe house nearby, but could she trust the FBI after what had happened to Whitney while in protective custody? Could she trust anyone but the man beside her?

This attack had been directly on them. They had been the target. Someone knew who they were, where they had been, who they were talking to, and probably where they lived.

For a split second, she felt overwhelmed, but she refused to give in to that feeling. She just needed to think. Finally, it came to her. She grabbed her phone out of her pocket and punched in Jess's number. "Please pick up," she muttered.

"Kara?" Jess said. "Hey, how are you?"

"Are you still handling properties in Westchester?" she asked abruptly.

"What? Well, my mom does. Why?"

"I need a house, Jess, an empty house where I can stay for a few hours with no one knowing. Some place where no one would question the lights being on."

"This sounds bad. Okay," Jess said immediately. "I'm checking our listings." A moment later, she added, "We have a listing in Pound Ridge. The owners are in Europe for six months. Big house, end of a private road, fully furnished. Showings are by appointment only."

"That's perfect."

"I'll text you the address and the code to get in. What else can I do?"

"Call my brother," she said. "Tell Hayden it's not for me, but I need a doctor at this address, and he can't ask questions, and he can't tell anybody. I'm going to turn my phone off, so he won't be able to reach me. Tell him I'll owe him big time, but I really need his help."

"God, Kara," Jess said worriedly. "Are you sure you're okay?"

"I am, but I'm with someone who's not. Tell Hayden to bring his medical bag."

"Okay. I'm not sure what he'll say."

"He'll ask you a million questions, and he'll complain, but he'll come. Thank you, Jess. I'll explain later."

"You better. Take care of yourself."

A text came through a second later, and she changed her GPS to that address. "Hang in there," she told Max, who gave her a weak smile.

"Told you I'm fine," he said. "I've been worse."

She hoped that was true, but she wasn't convinced.

Fifteen minutes later, she parked in front of a drugstore. She hated to leave Max for a second, but she needed supplies. She ran into the store, grabbed a first-aid kit and bandages, then threw some random food items and drinks into the cart before racing to the self-checkout. She didn't want to talk to anyone if she didn't have to.

When she got back in the car, Max's eyes were closed, but he was still breathing. And she was more than grateful for that. She pulled out of the lot and drove to the house, which was exactly as Jess had described. It was set away from the road, and the nearest neighbor was on the other side of a patch of trees. She pulled into the drive, opened the garage door with the code, then got back into the Jeep and drove inside. As the door closed behind them, she took her first full breath.

"We're safe," she told Max. She just didn't know for how long.

CHAPTER EIGHTEEN

An hour and a half later, she'd thrown a blanket over the top of the king-size bed in the primary bedroom and helped Max off with his jacket. The bleeding had slowed down thankfully, but both her shirt and his shirt were soaked in blood.

She removed her shirt and tossed it onto the blanket, then took some scissors out of the first aid kit and cut off his shirt. She cleaned his wound as best she could. It was still seeping, but the heavy bleeding had eased. She applied more pressure and a bandage, which caused Max to groan in pain. She felt terrible about hurting him, but she felt better that she'd cleaned him up a bit.

"Cold," Max mumbled.

She found another blanket and covered him, then went to the kitchen for ice and more towels. The house was beautifully appointed—granite counters, stainless steel appliances, a fully stocked wine fridge. The owners clearly had money. She unpacked the few groceries she'd purchased, grabbed a soft towel, which she ran cold water over, then went back to Max.

Putting her hand on his forehead, she realized he was blazing hot. Damn! He had a fever now. That wasn't a good sign. She pressed the cool, wet towel against his forehead, praying that her brother would show up, that Jess had reached him, that he was on his way. She'd turned off their phones long before they'd gotten to the house so that no one could track them. But now she felt lost without a way to contact her brother, and the more minutes that passed, the more worried she became. Maybe she needed to take Max to the hospital because he was getting worse instead of better.

Finally, she heard a knock at the door. Three quick knocks, silence, then a fourth. She checked the window and saw Hayden on the porch. She quickly went to let him in.

"Thank God," she said, looking past him to the quiet street. "Where's your car?"

"Two blocks away, by a park."

"Good job." She closed the door, looking at her younger brother with immense gratitude.

"I learned from the best. What's going on? You don't look hurt."

"I told Jess to tell you I wasn't."

"She did. I didn't quite believe her."

"It's my...partner," she said, stumbling a little over the word. "He was shot. And it looks like the bullet went clean through, but he's lost a lot of blood, and now I think he has a fever." She led him into the bedroom and waved her hand toward Max.

Hayden moved to the bed and sat down on the mattress next to Max. "What's his name?"

Max's eyes opened at the question. "Who are you?" he grumbled.

"I'm a doctor."

"I said no doctors," Max said, his gaze moving to hers.

"He's my brother," she said quickly. "This is Max."

"Hayden Reid," her brother added. "Let's see what you've got here, Max." He removed the temporary bandage she'd applied and checked both the front and back of his shoulder.

Max winced with every slight movement and began to shiver.

"Sorry," Hayden said as he finished his exam. "You need some stitches, Max. I can do that. And I can give you something for the pain and for the infection. But you'd be better off in a hospital."

"Can't go," Max mumbled. "Do what you gotta do."

Hayden looked at her as Max's eyes closed. His expression was serious. "You sure you want me to take care of this here?"

"If you can."

He nodded, then opened his medical bag. "It looks like the bullet missed the major arteries, but there's muscle damage, and he's lost a fair amount of blood. But right now, the biggest concern is the fever."

Hayden worked efficiently, numbing the area around both wounds before cleaning and stitching them. Max gritted his teeth but didn't complain, even when Hayden had to probe for fabric fragments that had been driven into the muscle.

"There," Hayden said finally. "Now for the antibiotic."

He prepared a syringe and injected it into Max's good arm, then handed Kara a bottle of pills.

"He should take two every eight hours." He glanced at his watch. "It's almost six. He can take the next dose at midnight. And then again in the morning. The fever should break in the next few hours. If it doesn't, go to the nearest hospital." He pulled out a sample packet of pain pills. "This will get you through today and tomorrow. After that, see another doctor, get a prescription."

"Thank you so much, Hayden. I know you're supposed to report gunshot wounds..."

"You're FBI, and you're my sister. I trust you know what you're doing." He packed up his medical supplies, then added, "Were you close to him when he got shot?"

"He pushed me out of the way," she said.

Hayden stared at her. "Is he the guy you took to Uncle Danny's birthday?"

"Mom told you?"

"Yeah. Said you have a good-looking boyfriend who seems to care about you. Was that real?"

She shrugged. "I don't know what we are. It's complicated."

"It always is with you," he said with a small smile. "But I have to say, you looked scared when I got here. Freaked me out a little. You're always so tough."

"I was feeling out of my depth."

"You did a good job cleaning his wound." He paused. "Do you want me to stay?"

"I don't," she said. "I don't think we're in danger here, but if we are, I don't want you in the middle of it. I know it was a risk to contact you."

"Which is why you had Jess do it."

She nodded. "I knew you'd come if you could."

"I will always come if I can, even if I shouldn't. You're my sister. You need me; I'm there."

"The same goes for you, Hayden. You need me; I'm there." She gave him a hug. "Be careful leaving here. If you see anything out of the ordinary, if anyone is following you..."

"I'll call the police because you don't have your phone on. But you don't have to worry. I may not be law enforcement, but I can take care of myself." He walked to the door, then paused. "I know it's not my business, but—"

"You're going to say something anyway."

"Mom said you looked happier than she'd seen you in a while. If that guy in there makes you feel that way, then don't second-guess it the way you always do. Get out of your own way and just be happy."

"I can't believe you're giving me relationship advice," she said. "You're single, too."

"Yeah, but I'm younger, and I'm a man. I've got more time."

She laughed. "Get out of here, Hayden."

"I'm going," he said. "On a more serious note, be careful."

"I will be."

After he left, she went back into the bedroom. Max was

asleep and no longer shivering. It was only seven, but she was suddenly exhausted, so she stretched out next to him in the bed, staying on the side of his good shoulder so she wouldn't accidentally fall asleep and bump into him.

At some point, she dozed off, but Max woke her up around ten, talking wildly in his sleep as he thrashed on the bed.

"Have to get him," he muttered, his head tossing restlessly. "Have to kill him. Should have done it years ago."

"Max?" She touched his forehead. He was still warm but no longer burning up.

"Qadir," he said clearly. "Have to find him. Have to make him pay for what he did to Nicole."

Nicole. Kara's chest tightened. *Who was Nicole? And what had Qadir done to her?*

"It should have been me," he muttered. "Not you, Nicole. My fault. Should have seen it coming."

His ramblings continued for the next several hours. By dawn, she had a lot of questions and a growing certainty that there were parts of Max's past he hadn't shared with her.

She'd always known he had secrets, but in the last several days, she'd felt like those secrets didn't matter. But they did. And she needed to stop burying her head in the sand and figure out what was really going on. Max had wanted to tell her something at the lake, just before he got shot, but he hadn't had the chance. As soon as he woke up for real, she was going to find out what he hadn't wanted to tell her. Because she had a feeling it was something she really needed to know.

———

Max woke up, feeling a stabbing pain in his shoulder, but the pounding in his head had stopped, and so had the endless shivers. He blinked his eyes open, seeing the sun coming through a crack in the blinds. He didn't recognize this room. But he did recognize the woman sleeping next to him on the bed, her cheeks rosy from sleep, her brown hair falling around her pretty face. Seeing Kara safe and right next to him drove the cloudy fear out of his head as his brain cleared and his memories sharpened.

He rolled over onto his good side, aware of the bandage on his shoulder and the throbbing pain in that part of his body. As his weight shifted, Kara woke up. She opened her eyes much faster than he had, alarm followed by relief as she met his gaze.

"You're awake," she murmured, putting her hand on his side. "How are you feeling?"

"Great," he murmured.

"Liar."

"Where are we?"

"At a house in Pound Ridge. I needed to get us somewhere safe, and my friend is a realtor. She has the listing on this house."

"Was your friend here?" He tried to remember what he'd seen and heard. "My memory is fuzzy."

"You had a fever, and you were in a lot of pain. My brother was here."

"Your brother?" he echoed in surprise. "Why?"

"You needed a doctor. He stitched you up, gave you antibiotics, and also left you a couple of pain pills. Do you need one?"

"Not right this second. Was it safe to bring him here?"

"My friend Jess called him. I turned off our phones miles before we got here. He took precautions. It was a risk, but I had to take it. You were burning up, Max. It was my brother or the ER."

"This was the better choice," he said. "Thanks for taking care of me."

"Well, you took a bullet for me, so I owed you."

"I think you more than paid me back by saving my life."

He let out a breath. "I remember being by the lake, and then I saw something."

"A gun," she reminded him. "You pushed me out of the way. We ran to your Jeep. A guy followed us for a while, but I lost him. Eventually, we came here. I have some snacks in the kitchen if you're hungry."

"Maybe in a minute. Do you know who shot at us?"

"No. But I know they weren't shooting at anyone else. We were the target. Someone wanted to kill us, and I can only think of a couple of people who knew where we were."

He met her gaze, following her thought. "Dominic. But he wouldn't have me killed."

"Maybe it was Caroline Rowe or one of Dominic's mysterious visitors. Maybe it was someone on his security team."

"Or someone on your team. You texted them. You said we were going to meet Dominic near his executive retreat."

She frowned at the reminder. "I didn't give the details, but you're right, I said something." She paused. "But that's not what I want to talk about now."

There was something about her tone that made him nervous. "What do you want to talk about?"

"Who's Nicole?"

Her question stole his breath away. "What?" he asked, stalling for time.

"Nicole. You talked about her. You apologized to her. You said it should have been you. And you said her name with Qadir's name about a hundred times. So, who was she?"

"She was another agent, and she was also my friend."

"She sounded like more than a friend. Like someone you were in love with."

He shook his head. "No, it wasn't like that. We had something a long time ago, right after we both joined the agency. But it didn't last. And then she got together with another agent a couple of years later. The three of us were close, and I cared a great deal about both of them. But Nicole and Brian were in love with each other, and they would have been together forever if I hadn't made mistakes."

She licked her lips. "Did Qadir kill Nicole?"

He slowly nodded, that truth always bringing him a great

deal of pain. "He killed both of them. First, Brian, then Nicole. She had to watch her love die right in front of her. And I had to watch..." His voice trailed away. "Qadir is evil, twisted. He has no conscience. He can't be turned. He can't be changed. He's a monster. And the CIA never should have put him back out in the world."

"How could they do that if he killed two of their agents?"

"Because they didn't believe he'd done it. But I knew he had."

"Why didn't they believe it? Why didn't they trust your judgement?"

He really didn't want to talk about it all, but what choice did he have? Kara had saved his life, and she wanted answers. He owed her that much. "Qadir drugged me for days. I was hallucinating for much of the time. But before I was really out of my mind, I was able to send our location out to the team. Unfortunately, by the time they arrived, I was delirious, and drug testing showed hallucinogenic drugs in my system. They put me into an immediate rehab center, and while I was recovering, Qadir told them a different story."

"What was the story?"

"That he'd come across the terrorists holding Nicole, Brian, and me, that he'd killed two of those men to save my life. Which wasn't true. He'd killed them to provide cover for his story, to make him look like someone who had decided he was tired of the bloodshed, that he wanted to change his life, be a better person."

"I still don't see how they could believe that?"

"It was beyond me. But Qadir was a con man, and they were blinded by the opportunity to get someone like him acting as an asset."

"And now he's back out in the world, doing terrible things."

"Yes, with more power than he had before."

"Why didn't he kill you, Max?"

"He had a plan to use me for leverage. Fortunately, the team got there in time to capture Qadir and save me, just not the others."

"I'm sorry about that. Was the team from your agency, or was it a team from Delta?"

"It was a mix," he said, meeting her gaze. "Tyler Brennan was part of it, although he wasn't at the rescue. He was someone I'd seen earlier that week, before it all went to hell. There was a break in the intelligence chain. That's how Qadir got to the three of us in the beginning. I don't know that Brennan had anything to do with it. But I also don't know that he didn't."

"Why would Tyler suspect you of being a traitor if you were the one who was responsible for sending Qadir's location?"

"Because I was the sole survivor. Brennan wasn't the only one to question why I was still alive."

She drew a breath and let it out, her eyes filled with confusion. "It sounds like a nightmare."

"It feels that way to me."

"Is it possible you don't really know what happened, Max? If you were hallucinating, how can you be sure of your memories?"

He thought about her question. "I'm sure of some things. I'm sure that our mission was to find Qadir's hideout and call for a drone strike. I'm sure that Nicole and Brian are dead. And I'm absolutely sure that Qadir has never been an asset. Do I know all the details? I don't. But in my gut, in my heart, and in my head, I am certain that Ali Qadir is responsible for the death of my friends and for the deaths of many other people. You can believe me or not. You wouldn't be the only one to doubt my story."

"I believe you," she said, easing his heart. But the puzzlement in her gaze didn't completely reassure him.

"But?" he challenged.

"You were saying a lot of things last night, and one of them was about killing Qadir. You quit the agency, but you still want to take down Qadir, don't you?"

"Yes."

She sucked in a breath of surprise. "I didn't think you were going to admit it."

"The agency was going to send me to Latin America. They didn't want me anywhere near Qadir's territory, so I quit. I hunted him on my own for six months, but I ran out of money and resources. I went back to the UK to visit my father, to take a moment to regroup and consider my options. That's when I ran into Dominic. We had dinner. Dominic told me it was fortuitous that he'd run into me, that he needed a security consultant for his upcoming trips and projects in dangerous areas in the Middle East. It was perfect. I could take the job, make a lot of cash, and have an opportunity to go back into an area where I thought Qadir might be hiding, and I would be under the cover of private security."

Kara sat up in bed, pushing her hair behind her ears. "So, taking the job with Dominic was just a way for you to get back to your mission? Or should I call it an obsession?"

"Call it whatever you want," he returned, seeing the sharp gleam in her eyes.

"You want revenge. You don't want to capture him; you want to kill him."

"I tried to bring him in before. I tried to do it the right way, Kara."

"Revenge isn't justice."

"It's the next best thing," he said, seeing disappointment run through her eyes. He wasn't surprised. She wasn't a person who would seek vengeance over justice. She still had ideals. "I'm sure you don't agree."

"I don't. I believe in justice, in punishment, in putting people away, not killing them."

"Sometimes, that's the only choice that allows good to triumph over evil. If there was another way, I would take it."

"There is another way. Your agency knows he can't be trusted now. If he's captured again, he won't be turned into an asset.

He'll go to prison. He'll pay for his crimes, for what he did to you, to your friends, to everyone."

"I'm not sure anyone will ever catch him, and if they do, I don't believe he'd allow himself to be taken alive."

"Well, that would be his choice, not yours."

As their gazes clung together, he saw a myriad of emotions run through her beautiful brown eyes. "I'm sorry," he said.

"For what?"

"Not being who you want me to be."

Her breath caught in her throat. "I don't know who I want you to be."

"Yes, you do. And I don't blame you. I was once like you. I believed in my power to change the world in a way that was honorable."

"I don't blame you for wanting Qadir dead. But there's time to make a different choice, Max. You just have to want to make that choice."

"Well, I may never get close enough to him to capture him or kill him. He's been very elusive so far."

Her expression suddenly shifted. "When you told me about Caleb being Malik Azrani's brother, and Malik being one of Qadir's top guys, you didn't tie that all together for me. You didn't say Qadir was the terrorist turned asset. Why not?"

He shrugged. "I was still trying to figure it out. My contact said the Azrani brothers have been estranged for years. Malik was raised by his father in the Middle East. Caleb was raised by his mother in the US. It's possible Caleb is not tied to Qadir."

"It's possible he is," she argued.

"I was going to talk to you about it yesterday, but then everything went to hell."

"You got a strange look on your face when we were talking to Dominic about the tower fire and the revenge plot, and he said he couldn't believe the bombs were about that. You were thinking the explosions are about Qadir."

"Qadir has power in Tajikistan. He's a threat to Dominic's

project and to Dominic's safety. Malik Azrani works closely with him, and if Caleb is tied to the explosions here, then it all seems to connect," he admitted. "But it also doesn't."

Kara thought for a moment. "You're right. It's confusing because it doesn't add up, not the victims, not the methods... nothing except that we have two Azrani brothers and a tie to Qadir and an established terrorist network."

"Caleb may have his own game going here in the US, and someone reached out to him to buy bombs and revenge that had nothing to do with Tajikistan. And the link to Qadir could be a stretch." He paused and then painfully shifted into a sitting position, his head spinning a little with the movement. "We should get out of here. There's too much to do. We can't hide out. We have to get in the fight."

"I'm not sure you're ready for that fight."

"I will be. I feel better now. And you said I have antibiotics and pain pills, so I'm good to go." He swung his legs over the side of the bed and then slowly stood up. "What happened to my shirt? My jacket?"

"Your shirt was cut to shreds and covered in blood. Your jacket is also pretty bloody and has a hole in it."

"It will do." He picked up his jacket from the bed where she'd put it. "The blood is dry," he added as he eased the jacket over his painful shoulder. "Where's my phone?"

She got out of bed, walked to the dresser, and got his phone. He turned it on to check his messages and was shocked to see a photo from Reza sent sometime last night. As he studied the image, he felt his world spin once more, but this time it wasn't from a loss of blood.

"What's wrong?" Kara asked, moving toward him.

"Qadir is in New York." He turned the phone around so she could see the photo.

"Oh my God! This is time-stamped yesterday."

"This is about him," he said, meeting her gaze. "We need to get back to the city, and then you need to get as far away from me as you can. This isn't just about Dominic or any of the others anymore. It's also about me"

"How does that make sense?" she asked in confusion.

"Qadir is a complex thinker. It's one of his gifts. Others go linear. He never sees opportunities in a straight line. Maybe this didn't start out to be about me or about New York. But whatever is happening has drawn his interest, and if there's one thing I can guarantee, however big and bad we think it's going to be, it will be worse."

CHAPTER NINETEEN

The drive back to Manhattan felt endless. Max sat in the passenger seat, his left shoulder a constant throb of pain. He hadn't taken the medication Hayden had left for him because he needed his head to be clear. But he had to admit that the pain was dulling his senses a little, too. But he'd get through it because he had to. Qadir was in New York.

The realization went around and around in his head. He couldn't quite believe it. Getting into this country would have been an incredible challenge, but somehow, he'd done it. Qadir was here. And he had a plan.

What that plan could be gave him a headache to match the pain in his shoulder. And as he shifted position, another thought entered his mind.

"Dominic," he muttered.

"What?" Kara asked.

He turned his head to meet her questioning gaze. "I'd like to know who he was meeting with yesterday."

Her eyebrow raised. "Are you suggesting it was Qadir?"

"Not him specifically. But maybe someone in the circle, someone Qadir has bought, someone with influence here and also in the region where Dominic wants to build."

"That could be many different people," she said.

As the car ran over a pothole, his seat bounced, sending a jolt of pain through his body.

"Sorry," Kara said quickly. "How are you doing? Are you sure you don't want to take something?"

"I'm fine."

"You're not fine. You're very pale, and I can see the pain in your eyes."

"Well, I don't have time to not be okay," he said with a shrug. "Don't worry. I'll get through this. I've been shot worse before."

"Yeah, I've seen a few of those scars," she murmured.

"They make me sexier, right?" he asked, trying to joke his way through the tension coming not only from his pain but also from their earlier conversation.

Kara hadn't said much since they'd left the house, her hands steady on the wheel, but her jaw was tight. The easy intimacy they'd shared just two days ago felt like it belonged to different people. Now there were walls between them again, built from secrets and moral differences that might be impossible to bridge.

"It's not funny," she said a moment later. "You could have been killed yesterday."

"So could you. We both live lives of danger, Kara. That doesn't make us stop doing our jobs."

"I know, but this felt...different." She let that thought linger, then gave him a quick look and said, "You pushed me out of the way. You saved me from being shot."

"And you saved me afterwards. We're even."

"I guess."

"Let's focus on the case. I want to go back to my place. I need some clothes."

She nodded. "Good idea. But I'm not sure your place is safe, or mine, for that matter. I didn't expect us to be targeted on our own. We've had some close calls, but that was because we were with someone else. But Dominic was long gone by the time we got to the lake. There was no one there but us."

"We're getting too close," he said. "That's a good thing. It means they're not feeling totally in control. And worried people try to move faster, which sometimes leads to mistakes."

"Do you think Qadir made a mistake when he walked in front of a security camera?" she asked.

He heard the doubt in her voice and understood where it was coming from. "I don't know," he admitted. "He could have wanted to make himself a distraction, but that would be incredibly risky and very dangerous. It's not just me who wants to get to him; his escape and defection are an embarrassment to the entire agency. And there are other agencies that have also been affected by his many crimes. Putting a target on himself makes little sense to me."

"I'm still leaning toward the idea that he wanted you to see him. Your history with him is intense."

She didn't even know the half of it. "That's true. But understanding why he's here isn't as important as finding him."

"I need to get my team involved," she said. "Probably 26 Fed, too. And you need to talk to the agency. Maybe also Dominic. Make him tell you who he was with at the lodge."

"Getting additional people involved doesnt always make things easier. There are more layers of bureaucracy, more chances that someone is a mole, that information will be leaked."

'That's a chance we have to take. Qadir is one of the most wanted terrorists in the world, and he's in New York City."

"Well, my former agency is already involved. That photo came from someone still working for the CIA."

"Then the FBI needs to catch up fast," she said decisively. "I'll drop you off at your apartment. Then I'll catch a cab and go to the office. It's Sunday, but I'm sure I can get some people in based on this information."

"Why don't I go with you to the office?" he suggested. "After I change clothes, of course. I'd like to talk to Tyler. He was in

Syria when my friends were killed. He was hunting Qadir, too. We need to compare notes."

"Now, you want to be friends with Tyler? You spent the past week telling me not to trust him."

"I'm not saying I'm going to trust him. But we need to find out what he knows and what side he's on."

———

Fifteen minutes later, Kara parked by Max's building, and they carefully walked down the block, both on high alert. Since she'd found Max's address with little trouble, she was concerned that someone else had as well. He hadn't been living a covert life recently. "I think you should pack a bag," she said as they entered the building. "You're a target now. You can't stay here."

"I agree," he said as he led the way up the stairs and unlocked his door.

She pulled her weapon, exchanging a silent look with him before he pushed the door open. She entered first, prepared to shoot, but there was no one inside the small apartment. She checked the bedroom as Max closed the door.

"It's clear," she said.

"I'm going to change and throw some clothes in a bag."

She nodded, putting her weapon away. While he was changing, she wandered around the living room, her gaze narrowing as she moved over to his desk. It wasn't the two computers and multiple monitors that surprised her; it was the map on the wall, marked with red pins and tags showing Qadir's known locations over the past two years. There were also photos under the map with men in robes and head wraps, sometimes in fatigues, sometimes in business clothes. Most were of Qadir, revealing how often he changed his look from dark hair to blonde hair to bald with a beard. There were a few other men in the photographs, too; some younger, some older.

Glancing down at the desktop, she saw intelligence reports, clippings of articles about bombings and terrorist attacks all over the world. He had an entire notebook filled with pattern analyses and predictions.

It was the work of a smart and thorough agent. It was also the work of someone obsessed. Someone who'd let a single mission consume his entire life.

When he emerged from the bedroom in a clean shirt and jacket, an overnight bag slung over his good shoulder, she turned to face him. His gaze moved from her to the desk, and then he shrugged. "I've been tracking him for a long time."

"I can see that."

"We should go."

"One second." She drew a breath and let it out, not really sure what she wanted to say. She'd never lost a partner in the field, but she had lost friends, people who were trying to do good, people who shouldn't have died. "I understand why you need to catch Qadir."

"Great. Then we don't have a problem." He paused. "Or do we?"

She took a moment to find the right words. 'I just want you to think about how all this started: a bomb in a café, a federal prosecutor tied to the Meridien Tower fire, a building inspector with the same connection. Small, targeted explosives not designed to kill a high number of people, small-time players like Jonas Cray hired to spill coffee, a Building Department admin paid to get someone into an electrical closet, a strip club owner and a gym manager tied to poker games, money laundering, maybe drugs..."

His jaw tightened. "I don't need a recap."

"I disagree. There is nothing about the two prior explosions that suggests the work of Qadir. You said that yourself."

"Caleb Azrani's brother, Malik Azrani, works for Qadir. That suggests a connection."

"But the brothers were estranged. They grew up in different parts of the world. I just don't want us to get lost in this obsession." She waved her hand toward the wall. "And not see what else might be occurring. Maybe Qadir is now involved, but I don't think it started with him."

"You're going back to the victim's families, to Hartford and Faulkner."

"Yes. We have today and tomorrow to figure out what's happening before that summit takes place, and while I want to run as fast as you do toward the idea of capturing Qadir, I want to make sure we're not running in the wrong direction for this case. I think I should go to my office, and you should go to your CIA friends, and then we should compare notes."

"The last thing we should do is split up. I have your back, Kara, and I know you have mine. We don't know about anyone else. I don't need a meeting with my contact right now. In fact, it's probably better that we communicate using a protocol that we've already set up. Let's go to your office, and we'll discuss everything and everyone, not just Qadir."

She wondered if he could really put his energy and thought anywhere else, but she'd made her point, so she'd just have to see. Taking out her phone, she texted her team saying that one of the world's most wanted terrorists was now in New York City, and they needed to meet.

———

Max had been in a lot of briefing rooms over the years—CIA buildings, military command centers, embassy conference rooms, where the air was thick with tension and the stakes were always life or death. But he'd never been in one where he was the outsider, the civilian consultant whose presence was barely tolerated.

Kara's team had assembled quickly for a Sunday afternoon. The field office was mostly empty except for the essential personnel Jason had called in: Agent Tyler Brennan, who sat across the table studying him with undisguised suspicion; Agent Alina Vokov, a sharp-eyed, beautiful blonde; and Wes Paulson, a tech specialist.

Jason Colter, the head of the unit, stood at the head of the conference table, his expression determined as he asked Kara to brief them on the situation.

Kara stood, her voice clear and authoritative as she laid out the situation: the connection between the local bombings, Caleb Azrani and Qadir's organization, ending with the photo that confirmed Qadir's presence in the city.

"The important thing to remember," she said, "is that this investigation started with specific, targeted attacks against people connected to the Meridien Tower fire seven years ago. Samantha Barkley and James Cooper both had roles in the aftermath of that disaster. We can't lose sight of that pattern just because a bigger fish has entered the water. To catch him, we need to pick up some of the smaller fish first. Unfortunately, some of those fish are dying before we can get to them. Elias Costa was apparently killed in a car crash last night in Maine."

"I'll look into that," Wes said.

"Thanks. The infrastructure summit is on Tuesday. If Qadir is planning something spectacular, that's the most likely target. Which gives us approximately thirty-six hours to find him."

Tyler spoke up. "What about the Azrani brothers? Any leads on their current location?"

"Malik was spotted in Berlin three days ago, but that could be a misdirection." Kara looked around the table. "Caleb is in the wind."

"All right," Jason said. "I'm calling in the rest of the team, and I'll talk to Damon as soon as we're done here. We'll need to get 26 Fed involved as well. I know we've had concerns about leaks, but at this point, it's all hands on deck. Alina, I want you to coordinate with Homeland Security and the ATF. Wes, I need you and your team to figure out how Qadir got here, where he could be staying, and what identity he might use now."

"What about the summit?" Tyler asked. "Are we recommending that they cancel?"

"We are, but that's not our call. I'm sure there will be further discussions today." He paused. "Anything you'd like to add, Mr. Malone?"

"Ali Qadir is a chameleon. He may not look like anything in that photo now. He can be charming, intelligent, and also completely evil. For him to be here in the US, knowing he's a hunted man, means the stakes are very high."

"On that note, let's get to work," Jason said.

As the meeting broke up, Kara said, "Max, Tyler, come with me."

She led them into a break room with fluorescent lights, vending machines, a coffee maker that had seen better days, and a small table with a bowl of fruit on it. She closed the door behind them and turned to face both men.

"Okay," she said, crossing her arms. "Before we go any further, we need to clear the air."

"We don't have time for this," he said.

"I agree," Tyler replied.

"We're making time," Kara said with a stubborn glint in her eye. "Max, you first. What's your problem with Tyler?"

"That's classified."

"You can say something, so talk."

"Joint operation," he said finally, "mission was compromised."

Tyler's face darkened with anger. "You think I sold you out? My team was ambushed, and you weren't where you were supposed to be. One of my team members almost died."

"And my team members were not that lucky. They died at Qadir's hands."

"But you didn't. You survived because my team got there in time to save you."

"My team," Max corrected. "And you weren't even there."

"Because I had to be somewhere else," Tyler snapped.

As silence fell between them, Kara said, "So, neither of you has any proof of anything? Is that what I'm hearing?"

"It was a complicated situation," he admitted.

"Trust is difficult to come by in that part of the world, especially with a spook," Tyler said.

"You were doing the same work," he returned, meeting Tyler's gaze.

Another silence stretched between them.

"So, your teams both got hit," Kara said. "Both teams were compromised. Is it possible it was an outside setup, that the ones who benefited from your mutual suspicion were the terrorists you were hunting?"

"It's possible," he conceded.

Kara turned to Tyler. "What do you think?"

"It's possible," Tyler echoed.

"Good," Kara said. "Then, can we all get on the same side and focus on stopping Qadir? Because that's all that matters right now."

"I can do that," Tyler said.

"Yes," he agreed.

"Then let's go stop a terrorist."

"I'm going to talk to a friend of mine who is well-connected in that part of the world," Tyler said. "I'll let you know what he says."

"Okay." Kara opened the door and stepped into the hallway.

Max gave Tyler a thoughtful look, wondering who that friend was and why he was taking off on his own. "I'm still keeping an eye on you, Brennan."

"Likewise," Tyler returned. "But I didn't set you up before, and I'm not setting you up now."

"Likewise," he echoed as he left the room and headed back into the bullpen to see what Kara wanted to do next.

———

Kara was happy that Max and Tyler had called a temporary truce, although she wasn't sure how long it would last. But she couldn't worry about them; the clock was ticking, and every minute counted. She'd no sooner gotten back to her desk when Wes came over, an unusual gleam in his usually unemotional gaze.

"Got a new lead on Hartford," he said.

She was happy to hear that since Hartford's phone had been disconnected, and he hadn't been back to his house in the last twenty-four hours. "What is it?"

"His former mother-in-law owns a rental house on Long Island and a vacation home on the Jersey Shore."

She thought about that. "Text me the Long Island address. I feel like Hartford would want to stay a little closer to the action." Then she turned to Max. "Let's go."

They headed down to the garage, and she grabbed the keys for one of the team's SUVs. Max's Jeep was too well known at this point. She slid behind the wheel as Max got in next to her. After putting the address into the GPS, she shot out of the parking garage, eager to find Hartford and figure out if her theory about him was correct.

"You were good back there," Max said, surprising her with his words.

"In the meeting? I was just relating the facts."

"In a way that made sense. But I was actually talking about the way you forced Tyler and me to talk to each other."

She flung him a smile. "That was easy. I have a stubborn younger brother, who I used to babysit. And when his friends came over, there was often some sort of dispute. I found the best way to handle it was to make them talk to each other. For some reason, males of all ages seem to prefer to avoid that."

"You're not wrong," he said. "I will say that Tyler's speedy exit to talk to an unnamed friend still raised my suspicious radar."

"I get it. But you have a lot of meetings with unnamed people, too. I'm going to trust Tyler to be on the right side, just as I trust you. If I'm wrong, I'll deal with that when it happens. But I don't think I am."

"You're probably not. When you made me look back in time, I have to admit my evidence for distrusting him was pretty flimsy."

"And his for you." She paused, changing the subject. "I really hope we can pick up Hartford today. If he's not guilty, then a lot of my assumptions are wrong."

"It seems unlikely he'd have done a disappearing act if he wasn't guilty of something."

"I agree. But if we're wrong, we could waste a lot of time."

"Always a risk, but I trust your instincts, Kara."

She was touched by his words. "I hope I don't let you down."

"You won't," he said confidently.

She turned her attention back to the road. Only one way to find out.

CHAPTER TWENTY

The house belonging to Hartford's former mother-in-law sat on twenty acres overlooking Oyster Bay, a sprawling Tudor mansion that spoke of generations of wealth and privilege. They parked at the end of the long driveway, using the landscaping to approach the house without being seen from the windows.

"There he is," Max said quietly, pointing toward a large window at the back of the house where they could see David Hartford stuffing papers into a leather briefcase.

"Back door," Kara whispered, spotting a service entrance partially hidden by ivy.

Max tested the handle. Locked, but it was an old lock that yielded quickly to the lock picks Kara pulled out of her bag. They slipped inside through what appeared to be a mudroom, then moved silently through the house toward the study.

As they reached the open door, Kara pulled her weapon, as did he. Then she moved into the room with purpose. "David Hartford, FBI. We need to talk."

David's head jerked up in surprise. "You?" he said. "You're FBI?"

"Yes."

David's shoulders sagged, and he looked suddenly older than

his forty-five years, his expensive suit hanging loose on his frame, as if he'd lost weight along with everything else he'd lost. She glanced at the open briefcase. There were papers and also framed photographs.

"How did you find me?" he asked, sinking down in the chair behind the desk.

"That doesn't matter," she said. "You need to tell me what's going on, David. Why you hired people to blow up a café and a building."

He stared at her, then his gaze moved to the photograph in his briefcase. He picked it up, gave it a long look, then turned it around. "This is my wife, Tori, and our daughter, Ariel. It was taken at Christmas, six weeks before they died. This was the last photo taken of all three of us."

It was a heartbreaking picture of a once-happy family. David looked young and confident, on top of the world. Tori was a stunning redhead. Ariel had the sweet beauty of an innocent six-year-old.

"They're beautiful," she said, still keeping her weapon trained on him.

"They were my everything. They didn't deserve to die. They didn't deserve for their last minutes to be filled with smoke and fire and terror, trapped by a system that was supposed to protect them but prevented them from escaping."

"So you decided to punish the people responsible for their deaths. But Samantha Barkley wasn't responsible."

"She let them walk," he said, energy returning along with his hatred. "She made plea deals to keep her rich friends out of trouble. And Cooper signed off on the building construction after taking a bribe. They weren't innocent. They were criminals. Someone had to make them pay."

"Why now?" Max asked. "That was seven years ago."

"Because they were happy. I saw Samantha Barkley at a charity gala with Dominic. She was laughing, flirting, and having the time of her life. I realized she probably didn't even remember my wife and daughter. Or any of the others. She'd moved on with her life. They all had. Redstone changed its company name, but it kept making smart systems. Wexler Properties built more buildings, using the renamed systems, bribing the city to look the other way while they cut corners."

"Who's next?" she asked. "Do you blame Dominic for what happened?"

David's gaze narrowed. "He's the one who funded Redstone in the beginning. If he hadn't given them money, maybe they wouldn't have been able to build the system that killed my family."

"Why not go after him directly?" Max challenged.

"I was building up to it. I wanted him to feel pain first: the loss of a loved one, the worry that danger was coming for him, the realization that he might not be as untouchable and invincible as he might think. But..." His voice trailed away. "He's going to get away."

"Why?" Max asked. "Because your plan is falling apart?"

"Because my plan has been taken over," he said, anger and fear burning in his eyes now. "And they don't want Dominic dead. He's too valuable to them. They don't care about my other targets. They took my money to fund their own plan, and there's not a damn thing I can do about it."

"Who took your money? How did this start?" she asked, eager to finally get some answers.

"After the civil case was over, I was venting to Elias about how no one paid for what happened to my wife and daughter, and he said he might be able to help me. He knew someone who could handle jobs like that."

"How did you know Elias?" she interrupted.

"I have a personal training session at Forge Fitness every week. Sometimes, Elias stepped in when my trainer was unavailable. And at times, I gave him some personal financial advice. Anyway, he connected me to Alex Novik, who got me onto an encrypted site where I could post a job." David paused. "I wanted people to feel what Tori and Ariel felt. It couldn't be a bullet or a blade. It had to be an explosion. And I found someone who could do that." He took another breath. "I thought about it for a long time. Didn't really decide to do it until I saw Samantha with Dominic, and her smile made me crazy. It was so unfair, so wrong."

"Who took the job? Caleb Azrani?" Max asked.

"I know that's his name now, but at the time, it was someone named Cal475. He said he could make bombs. And he had people to place them. But he would need me to double my offer. I didn't care what the cost was."

"He must have loved that," Max said dryly.

"I became a mark," David agreed. "I thought I was in charge, but I wasn't. I realized that too late. Other people were getting hurt. The explosions weren't as targeted as I wanted them to be. And I was worried that once the FBI started looking around, they could trace everything back to me. Cal assured me that wouldn't happen. I paid him more money to make sure he tied up any loose ends."

"Was Jonas Cray one of those loose ends?" she asked. "Was he the one who placed the bomb?"

"I found out later that he was, but that was after I heard he was dead, and I realized that Cal had hired Jonas. I had left it up to Cal to do whatever he needed to do and use whoever he needed to use to get the job done. I didn't want names or details."

"Cal also tried to kill a woman named Whitney Holden," Kara said. "She works in the Building Department. She got James to reschedule his inspection and check out the closet where the electrical boxes were placed."

"I don't know about that. Look, I wanted to be done after the last bomb went off. Nothing was going the way I thought, and I wanted it to end, but Cal said he wasn't done. I would have to keep paying him, or he'd turn me in. He had everything on me. He could send me to prison. Or he could kill me. I'm not sure which he had in mind. But he told me there would be more explosions, that everyone on my target list would eventually die or suffer terribly, but other people would, too, because this was bigger than both of us now."

"Was he talking about the summit on Tuesday?" Max asked. "Where Dominic is the headliner, where the city officials will be, and some of the other investors and builders tied to Wexler and Redstone and all the others?"

"I think so, but I'm not sure. Cal said something about not being obvious."

"When did you last communicate with Cal?" she asked. "And did he mention who else he was working with?"

"Yesterday. He requested another payment, even bigger than the last. He said the people in charge now needed cash, and the only way he could stop them from killing me was to pay up. I paid him last night, and then I got a motel room. I was afraid to go home. I drove out here a few hours ago. I had decided to leave the country, but I needed to get some photos to take with me and I couldn't go back to my house. I knew Amelia, Tori's mother, had some here."

She couldn't believe he'd halted his escape plan to get a few family photos. But clearly, David Hartford had been obsessed with his wife and his child and their tragic deaths.

"I don't like it," Max said suddenly.

Her gaze swung to his. "What do you mean?"

"He wasn't that hard to find. And it's too quiet." Max shook his head. "We need to get out of here. Get up," he ordered Hartford. "If you don't want to die, you better come with us, because we're the only ones who can protect you."

Hartford stood up, grabbing the photo and holding it close to his chest as they ran through the house to the back door. They had just cleared the house and gotten into the middle of the driveway when David stopped abruptly, his face panicked. "Wait. The letters Tori wrote to Ariel when she was a baby. They're in my briefcase. I have to get them."

"Stop," she yelled, but he was already running back to the house. "We have to get him."

Max grabbed her arm as another heart-stopping, ear-ringing blast knocked them off their feet and onto the paved drive. The pain in her ears was even worse than before. And she could barely breathe with dust and debris falling around her. When the smoke finally cleared a little, she looked for Max, terror entering her heart once more.

"Max," she yelled as she struggled to get to her feet.

She didn't see him anywhere, but he had been right beside her. He had stopped her from going after David. *God, David!*

She pressed her hands to her ears in a desperate attempt to stop the painful ringing and moved forward, but it was hard to see more than a foot in front of her. And then she heard him call her name.

"Kara!"

"Max," she yelled back, a wave of relief running through her as he came toward her. He looked into her eyes, then wrapped his arms around her and held her tightly against his chest. She breathed him in, feeling the safety of his embrace, but she couldn't linger there as much as she wanted to. "Are you hurt?" she asked.

"No. You?"

"I'm fine."

They turned to look at the house, which was engulfed in flames. And there, by the side door, was David. He wasn't moving.

But when she got to his side, she dropped to her knees and saw his eyes were open, flickering, his hand against his chest, his whole body shaking as a sharp, jagged piece of metal was coming out of his chest.

"Call 911," she told Max, but he was already on his phone, calling it in. "You're going to be okay, David. Help is coming."

"I just wanted someone to pay," he gasped. "Just the bad people, the ones who didn't care about the loss of life, who didn't know that my daughter was about to have her seventh birthday, and my wife thought she was pregnant."

The pain and grief in his gaze were difficult to see. "I understand," she told him, even though she didn't. Because he'd tried to kill those people and had hurt others in the process. But she needed him to calm down, to hang in there. He still had the information they needed. But his breath was coming in strangled gasps.

"Better this way," he stuttered. "Now I'll see them again."

"David, hold on," she ordered. "Where is the next explosion going to be? Tell me so I can stop it, so you can make up for what you did."

"Too late," he said, the last word barely getting off his tongue before his breath stopped and his eyes turned glassy and unseeing.

He was gone, and they still didn't have the answers they needed. Someone had made sure of that.

It was more than an hour later and a little after six o'clock when they finally drove back to the city in grim silence. After communicating what had happened to the various agencies that had shown up, including her own, Kara had driven away from the scene of yet another explosion, another blast that had rocked the world and taken a life.

"Does this make sense?" she asked Max. "Why kill Hartford in such an explosive way?"

"It's a good way to destroy evidence. They might have gotten lucky and killed us, too."

"I didn't see a car. Maybe the bomb was on a timer."

"Probably, or they would have set it off before we could get out of the house." She glanced over at him and saw him wince as he shifted positions. "Are you sure you're okay?"

"I fell on my shoulder."

"Sorry. I have to say I'm getting damn tired of being thrown into the air and landing hard on the ground, not to mention my ears are still ringing."

"I feel the same way."

She drew a breath and let it out, thinking about David's last words. "David really loved his wife and child."

"Doesn't excuse what he did."

"I know. He wanted to hurt other people in exactly the same way his family was killed, and the way he ended up being killed. It's a terribly sad irony."

"I'm more concerned with what's coming next," Max said. "David mentioned Costa was his first lead. Costa is dead, so he can't help us. Alex Novik was the one who got David onto the site where he connected with Caleb. We need to find him."

"He hasn't been at the club in days."

"Where does he live?"

"Midtown. We alerted the team there to notify us when he came back to his apartment, but that hasn't happened."

"Maybe he's dead, too," Max said grimly.

"I hope not." She paused as her phone buzzed. "This is Tyler." She punched a button and said, "Hello?"

"Just heard what happened," Tyler said. "How are you and Malone?"

"We're fine. What's up?"

"I think Alex Novik may be at the Bayside Marina. His ex-girlfriend has a boat called the Isabelle. I'd go there myself, but I'm in Newark. If you're closer..."

"We are. We can check it out. What are you doing in Newark?"

"I had a meeting with a guy who worked on Sergei Novik's security team a few years back. He told me Sergei is clean, that his brother is the bad seed, as Sergei put it. He only invested in the Crimson Club to get his brother into a more legitimate business, although it hasn't turned out that way. My friend got in touch with Sergei and told him that Alex was in trouble and it would be better if the FBI found him before anyone else. He suggested we check the boat."

"We're on our way," she said as Max typed the marina into the navigation screen. "We should be there in about thirty minutes. Good work, Tyler."

"Let me know what happens."

She ended the call and glanced at Max. "I hope Alex Novik is still alive. It would be nice to get some good luck for a change."

"I agree."

"So, Tyler was helpful," she added.

"Yeah, we'll see."

"You're great at holding a grudge, aren't you?"

"I have a long memory," he admitted. "But I'm willing to give Tyler the benefit of the doubt. As you pointed out earlier, I really don't know what happened back in the day. And it also doesn't matter anymore, although it involves some of the same people."

"I would imagine that there are hundreds, maybe thousands of people whose lives have been irrevocably changed by Ali Qadir. You're not the only one, Max."

"I never thought I was. But most people don't have the power to stop him. If I can find him, I will stop him."

His vow sent a shiver down her spine, and she didn't want to ask any more questions because she wasn't sure she wanted to hear his answers.

———

The Bayside Marina sat on a protected inlet in the Bronx, a mid-sized facility that catered to weekend boaters and fishing enthusiasts rather than luxury yacht owners. As they pulled into the gravel parking lot, Kara could see maybe fifty boats of various sizes tied up along a series of floating docks—cabin cruisers, fishing boats, a few sailboats with their masts reaching toward the darkening sky.

At seven o'clock on a Sunday evening in January, the place was nearly deserted. Most recreational boaters had already pulled their vessels in for the winter, and those that remained were battened down for the night. The marina office was dark, and only a few boats showed lights on in their cabins.

They got out of the car and walked carefully down to the floating docks, their footsteps muffled by the gentle lapping of waves against the hulls.

"There," Max said, pointing toward the furthest dock where a sleek white cabin cruiser sat at the end of the pier with the name Isabelle painted on the side. It was bigger than most of the other boats, maybe forty feet long. As they approached the boat, they could see a light on inside the main salon.

They paused for a moment as Novik came into view, a phone pressed to his ear, gesturing wildly as he spoke.

"Wonder if he's alone," she whispered.

"Let's get closer," Max said, casting a look around as they crept down the dock. And suddenly Novik's voice ran through the air.

"I told you, I don't have a boat that can make it to the Bahamas," he said. "I need a plane and a private airfield."

He was looking to run, and they needed to stop him. Max stepped aboard first, and she followed. They both drew their weapons. Novik was a big man, broad-shouldered and thick around the middle.

"I need to get out of the country," Novik continued. "Tonight, if possible. Yes, my brother will pay anything. He owes —" Novik stopped mid-sentence when he saw them enter the cabin. He threw down his phone and started to reach for a gun on the table.

"FBI," she shouted. "Don't do it, Novik. We just saw Hartford die. You don't want to be next."

He froze, turning his head at her words, his eyes cold but also scared. "Hartford is dead?"

"Yeah. His house was blown up," Max said as he moved across the room and grabbed Novik's gun before he could reach for it again. "Costa was killed last night. I'm guessing you're next, unless you make a deal."

"What kind of deal?" he asked warily.

"You tell us where to find Caleb Azrani and Ali Qadir."

"I don't know where Caleb is, or his brother, or anyone else. I had nothing to do with any of this. All I did was tell Hartford about an internet site."

"Where he could hire someone to build bombs, blow up buildings and kill people," she said, still pointing her gun at his face. "Start talking."

"I can't help you. They didn't tell me anything. And when I heard about Elias, I got scared, so I went into hiding. I'm trying to get out of town."

"Where does Caleb live?"

"He's always changing his address. I only know how to reach him through the site."

"You're not in charge?" she asked.

"God, no! Caleb is in charge. Well, actually, I don't think he's on top anymore either. His brother is in town with a lot of other bad people."

"What are they here to do?" Max asked.

"I don't know, but Cal's brother hates America. That's why I was shocked when I heard he was in town. I didn't think he could get into the country."

"You need to come with us," she told him. "We'll protect you as long as you tell us the truth."

"You'll put me in jail," he said, but the resignation in his gaze told her he knew he had no other option.

"At least you'll be alive."

Before he could respond, they heard approaching engines. Fast boats, more than one.

Max moved to the window and swore under his breath. "We've got company. Two speedboats coming in fast."

"Back exit?" Kara asked.

"Engine compartment leads to the stern deck," Novik said, already moving.

The first shots came through the cabin windows before they could reach the rear of the boat. Kara dove to the floor, pulling Novik with her, while Max returned fire through the broken glass.

They squeezed through the narrow opening into the engine room, the sound of automatic weapons fire echoing behind them.

They emerged onto the stern deck just as one speedboat pulled alongside, its occupants spraying bullets at the cabin where they'd been hiding moments before.

"Jump!" Max shouted.

They went over the side together, hitting the cold water of the bay with a shock that drove the air from her lungs. Behind them, the cabin cruiser erupted in flames as someone threw an incendiary device through the broken windows.

They swam underwater as long as they could, surfacing near another dock as the speedboats circled back, searching. But in the confusion and smoke from the burning boat, they slipped away unseen. For a moment, she thought they might have lost Novik, but then he came to the surface, looking even more terrified.

Sirens rang through the air. She could hear yelling as people came out of their boats, and within seconds, the two speedboats were out of the harbor. They paddled to the dock. Max helped her out as Novik climbed onto the boat, and then Max followed. She was afraid Novik might try to run, but the sight of the burning boat seemed to make him realize they were his only hope of staying alive.

CHAPTER TWENTY-ONE

After dropping Novik off at her office, where Tyler was waiting to interrogate him and get him into protective custody, she and Max went down to the parking garage. "I think we should leave your car here," she said. "Why don't you grab your bag from your Jeep?"

He nodded and walked over to his Jeep and got his overnight bag. As they got into the SUV, she started the engine and then said, "I don't want to go to my place, and I don't think you should go to yours. Our addresses are probably known, and I really don't want to deal with any more explosions."

"I agree. Do you have another safe house?"

"No. We'll have to go to a hotel. Maybe one with room service," she added. "Something medium-sized, clean, safe. Hopefully, it's just for a night, and we can find Qadir tomorrow."

"Hopefully. But there is no way we are doing that kind of hotel," he said. "Let's go to the Castleton."

"Excuse me? That's a new five-star luxury hotel by the park."

"And you don't think we deserve it?"

"It's way out of my range. How much does Dominic pay you?"

He laughed. "Enough. And I have an ID and credit cards we

can use that won't be traced back to us. If we're going to hide out, let's do it in style."

"Is that the way they do it in the CIA?"

"No, but it's the way I'd like to do it now. It's been a long day."

"We look pretty bad," she said, her clothes still damp from jumping into the water, her hair still wet and tangled. "Or at least I do."

He shot her a quick look. "You do look a little ragged. I'll check us in. You can go into one of the shops and buy whatever you need for the night."

The thrifty, responsible part of her wanted to tell him there was no need to waste money at an expensive hotel, but the thought of gourmet room service, a thick robe, and maybe even a Jacuzzi tub was too enticing to resist. So, she kept her mouth shut and drove to the Castleton.

They left the car with the valet. Max gave his last name as Anderson, and then they headed into the hotel. The lobby was spectacularly beautiful: shiny marble floors, glittering chandeliers, wood-paneled walls with incredible art, and the furniture looked like it had come straight from a showroom.

"There's a boutique," Max said, handing her a credit card. "Use this. And for God's sake, buy some nice things. You deserve that, too."

"I'm not ordinarily a big spender."

"Neither am I. You've seen my apartment."

"That's true," she said, thinking about that. "You don't live like a rich person."

"Tonight, I'm going to live exactly like that, and so are you. If you come out empty-handed, I'm going to go into that store after we get a room and buy some things for you myself."

She smiled. "That's quite a threat. If you don't do what I say, I'm going to shower you with gifts."

He grinned back at her. "You know what I mean. I'll come find you after I get the keys."

"They're going to look at me like I'm a drowned rat. I wish I could say it was raining outside."

"Tell them a pipe burst in your apartment. You got soaked, and so did your clothes, and you had to move out for a night."

"That's not bad. I'm impressed with the quick lie. Also, a little scared."

He gave her a gentle push toward the store. "Go crazy."

It felt a little strange to walk even a few feet away from him, but she felt pretty safe even in the lobby. She'd been careful on the way over, keeping an eye out for any tails. She thought they were good, at least for a while.

The boutique actually had an excellent selection of clothes, including silky pajamas, undies, jeans, and T-shirts. She didn't go crazy as Max had suggested, but she bought enough to make her feel like she could hit the ground running tomorrow. When she was done, Max was waiting just outside the door.

"Looks like the shopping was a success," he said. "Did you buy something sexy to sleep in?"

"Maybe," she said, not willing to admit she had thought about him when she was picking out sleepwear. "Did you get us a nice room?"

"I did. Let's check it out."

They had to show their key to a security man at a podium by the elevator bank and had to use the key again to access the thirty-fifth floor. She couldn't help noticing discreetly placed cameras everywhere they went, which actually made her feel even safer. But she stopped worrying about safety when Max threw open the door to an incredibly luxurious suite that was unlike any place she had ever stayed before.

The suite looked like something from a magazine—easily twice the size of her entire apartment, with soaring ceilings and floor-to-ceiling windows that offered a breathtaking panoramic view of Manhattan. In the living area, plush cream-colored sofas were arranged around a marble coffee table, original artwork on the walls, and a dining area that could easily seat eight people.

"Wow," she said, moving toward the windows. "This is amazing."

The view was as incredible as their suite, with Central Park stretched out directly below them, a dark rectangle of trees bordered by the glittering lights of the Upper East Side and the Upper West Side. Beyond the park, the city extended in every direction, millions of lights twinkling in the gathering dusk. She could see the spire of the Empire State Building to the south, and the George Washington Bridge spanning the Hudson River to the north.

"It's beautiful," she murmured as Max stood next to her. "This city is everything and more."

"This is a magnificent view."

She turned to look at him. "We have to protect it, protect all the hopes and dreams out there."

He met her gaze. "That's what we're going to do. Tomorrow."

"I hope tomorrow won't be too late." At his frown, she added, "Sorry. I'm not trying to be a downer."

"I get it. But we have another day before the summit on Tuesday, and I think we need a break so we can regroup and re-energize."

"Well, this is the perfect place to do that. Do you want to take a shower and change, or order room service?"

"Let's start with room service. I'm starving." She moved over to the dining room table, where an elegant menu was encased in a thick leather folder. "This looks good, too. I could get used to living like this. What shall we get?"

He smiled at her enthusiasm. "Order whatever you want. I'm going to take a few minutes to try to reach Dominic."

"I thought we were taking a break."

"I'm just surprised he hasn't returned my calls, so I'm going to give it one more shot. See if they have a good fillet on that menu. I wouldn't mind getting a steak."

"They do. I'll put in an order." As he walked into the

bedroom, she wondered a little at his need for privacy, but she wasn't going to let doubts creep in. She knew the man she was with. She'd already trusted him with her life; she could trust him with a phone call to his boss.

While he was gone, she ordered steak for him, salmon for her, and an array of side dishes and dessert; and for good measure, she threw in some beers and a really expensive bottle of wine. Her stomach was rumbling, and she was thrilled to hear the room service operator tell her the food would be there within twenty minutes.

She'd just put down the phone when Max returned to the living room. She gave him a questioning look. "Well?"

"He finally picked up. He just left the hospital. They took Samantha off the ventilator. She's breathing on her own but apparently still heavily sedated, so he wasn't able to talk to her."

"Still, that sounds like good news. Why don't you look happier?"

"I got a bad feeling from Dominic. The Samantha news was good, but I felt like he used it to change the subject."

"And the subject was..."

"I told him what happened to us at the lake. I asked him why he hadn't called me back. He made some excuse about having locked his phone away during his meetings. He uttered the appropriate amount of surprise and concerned words and all that, but it felt hollow. Like there's something else going on."

She frowned. "You don't really think he was meeting with Qadir, do you? I mean, Dominic is a billionaire. He's a global leader, a philanthropist. Why would he risk meeting with a renowned terrorist?"

"The obvious answer is that he wouldn't. But Dominic has run into a lot of issues with his project in Tajikistan. He lost two men in an ambush, and he's received a lot of threats. If Qadir had the power to pave his way, I'm sure he'd pay to make that happen."

"He'd make a deal with the devil."

"I'm sure he wouldn't see it that way. He always tells me to look at the bigger picture. Look at the end, not at the means. He was that way when we were in boarding school together. He will use people to get what he wants. I'm not sure that he knows how to live any other way."

"Did you tell him about David Hartford?"

"I just said that he'd been killed in an explosion; I didn't get into details. He asked me if that meant everything was over. I told him I wished it did, but it appeared that David's targeted revenge bombings had been taken over by someone else who decided to use his massive bank account to launch their own attacks. I told him again that he should cancel the summit. He said he would consider it after talking to other people tomorrow."

"He's a stubborn man."

"He is. And I shouldn't judge him for using people since I have been using him."

"Well, I assume you are actually trying to protect him on his next trip, so maybe you're using him for resources and access, but you're still doing your job. How do you manage all that? Do you have a team?"

"I have a woman who helps me. Her name is Kai. She used to be at the agency. She came out of retirement for me."

"Does she know about your hidden agenda?"

"She does."

"Is she who you contact when you say you need to talk to people?"

"She's one of two people I've been talking to. The other is still an active agent." He cleared his throat. "Did you order dinner?"

"I did. I think I'm going to take a shower before it gets here. I'm hoping there's one of those fluffy robes in the bathroom."

"There is. Want some company?"

"That might make the shower a little too long, and dinner should be here shortly. Can I have a rain check?"

"Any time," he said with a sexy smile.

When she walked into the bathroom and saw more luxury, she let out a little sigh of pleasure. She turned on the shower, stripped off her clothes, and stood under the hot stream of water, lathering herself with expensive bath products that smelled incredible. It felt good to wash off the dirt of the day, to feel warm and safe. It might not last long, but she was going to hang on to the feeling as long as she could.

After getting out of the shower and drying her hair, she put on her new undies and then wrapped herself in the deliciously warm robe and went back into the living room.

The dining room table was now covered in covered dishes, and Max was opening the wine. "How was it?" he asked. "You look a lot better than you did before."

"It was great. The splurge idea was one of your best ones ever."

He laughed at that. "Good. I'm glad you're enjoying it."

She pulled the lid off a plate and saw a nicely grilled salmon, and her mouth watered. "The good just keeps getting better," she said as she sat down.

He handed her a glass of wine. "I thought this meal deserved wine instead of beer. You made a good choice."

"I don't know much about wine, but it was expensive, so fingers crossed." She took a sip. "Nice."

He sat down across from her and opened the plate with his steak. "I have to admit I'm hungry, too," he said. "When did we eat last?"

"I can't even remember." She swallowed a bite of salmon, then said, "I can split all this with you, Max. It may be a different name on the credit card, but I'm assuming you're still paying the bill."

"Don't worry about it."

"I like to pay my way."

"We'll settle up later. Just eat."

She was too hungry to argue, and for the next thirty minutes she tasted everything on the table, including Max's steak. She was happy to see he was a man who was willing to share his food, something she loved to do. If two people were eating, it only made sense to order two things and share. But her ex had not been big into sharing. He just couldn't understand why she couldn't just order her own meal and stick to it.

"What are you thinking about?" Max asked. "You suddenly got a frown on your face."

"Nothing really," she said, not wanting to talk about her ex. "I think I'm finally full."

"Me, too."

"Should we take our wine glasses and sit on the couch?" he asked.

She followed him over to the couch, which was facing the windows. He turned the lights in the room down so they had a better view of the city.

"I'm starting to feel like I can relax," she murmured a few minutes later. "How's your shoulder feeling?"

"It's fine."

"You're pretty low maintenance when it comes to injuries."

"Your brother did a nice job stitching me up. Have you talked to him again?"

"I sent him a text saying you were good, and I was fine. He didn't ask questions."

"He has faith in you. Smart guy."

"Thanks." She gave him a smile. "Can you believe how many near-death experiences we have had together? When is our luck going to run out?"

"That's not a question you should put out into the universe."

She was a little surprised by his answer. "Does that mean you believe in the power of the universe, or in fate? You seem too cynical and pragmatic for that."

He didn't answer right away, then said, "I've been around a lot of different people in my life: cultures, religions, spiritual beliefs. Sometimes it makes me crazy how many people will kill in the name of whatever they believe in, which is usually against what they believe in. And it's not like there's just one group to blame."

"No, there's not, and there's always a personal element, isn't there? The people who want to terrorize the world, who want to destroy anyone who doesn't believe like they believe or act like they want them to act, are usually all about themselves. It's not the greater power they are touting; it's their own power. It's their vision of personal greatness. Of course, I'm speaking in general terms."

"Well, Qadir certainly fits that bill," he said heavily.

"I understand why you want to take him down; I do, too." She turned sideways on the couch, snuggling up next to him. "But I'm worried about what it's doing to your heart." She put a hand on his chest.

He covered her hand with his as he met her gaze. "I haven't thought about my heart in a long time."

"Because it's painful to love people and lose them. But...'

He gave her a wary look. "I have a feeling you're going somewhere with this that I don't want to go."

"Well, let's find out," she said, unwilling to let him shut her down. "Look what revenge has brought... David Hartford loses his wife and child and goes from a family man, a businessman, to a murderer. All because he can't let his family's pain go unpunished. And now he's dead. And his plan has taken on a life of its own."

"That was a terrible revenge plan," he said.

"I don't know who said this, but I heard it once, and it stuck with me: Revenge is like drinking poison and expecting the other person to die. That's what happened to David." She paused, seeing the stubborn glint in his eyes. "Revenge is driving Qadir, too. He wants to inflict pain on Americans because of what happened to his family."

"And hopefully, he will die because of that," Max said harshly.

His words sent a chill down her spine. "I don't want revenge to kill you, too, Max. Killing Qadir isn't going to bring anyone back."

"I'm not trying to bring anyone back; I'm trying to stop him from killing anyone else. I know you're going to tell me he should be in jail, that revenge isn't justice, and that's what I believed. Until my agency sent a killer back out in the world to gather intelligence that he was never going to give to us."

"That was a terrible calculation on their part. But it wouldn't happen again. We can bring him in and put him in jail."

"Why do you care if he's dead or alive?"

"I don't actually care about that," she admitted, bringing surprise to his gaze. "I care about you, about what revenge might do to you."

His fingers tightened around hers as he gazed deep into her eyes. "I care about you, too, Kara."

"It's strange isn't it, how we came to know each other, how we got here... I struggle with the whole idea of fate and things happening for a reason, because I lost my dad when I was young, when he was young. And I see so many other deaths that really don't seem to have a reason. But maybe that's what faith is about. I don't know."

"Neither do I, and that's too heavy of a question to ponder right now. You're a deep thinker, aren't you, Kara?"

"I am. I have a feeling you are, too."

"Sometimes," he admitted. "My brain can get me into trouble. My ideas aren't always the best. In fact, I have an idea right now that I can't seem to shake."

As the heat between their fingers ran through the rest of her body, she knew exactly what he was thinking, and here in this quiet apartment, so high above the city, she felt like they were in a special safe place that was just about the two of them and not at all about reality. And she needed that escape.

"We've had a lot of close calls in the past couple of days," she murmured.

He nodded in agreement. "Those close calls are a reminder of how fragile life can be. I don't know what's going to happen tomorrow, Kara."

"Maybe nothing. Maybe we find Qadir, shut down his plan, save the world, and everything is great."

"There's my positive thinker. I like the sound of that," he said.

"Me, too. But just in case it isn't exactly like that..." she began. "Let's go into the bedroom and see what making love in a five-star luxury hotel room bed is all about. It could be a once-in-a-lifetime experience."

"Are you talking about the bed or me?" he asked with a laugh.

She grinned back at him. "I don't know. Maybe you should take that as a challenge. I know you like to win."

"You're going to win, too," he promised as he pulled her in for a hot kiss. And then they scrambled to their feet and ran into the bedroom.

The teasing turned to passion as she shed her robe and he stripped off his clothes, and they tumbled onto the soft, enveloping mattress with a desperate, passionate need to be together. But Max was determined to beat the bed, tasting and touching her in a way that rocked her world more than any explosion. She didn't know what the future would bring, but tonight she was with a man who challenged her and protected her and also knew how to love her in a way she'd never thought was possible.

Afterward, they lay tangled together in the hotel room darkness, the city lights painting patterns on the surrounding walls. She rested her head on Max's chest, soothed by the sound of his heartbeat, by the safe bubble of happiness that surrounded them, if only for a few more hours...

CHAPTER TWENTY-TWO

Monday morning arrived far too fast for Kara, but the sun streaming through the open curtains woke her up, and when she glanced at the clock and saw it was almost eight, she immediately sat up, disturbing the very handsome, very naked man sleeping next to her.

"Is it morning?" he mumbled as he opened his eyes.

She smiled, wishing she could slide back under the covers and make love to him again. "It's eight o'clock. We have to get up, get to work."

He gave her a sleepy grin as he rolled over onto his side, hooked one hand around her neck, and brought her back down for a kiss that immediately sent a wave of desire through her. But she somehow found the strength to pull away. "We have to get up, Max. I need to get to the office and go over everything with my team, see if we can figure out where Caleb and Qadir and everyone else are hiding."

His expression grew more serious with each passing word, and he sat up now, fully awake. "You're right. We have a lot to do. I need to touch base with Reza—"

"Reza?" she interrupted. "Is that the person who shall not be named?"

"Since I just named him, yes," he said with annoyance, which was directed more at himself than at her.

"I won't tell anyone. You can trust me."

"I know that, Kara," he said, the look they exchanged going far deeper than the words. "Anyway, Reza and I are working on something that may come in handy later."

"That sounds interesting. You're not going to tell me what that is, are you?"

"Not right now."

"Okay, fine. I'll wait. We should turn our phones back on." She got out of bed, grabbed the beautiful robe from the floor, and pulled it around her before walking back out to the living room to get her phone from her bag. She had a couple of messages from her team, the most important one being a joint task force meeting with Damon's team at 26 Fed scheduled for ten. She texted back that she'd be there.

As she did that, Max came into the room, wearing briefs, his phone in his hand, a puzzled look in his gaze. "Caroline Rowe wants me to meet her this morning. She doesn't say why. Just says it's important."

"Where does she want to meet?"

"Garden Court at the Fritz Collection."

"A museum? That's strange. Maybe you should just call her back."

"I tried. She didn't answer."

"I don't think you should go, Max. Look what happened the last time a woman sent you an urgent text message needing to talk to you."

He frowned at the reminder of Samantha's text. "Fair point. But it's a big public venue, with security, certainly a different scene than the café."

"It's also a well-known museum in the city that someone might want to blow up."

"I need to hear what she has to say. I'm going to have to take that risk."

"What time?"

"Ten."

"See if you can change it to eleven thirty or twelve. There's a joint task force meeting at ten that I need to be at. But I want to go with you to meet her."

He sent a text and then waited. "She's writing back." A moment later, he looked up and shook his head. "She said it has to be ten."

"That's even more concerning."

"If she can't change the time, change the location. Meet her in the park." At his frown, she added, "I'm just worried, Max."

"It's a good idea. I'll have her meet me at Bryant Park."

"I hate us splitting up."

"Me too, but I doubt I'll be allowed into a joint task force meeting, and maybe Caroline has important information."

"Do you think it's about Dominic?"

"Probably. I suspect she wants me to talk him into bailing on the summit tomorrow."

"I hope it's more than that."

"I'll find out." He walked forward and took her hand in his. "Next time we spend the night together, we're going to spend the morning in bed."

"I like the sound of that." She let go of his hand. "I need to take a shower."

"Hang on."

She turned in surprise. "What?"

"Did I win? Me versus the bed?" he asked with a sexy smile on his lips.

"Definitely you," she returned.

"Good. Then let's see how I do in the shower."

"Max, we don't have time," she protested, but it was a weak protest at best.

"Then we'll have to be fast." As he stripped off his briefs and headed back to the bedroom, she had absolutely no willpower to say no.

It would be fast, she told herself, but as they got into the steamy shower together, she thought they might need just a little longer...

———

Max arrived at Bryant Park twenty minutes early. Kara had dropped him off on her way to work, and it had felt strange to say goodbye to her. But they planned to meet up after their meetings and compare notes, so it wouldn't really be that long. And he needed to get his mind back on work. He walked the perimeter of the park, checking for any potential issues. But everything looked normal for a Monday morning.

Located in Midtown, the park was always busy with people cutting through on their way to work, tourists clustered around the coffee and hot chocolate kiosk, and the usual collection of chess players, and people-watchers, occupying the movable chairs scattered through the space.

He positioned himself near the fountain at the center of the park, where he could see all the main entrances and keep his back to the New York Public Library's imposing presence.

Caroline appeared at exactly the appointed time, entering from the Sixth Avenue side. She looked completely out of place among the casual parkgoers—her tailored black wool coat and leather gloves were perfectly appropriate for a business meeting in a climate-controlled office but made her stand out like a beacon among the joggers and dog walkers.

As she approached, she scanned the crowd, her movements tight with nervous energy. She clutched her purse against her body like a shield, and her usually perfect composure showed cracks of genuine anxiety. When she finally spotted him near the fountain, her relief was visible even from a distance.

"Why the change in location?" she asked.

'Museums are too contained. Here, we can see trouble coming."

He tipped his head toward a nearby empty table. "Let's sit."

Caroline did as he requested, perching on the edge of a chair, but she didn't relax. Her posture remained rigid, alert, like someone who expected to run at any moment.

"What's going on?" he asked.

"Dominic is in trouble. I think he's been lying to you, to both of us."

"About what?" he asked, his pulse speeding up. But he cautioned himself to proceed carefully. Caroline was extremely loyal to Dominic, maybe even in love with him, as Kara had suggested. Whatever she was about to tell him could be a setup.

"Last night after he got off the phone with you, he told me that David Hartford is dead, that he was plotting revenge against everyone connected to the tower fire several years ago, that David was responsible for Samantha's injuries, the bomb at the café."

"You're not telling me anything I don't already know."

"Dominic started drinking heavily. Like I've never seen him drink before. I thought maybe it was the shock of one of his friends wanting his girlfriend dead, wanting him dead. But it was more than that. After a couple of shots, he started talking about mistakes he's made, that maybe he had finally crossed a line he couldn't come back from." She cleared her throat. "I feel like I'm betraying him, but I'm scared. I know you're his friend, not just a security guy, and I hope you'll want to help him. Promise me you'll try."

"I can't promise anything. What else did he say?"

She gave him a troubled look. "He said that he never should have made a deal with the devil."

"Who's the devil? Qadir?"

Her eyes widened. "You know?"

"I'm guessing. What deal did he make?"

"I'm not entirely sure. But he said after Cody and Ray were

killed that he knew he was going to have to work with someone or he was going to have to give up on the project in Tajikistan."

"So, he made a deal with a terrorist for protection? Why wouldn't he tell me that?" His gaze narrowed on her nervous face. "I'm supposed to protect him at the groundbreaking. Why wouldn't I know about this deal?"

"Because you're part of it," she breathed, her words coming out in a quiet rush. "I didn't know. I swear I didn't. I'm not even sure I'm putting it all correctly now. But—"

"What did you say?" He interrupted her rambling with a piercing stare. "What exactly are you saying?"

"I think Dominic hired you because he was told to do that. This Qadir wanted Dominic to bring you to Tajikistan."

His mind raced, spinning back to the past, to the casual meeting in London, the job offer that was absolutely perfect, the timing of everything that had followed. He'd thought he was using Dominic, but Dominic had been using him. "He was setting me up. That's why he has never really cared about my plans. He doesn't need me to be safe; he needs Qadir." He paused. "But that plan was about getting me into Qadir's territory, and I don't think he's in Tajikistan anymore. I believe he's in New York City."

"I think you're right. And I think Dominic talked to him last night, right after he spoke to you. That's when he really started drinking. He also told me he wasn't going to the summit, but no one could know that until the last minute. And he wanted me to pack my bags, get his plane ready, make sure we could leave at any moment."

"Dominic thinks Qadir is going to blow up the summit.'

"I'm not sure he knows what this person is going to do." She licked her lips. "I talked to him an hour ago, and I wasn't sure what he remembered telling me. He said he was exhausted and drunk, so whatever he'd said was just part of some fever dream. I told him what he'd said about having the plane ready, cancelling out of the summit at the last second, and he said that was ridiculous; he wasn't going anywhere. Now, I'm totally confused. He asked me to forget whatever I thought I'd heard and reassured me that everything was fine, and that we would all be safe. I don't know if that's because something changed since last night, or if he was just drunk and hallucinating, or if he's lying to me."

There was a lot of self-interest in her story. The person she was most concerned with protecting was herself. And she probably should be worried. If anyone caught wind of what Dominic had let slip, her life would be over.

"What do I do, Max?" she asked, looking nowhere near the self-assured person he'd always thought her to be.

"Just act normally for now. If Dominic asks, reassure him you didn't really understand what he was saying, but he knows you're always there for him. Make him feel that you're still loyal to him. And do not mention that you spoke to me."

"What are you going to do?"

He thought about that. She'd dropped some breadcrumbs they could follow. "Find out who Dominic was talking to last night, for one," he said. "Did he mention anyone by name?"

She shook her head. "I just heard Qadir, but nothing else."

"What about a location? Qadir is in New York City, and he needs money and a place to stay. If Dominic helped him with those issues, how could we figure that out? Dominic would have had to use an intermediary. Who would that be? His security team? Someone else he trusts?" He watched her face. Caroline knew Dominic probably as well as anyone did. "His chief of staff, Nina Willey. She's been with him for eight years. She's practically a second mother to him, but not a nurturing one She's cold and ruthless, and a lot of people think Dominic has fired them based on her opinion."

He'd met Nina a few times, and she'd always given him an assessing stare as if she wasn't too impressed or too certain that he should be working for Dominic. In fact, she'd offered him little help even when he'd asked for more details on Dominic's trip. Maybe that's because she'd always known he was just a pawn." That realization stung. But he didn't have time to get emotional about anything. Because that plan had clearly changed. Once Caleb's operation had begun, and the money had started flowing from Hartford to Caleb, Qadir had seen an opportunity to create a different plan, one that would be funded by a couple of billionaires whose ambition or revenge plans had made them so easy to use.

"I should go. I'm supposed to meet Dominic at eleven thirty."

"In the office or at his house?"

"His house. He's working remotely today."

"You need to stay in touch with me," he said. "Report exactly what Dominic is saying and doing. You work for me now."

She bristled at that. "I don't work for you."

"If a bomb goes off in this city and kills people, and Dominic is part of it and you don't help us, I will make sure you go down with him."

"I came to you for help, not for threats."

"I am helping you. I just want you to know what's at stake."

"I already know. I'm not stupid, Max. Well, not about this anyway. I must admit that I never thought Dominic would make a deal with a terrorist that involved turning over a friend of his."

"Did you specifically ask him about that?"

"I hedged around about it. He laughed and said I must have been drunk, too, because that didn't make any sense at all." She got to her feet. "I'll text you later with an update, but you need to find this Qadir person fast."

As Caroline left, he took out his phone and called Kara. Her phone went to voicemail. She'd probably turned it off for the meeting. He glanced at his watch. It was ten forty-five. He got to his feet, debating his next options. And then his phone rang.

"Hello?" he asked, not recognizing the number.

"It's Tyler."

His stomach twisted into a knot. He knew immediately that

Tyler wouldn't call him unless he had a very good reason. "What's up?"

' Is Kara with you?" Tyler asked.

' No. She went to a meeting almost an hour ago."

' She never showed up," Tyler said. "Dammit! I knew something was wrong. I just thought she was running late and still had her phone off from last night. When did you last see her?"

' She dropped me off about a block away from Bryant Park at nine-forty. She's in one of the team SUVs. You should be able to track it."

'On it now. Hang on."

His hand tightened as he could hear Tyler talking to someone in the background. There was no way Kara wouldn't show up for a meeting of the joint task force. So where was she?

Tyler came back on the phone. "Her car is at the corner of Ninth and Jackson."

He started running even before Tyler finished speaking. That was only three blocks away. "I'm going there now."

"Keep your phone on. Wes and I are pulling up security cameras from the area."

His heart was in his throat when he turned the corner and saw a black SUV on the side of the road with a smashed rear fender and an open door.

"Found the car," he yelled as he ran across the street, dodging traffic and horns. When he got to the vehicle, it was empty, but Kara's bag was on the seat. "She's not here." His gaze scanned the surrounding area. "But someone smashed into her car." The truth hit him hard. "Someone grabbed her." He suddenly felt sick. "Qadir," he breathed. "It had to be him. He's taken Kara."

"We've got the accident on camera,' Tyler said. "A van pulled up next to her. We have a partial plate, but a bus blocks the camera. And when it's gone, the door is open, and there's no sign of her. We're going to look for different cameras, different angles."

"We have to find her," he said, filled with a raging fear that was almost overwhelming. "Before it's too late."

———

Max's anger was still raging when he got to Dominic's townhouse, but he tried to tamp down his emotions as he nodded to the security team in the lobby and then the guards outside Dominic's front door.

"Mr. Ashford's expecting you?" Brett Connors asked, his tone more courtesy than suspicion.

"He is," Max replied as the guard opened the door and let him in.

He could hear voices from the study. It sounded like Dominic and Caroline. He didn't bother to knock. He pushed open the heavy wooden door and stepped inside.

Dominic was standing behind his desk, dressed in dark slacks and a white dress shirt, but he looked like he'd aged ten years overnight.

Caroline stood across from Dominic. They both looked at him in startled surprise.

"Max, what are you doing here—"

Before Dominic could finish that sentence, he'd crossed the room in three long strides, grabbed Dominic's arms, and slammed him against the floor-to-ceiling bookshelf next to the desk. Books tumbled to the floor as Dominic's head hit the wooden shelving.

"What the—"

Dominic yelled in disbelief, stopping abruptly as Max put his gun against Dominic's throat in one smooth motion.

Caroline gasped. "Max, no."

"Where is she?" he said, his gaze boring into Dominic's. "Where is Kara?"

"How the hell would I know where your FBI agent friend is?" Dominic asked, instilling some bravado in his voice, but his eyes were filled with fear.

"Because Qadir is holding her. And he's your friend, right? Your new partner? The one you're selling me out to?"

"Max, stop," Caroline implored. "Let's talk about this calmly."

"You told him?" Dominic asked, his gaze shooting to Caroline, betrayal in his voice.

"I'm scared for you, Dominic," Caroline said. "I did it to save you."

"No, you didn't," he said coldly.

"Shut up," he told Dominic. "This isn't about her. This is about Kara. She's missing. Qadir has her. You tell me where she is and I'll let you live."

"You're not going to shoot me," Dominic said, but there was a trace of uncertainty in his voice. "Caroline, get the guard, for God's sake."

"Don't go," he told Caroline. "You have one choice to get it right, and that choice is now."

"I'm sorry, Dominic," Caroline said.

"Tell me where Kara is," he ordered again.

"I don't know where she is. I don't know where Qadir is," Dominic said, pleading for him to understand. "None of this was supposed to happen, Max. This wasn't my plan. It was Hartford's. He's the one who started this."

"But Qadir came to you to finish it because he already had you in his pocket. You'd already sold your soul to him, and for what? To build a fucking bridge?" He shook his head in disgust, no longer seeing a strong, powerful, intelligent man in front of him but a weak, narcissistic coward.

"The people of Tajikistan need that bridge, that highway. I made a deal with him to protect important infrastructure and the people who would build it. I was never going to turn you over, Max, but I wasn't going to tell him that. I was going to use him until I didn't need him anymore." Dominic paused. "It's not like you weren't using me. You needed my money. You took that job so you could get back into Tajikistan, so you could keep hunting Qadir. So, don't act like I betrayed you."

"You're right. I took your job and your money, but I wasn't going to take your life." He shook his head. "I don't care about that anymore. Where is Qadir?"

"I told you I don't know. Do you think I'd be alive if I knew?"

Dominic made a good point. "What's Qadir's plan? Is he bombing the summit?"

"He won't be able to. I just told the organizers to cancel."

"Your new best friend won't like that."

"He's not my friend, and I'm not going to let hundreds of people die."

"Well, I don't think Qadir is going to leave empty-handed, so what's his backup plan?"

"How many times do I have to tell you I don't know?" Dominic asked wearily.

"You know something. There's no way he got into this country without some help."

Dominic stared back at him. "He demanded an extra cash payment three days ago. It was deposited in an offshore account."

There was something Dominic wasn't telling him. "And..."

"He contacted me when I was at the lodge yesterday. He told me he needed another payment, a cash drop in Manhattan. I sent one of my guys to take care of it."

"You knew he was here."

"I suspected, but I wasn't positive."

He didn't believe him for a second. Dominic had funded Qadir's trip to the US. "You have no idea what he's capable of. You think he's going to play by any rules you set up?"

"I've become aware of that," Dominic admitted. "And I would like nothing better than for you to catch him."

"Oh, I don't think you want me to catch him; you want me to kill him, so he can't turn you in."

"I told you, Max. I just thought I was buying protection in Tajikistan."

His phone buzzed, and he pulled it out of his pocket. Seeing Tyler's name, he immediately answered. "Tyler, have you found her?"

"We tracked the van to an industrial area in Long Island City, near the waterfront. But there are a dozen warehouses in that area, and the van could have disappeared into any of them. I'm on my way there now, but if you can narrow anything down..."

Max looked at Dominic. "Long Island City? Does that mean anything to you? Do you own any warehouses in that area?"

"No, but Hartford had two buildings in that area."

That made perfect sense. Qadir had turned the tables on Hartford. They'd have access to his properties, his security codes.

"Check property records for David Hartford in Long Island City," he told Tyler. "I'm on my way." He ended the call. "I'm going to need your car." He'd taken a cab from the park to Dominic's building.

"My car?" Dominic echoed.

"Take mine," Caroline said, throwing him the keys. "It's the Audi out front. I hope you find Kara."

"I'll find her," he vowed, then turned back to Dominic. "If you find out where Qadir is and what he's planning to do, you sure as hell better send me a text. Because if he blows up this city, if he hurts Kara, Qadir is going to be the least of your worries."

CHAPTER TWENTY-THREE

Kara blinked her eyes open, a metallic taste in her mouth, a sharp pain in her head. The room in front of her spun for a moment and then finally settled as her brain tried to define where she was and what had happened to her. She was sitting in a straight chair, and her hands were tied behind her back. There was a vest around her chest, a heavy black vest with blocks of what appeared to be C-4 plastic explosives wired to a digital timer that currently read 35:23...35:22...

Oh, God! The memories came flooding back starting with the rear-end collision. She'd pulled over to the side so she wouldn't block traffic. She'd gotten out of her car. Then a van had pulled up next to her. The side door had opened. A man had grabbed her and pulled her inside. It had happened so quickly. He'd had black hair and black eyes. *Caleb!* It had to have been him.

She'd tried to fight, but he'd jabbed a needle into her arm, and the world had faded away.

Now reality was back, and panic ran through her as she realized that someone had put a suicide vest on her, a bomb that was going to explode in...thirty-four minutes, fifteen seconds.

Her heart almost jumped out of her chest. She told herself to stay calm. It was possible that any wild movement could also set off the bomb.

She looked around, thinking she was in some sort of warehouse. There were pallets of boxes along one wall, and a table along another. The table was covered with wires and metals and other bomb-making materials. The light was dim and the only windows were at least twelve feet off the ground. She had to find a way out of this, but how? She was a human bomb. She couldn't fight anyone. She'd blow herself up.

A door suddenly opened, and three men came into the room. The man who'd grabbed her in the van was first, a similar-looking man right behind him, but not as tall, not as dark. But it was the third man that made her breath catch in her chest. She recognized him from the photos in Max's apartment and the one she'd seen on Max's phone when he'd learned that Ali Qadir was in New York City.

Caleb, and, who she could only guess was his brother, Malik, moved to the side as Qadir strode forward, clearly the boss. For a world-renowned terrorist, he wasn't that big or that scary looking. He was average height, with dark hair going gray at the temples, and tanned, weathered skin that suggested he spent a lot of time outside in harsh environments. He was dressed like an American businessman in dark slacks, a gray sweater, and a winter coat. But the intelligence and cruelty in his gaze did not match his sophisticated look.

"Ah, you're awake," he said with a slight accent. "Special Agent Kara Reid. You've become quite annoying to our plans."

"To blow up the city?" she challenged, lifting her chin as she gave him a defiant look. "The FBI is going to stop you."

"I don't think so," he said with an evil smile. "But I like your fire. It's...amusing how so many of you think you can beat me, and yet you never do."

"The day isn't over yet."

"No, and it will be a glorious day. You'll be a martyr, Agent Reid. You'll die for something, or at least that's what they'll say about you. Your name will be in the paper. The people in New York who aren't grieving the loss of their loved ones will read about you and say how brave you must have been. Or perhaps they'll believe I turned you, that you got into the suicide vest willingly, that you had turned your back on America, that you knew this country to be the biggest war criminal of all."

His voice and words had an educated cadence. "Where did you grow up?" she asked.

"You mean after my family was completely shattered by an American bomb at a family wedding? My sister was getting married that day. My parents were standing right next to her when the bomb dropped. I was unfortunately not with them."

"Sounds like you were fortunately not unfortunate."

"I would have preferred to die with them than live without them. But that wasn't my choice. I was left alive so that one day I could get justice. And some of that justice will come today."

"Killing innocent people isn't justice, and no one would ever believe I became a terrorist. I had the same experience as you. My father was killed on 9/11."

Unexpected surprise ran through his gaze, and she enjoyed being able to rattle him with information he didn't have. She needed to keep him talking, give someone a chance to find her. When she didn't show up at the task force meeting, surely her team would notice. And Max would try to find her at some point. They'd be able to trace the car she was driving. She just had to hang on for as long as she could. But a quick glance down at her vest showed the danger of that plan. The time was ticking away: Thirty minutes, twelve seconds.

Was that really all she had left of her life?

"Is this the plan?" she asked. "I die in this warehouse alone. What's the drama in that?"

"You're just the warm-up. The main act will be glorious and visible for miles. It will be much bigger than 9/11. No one will ever forget it. At least, those who are alive and still able to remember."

Her stomach flipped over. He could be talking about so many different sites. But it didn't sound like he was speaking about the conference, more like something iconic...the Empire State Building, the Statue of Liberty, one of the bridges, maybe...

She turned to Caleb. "I heard he took over your plan. You had a nice deal going with David Hartford, lots of money, little effort, not a high body count, just enough to be satisfying. And now you've handed it all off. No credit will go to you, that's for sure."

Caleb stiffened with her words, and while he didn't say anything, she could see that her words had struck a nerve.

"Maybe it was your brother's idea to take over and hand it all off to his friend. What do they even need you for anymore? You're going to end up just like all the people you killed."

"Shut up," Caleb said.

Qadir sighed. "You are so easy, Caleb, so Americanized, so soft. Go. Now."

Caleb's jaw tightened. He looked at his brother, who refused to meet his eye, and then he turned and left.

Malik stepped up with a phone in hand. "Shall we do this?"

"Yes." Qadir moved toward her.

As he drew closer, she cringed, not sure what was coming next. And then the flashes blinded her as Malik shot several photos of her with Qadir in the background.

"Why do you need photos?" she asked.

"Proof of life, of course. I want Max Malone to see you in all your glory."

She drew a quick breath as Qadir's evil voice twisted around Max's name.

"He will come running to protect you," Qadir continued. "He should be able to find you in time, especially with this photo. I'm sure your team will help him trace the call." He tipped his head to Malik. "Is it sent?"

Malik nodded and set the phone down on the nearby table.

"Max isn't coming. He probably isn't even aware that I'm missing," she said.

"He knows, and he's frantic."

"How would you know that?"

"Because I have people everywhere. You and Max have been together this past week. I've seen photos of you together. He'll come to save you. He can't resist playing the hero."

She had both the happy and terrible feeling that he was right. But Qadir wasn't going to let Max rescue her. She was the bait in his trap. He wanted Max to come to him, and then he would kill them both.

Despair hit her hard. Tears blurred her vision, but she couldn't let them drop, couldn't let Qadir have the satisfaction of seeing her cry or hearing her beg for her life. She hoped Max wouldn't get to her in time, that the bomb would go off before then, that he would be safe. But even as that thought crossed her mind, she remembered that this wasn't the only bomb.

The sound of a gunshot outside made everyone jump.

Qadir spun toward the sound, his face darkening with anger as he swore, "Dammit! They're early."

———

Max, Tyler, and members of an FBI SWAT team moved fast, taking down the men outside the warehouse with deadly precision, but each shot made him fear more for Kara's life. The horrific photo had come in just seconds before they'd launched their attack, and seeing her in the suicide vest...

He shook that thought away as they cleared the loading dock and headed into the warehouse. He didn't know how many more were inside, but it seemed a little too quiet. The warehouse was vast and dimly lit, filled with shipping containers and machinery that created a maze of shadows and blind spots.

"I'll take the north corridor, you sweep south," he told Tyler as they broke apart, working in sync in surprising unison, with only one goal: save Kara's life.

He moved through the warehouse like a predator, every one of his senses focused on the hunt.

Another shot came from Tyler's direction, and his voice crackled through his earpiece. "Malik Azrani down."

He didn't respond as he heard footsteps. Someone moving fast, trying to escape.

That's when he saw him—a figure in dark clothing slipping through the shadows toward a rear exit door. He didn't hesitate, sprinting across the open floor, weaving between pallets and machinery, closing the distance.

Qadir spun around just as Max launched himself forward, tackling him to the concrete floor. They rolled, struggling for position, until Max pinned Qadir down, putting a gun to his throat.

"Where is she?" he demanded.

Qadir looked up at him with those cold, intelligent eyes and smiled through the blood on his split lip. "Hello, Max. Right on time."

"I asked you a question."

"She's close by. She's waiting for you to save her. I told her you would try. She's feisty and brave, just like the other one. But you know what happened to her."

His finger tightened on the trigger at Qadir's taunting words, but he couldn't pull it, couldn't kill him—not yet.

Instead, he pulled Qadir to his feet and cuffed his hands behind his back. "Move."

Qadir didn't resist. That bothered Max on a lot of levels, because he wanted to believe he had the upper hand, that this was almost over, but he didn't think it was.

He spoke into the radio. "I have Qadir. He's taking me to Kara."

Tyler responded. "Rest of the building is clear."

"It's just you now," he told Qadir. "All your men are dead."

"Perhaps the ones who were still here when you arrived," Qadir said.

He bit down on his lip at that statement. He'd known all along Qadir had taken Kara to set him up, and as much as he wanted to shut him up, he needed to keep him alive until he could get Kara out of that vest and find out what the hell else was going on.

———

The silence was almost more terrifying than the gunfire, Kara thought. Had Qadir gotten away? Was everyone dead? Why was she still alone?

She glanced at the timer, hating to look, but knowing she had to. Twenty-one minutes and five seconds. She squeezed her eyes shut for a moment, saying a prayer, putting the images of everyone she loved into her head: her mom, her brother, her big, crazy family, the people she worked with...Max. His image stayed with her until she heard a crash.

Her eyes flew open as Max dragged Qadir through the now open door, his gun at his back. Tyler, Jason, and Alina, along with several SWAT officers, came in seconds behind them.

She was both happy and terrified to see them all.

Max shoved Qadir forward with the barrel of his gun. "Get her out of that," he ordered.

"I'm afraid that's not possible," Qadir replied with an evil calm.

"The hell it isn't. Disarm it. Now."

"Or what? You'll kill me?" Qadir's laugh was genuinely amused. "Look at the timer, Max. Nineteen minutes and counting. Kill me now, and she dies anyway. Along with everyone else."

A bomb technician came forward, squatting down next to her to inspect the device. His grim look told a terrible truth.

"He's right. I can't disarm this without a code. And even without the timer, one wrong move, and it could detonate immediately."

A shocked hush filled the room. She wasn't as surprised as they were, because she'd had time to understand exactly what was happening. She could see the war playing out on Max's face—the desire to put a bullet in Qadir's head warring with the knowledge that her life depended on keeping the terrorist alive. It was exactly the position Qadir had wanted to put Max in, and she was simply the pawn. But she wasn't the only one.

' There's another bomb," she said quickly.

Max's jaw tightened as he met her gaze. "Where?"

"I'm guessing it's somewhere symbolic. Somewhere that would make the whole world watch."

"What the hell have you done?" Max gritted out, turning back to Qadir.

Qadir smirked. "The city is always so busy, the bridges packed with traffic, especially the Brooklyn Bridge. It's such a beautiful piece of American engineering, don't you think? Like the bridge your friend Dominic wants to build in my country, a bridge to show his American strength and power. But he doesn't have the power there, and you don't have the power here—I do."

She almost had to marvel at Qadir's confidence, but the sad fact was that he wasn't wrong.

"Son of a bitch," Tyler muttered, looking to Jason.

Jason turned to Alina. "Send everyone to the bridge. Start an evacuation."

"You'll never clear the bridge in time," Qadir said, making Alina pause by the door. "Only I can help you."

"What do you want?" Max demanded.

"Safe passage out of the city. There's a helicopter and a pilot waiting on the roof of the building next door. I walk out of here, and once I'm safely airborne, I'll text the disarm codes for both devices."

"And if we say no?" Max challenged.

Qadir gestured toward Kara. "Then she'll die in seventeen minutes. And thirty seconds later, half the Brooklyn Bridge collapses into the East River."

"Where's the bomb on the bridge?" Jason asked.

"The main suspension cable on the Manhattan side. Two-thirds up the tower. It can't be disarmed without the code. Neither can this one. I didn't come just to play," Qadir continued. "I came to win."

Kara was terrified he was going to win, and they were all going to die. "You need to go. All of you," she said. "Get out of here. Go to the bridge. Get as many people away from there as you can."

"I'm not leaving you," Max told her.

"Fourteen minutes," Qadir said.

She couldn't believe what she was about to say, but she had to say it. "Let him go," she said. "Let Qadir go. Not for me. For everyone else. Thousands will die."

"He can't be trusted," Tyler said. "He'll escape, and he won't send the codes."

"Is there another choice?" Jason asked Max.

"No," Max replied through tight lips. "We have to let him go. But we'll do so with insurance."

"What are you talking about?" Qadir asked, sounding surprised for the first time.

"I have a photo, too," Max said, taking out his phone. "Of your wife and child being held by the CIA."

"That's a fake," Qadir said, but she could see the uncertainty in his eyes as he looked at the photo.

"Look at the newspaper in your wife's hands," Max added. "It has today's date on it. Did you really believe you could come into this city without us knowing, without us taking advantage of the fact that you'd left your family far behind?"

She wondered if the photo was real, how the CIA would have gotten to Qadir's family so quickly.

The two enemies exchanged a long, measuring look.

"I will send the codes to that phone," Qadir said, pointing to the one he'd used to take her picture. "As soon as we are away from the area. But I'll need my hands to be free."

He uncuffed him and then turned him over to Jason, who escorted Qadir out of the room.

"Everyone else needs to leave, too," Kara told the others. "Go to the bridge. Save however many people you can just in case Qadir doesn't send the codes in time."

There were murmurs of protest and also words of encouragement, promises she would be okay, but she didn't really believe any of them.

And then she and Max were alone. He came forward, squatting down in front of her. "I'm so sorry, Kara."

"You have nothing to apologize for. I'm the one who let myself get taken. This is on me, not on you. I don't want you to ever think you're responsible," she said fiercely. "Whatever happens to me is not your fault. And now you have to leave. Take that phone and go outside. Don't come back in unless you have the codes."

"I'm not leaving you. I'm staying with you until he sends the codes."

"If he does. Was that photo real, Max?" She searched his face for the truth.

He shook his head. "No. It's a fake. When I knew Qadir was here, I had my contact at the CIA make it up. It was a long shot that I'd ever use it or that he'd buy it. But it was good enough to make him want to call this off and live to fight another day."

"I'm not sure that's true. He wants to kill us, Max. He wants to blow up that bridge. He wants to make a huge statement. Will he really give all that up based on a photo?"

"If he loves anyone, it's the two people in that photo. I actually got close enough to take their picture a few months ago. That's why I was able to send Reza something that would look real to Qadir. At the time, Qadir wasn't there, and I staked out the place for almost a week, ready to get him as soon as he appeared. But he didn't return. I think he has been staying away from them to keep them safe." He drew a ragged breath. "I should have stayed away from you, Kara. I made you a target."

"I told you this isn't your fault. And when the time on this vest gets down to four minutes, you are going to run like hell. Because I don't want you to die, and if you want to do something for me, if you want to give me some peace before my life ends, then you'll go."

"Kara, I can't," he said, his voice breaking. "I can't leave you. I don't want to be alive if you're not."

"But I want you to be alive, and that's the promise you have to give me. That's the only thing that will make me happy right now. Promise me you'll go. And you'll tell my mom and my brother that I love them, that they were the best family in the world." Tears slipped from her eyes, and she wanted to wipe them away, but she couldn't move. "Max, please."

He gently wiped away her tears with his thumb. "You are so brave, Kara."

"Don't tell anyone I cried, okay? Let them think I was tough until the end."

"There's not going to be an end," he said desperately. "Qadir will send the codes. He'll make the trade. He has to."

She really wanted to believe that.

Max's gaze roamed her face, as if he were memorizing every detail, and she was doing the same. His face was the image she wanted to see when she took her last breath.

Max's earpiece crackled, and he took it out of his ear so she could hear Jason.

"Helicopter is airborne," Jason said. "We should have the codes in the five minutes."

She looked at the timer. It was down to eight minutes. She felt a strange sense of calm, of acceptance. If death came, it would be quick. Maybe that was the blessing. "I love you, Max," she said suddenly. "I want you to know that. It's kind of crazy that I could feel this way for someone I've only known for a week. But I'm glad I got to feel it."

"I love you, too."

"Even if you don't mean it, I like hearing it."

"I mean it, Kara. It's fast, but it's also real."

"You need to go, Max. It's down to seven minutes."

"You said four," he argued.

"Three more minutes won't make a difference."

"The code is coming. It has to," he said fiercely.

She smiled through her tears. "And you said I was the optimistic one."

He cupped her face with his hands, still being careful, then pressed his lips against hers in one last emotional kiss.

And then the phone on the table buzzed.

She couldn't quite believe it. "Is that it?" she asked in disbelief.

Max grabbed the phone. "Two sets of numbers," he said, taking a photo of the code and sending that one to Jason, before he came to her.

She could hear Jason confirm receipt of the code.

Max looked at the keypad on her vest. "Here we go."

"Don't you want to send a bomb tech in here?'

"I can do it. Trust me."

"With my life," she breathed.

He carefully pressed each number on a code that felt ridiculously long. Her heart was thundering against her chest. She felt like she was going to pass out, which might be a blessing. But she was still awake when Max finished the sequence.

"Done," he said.

Nothing happened. The timer kept counting.

"It's not working," she said with despair. "He probably just wanted to stall us."

Jason's voice came across the radio, tight with stress: "Timer is still running on the bridge device."

"Maybe there's a delay," Max said, but she could hear the fear.

"Max, get out of here," she pleaded. "It's down to four minutes. Go."

"No."

He put his arms around her. "If you die, I die. Just look at me."

They held each other's gaze for a long minute, and then she heard a click.

Max pulled slightly away from her so he could see the timer. "It stopped," he said in amazement. "The screen is blank."

"Oh my God!" she said, not quite able to believe it. "Are you sure?"

"I'm sure," he said with a joyful smile.

"Bridge device is down!" Jason's voice exploded through the radio.

"All good here, too," Max replied, a smile lighting up his face. "We made it, Kara. It's over."

"Qadir believed the photo. That was a brilliant move, Max."

"I'm glad it worked."

"But he's still free. And once he knows that his family is safe, he'll come for all of us again."

"We'll stop him before he can do that. Let's get you out of this vest." He pulled a knife out of his pocket and cut the zip ties as the bomb squad came into the room to remove the vest.

Alina followed a moment later, her gaze happy and triumphant. "Thank God you're all right, Kara."

"I am thanking God," she said as the heavy weight was finally taken from her body. "That was the longest and shortest thirty minutes of my life." She stretched her aching arms in front of her, still feeling a little too weak to stand up.

"Was the picture real?" Alina asked Max.

He gave a negative shake of his head. "I took the picture a few months ago. The newspaper, the CIA agents holding them, was doctored."

"That was quite a gamble," Alina said. "But also impressive. When did you have time to do that?"

"As soon as I knew Qadir was in New York City, I had a friend of mine at the agency create it. I wasn't sure if I'd ever use it or not, but I had a feeling Qadir would come after me at some point. I've been making him move locations every couple of weeks."

"So, you've been a pain in the ass," Alina said lightly.

"You could say that." Max paused. "Were you at the bridge?"

"No. Jason asked me and some of the team to stay here to guard some of the injured combatants and the deceased."

"There are survivors?" Kara asked.

"Two," Alina replied. "Six men are dead, including Caleb Azrani and his brother, Malik. Obviously, the terrorists who delivered the bomb to the bridge are still out there, but we'll do everything we can to find them. In the meantime, the city is safe for at least one more day." Alina paused. "I have to say that you impressed the hell out of me, Kara. I would not have been nearly as calm in your position."

"I'm sure that's not true."

"Let's get out of here," Max said, offering her a hand. "I'm sure Kara would like to see some daylight."

"I really would." She got to her feet, but before they could move, one of the SWAT members came back into the room with an odd expression on his face.

"What's wrong?" Alina asked sharply.

"We've been clearing the buildings in the area," he said. "We found two men next door. One was deceased, the other was half naked and unconscious behind a dumpster at the helipad. He said he was supposed to fly Qadir out of the area, but someone knocked him out and apparently stole his clothes.'

"What?" she said in shock. "The helicopter pilot was knocked unconscious?" She turned to Max. "Who the hell is flying Qadir's helicopter?"

He stared at her for a long minute. Then his gaze swept the room. "Where's Tyler?"

"He went to the bridge," Alina said.

A moment later, Max's earpiece came to life, Tyler's calm voice coming across the radio. "I just landed a helicopter at Morris Field in Westchester. Ali Qadir is deceased. Repeat, Ali Qadir is dead."

She sucked in a breath as she met Max's gaze.

Then Max said, "Copy that."

CHAPTER TWENTY-FOUR

It was after five p.m. when they returned to the Castleton Hotel. They'd planned to pick up their things and go back to her place, but once she sat down on the soft couch in the living room, Kara didn t think she could get up again any time soon. "Maybe we can spend one more night here," she said. "It's so much nicer than my apartment."

"I could do that," Max said, sitting down next to her and grabbing her hand.

He'd been holding her hand for most of the day. After they'd left the warehouse, they'd gone back to her office, where they'd met up with the rest of her team for a lengthy debrief.

Qadir's men, who had not been killed at the warehouse, were already talking, giving names and contact information for those who had escaped after setting up the bomb on the bridge.

There would be a long investigation into everything else that had happened, including Hartford's original revenge plot, including the café bomb, and the explosion that had killed James Cooper as well as Dominic's shady deal with Qadir. There was a lot to be sorted out over the next several weeks, and her team would be on it.

Kara had also been relieved to hear that the safe house leak had been tied to a low-level analyst at 26 Fed, who happened to be David Hartford's cousin, and who owed Hartford a great deal of money for canceling his gambling debts. That analyst had been Hartford's eyes inside the investigation. Thankfully, most of the investigation had been done by her team, but the analyst had been able to access the safe house location, which was used by the New York field office. Kara was thrilled that no one on her team had been responsible.

The most important update had come from Tyler, who had escorted Qadir's body back to New York City for confirmation of his death. Then he'd told them what had happened. Once he'd learned Qadir's escape plan, he'd slipped out of the warehouse, taken out the guard at the helipad, knocked out the pilot, and put on his clothes and flight gear. He'd been waiting in the helicopter when Jason had escorted Qadir to the helipad. He'd wondered if Jason had recognized him.

Jason said he had, and he was on board with the idea and with Tyler's initiative to think that quickly. He was also impressed that Tyler knew how to fly a helicopter.

Kara had been impressed by that, too. Apparently, Tyler had a lot of talents, and she was happy that he was not only someone she could trust but someone she could count on to be extremely good at his job.

After Qadir sent the codes, Tyler said he'd landed the helicopter in the field instead of the small airport where Qadir had wanted to go. Qadir attacked him with a knife that he'd hidden in his shoe, and he shot him in self-defense.

She wondered about that part of the story, but no one had seemed interested in discussing the details of Tyler's actions since he'd killed one of the most wanted terrorists in the world.

"Kara?"

She suddenly realized how long she'd been lost in thought. "Sorry, what did you say?"

"Just wondering what you're thinking about?"

"Everything," she said with a helpless shrug. "There's a lot to process."

"You don't have to do that tonight."

"I know." She paused. "What did you think about Tyler's actions?"

"I thought he was brilliant," Max admitted. "And I was impressed Jason let him do it. There was a lot at stake."

"We had more control with Tyler in the pilot's seat. If Qadir hadn't sent the codes, if the bombs hadn't been disarmed, he was going to kill him."

"He was always going to kill him," Max said, meeting her gaze. "Maybe that won't be the official story, but I think it's the truth."

"So do I. Are you sorry you didn't get to be the one to do that?"

"Absolutely not. I was where I wanted to be—with you."

"You should have left. You are too brave and too protective for your own good." She paused, gazing into his eyes. "Thank you."

He squeezed her hand. "I didn't want to live without you."

"Not even to hunt down Qadir if he got away?"

"I wasn't thinking about him. But I'm very glad he's dead, and that the Azrani brothers are also deceased. Qadir's organization will splinter now. They'll be far less lethal."

"But more will come in his place."

"Let's not think about that now." He paused. "Do you want to call your mom or your brother? I couldn't help noticing your phone has been lighting up all day."

"Whenever my family hears bad news in the city, they text me. I told them I was fine. I didn't tell them what happened. They don't need to know. But they still keep texting."

"I don't blame them. They love you. And they should, because you are an incredible woman."

She felt touched and flattered by the admiration and respect in his gaze. "I just survived. You and Tyler and Jason did the hard work."

"Are you kidding? None of us were trapped in a suicide vest. I can't imagine how that felt."

"You don't want to imagine it, and I don't want to think about it anymore. I'm actually feeling hungry."

"Room service," he said with a smile. "I say we order everything on the menu."

"Including dessert. And then I want to try out that Jacuzzi tub. I'm hoping you'll join me."

"Well, considering I can't seem to let go of your hand, I'd say that's going to happen," he said dryly.

"It's funny. I didn't think you would be a hand-holder."

"I never have been."

"I haven't either. But this feels right." She licked her lips. "We said a lot of things to each other in the heat of the moment, Max. It's going to be okay if you want to back off on any of them."

"Do you want to back off?" he challenged.

"No, but I'm pragmatic enough to know that people say things when they're scared, and then when they're not—"

"I didn't say anything that wasn't true or that I didn't mean," he said with certainty in his voice. "But we can go as fast or as slow as you want. I just want to be with you, figure things out together."

"I like the sound of that. And there will be things to figure out for you, like whether you ever work for Dominic again. I wonder what's going to happen to him."

"Probably not much," he said. "I doubt there's any evidence linking him to some deal with Qadir that involved me. And bribes in that part of the world are so common, it would be stranger if Dominic hadn't paid people for protection. But we'll see what happens. I'd like to make sure that every part of his organization is investigated."

She laughed at his wicked smile. "Put him through hell."

"It's only right, don't you think?"

"I absolutely do think it's right."

"Even if you don't believe in revenge?" he challenged.

"I don't believe in revenge that includes killing people. Making their life miserable...I'm okay with that."

"We'll see how it plays out. Revenge is no longer a priority for me. I don't want to wake up every day filled with anger."

"How do you want to wake up?"

"I want to wake up with you, Kara."

She leaned her head against his good shoulder as he put his arm around her. "That sounds wonderful. I never thought I'd meet someone I could really count on to be there for me. But you blew that thought out of the water."

"And I never thought I'd want to commit to anyone, but I can't imagine not seeing you every day of my life."

"What if our life becomes ordinary after the adrenaline wears off?"

"Ordinary sounds amazing to me. And I want to get to know your family for real. I don't want to be your fake boyfriend. I want to go to your uncle's poker games, let your mother feed me too much food, and ask when we're going to get married."

"She will ask—a lot."

He laughed. "I can handle your mother."

"We'll see. I'd like to meet your dad, too, Max."

"We have time for everything now."

"Time," she murmured. "What a beautiful thing." She lifted her head from his shoulder and gave him a kiss that drove all thoughts of dinner and Jacuzzi tubs out of her head. "Maybe we'll eat later," she said.

"Much later," he agreed as he pulled her into his arms.

The softball game had been Hayden's idea. "Family bonding," he'd called it, though Kara suspected it was really an excuse for her brother to determine whether her new boyfriend had the goods to compete on his men's softball team starting next month.

Softball had always been a tradition in their family. Every spring they gathered for a game in the park to kick off baseball season. Kara was a pretty good player, but rarely had time to play on a team, so her skills were rusty. Not that she cared much about this game at all; she was more interested in seeing how Max fit in with her large, extended family. Until now, she'd been introducing him to people in smaller groups. But this was everyone and their friends. And Max seemed to be loving it.

He waved to her from second base, where he'd landed after hitting a double. He looked more relaxed than she'd ever seen him. Three weeks of sleeping through the night without nightmares of Qadir and waking up next to someone who loved him despite knowing all his secrets, had taken a lot of weight off him.

She felt lighter herself, no longer feeling the need to prove anything to anyone. She realized now how the incident at the NYPD, the breakup with her boyfriend, and the blacklisting by former friends had taken a serious toll on her. She'd buried herself in work, so she didn't have to think about friendship or love. She'd thought proving she was an excellent agent would make everyone realize they were wrong about her, but now she knew she hadn't really been trying to prove that to others, but to herself. She didn't have to do that anymore. She knew who she was, and she was good with herself.

"Strike three!" Uncle Danny called from behind home plate, grinning as Hayden walked back to the bench after striking out spectacularly. "Medical school didn't teach you how to hit a curveball!"

"That wasn't a curveball!" Hayden protested. "That was barely a strike!"

"I'm the umpire. My rules."

"Max is fitting in well," her mother said, settling down beside her on the blanket Kara had spread on the grass when she'd decided to sit out so that the two teams would have even numbers. "Look at him, he's having the time of his life," her mom added as Max ran home on her cousin Laurel's long fly ball.

"He likes our big, chaotic family."

"We like him. So, when are you going to make this official?"

"Mom!"

"What? I'm just saying, you're not getting any younger, Kara. And he clearly adores you."

"We've known each other for a month."

"That doesn't matter. I've never seen you look so happy. I want that to continue."

"It will," she said. "Stop pushing. I've got this."

"I'm glad," her mother said. "Do you want something to eat or drink?"

"No, I'll wait for Max."

Her mother stood up, then paused. "Your father would have liked him, Kara."

"Really?"

"Yes. Not because he's strong and brave and handsome, but because he loves you, and he wants to protect you."

"I don't need him to protect me."

Her mother smiled. "I know that, but there is always a time in life when you need someone to have your back."

"Well, I know that Max will always have my back," she said, remembering how he'd bravely stood by her side as they both faced death. But her mother was never going to hear that story.

"That's what I think, too," her mom said with a satisfied smile. Then she went to join her sister-in-law at the dessert table.

A moment later, the game ended, and Max came over to join her.

"I think we won," he said, flopping down on the blanket beside her. "But I'm not entirely sure. The game seems to be starting again with new teams, so who knows?"

"That's how these games go," she said with a laugh. "They never end, and my uncle makes up rules so everyone will feel like they've won. By the way, my family loves you."

"I love them too."

"So, you said you had some news," she reminded him. "Can you share it?"

"I'm not sure this is the right time."

"We're alone. And I want to hear it."

"Okay. I've decided to make my fake security firm real," he said. "My friend Reza is leaving the agency; he's going to join me. So will Kai, who was helping me with Dominic's business. She's willing to commit to full-time as long as I don't make her travel. Reza has another friend who's leaving the ATF. He'll come on board as well, and we'll see where we go from there. It looks like I'm going to need an actual office."

"Are you focusing on overseas work?"

"No. I'm happy to focus on the city. I'm starting to like it almost as much as you do."

"It is an amazing city." Her gaze drifted to the Brooklyn

Bridge in the distance. "I still sometimes wonder how we didn't lose that bridge. But I'm so glad it's still there." She looked back at him. "I've been thinking about a few things, too."

"Like..."

"Maybe we should get an apartment together. We're together most nights, and going back and forth is getting to be a pain. I think we should find a place to share."

"I already started looking," he said, surprising her again.

"Really?"

"Yes. But before we move in together, I want to make things more official."

She gave him a warning look. "Stop right there, Max Malone. You are not going to propose to me at a family softball game with everyone watching."

He laughed. "That would be perfect, wouldn't it?"

"No. I don't enjoy being the center of that kind of attention."

"I know you don't." He gave her a look that suggested he knew her as well as she knew herself. "I'm not proposing here, but soon. I want you to know that I'm committed to you and me. This is going to be a long-term deal."

"I thought you didn't like long-term."

"Well, you changed my mind. And when I ask you to marry me, it will be a surprise."

"As long as it's just you and me, I don't care where it is or when it happens. Because I love you, and I'm all in. In fact, I could just ask you right now," she said.

"No way. You don't want a family proposal, and I don't want you to ask me."

"So, we make a deal that I propose when your family is not around."

"It's a deal," she said with a grin. "We negotiate pretty well."

"We do a lot of things pretty well." He leaned over and gave her a kiss. "By the way, I heard that the investigations into Dominic's global empire are revealing quite a few skeletons in the closet. He's going to be facing charges for all kinds of things."

"Good," she said with satisfaction. "I can't stand that he used you to make a deal with Qadir. I know he's acting like he wasn't going to honor it, and that it only had to do with getting you to Tajikistan, but I don't buy it, and I don't trust him."

"Samantha doesn't trust him, either," he said. "I stopped at the hospital this morning on my way here."

"Really? How is she doing?" She knew that Samantha had been recovering from her near-death experience but still had a long road back to recovery.

"She's now aware of everything that happened, and her newfound appreciation for life has apparently given her a conscience. She said she's asked the DA to reopen investigations into the fire and all the people who were involved."

"Too little, too late for David Hartford and his family, not that he deserves any compassion, but the victims of that fire do. By the way, did Samantha ever tell you why she sent you that text asking you to meet her at the café?"

"It was what we thought. She was concerned about Dominic. Actually, it wasn't just concern; she'd overheard him talking to someone, and it had sounded like he was paying for protection. She didn't like that idea. She was concerned that Dominic's ambition would lead him and possibly her into a dangerous situation, as she was planning to attend the groundbreaking with him."

"She is a smart woman."

"Smart enough to end things with him as soon as she realized how deeply he'd gotten involved with Qadir."

"Well, I'm glad she's recovering."

"She told me she's hoping to be back to work within the next two months."

"She's a workaholic—kind of like us."

He smiled. "We're talking too much about work, aren't we?"

"Maybe. I'm excited about your new company, Max, and I

really enjoy working with my team, but I hope we can find some balance going forward. I want more in my life than just work. I want a real relationship, and I want to make that relationship a priority, too. I know it won't be easy for either of us. When there are lives on the line, we'll go all in. But maybe when there aren't lives on the line, we don't obsess over work."

"I like the sound of that. I've spent too many days and years chasing Qadir, looking for revenge, justice, whatever you want to call it. I don't want to do that anymore."

"It's all really pointless, isn't it? No one can change the past. All any of us can do is just move on. The best revenge is being happy, right?"

"Right. And we are going to be so happy." He leaned forward and gave her a long, passionate kiss.

"Hey!" Danny called from home plate. "No kissing in the outfield! This is a family game!"

"We're not in the outfield!" she yelled back.

"Close enough! Save it for later!"

She ignored him and went back to kissing Max, because if she'd learned anything about time, some things couldn't and shouldn't wait.

WHAT TO READ NEXT...

Next up is Tyler's story in **CROSS THAT LINE
FBI SERIES: STRIKE TEAM EAST**

FBI Agent Tyler Brennan has never hesitated to cross a line in the name of justice. Rules are flexible. Failure isn't.

Dr. Rachel Thorne believes lines exist for a reason. The last time she stood her ground against Tyler, sparks flew—and not the good kind.

Now a disturbing incident at a veterans hospital forces them back into each other's orbit. Rachel is certain a decorated soldier didn't simply walk away, and she needs someone to listen to her, even if that someone is Tyler Brennan.

As the investigation deepens and the danger closes in, old resentment ignites into something far more dangerous. Because this time, the truth isn't just buried—it's protected. And crossing that line could cost them everything.

From #1 New York Times *bestselling author Barbara Freethy comes the next electrifying installment in the FBI Series: Strike Team East—a thrilling romantic suspense filled with high-stakes danger and a slow-burn sizzling romance!*

ABOUT THE AUTHOR

Barbara Freethy is a #1 New York Times Bestselling Author of 90 novels ranging from mystery thrillers to romantic suspense, contemporary romance, and women's fiction. With over 15 million copies sold, twenty-eight of Barbara's books have appeared on the New York Times and USA Today Bestseller Lists.

Barbara is known for her twisty thrillers and emotionally riveting romance where ordinary people end up having extraordinary adventures.

For further information, visit www.barbarafreethy.com

www.ingramcontent.com/pod-product-compliance
Lightning Source LLC
Chambersburg PA
CBHW020912060726
47591CB00004B/1207